Also by

GILES BLUNT

BY THE TIME
YOU READ THIS

GILES BLUNT

St. Martin's Paperbacks

Published in Canada in 2006 by Random House Canada
Published in Great Britain in 2006 by HarperCollins

This is a work of fiction. All of the characters, organizations, and events portrayed in this novel are either products of the author's imagination or are used fictitiously.

BY THE TIME YOU READ THIS

Library of Congress Catalog Card Number: 2006048563

ISBN: 0-312-94548-5
EAN: 978-0-312-94548-0

Printed in the United States of America

Henry Holt and Company hardcover edition / February 2007
St. Martin's Paperbacks edition / August 2008

St. Martin's Paperbacks are published by St. Martin's Press, 175 Fifth Avenue, New York, NY 10010.

10 9 8 7 6 5 4 3 2 1

To Janna

*I know I could kill someone. I know
I could kill myself.*

—THE JOURNALS OF SYLVIA PLATH

1

Nothing bad could ever happen on Madonna Road. It curls around the western shore of a small lake just outside Algonquin Bay, Ontario, providing a pine-scented refuge for affluent families with young children, yuppies fond of canoes and kayaks, and an artful population of chipmunks chased by galumphing dogs. It's the kind of spot—tranquil, shady, and secluded—that appears to offer an exemption from tragedy and sorrow.

Detective John Cardinal and his wife, Catherine, lived in the smallest house on Madonna Road, but even that tiny place would have been beyond their means were it not for the fact that, being situated across the road from the water, they owned neither an inch of beach nor so much as a millimeter of lake frontage. On weekends Cardinal spent most of his time down in the basement breathing smells of sawdust, paint, and Minwax, carpentry affording him a sense of creativity and control that did not tend to flourish in the squad room.

But even when he was not woodworking, he loved to be in his tiny house, enveloped in the serenity of the lakeshore. It was autumn now, early October, the quietest time of the year. The motorboats and Sea-Doos had been hauled away, and the snowmobiles were not yet blasting their way across ice and snow.

Autumn in Algonquin Bay was the season that redeemed the other three. Colors of scarlet and rust, ocher and gold swarmed across the hills, the sky turned an alarming blue, and you could almost forget the sweat-drenched summer, the bug festival that was spring, the pitiless razor of winter. Trout Lake was preternaturally still, black onyx amid fire. Even having grown up here (when he took it completely for granted), and now having lived in Algonquin Bay again for the past dozen years, Cardinal was never quite prepared for how beautiful it was in the fall. This time of year, he liked to spend every spare minute at home. On this particular evening he had made the fifteen-minute drive from work, even though he only had an hour, affording him exactly thirty minutes at the dinner table before he had to head back.

Catherine tossed a pill into her mouth, washed it down with a few swallows of water, and snapped the cap back on the bottle.

"There's more shepherd's pie, if you want," she said.

"No, I'm fine. That was great," Cardinal said. He was trying to corner the last peas on his plate.

"There's no dessert, unless you want cookies."

"I always want cookies. The question is whether I want to be hoisted out of here by a forklift."

Catherine took her plate and glass into the kitchen.

"What time are you heading out?" he called after her.

"Right now. It's dark, the moon is up. Why not?"

Cardinal glanced outside. The full moon, an orange disk riding low above the lake, was quartered by the mullions of their window.

"You're taking pictures of the moon? Don't tell me you're going into the calendar business."

But Catherine wasn't listening. She had disappeared down to the basement, and he could hear her pulling things off the shelves in her darkroom. Cardinal put the leftovers in the fridge and slotted his dishes into the dishwasher.

Catherine came back upstairs, zipped up her camera bag, and dumped it beside the door while she put on her coat. It was a golden tan color with brown leather trim on the cuffs and collar. She pulled a long scarf from a hook and wrapped it once, twice, about her neck, then undid it again.

"No," she said to herself. "It'll be in the way."

"How long is this expedition of yours?" Cardinal said, but his wife didn't hear him. They'd been married nearly thirty years, but she still kept him guessing. Sometimes when she was going out to photograph, she would be chatty and excited, telling him every detail of her project until he was cross-eyed with the fine points of focal lengths and f-stops. Other times he wouldn't know what she was planning until she emerged from her darkroom days or weeks later, clutching her prints like trophies from a personal safari. Tonight she was subdued.

"What time do you think you'll get back?" Cardinal said.

Catherine tied a short plaid scarf around her neck and tucked it inside her jacket. "Does it matter? I thought you had to go back to work."

"I do. Just curious."

"Well, I'll be home long before you." She pulled her hair out from under her scarf and shook her head. Cardinal caught a whiff of her shampoo, a faint almondy smell. She sat down on the bench by the front door and opened her camera bag again. "Split-field filter. I knew I forgot something."

She disappeared downstairs for a few moments and came back with the filter, which she dropped into the camera bag. Cardinal had no idea what a split-field filter might be.

"You going to the government dock again?" In the spring Catherine had done a series of photos on the shore of Lake Nipissing when the ice was breaking up: great white slabs of ice stacking themselves up like geological strata.

"I've done the dock," Catherine said, frowning a little. She strapped a collapsible tripod to the bottom of the camera bag. "Why all these questions?"

"Some people take pictures, other people ask questions."

"I wish you wouldn't. You know I don't like to talk about stuff ahead of time."

"Sometimes you do."

"Not this time." She stood up and slung the camera bag, bulky and heavy, over her shoulder.

"What a gorgeous night," Cardinal said, when they were outside. He stood for a moment looking up at the stars, but the glow of the moon washed most of them out. He took a deep breath, inhaling smells of pine and fallen leaves. It was Catherine's favorite time of year too, but she wasn't paying attention at the moment. She got straight into her car, a maroon PT Cruiser she'd bought used a couple of years earlier, started the engine, and pulled out of the drive.

Cardinal followed her in the Camry along the dark curving highway that took them into town. As they approached the lights at the Highway 11 bypass, Catherine signaled and shifted into the left lane. Cardinal continued on through the intersection, heading down Sumner toward the police station.

Catherine was headed toward the east end of town, and he wondered briefly where she was going. But it was always good to see her involved in her work, and she was taking her medication. If she was a little moody, that was okay. She'd been out of the psychiatric hospital for a year now. Last time, she had been out for nearly two years when she suddenly embarked on a manic episode that put her back in for three months. But as long as she was taking her medication, Cardinal didn't let himself worry too much.

IT WAS A Tuesday night, and there was not a lot going on in the criminal world. Cardinal spent the next couple of hours catching up on paperwork. They'd had the annual carpet cleaning done, and the air was rich with flowery chemicals and the smell of wet carpet. The only other detective on duty was Ian McLeod, and even McLeod, the station loudmouth during the day, maintained a comparative solemnity at night.

Cardinal was putting a rubber band around a file he had just closed when McLeod's florid face appeared over the acoustic divider that separated their desks.

"Hey, Cardinal. I have to give you a heads-up. It's about the mayor."

"What's he want?"

"Came in last night when you were off. He wanted to put in a missing-person report on his wife. Problem is, she's not really missing. Everybody in town knows where she is except the goddamn mayor."

"She's still having the affair with Reg Wilcox?"

"Yeah. In fact she was seen last night with our esteemed director of sanitation. Szelagy's on a stakeout at the Birches Motel, keeping an eye on the Porcini brothers. They got out of Kingston six months ago and seem to have the idea they can actually get back into business up here. Anyways, Szelagy's reporting back and happens to mention he sees Feckworth's wife coming out of Room Twelve with Reggie Wilcox. I was never keen on the jerk myself. I don't know what women see in him."

"He's a good-looking guy."

"Oh, come on. He looks like one of those Sears guys modeling the suits." By way of imitation, McLeod gave him a three-quarter profile with a fake-hearty grin.

"Some people consider that handsome," Cardinal said. "Though not on you."

"Well, some people can kiss my—anyway, I told His Worship last night, I said, 'Look, your wife is not missing. She's an adult. She's been seen downtown. If she's not coming home, that's apparently her choice at this particular moment in time.'"

"What'd he say to that?"

"'Who saw her? Where? What time?' Same questions anybody'd ask. I told him I wasn't at liberty to say. She'd been seen in the vicinity of Worth and MacIntosh, so we could not file a missing-person report. She's at the Birches again tonight with Wilcox. I told Feckworth to come on down, you'd be happy to talk to him."

"What the hell did you do that for?"

"He'll take it better from you. Him and me don't get along so good."

"You don't get along with anyone so good."

"Now, that's just hurtful."

WHILE HE WAS waiting for the mayor to arrive, Cardinal made out an expense report for the previous month and wrote up the top sheet on a case he had just closed. He found his thoughts wandering to Catherine. She had been doing well for the past year and was back teaching at the community college this semester. But she had seemed a little distant at dinner, a little impatient, in a way that might indicate some preoccupation other than her photographic project. Catherine was in her late forties and going through menopause, which played havoc with her moods and necessitated constant tweaking of her medication. If she seemed a little distant—well, there was no shortage of plausible reasons. On the other hand, how well do we really know the people we love? Just look at the mayor.

When the mayor, Lance Feckworth, arrived, Cardinal took him to one of the interview rooms so they could talk in private.

"I want to get to the bottom of this," the mayor told him. "A full investigation." Feckworth was a lumpy little man, much given to bow ties, and was perched uncomfortably on the edge of a plastic seat that was usually occupied by suspects. "I know I'm mayor, and that doesn't give me the right to more attention than any other voter, but I don't expect less, either. What if she's had an accident of some kind?"

Feckworth was not much of a mayor. During his tenure, all the city council seemed to do was study problems endlessly and agree to let them drift. But he was usually an affable man, ready with a joke or a slap on the back. It was unsettling to see him in pain, as if a building one had grown used to over the years had suddenly been painted a garish color.

As gently as possible, Cardinal pointed out that Mrs. Feckworth had been seen in town the previous night and there had been no major accidents that week.

"Damn it, why is my entire police force telling me she's been seen around town but you won't say where or by who? How would you feel if it was your wife? You'd want to know the truth, right?"

"Yes, I would."

"Then I suggest you explain to me exactly what is going on, Detective. Otherwise, I'll just have to deal directly with

Chief Kendall, and you can be sure I won't have anything good to say about you *or* that lunkhead McLeod."

WHICH WAS HOW Cardinal came to be sitting in his car with the mayor of Algonquin Bay in the courtyard of the Birches Motel. Despite its name, the Birches was nowhere near a birch tree. It was not near a tree of any kind, being located in the heart of downtown on MacIntosh Street. In fact, it was no longer even the Birches Motel, having been taken over by Sunset Inns at least two years previously, but everybody still called it the Birches.

Cardinal was parked a dozen paces from Room 12. Szelagy was parked across the lot, but they didn't acknowledge each other. Cardinal rolled the window down a little to keep the glass from fogging up. Even here in the middle of downtown, you could smell fallen leaves and, from someone's fireplace, the comforting smell of wood smoke.

"You're telling me she's in there?" the mayor said. "My wife's in that room?"

Surely he must know, Cardinal thought. How could it get to this stage—his wife staying out for days at a time and renting motel rooms—without his knowing?

"I don't believe it," Feckworth said. "It's too tawdry." But there was less conviction in his voice, as if seeing the actual motel room door was beginning to shatter his faith. "Cynthia's a loyal person," he added. "She prides herself on it."

Cynthia Feckworth had in fact been sleeping her way around Algonquin Bay for at least the past four years; the mayor was the only one who didn't know it. And who am I to tear off his blinders? Cardinal asked himself. Who am I to refuse anyone the sweet anesthetic of denial?

"Oh, she couldn't be screwing someone else. That would be—if she's letting another man—that's it. I'll dump her. You watch me. Oh, God, if she's doing those things. . . ." Feckworth groaned and hid his face in his hands.

As if summoned by his anguish, the door to Room 12 opened and a man stepped out. He had the perfectly groomed look of a catalog model: *Take advantage of our mid-autumn sale on men's windbreakers.*

"It's Reg Wilcox," the mayor said. "Sanitation. What would Reg be doing here?"

Wilcox ambled to his Ford Explorer with the slouchy, smug air of the well laid. Then he backed out of his space and drove off.

"Well, at least Cynthia wasn't in there. That's something," Feckworth said. "Maybe I should just head home now and hope for the best."

The door to Room 12 opened again, and an attractive woman peered out for a moment before closing the door behind her. She buttoned up her coat against the chill night air and headed toward the exit.

The mayor jumped out of the car and ran to block her path. Cardinal rolled up his window, not wanting to hear. His cell phone buzzed.

"Cardinal, why the hell don't you answer your bloody radio?"

"I'm in my own car, Sergeant Flower. It's too boring to explain."

"All right, listen. We got a caller says there's a dead one behind Gateway condos. You know the new building?"

"The Gateway? Just off the bypass? I didn't even realize it was finished yet. Are we sure it isn't a drunk sleeping it off?"

"We're sure. Patrol on the scene already confirmed."

"All right. I'm just a few blocks away."

The mayor and his wife were quarreling. Cynthia Feckworth had her arms folded across her chest, head bowed. Her husband faced her, hands extended, palms out, in the classic gesture of the pleading mate. An employee was outlined in the doorway of the motel office, watching.

The mayor didn't even notice as Cardinal drove away.

THE GATEWAY BUILDING was in the east end of town, one of the few high-rises in an area that was breaking out in new strip malls every day. In fact, the ground floor of the building was a mini-mall with a dry cleaner, a convenience store, and a large computer-repair concern called Compu-Clinic that had moved over from Main Street. The businesses had been open for a while, but many of the building's apartments were still unsold. Road crews were working on a new cloverleaf to accommodate traffic to and from the burgeoning neighborhood, if it could be called a neighborhood. Cardinal had to drive through a gauntlet of orange cones and then detour by the new Tim Hortons and Home Depot to get there.

He passed a row of newly built "townhomes," most still unoccupied, although lights were on in a few of them. There was a PT Cruiser parked in front of the last one, and Cardinal thought for a second that it was Catherine's. Once or twice a year he had such moments: a sudden worry that Catherine was in trouble—manic and somewhere dangerous, or depressed and suicidal—and then relief to find it was not so.

He pulled into the Gateway's driveway and parked under a sign that said RESIDENT PARKING ONLY; VISITORS PARK ON STREET. A uniformed cop was standing beside a ribbon of crime-scene tape.

"Oh, hi, Sergeant," he said, as Cardinal approached. He looked about eighteen years old, and Cardinal could not for the life of him remember his name. "Got a dead woman back there. Looks like she took a nasty fall. Thought I'd better secure a perimeter till we know what's what."

Cardinal looked beyond him into the area behind the building. All he could see were a Dumpster and a couple of cars.

"Did you touch anything?"

"Um, yeah. I checked the body for a pulse and there wasn't one. And I searched pockets for ID but didn't find any. Could be a resident, I guess, went off one of those balconies."

Cardinal looked around. Usually there was a small crowd at such scenes. "No witnesses? No one heard anything?"

"Building's mostly empty, I think, except for the businesses on the ground floor. There was no one around when I got here."

"Okay. Let me borrow your flashlight."

The kid handed it over and let Cardinal by before attaching the end of the tape to a utility pole.

Cardinal walked in slowly, not wanting to ruin the scene by assuming the kid's idea of a fall was correct. He went by the Dumpster, which seemed to be full of old computers. A keyboard dangled over the side by its cable, and there were a couple of circuit boards that appeared to have exploded on the ground.

The body was just beyond the Dumpster, face down, dressed in a tan fall coat with leather at the cuffs.

"I don't see any of the windows or doors open on any of the balconies up there," the young cop said. "Probably the super'll be able to give us an ID."

"Her ID's in the car," Cardinal said.

The young cop looked around. There were two cars parked along the side of the building.

"I don't get it," he said. "You know which car is hers?"

But Cardinal did not appear to be listening. The young cop watched in astonishment as Sergeant John Cardinal— star player on the CID team, veteran of the city's highest-profile cases, legendary for his meticulous approach to crime scenes—went down on his knees in the pool of blood and cradled the shattered woman in his arms.

2

Normally, Lise Delorme would have been irritated at being called in on her day off. It happened all the time, but that didn't make it any less annoying to be hauled out of whatever you were doing. She had been at a pub, enjoying a particularly pungent curry with a new boyfriend—a very good-looking lawyer only a year or two her junior—whom she had met when he unsuccessfully defended a longtime thug whom Delorme had nabbed for extortion. This was their third date, and even though the concept of sleeping with a lawyer was extremely hard for her to accept, Delorme had been planning to invite him in for a drink when he took her home. Shane Cosgrove was his name.

It would have been sexier if Shane had been a *better* lawyer. Delorme actually thought his thuggy client should have gotten off, considering the meager pile of evidence she had managed to put together. But still, he was good-looking and good company and such men, single, were hard to come by in a place the size of Algonquin Bay.

When she returned to the table, Shane asked her if she needed to lie down, she had turned so white. Detective Sergeant Chouinard had just told her that the victim was John Cardinal's wife and that Cardinal himself was at the scene. A patrol unit had called Chouinard at home and Chouinard had in turn called Delorme.

"Get him out of there, Lise," he had said. "Whatever else is going on inside him right now, Cardinal's been a cop for thirty years. He knows as well as you and me that until we rule out foul play, he's suspect number one."

"D.S.," Delorme said, "Cardinal's been absolutely loyal to his wife through a lot of—"

"A lot of shit. Yes, I know that. I also know it's possible he finally got fed up. It's possible some little straw broke the camel's back. So get your ass over there and make sure you think dirty. That place is a homicide scene until such time as we rule out foul play."

So there was no irritation in Delorme's heart as she drove across town, only sorrow. Although she had met Cardinal's wife on social occasions, she'd never gotten to know her well. Of course, she knew what everyone in the department knew: that every couple of years Catherine went into the psychiatric hospital following a manic or depressive episode. And every time Delorme had encountered Catherine Cardinal, she had wondered how that was possible.

For Catherine Cardinal, at least when she was well, was one of the few women Delorme had ever met who could with any degree of accuracy be described as radiant. The words *manic* and *depressive*—not to mention *bipolar* or *psychotic*— evoked images of the frazzled, the wild-eyed. But Catherine had radiated gentleness, intelligence, even wisdom.

Delorme, single for more years than she cared to count, often found the company of married couples tedious. In general, they lacked the spark of people still on the hunt. And they had an exasperating way of implying that single people were in some way defective. Most upsetting of all, many seemed not even to like each other, treating their partners with a rudeness they would never dream of inflicting on a stranger. But Cardinal and his wife, married God knew how long, seemed genuinely to enjoy each other's company. Cardinal talked about Catherine almost every day, unless she was in the hospital, and then his silence had always struck Delorme as an expression not of shame but of loyalty. He was always telling Delorme about Catherine's latest photograph, or how she had helped some former student get a job, about an award she had won, or something funny she had said.

But in Delorme's experience there was something impos-
ing about Catherine, something commanding, even when
you knew her psychiatric history. In fact, it may partly have
been an effect of that very psychiatric history: the aura of
someone who had traveled into the depths of madness and
come back to tell the tale. Only this time she hadn't come
back.

And maybe Cardinal's better off, Delorme thought. Maybe
it's not the worst thing for him to be free of this beautiful albatross. Delorme had witnessed the toll on Cardinal when his
wife had been hospitalized, and at such times she found herself surprisingly angry at the woman who could make his life
a misery.

Lise Delorme, she told herself as she came to a stop at the
crime-scene tape, sometimes you can be a hundred-percent
unforgivable unmitigated bitch.

If Chouinard had been hoping his speedy dispatch of
Delorme would prevent suspect number one from messing
up a crime scene, he was too late. As she got out of the car,
she could see Cardinal holding his wife in his arms, blood
all over his suede jacket.

A young cop—Sanderson was his name—was standing
guard by the crime-scene tape.

"You were first on the scene?" Delorme asked him.

"Got an anonymous call from someone in the building.
Said there appeared to be a body out back. I proceeded here,
ascertained that she was dead, and put in a call to the sarge.
She called CID and Cardinal got here first. I had no idea it
was his wife." There was a trill of panic in his voice. "There's
no ID on the body. There's no way I could've known."

"That's all right," Delorme said. "You did the right
thing."

"If I'd have known, I'd have kept him away from her. But
he didn't know either till he got up close. I'm not gonna get
in trouble over this, am I?"

"Calm down, Sanderson, you're not in trouble. Ident and
the coroner will be here any second."

Delorme went over to Cardinal. She could tell from the

damage to his wife that she had fallen from a high floor. Cardinal had turned her over and was holding her up in his arms as if she were asleep. His face was streaked with blood and tears.

Delorme squatted beside him. She gently touched Catherine's wrist and then her neck, establishing two things: there was no pulse, and the body was still warm, though beginning to cool at the extremities. There was a camera bag nearby, some of its contents spilling out onto the asphalt.

"John," she said softly.

When he did not respond, she said his name again, her voice even softer. "John, listen. I'm only going to say this once. What we have here, this is breaking my heart, okay? Right now I feel like curling up in a corner and crying and not coming out till somebody tells me this isn't real. You hear me? My heart is going out to you. But you and I both know what has to happen."

Cardinal nodded. "I didn't realize it was . . . till I got up close."

"I understand," Delorme said. "But you're going to have to put her down now."

Cardinal was crying, and she just let him. Arsenault and Collingwood, the Ident team, were heading toward them. She held up her hand to ward them off.

"John. Can you put her down for me now? I need you to put her back just the way she was when you found her. Ident's here. The coroner's going to be here. However this happened, we need to do this investigation by the book."

Cardinal shifted Catherine off his knees and, with futile tenderness, turned her face down. He arranged her left hand over her head. "This hand was up like this," he said. "This one," he said, taking her other arm by the wrist, "was down by her side. Her arms are broken, Lise."

"I know." Delorme wanted to touch him, comfort him, but she forced her professional self to keep control. "Come with me now, John. Let Ident do their work, okay?"

Cardinal got to his feet, swaying a little. Sanderson had been joined by lots of uniformed colleagues, and Delorme was aware of one or two people watching from balconies as she led Cardinal past the crime-scene tape and over to her car. Bits of computer crunched underfoot. She opened the passenger door for him and he got in. She got in on the driver's side and shut the door.

"Where were you when you got the call?" Delorme said.

She couldn't be sure from Cardinal's expression if he was taking anything in. Was he aware of the ambulance, its lights uselessly flashing? Did he see the coroner heading toward the body with his medical bag? Arsenault and Collingwood in their white paper jumpsuits? McLeod slowly pacing the perimeter, eyes to the ground? She couldn't tell.

"John, I know it's a terrible time to ask questions." It was what they always said. She hoped he understood that she had to do this, probe the wound with the knife still in it.

When he spoke, his voice was surprisingly clear; he just sounded exhausted. "I was at the Birches Motel, in my car, with the mayor."

"Mayor Feckworth? How come?"

"He was demanding a full missing persons on his wife, threatening to go to the chief, the papers. Someone had to break the bad news to him."

"How long were you with him?"

"About two and a half hours, all told. He came to the station first. McLeod can confirm all this. Szelagy too."

"Szelagy was still staking out the motel on the Porcini case?"

Cardinal nodded. "He may still be there. He'll have his radio off. You would too, if you were watching the Porcinis."

"Do you know why Catherine would be here at this building?"

"She went out to take photographs. I don't know if she knew anybody here. Must have, I guess, to get access."

Delorme could almost hear Cardinal's cop mind trying to click back into gear.

"We should be checking out the roof," he said. "If that's not where she went over, we should be canvassing the upper floors. You should be, I mean. I can't be involved."

"Wait here a minute," Delorme said.

She got out of the car and found McLeod over by the Dumpster.

"Lot of crap all over the place," he said. "Looks like someone blew up a computer back here."

"CompuClinic's out front," Delorme said. "Listen, did you see Cardinal earlier this evening?"

"Yeah, he was in the office till seven-thirty or so. Mayor showed up around seven-fifteen and they went out together. Probably to the Birches Motel, where his wife's been boinking the Sanitation Department. You want me to call the mayor?"

"You have his number?"

"Do I ever. Guy's been bugging me all week." McLeod had already pulled out his cell phone and selected a number from a list that glowed lilac in his palm.

Delorme went over to the Ident guys. They were down on their knees picking up small items and dropping them into evidence bags. The moon was higher now, and no longer orange. It lit the scene with a silvery light. A cool breeze carried smells of old leaves. Why do the worst horrors occur on the most beautiful nights? Delorme wondered.

"You bagged her hands?" she said to Arsenault.

He looked up at her. "Well, yeah. Until we actually rule out foul play."

Collingwood, the younger member of the Ident team, was extracting objects from the camera bag that lay a few feet from the body. He was young, blond, and laconic almost to the point of hostility.

"Camera," he said, holding up a Nikon. The lens was smashed.

"She was a photographer," Delorme said. "Cardinal said she went out this evening to take pictures. What else?"

"Spare rolls of film. Battery. Lenses. Filters. Lens tissue."

"About what you'd expect, in other words."

He didn't reply. Sometimes it was as if you hadn't quite hit Collingwood's ENTER button.

"Found car keys in her coat pocket," Arsenault said, handing them over.

"I'll check out her car," Delorme said, reaching for them.

The coroner was getting up from the body, whacking dust from the lower part of his overcoat. It was Dr. Claybourne, already balding in his early thirties. Delorme had worked with him a couple of times before. He had asked her out once, but she had declined, saying she was already seeing someone, untrue at the time. Some men were too nice, in Delorme's view, too harmless, too bland. It was like being alone but without privacy.

"What do you think?" Delorme said.

Dr. Claybourne had a ring of red hair around his pate and pale, almost translucent skin. He blushed a lot, Delorme had noticed, which she put down to his complexion.

"Well, she's taken a terrible fall, obviously. And from the amount of blood, she was certainly alive when she fell."

"Time of death?"

"I only have body temperature to go on, at the moment, and the lack of rigor. I'd say she's been dead about two hours."

Delorme looked at her watch. "Which would put it at about eight-thirty. What do the measurements tell you?"

"Oh, I'd have to bow to your forensics experts on that. She's eight feet from the edge of the building. The balconies extend five feet. She could have fallen from a balcony or a window."

"From how high, do you think?"

"Hard to say. Somewhere around ten stories is my guess."

"The building's only nine. We should probably start with the roof."

"All right. I'm not seeing any evidence of foul play, so far."

"I have a feeling you won't find any. The victim is known to me, Doctor: Catherine Cardinal. Are you aware of her medical history?"

"No."

"Call the psychiatric hospital. She's been hospitalized up there at least four times in the past eight years. Her last stay was about a year ago and lasted three months. When you've done that, why don't we go up to the roof?"

McLeod was waving her over. She left Claybourne dialing his cell phone.

"Feckless Feckworth was not happy to hear from me. I could hear the wife screaming at him in the background. Naturally I brought all my diplomatic and social skills to bear."

"I can imagine."

"His Worship says Cardinal was with him at the Birches till nine-thirty. Szelagy says the same."

"You heard from Szelagy?"

"Yeah, he's off the Porcinis for the night. He's on his way."

Delorme went to her car. Cardinal was where she had left him, looking as if he had taken a large-caliber round in the gut. Delorme led him over to the ambulance.

The paramedic was a hard-looking woman with very short blond hair. Her uniform was tight on her.

"Victim's husband," Delorme said. "Take care of him, will you?" She turned to Cardinal. "John, I'm heading up to the roof now. Stay here and let these people look after you. I'll be back in about ten minutes."

Cardinal sat down on the folded-out tail of the ambulance. Once again Delorme suppressed an urge to put her arms around him: her friend in agony and she has to remain all business.

McLeod and Dr. Claybourne went with her in the elevator to the top floor. Then they had to take the stairwell up another flight to a door marked PATIO. The door was propped open with a brick. McLeod found a switch and turned on the exterior lights.

The roof had been covered with pressed wood flooring, and there were picnic tables with holes for umbrellas. The umbrellas had been taken in; the autumn breezes were already too cold for anyone to enjoy sitting outside for more than a few minutes.

"I can see why she might have come up here to take pictures," Delorme said, looking around. To the north, a string of highway lights wound up the hill toward the airport. Slightly to the east was the dark shoulder of the escarpment, and to the south, the lights of the city, the cathedral spire, and the post office communications tower. The moon was rolling out from behind the twin belfries of the French church.

McLeod pointed to an unadorned concrete wall, waist high, that surrounded the roof. "Doesn't look like the kind of thing you could easily fall over. Maybe she was leaning over to take a picture. Might want to look at what's on her camera."

"The camera was in the bag, so I don't think she was shooting when she fell."

"Might wanna check anyway."

Delorme pointed in the direction of the moon. "That's where she went off."

"Why don't you examine it first?" Dr. Claybourne said. "I'll take a look when you're done."

Delorme and McLeod, careful where they stepped, walked slowly toward the edge of the roof. McLeod said in a low voice, "I think the doc's sweet on you."

"McLeod, really."

"Come on. Did you see the way he blushed?"

"McLeod!"

Delorme approached the railing, head bowed, looking at the flooring in front of her. The area was well lit by the moon and by the roof lights. She paused at the wall and peered over, walked slowly to the left, and then back to the right beyond where she had started.

"I'm not seeing any obvious signs of struggle," she said. "No signs at all, in fact."

"Here's something." McLeod had spotted a piece of paper wedged under a planter and stooped to pick it up. He brought it over to Delorme, a lined page about four by six, torn from a spiral notebook.

It contained a few sentences, in ballpoint, written in a small intense hand.

Dear John,

By the time you read this, I will have hurt you beyond all forgiveness. There are no words to tell you how sorry I am. Please know that I've always loved you—never more so than at this moment—and if there had been any other way . . .

Catherine

3

When Delorme got back downstairs, she found Szelagy just entering the lobby with a distraught woman in black: black skirt, black blazer, black hat, black scarf.

"Sergeant Delorme," Szelagy said, "this is Eleanor Cathcart. She lives on the ninth floor, and she knows Catherine."

"I can't believe this is happening," the woman said. She removed her hat and swept black hair from her forehead in a dramatic gesture. Everything about her seemed exaggerated; she had dark eyebrows, dark lipstick, and skin as pale as china, though there was nothing remotely fragile about her. Her pronunciation of certain words hinted at a cozy familiarity with Paris. "I let her into the building and she goes off the roof? It's just too—too *macabre*."

"How do you know Catherine Cardinal?" Delorme said.

"I teach up at the community college. Theater Arts. Catherine teaches photography there. *Mon Dieu*, I can't believe this. I just let her in a couple of hours ago."

"Why did you let her in?"

"Oh, I'd been raving about the views from my apartment. She asked me if she could come up and take photographs. We're the only building of any height this side of town. She's been talking about it for months, but we'd just recently set up an actual rendezvous."

"For her to come to your apartment?"

"No, she just needed access to the roof. There's a patio thingy up there. I showed her where it was and showed her how to prop the door open—it locks you out otherwise, as

I've learned from bitter experience. I didn't linger. She was working, she didn't want company. The arts demand a great deal of solitude."

"You're quite sure she was alone?"

"She was alone."

"Where were you going?"

"Rehearsal at the Capital Centre. We're opening *A Doll's House* two weeks from now and, believe me, some of us are not ready for prime time. Our Torvald is still on book, for God's sake."

"Was Catherine showing any signs of distress?"

"None. Well, wait. She was very intense, very anxious to get to the roof, but I took that as excitement about her work. Then again, Catherine is not an easy read, if you know what I mean. She regularly gets depressed enough to be hospitalized, and I never saw that coming either. Of course, like most artists, I'm somewhat prone to self-absorption."

"So it wouldn't surprise you if she committed suicide?"

"Well, it's a shock, I mean, *mon Dieu.* You imagine I'd just hand her the key to the roof and say, 'Ta-ta, darling. Have a nice suicide while I just pop out to rehearsal'? Please."

The woman paused, tossing her head back and looking up at the ceiling. Then she leveled a look at Delorme with dark theatrical eyes. "Put it this way," she said. "I stand here thunderstruck, but at the same time, out of all the people I know—and I know a *lot*—I'd say Catherine Cardinal was the most likely to kill herself. You don't get hospitalized for a simple case of the blues, you don't get slapped into the ward for a slight disappointment, and you don't take lithium for PMS. And have you seen her work?"

"Some," Delorme said. She was remembering an exhibition at the library a couple of years ago: a photograph of a child crying on the cathedral steps, an empty park bench, a single red umbrella in a landscape of rain. Photographs of longing. Like Catherine herself, beautiful but sad.

"I rest my case," Ms. Cathcart said.

Just as Delorme's inner magistrate was condemning the woman for displaying an unforgivable lack of sympathy, she exploded into tears—and not the decorous weeping of the stage but the messy, mucus-y wails of real, unrehearsed pain.

DELORME WENT WITH Dr. Claybourne to the ambulance, where they found Cardinal still sitting in the back. He spoke before they even reached him, his voice thick and oppressed.

"Was there a note?"

Claybourne held it out so he could read it. "Can you confirm whether this is your wife's handwriting?"

Cardinal nodded. "It's hers," he said, and looked away.

Delorme walked Claybourne over to his car.

"Well, you saw that," the coroner said. "He identifies the handwriting as his wife's."

"Yeah," Delorme said. "I saw."

"There'll have to be an autopsy, of course, but it's suicide as far as I'm concerned. We have no signs of a struggle, we have a note, and we have a history of depression."

"You spoke to the hospital?"

"I got hold of her psychiatrist at home. He's distressed, of course—it's always upsetting to lose a patient—but he's not surprised."

"All right. Thanks, Doctor. We'll finish canvassing the building, just in case. Let me know if there's anything else we can do."

"I will," Claybourne said, and got into his car. "Depressing, isn't it, suicide?"

"To put it mildly," Delorme said. She had attended the scenes of two others in the past few months.

She looked around for Cardinal, who wasn't by the ambulance anymore, and spotted him behind the wheel of his car. He didn't look like he was leaving.

Delorme got in the passenger side.

"There'll be an autopsy, but the coroner's going to make a finding of suicide," she said.

"You're not going to canvass the building?"

"Of course. But I don't think we're going to find anything."

Cardinal dipped his head. Delorme couldn't imagine what he was thinking. When he finally did speak, it wasn't what she was expecting.

"I'm sitting here trying to figure out how I'm going to get her car home," he said. "There's probably a simple solution, but right now it seems like an insurmountable problem."

"I'll get it to your place," Delorme said, "when we're done here. In the meantime, is there anyone I can call? Someone who can come and stay with you? You shouldn't be alone at a time like like this."

"I'll call Kelly. I'll call Kelly soon as I get home."

"But Kelly's in New York, no? Don't you have anyone here?"

Cardinal started his car. "I'll be all right," he said.

He didn't sound all right.

4

"Do those shoes hurt?"

Kelly Cardinal was sitting at the dining room table, wrapping a framed photograph of her mother in bubble wrap. She wanted to take one to the funeral home to place beside the casket.

Cardinal sat down in the chair opposite. Several days had passed, but he was still stunned, unable to take the world in. His daughter's words hadn't organized themselves into anything he could decipher. He had to ask her to repeat herself.

"Those shoes you're wearing," she said. "They look brand new. Are they pinching your feet?"

"A little. I've only worn them once—to Dad's funeral."

"That was two years ago."

"Oh, I love that picture."

Cardinal reached for the portrait of Catherine in working mode. Dressed in a yellow anorak, her hair wild with rain, she was burdened with two cameras—one around her neck, the other slung over her shoulder. She was looking exasperated. Cardinal remembered snapping the photo with the little point-and-shoot that remained the only photographic apparatus he had ever mastered. Catherine had indeed been exasperated with him, first because she was trying to work, and second because she knew what the rain was doing to her beautiful hair and didn't want to be photographed. In dry weather her hair fell in soft cascades to her shoulders; when it rained it went wild and frizzy, which pricked her vanity. But Cardinal loved her hair wild.

"For a photographer, she sure hated getting her picture taken," he said.

"Maybe we shouldn't use it. She looks a little annoyed."

"No, no. Please. That's Catherine doing what she loved."

Cardinal had at first resisted the idea of having a photograph; it had struck him as undignified, to say nothing of the fact that the sight of Catherine's face tore his heart open.

But Catherine thought in photographs. Come into a room when she was working, and before you could open your mouth she had taken your picture. It was as if the camera were a protective mechanism that had evolved over the years solely to provide a defense for elusive, breakable people like her. She wasn't a snob about photographs, either. She could be as ecstatic over a lucky snap of a street scene as over a series of images she had struggled with for months.

Kelly put the wrapped picture into her bag. "Go and change your shoes. You don't want to be standing around in shoes that don't fit."

"They fit," Cardinal said. "They're just not broken in yet."

"Go on, Dad."

Cardinal went into the bedroom and opened the closet. He tried not to look at the half that contained Catherine's clothes, but he couldn't help himself. She mostly wore jeans and T-shirts or sweaters. She was the kind of woman, even approaching fifty, who still looked good in jeans and T-shirts. But there were small black dresses, some silky blouses, a camisole or two, mostly in the grays and blacks she had always preferred. "My governess colors," she called them.

Cardinal pulled out the black shoes he wore every day and set about polishing them. The doorbell rang, and he heard Kelly thanking a neighbor who had brought food and condolences.

When she came into the bedroom, Cardinal was embarrassed to realize he was kneeling on the floor in front of the closet, shoe brush in hand, motionless as a victim of Pompeii.

"We're going to have to leave pretty soon," Kelly said. "We have an hour to ourselves there before people start arriving."

"Uh-huh."

"Shoes, Dad. Shoes."

"Right."

Kelly sat on the edge of the bed behind him as Cardinal started brushing. He could see her reflection in the mirror on the closet door. She had his eyes, people always told him. But she had Catherine's mouth, with tiny parentheses at the corners that grew when she smiled. And she would have Catherine's hair too, if she let it grow out from the rather severe bob of the moment, with its single streak of mauve. She was more impatient than her mother, seemed to expect more from other people, who were always disappointing her, but perhaps that was just a matter of being young. She could be a harsh judge of herself too, often to the point of tears, and not so long ago she had been a harsh judge of her father. But she had relented the last time Catherine had been admitted to the hospital, and they had been getting along pretty well since then.

"It's bad enough for me," Kelly said, "but I really don't understand how Mom could do this to you. All those years you stood by her when she was such a loony."

"She was a lot more than that, Kelly."

"I know, but all you had to go through! Looking after me when I was a little kid—raising me practically by yourself. And the stuff you put up with from her. I remember one time—back when we were living in Toronto—you'd been building this really complicated cabinet, full of drawers and little doors. I think you'd been working on it for like a year or something, and one day you come home and she's smashed it to pieces so she could burn it! She was on some trip about fire and creative destruction, some manic rap that made no sense at all, and she destroyed this thing you were creating with such devotion. How do you forgive something like that?"

Cardinal was silent for a time. Finally he turned to look at his daughter. "Catherine never did anything I didn't forgive."

"That's because of who *you* are, not because of what *she* was. How could she not realize how lucky she was? How could she just throw it all away?"

Kelly was crying now. Cardinal touched her shoulder and she leaned against him, hot tears soaking through his shirt the way her mother's had so often done.

"She was in pain," Cardinal said. "She was suffering in a way no one could reach. That's what you have to remember. Difficult as she could be sometimes to live with, she's the one who suffered the most. No one hated her disease more than she did.

"And if you think she wasn't grateful to be loved, you're wrong, Kelly. If there was one phrase she used more than any other, it was 'I'm so lucky.' She said it all the time. We'd be having dinner or something and she'd touch my hand and say, 'I'm so lucky.' She used to say it about you, too. She felt terrible that she missed so much of your growing up. She did everything she could to fight this disease and in the end it just beat her, that's all. Your mother had tremendous courage—and loyalty—to last as long as she did."

"God," Kelly said. She sounded like she had a cold now, nose all stuffed up. "I wish I was half as compassionate as you. Now I've gone and ruined your shirt."

"I wasn't going to wear this one anyway."

He handed her a box of Kleenex and she plucked out a handful.

"I gotta go wash my face," she said. "I look like Medea."

Cardinal wasn't sure who Medea was. Nor was he at all sure about the comforting things he had just told his daughter. What do I know about anything? he thought. I didn't even see this coming. I'm worse than the mayor. Nearly thirty years together, and I don't see that the woman I love is on the verge of killing herself?

PROMPTED BY THAT very question, Cardinal had the previous day driven into town to talk to Catherine's psychiatrist.

He had met Frederick Bell a couple of times during Catherine's last stay in the hospital. They had not talked long enough for Cardinal to form much more than an impression of intelligence and competence. But Catherine had been delighted to discover him because, unlike most psychiatrists, Bell was a talk therapist as well as a prescriber of drugs. He was also a specialist in depression who had written books on the subject.

His office was in his house, an Edwardian monstrosity of red brick located on Randall Street, just behind the cathedral. Previous owners included a member of Parliament and a man who went on to become a minor media baron. With its turrets and gingerbread, not to mention its elaborate garden and wrought-iron fence, the house dominated the neighborhood.

Cardinal was met at the door by Mrs. Bell, a friendly woman in her fifties, who was on her way out. When Cardinal introduced himself, she said, "Oh, Detective Cardinal, I'm so sorry for your loss."

"Thank you."

"You're not here in any official capacity, are you?"

"No, no. My wife was a patient of your husband's, and—"

"Of course, of course. You're bound to have questions."

She went off to find her husband, and Cardinal looked around at his surroundings. Polished hardwood, oak paneling and moldings—and that was just the waiting area. He was about to sit down in one of a row of chairs when a door swung open and Dr. Bell was there, bigger than Cardinal remembered him, well over six feet, with a curly brown beard, gray at the jawline, and a pleasant English accent that Cardinal knew was neither extremely posh nor working class.

He took Cardinal's hand in both of his and shook it. "Detective Cardinal, let me say again, I'm so terribly sorry about Catherine. You have my deepest, deepest sympathy. Come in, come in."

Except for a vast desk and the lack of a television, they might have been in somone's living room. Bookshelves, crammed to the ceiling with medical and psychology texts, journals, and binders, covered all four walls. Plump leather chairs, battered and far from matching, were set at conversational angles. And of course, there was a couch: a comfortable home-style sofa, not the severe geometric kind you saw in movies featuring psychiatrists.

At the doctor's urging, Cardinal took a seat on the couch.

"Can I get you something to drink? Coffee? Tea?"

"Thanks, I'm fine. Thank you for seeing me on such short notice."

"Oh, no. It's the least I can do," Dr. Bell said. He hitched his corduroy trousers before sitting in one of the leather chairs. He was wearing an Irish wool sweater and didn't look at all like a medical man. A college professor, Cardinal thought, or perhaps a violinist.

"I imagine you're asking yourself how it is you didn't see this coming," Bell said, expressing exactly what had been running through Cardinal's mind.

"Yes," Cardinal said. "That pretty much sums it up."

"You're not alone. Here I am, someone with whom Catherine has been discussing her emotional life in detail for nearly a year, and *I* didn't see it coming."

He sat back and shook his woolly head. Cardinal was reminded of an Airedale.

After a moment the doctor said softly, "Obviously, I would have admitted her if I had."

"But isn't it unusual?" Cardinal said. "To have a patient who keeps coming to see you but doesn't mention that she's planning to. . . . Why would anyone continue seeing a therapist they couldn't, or wouldn't, confide in?"

"She did confide in me. Catherine was no stranger to suicidal thoughts. Now don't get me wrong, she gave no indication of any imminent plan. But certainly we discussed her feelings about suicide. Part of her was horrified by the idea, part of her found it very attractive—as I'm sure you know."

Cardinal nodded. "It's one of the first things she told me about herself, before we were married."

"Honesty was one of Catherine's strengths," Bell said. "She often said she would rather die than go through another major depression—and not just to spare herself, I hasten to add. Like most people who suffer from depression, she hated the fact that it made life so difficult for the people she loved. I'd be surprised if she hadn't expressed this to you over the years."

"Many times," Cardinal said, and felt something collapse inside him. The room went blurry, and the doctor handed him a box of Kleenex.

After a few moments, Dr. Bell knit his brows and leaned forward in his chair. "You couldn't have done anything, you know. Please let me set your mind at rest on that point. It's quite common for people who commit suicide to give no sign of their intention."

"I know. She wasn't giving away objects that were precious to her or anything like that."

"No. None of the classic signs. Nor is there a previous attempt in her medical records, although there is plenty of suicidal ideation. But what we do have is an ongoing decades-long battle with clinical depression, part of her bipolar disorder. The statistics are indisputable: people who suffer from manic depression are *the* most likely to kill themselves, bar none. God, I almost sound like I know what I'm talking about, don't I?" Dr. Bell held his hands up in a gesture of helplessness. "Something like this—well, it makes you feel pretty incompetent."

"I'm sure it's not your fault," Cardinal said. He didn't know what he was doing here. Had he come to listen to this rumpled Englishman talk about statistics and probabilities? Clearly, *I'm* the one who sees her every day, he thought. *I'm* the one who's known her longest. *I'm* the one who didn't pay attention. Too stupid, too selfish, too blind.

"It's tempting to blame yourself, isn't it?" Bell said, once again reading his thoughts.

"Merely factual in my case," Cardinal said, and could not miss the bitterness in his own voice.

"But I'm doing the same thing," the doctor said. "It's the collateral damage of suicide. All people close to someone who commits suicide are going to feel they didn't do enough, they weren't sensitive enough, they should have intervened. But that doesn't mean those feelings are accurate assessments of reality."

The doctor said some other things that Cardinal seemed to miss. His mind was a burned-out building. A shell. How could he expect to know what was going on around him at any given moment?

As Cardinal was leaving, Bell said, "Catherine was fortunate to be married to you. And she knew it."

The doctor's words threatened to undo him all over again. He just managed to hold himself together, like a patient fresh off the operating table clutching together his stitched halves. Somehow he blundered his way out through the waiting room and into the gold autumn light.

5

Desmond's Funeral Home is centrally located at the corner
of Sumner and Earl streets, which pretty much means anyone coming in or out of town has to drive past it, turning it
into a daily memento mori for the citizens of Algonquin
Bay. It's not a pretty building, little more than a cement-
block rhomboid, painted a cream color to soften the severity
of its outlines and lighten the darkness of its implications.
Whenever Cardinal's father had driven by, he would always
wave and yell, "You haven't got me yet, Mr. Desmond! You
haven't got me yet!"

But of course Mr. Desmond *had* got Stan Cardinal in the
end, just as he had got Cardinal's mother before him and would
get every other resident of Algonquin Bay—the Catholics,
anyway. There was another funeral home a few blocks east that
got the Protestants, and still another, newer, establishment that
seemed to be doing a brisk business with recently deceased
Jews, Muslims, and "others."

Mr. Desmond was not in fact one man, but a many-per-
soned entity whose sad but necessary tasks were vigorously
carried out by numerous Desmond sons, daughters, and in-
laws.

As Cardinal stepped through the funeral home entrance
with Kelly, thick clouds of emotion gathered in his chest.
His knees began to tremble. David Desmond, a neat young
man married to precision, shook hands with them. He wore
a trim gray suit with just the right rectangle of perfectly
starched handkerchief showing above the breast pocket. His

shoes were gleaming black brogues more suited to an older man.

"You have forty-three minutes before people start arriving," he said. "Would you like to go in now?"

Cardinal nodded.

"All right. You're in the Rose Room just over that way, the second pair of oak doors on the right, just past the highboy with the head-and-shoulders clock." The directions were delivered as if they were embarking on a journey of some miles instead of thirty feet of pastel carpet. In any case Mr. Desmond Jr. escorted them and slid open the doors.

"Please go in," he said. "I'll be right here if you need anything."

Cardinal had been in this room before and knew what to expect: walls a soothing dusty pink, matching couches and armchairs, tasteful end tables dominated by gauzy lamps that bathed everything in diffuse, benevolent light. But when he stepped through the doorway he stopped, emitting one syllable—actually a sigh, a sudden expulsion of breath not intended as speech.

"What is it?" Kelly said from behind him. "Is something wrong?"

"I asked for a closed casket," Cardinal managed to say. "I wasn't expecting to see her again."

"Uh—no. Me either."

The two of them stood just inside the doorway. The room stretched into a rose-colored tunnel, at the other end of which Catherine, impossibly beautiful, lay waiting.

Finally Kelly said, "Do you want me to ask them to close it?"

Cardinal didn't answer. He crossed the room with slow, tentative steps, as if the floor might give way at any moment.

Years previously, when Cardinal's mother had been laid out in this same room, the figure in the coffin had scarcely resembled her. The disease that had consumed her had left no vestige of the chirpy, strong-willed woman who had loved him all his life. And his father too, minus his glasses and his combative manner, might have been a complete stranger.

But Catherine was Catherine: the wide brow, the full mouth with its tiny parentheses, the brown hair curling gracefully to her shoulders. How the Desmonds had repaired the damage inflicted by the fall, Cardinal didn't want to know. The left cheekbone had been completely smashed, but now here was his wife, face whole, cheekbones intact. The sight yanked Cardinal into yet another dimension of pain. *Pain* was not a big enough word for this country of agony, this Yukon of grief.

A bend in time, and he was huddled on one of the pink couches, exhausted and sighing. Kelly was beside him, clutching a soggy ball of Kleenex.

Someone was speaking to him. Cardinal rose unsteadily and shook hands with Mr. and Mrs. Walcott, neighbors on Madonna Road. They were retired schoolteachers who spent most of their time bickering. Today they had apparently agreed to a cease-fire and presented a united front that was formal and subdued.

"Very sorry for your loss," Mr. Walcott said.

Mrs. Walcott took a nimble step forward. "Such a tragedy," she said. "At such a lovely time of year, too."

"Yes," Cardinal said. "Autumn was always Catherine's favorite season."

"Did you get the casserole all right?"

Cardinal looked at Kelly, who nodded.

"Yes, thank you. It's very kind of you."

"You just have to reheat it. Twenty minutes at two-fifty ought to do it."

Others were arriving. One at a time they went to stand by the coffin, some kneeling and crossing themselves. There were teachers from Northern University, and the community college where Catherine had taught, and former students. There was white-haired Mr. Fisk, for decades the proprietor of Fisk's Camera Shop until it was put out of business, like half of Main Street, by the deadly munificence of Wal-Mart.

"That's a great picture of Catherine, with the cameras," Mr. Fisk said. "She used to come into the store looking just like that. Always she'd be wearing that anorak or the fishing

vest. Remember that fishing vest?" Nervousness was mani-
festing itself in Mr. Fisk as jauntiness, as if they were discussing an eccentric friend who had moved away. "Nice
turnout," he added, looking around with approval.

Catherine's students, middle-aged some of them, others
young and teary-eyed, murmured kind words at Cardinal.
No matter how conventional, they pierced Cardinal in a way
that surprised him. Who would have thought mere words
could be so powerful?

His colleagues showed up: McLeod in a suit that had
been cut for a smaller man, Collingwood and Arsenault looking like an out-of-work comedy duo. Larry Burke made the
sign of the cross in front of the coffin and stood before it
with head bowed for some time. He didn't know Cardinal all
that well—he was new to the detective squad—but he came
over and said how sorry he was.

Delorme showed up in a dark blue dress. Cardinal couldn't
remember the last time he'd seen her in a dress.

"Such a sad day," she said, hugging him. He could feel her
trembling slightly, fighting tears of sympathy, and he couldn't
speak. She knelt before the coffin for a few minutes, and then
came back to give Cardinal another hug, her eyes wet.

Police Chief R. J. Kendall came, along with Detective
Sergeant Chouinard, Ken Szelagy—everyone from CID—
and various patrol constables.

Another bend in the afternoon, and they were at High-
lawn crematorium. Cardinal had no memory of the drive out
into the hills. It had been Catherine's request that there be no
church service, but in the will she and Cardinal had had
drawn up, she had asked that Father Samson Mkembe say a
few words.

When Cardinal had been an altar boy, all of the priests
had been of Irish descent or French Canadian. But now the
church had to recruit from farther afield, and Father
Mkembe had come all the way from Sierra Leone. He stood
at the front of the crematory chapel, a tall bony man with a
face of high-gloss ebony.

The chapel was almost full. Cardinal saw Meredith Moore,

head of the art department up at the college, and Sally Westlake, a close friend of Catherine's. And he could make out among the mourners the woolly head of Dr. Bell.

Father Mkembe talked about Catherine's strength. Indeed, he got most of her good qualities right—no doubt because he had phoned earlier asking Kelly for tips. But he spoke also about how Catherine's faith had sustained her in adversity: a patent falsehood, as Catherine only went to church for the big occasions and had long ago stopped believing in God.

The furnace doors opened and the flames flared for an instant. The coffin rolled in, the doors closed, and the priest said a final prayer. A doomsday bell was tolling in Cardinal's heart: *You failed her.*

The colors of the world outside were unnaturally bright. The sky was the blue of a gas flame, and the carpet of autumn leaves seemed to emit light, not just reflect it—golds and yellows and rusty reds. A shadow passed over Cardinal as the smoke that had been his wife dimmed the sun.

"Mr. Cardinal, I don't know if you remember me. . . ."

Meredith Moore was shaking Cardinal's hand in her dry little palm. She was a wisp of a woman, so dehydrated she looked as if she should be dropped in water to expand to her natural size.

"Catherine and I were colleagues."

"Yes, Mrs. Moore. We've met a few times over the years." In fact, Mrs. Moore had fought a nasty battle with Catherine over control of the art department. She had not been shy about raising Catherine's psychiatric history as an impediment, and in the end she had prevailed.

"Catherine will be sorely missed," she said, adding, "The students are so fond of her," in a tone that implied the complete bankruptcy of student opinion.

Cardinal left her to find Kelly, who was being hugged by Sally Westlake. Sally was an outsized woman with an outsized heart and one of the few people Cardinal had called personally about Catherine's death.

"Oh, John," she said, dabbing her eyes, "I'm going to miss her so much. She was my best friend. My inspiration.

That's not just a cliché; she was always challenging me to think more about my photographs, to shoot more, to spend more time in the darkroom. She was just the best. And she was so proud of *you*," she said to Kelly.

"I don't see why," Kelly said.

"Because you're just like her, talented and brave. Pursuing a career in art in New York? Takes guts, my dear."

"On the other hand, it could be a complete waste of time."

"Oh, don't say that!" For a moment, Cardinal thought Sally was going to pinch his daughter's cheek or ruffle her hair.

Dr. Bell came up to give his condolences once more.

"It's kind of you to come," Cardinal said. "This is my daughter, Kelly. She's just up from New York for a few days. Dr. Bell was Catherine's psychiatrist."

Kelly gave a rueful smile. "Not one of your success stories, I guess."

"Kelly—"

"No, no, that's all right. Perfectly legitimate. Unfortunately, specializing in depression is a bit like being an oncologist; a low success rate is to be expected. But I didn't want to disturb you, I just wanted to pay my respects."

When he was gone, Kelly turned to her father. "You said Mom didn't seem particularly depressed."

"I know. But she's fooled me before."

"EVERYONE'S BEING SO kind," Kelly said, when they were back home. Troops of sympathy cards stood in formation across the dining room table, and in the kitchen the counter and table were heaped with Tupperware containers of casseroles, risottos, ratatouilles, meat loaves, tarts, and *tourtières*, even a baked ham.

"A nice tradition, this food thing," Cardinal said. "You start to feel all hollow and you know you must be hungry, but the thought of cooking is just too much. The thought of anything's too much."

"Why don't you go and lie down?" Kelly said, taking off her coat.

"No, I'd only feel worse. I'm going to put something in the microwave." He picked up a plastic container and stood contemplating it in the middle of the kitchen as if it were a device from the neighborhood of Arcturus.

"Even more cards," Kelly said, dropping a fistful on the kitchen table.

"Why don't you open them?"

Cardinal put the container in the microwave and faced the rows of buttons. Another hiatus. The simplest tasks were beyond him; Catherine was gone. What was the point of food? Of sleep? Of life? *You won't survive,* an inner voice told him. *You've had it.*

"Oh, my God," Kelly said.

"What?"

She was clutching a card in one hand and covering her mouth with the other.

"What is it?" Cardinal said. "Let me see."

Kelly shook her head and pulled the card away.

"Kelly, let me see that."

He took hold of her wrist and plucked the card from her hand.

"Just throw it out, Dad. Don't even look at it. Just throw it away."

The card was an expensive one, with a still life of a lily on it. Inside, the standard message of condolence had been covered by a small rectangle of paper, on which someone had typed:

How does it feel, asshole? Just no telling how things will turn out, is there.

6

The planet Grief. An incalculable number of light-years from the warmth of the sun. When the rain falls, it falls in droplets of grief, and when the light shines, it is in waves and particles of grief. From whatever direction the wind blows—south, east, north, or west—it blows cinders of grief before it. Grief stings your eyes and sucks the breath from your lungs. No oxygen on this planet, no nitrogen; the atmosphere is composed entirely of grief.

Grief came at Cardinal not just from the myriad objects that had been Catherine's: photographs, CDs, books, clothes, refrigerator magnets, the furniture she had chosen, the walls she had painted, the plants she had tended. Grief squeezed its way in through the seams of the house, under the doors, and around the windows.

He couldn't sleep. The note repeated itself over and over in his head. He got up from his bed and studied it under the bright lights of the kitchen. Kelly had thrown out the envelope, but he retrieved it from the trash. The type was clearly the work of a computer printer, but there was nothing distinctive about it—at least, nothing he could detect with the naked eye.

Nor was there anything remarkable about the card itself: a Hallmark sympathy card and envelope, available at any drug or stationery store across the country.

The postmark showed the date and time—that would be the date and time it was processed, of course, not the date and time of mailing—and the postal code. That code, Cardinal knew, indicated not the exact location of mailing but the location of the processing plant where the card was handled. The postal code was followed by a three-digit number for the individual machine. Cardinal recognized the postmark as Mattawa's. He knew a few people who lived there, acquaintances who could have no possible reason to hurt him. Of course, Mattawa was prime cottage country; lots of people went there from all over Ontario for weekends by the river. But it was well into October, and most people had closed their cottages for the winter.

Of course, if you wanted to disguise your true whereabouts, there was nothing to stop you from driving to Mattawa and mailing a card from there; it was right on Highway 17, little more than half an hour east of Algonquin Bay.

LISE DELORME WAS surprised to see him. It was Sunday, and he had caught her in the middle of washing her windows. She was wearing jeans with huge rips at the knees and a paint-stained gingham shirt that looked at least twenty years old. Her house, a bungalow at the top of Rayne Street, smelled of vinegar and newsprint.

"I've been meaning to wash them since August," she said, as if he had asked, "and only just got around to it."

She made coffee.

"Decaf for you," she said. "Obviously you haven't been sleeping."

"That's true, but there's a reason. I mean another reason."

Delorme brought the coffee and a plate of chocolate chip cookies into the living room.

"Why don't you ask your doctor for some Valium?" she said. "There's no point making things worse with lack of sleep."

"Tell me what you think of this." He pulled the card and envelope out of a manila folder and placed them on the coffee table. They were in a clear plastic sleeve now, the card open, the envelope address-side up.

Delorme raised an eyebrow. "Work? How can you be bringing me work? I thought you were off for a week or two. Hell, if I were you, I'd be gone for months."

"Just take a look."

Delorme leaned over the coffee table. "Somebody sent you this?"

"Yeah."

"Oh, John. I'm so sorry. It's sick."

"I'd like to know who sent it. I thought you could give me your first impressions."

Delorme looked at the card. "Well, whoever it is went to the trouble of printing out this two-line message instead of writing it by hand. That tells me it's someone who thinks you might recognize his handwriting—or at least be able to match it up."

"Any candidates spring to mind?"

"Well, anyone you've put in jail, of course."

"Anyone? I'm not so sure. I put Tony Capozzi away for assault a couple of months ago, and sure, he's pissed off, but I don't see him doing something like this."

"I meant guys who are doing serious time. Five years or more, maybe. There's not so many of those."

"And of those, it's got to be someone who's sophisticated enough—and persistent enough—to find out my home address. It's not like I'm listed in the phone book. I'm thinking maybe someone connected with Rick Bouchard's gang."

Rick Bouchard had been one of the world's natural-born creeps—even by the low standards of drug dealers—until he was killed in prison a couple of years previously. Cardinal had helped put him there for a fifteen-year stretch and Bouchard, who, unlike most criminals, had many resources and a good deal of natural intelligence, had pursued him until the day he died.

"Possible," Delorme said, "but how likely is that? With Bouchard dead and all."

"They know my address, and it's their style. Kiki B showed up at my door with a threatening letter a couple of years ago."

"But Bouchard was still alive then, and Kiki has since retired, you told me."

"Do guys like Kiki ever really retire?"

"Lots of bad guys are going to know your address. There's the Internet, for one thing. And remember when that idiot reporter a few years ago did a stand-up right outside your house? That was a huge case. Who knows how many people saw that?"

"They didn't use that clip nationally. I checked. It was just local."

"Local covers a lot of territory, John." Delorme took his hand between her warm palms, one of the few times she had ever touched him. Her face was soft, and even through the blur of pain—perhaps *because* of his pain—Cardinal thought her at that moment extraordinarily beautiful. He realized she must put on an entirely different face for work, armored for the daily sarcasm festival of the squad room. Of course, so did he, so did everyone, but he had a sudden sense of Delorme, the only woman of the group, as a dolphin in a tank full of sharks.

"It could just as easily be some sick neighbor," she said. "Somebody with a grudge against the police. It isn't necessarily personal."

Cardinal picked up the plastic folder. "The postmark indicates Mattawa."

"Yeah, well. . . . Why don't you let this go? It isn't going to help you. It's not going to make you feel any better. And you'd have to go to one hell of a lot of trouble. I'm not even sure you could."

"I was going to ask you to do it."

"Me." She regarded him, her eyes a little less soft.

"I can't do it, Lise. I'm involved."

"I can't investigate this. It's not a crime to send a nasty card through the mail."

"*Just no telling how things will turn out,*" Cardinal read. "You don't see that as a threat—given the circumstances?"

"Me, I'd call it a statement. About life in general. It doesn't contain any threat of future harm."

"You don't find it ambiguous, even?"

"No, John, I don't. The first part is obviously nasty, but it's not a threat. The whole thing amounts to a sneer. You can't go investigating people for sneering."

"Suppose Catherine didn't kill herself," Cardinal said. "Suppose she was actually murdered."

"But she wasn't murdered. She left a *note*. She has a *history*. People who suffer from manic depression kill themselves all the time."

"I know that—"

"You saw the note. I searched her car afterward. I found the spiral notebook she wrote it in. The pen was there too. You recognized it right away as her handwriting."

"Yeah. Well, it's not like I'm an expert."

"No one saw or heard anything suspicious."

"But the building just opened. How many people live there, five?"

"Fifteen of the apartments have been bought. Ten of them are occupied so far."

"It's a ghost town, in other words. What were the chances of anyone seeing or hearing anything?"

"John, there were no signs of a struggle. None. I searched that roof myself. No blood, no scrape marks, nothing broken, nothing cracked. The Ident guys and the coroner found her position on the ground consistent with a fall."

"*Consistent* with a fall. Meaning she *could* have been pushed."

"The autopsy didn't show anything either. Everything is consistent with suicide. Nothing points to anything else."

"I want to know who sent that note, Lise. Are you going to help me or not?"

"I can't. The moment we heard back from the pathologist, Chouinard closed the case. If there's no case, that means there's no case *number*. What do I tell people? We're talking about my *job* here."

"All right," Cardinal said. "Forget I asked." He got up and retrieved his jacket from the chair. He stood in front of the window, doing up the buttons. Outside, the sky was still an otherworldly blue, and the fallen leaves made a duvet of ocher and gold.

"John, no one wants to believe the person they love killed themself."

"You missed a spot," Cardinal said, pointing to the window. Two little girls were playing in a pile of leaves next door, wriggling around in them like puppies.

"You don't have to do this. There's no need to find a culprit. It's not your fault she's dead."

"I know that," Cardinal said. "But maybe it's not Catherine's fault either."

7

All the next morning, Delorme couldn't get Cardinal out of her mind. She had a stack of reports to excavate, various assault and burglary charges to follow up, and a rapist who was coming to trial the next week. Her best witness was getting cold feet, and the whole case was threatening to come apart.

And then Detective Sergeant Chouinard dropped a new one in her lap.

"You're gonna get a call from Toronto Sex Crimes," he said. "Looks like they've got something for us."

"Why would Toronto Sex Crimes have something for Algonquin Bay?"

"They're envious of our worldwide reputation, obviously. But, don't thank me. You're not going to like this one."

The call came half an hour later from a Sergeant Leo Dukovsky, who claimed to remember Delorme from a forensics conference in Ottawa a couple of years earlier. He'd been giving a talk on computers; Delorme had been on a panel discussing accounting.

"Forensic accounting?" Delorme said. "That would make it almost ten years ago. I must've done something awful for you to remember me after so long."

"Nope. I just remember you as a very attractive French person, with a—"

"French-Canadian," Delorme corrected him. She was willing to be charmed, but there were limits.

Sergeant Dukovsky didn't waver for a moment. "—with a very French name and no accent whatsoever."

"Why? You think we all live in the backwoods? Talk like Jean Chrétien?"

"That's another thing I remember about you. Kinda prickly."

"Maybe it's something you bring out in people, Sergeant. Did you ever think of that?"

"See, that's just the kind of remark that makes a man remember you," Dukovsky said, "when he has some really nasty work to be done. Although you may end up actually liking this one. It's going to be a lot of plodding, but the pay-off—assuming there is one—could be pretty good. We've been monitoring child pornography on the Web for a long time now. One particular little girl keeps cropping up. She was around seven when we first started seeing her. We think she might be thirteen or fourteen by now."

"She's showing up in different settings? With different abusers?"

"No, it's always the same guy. Naturally, he's pretty careful to keep his face out of the pictures, but it always seems to be the same few locations. We've been trying to isolate elements in the background—furniture, views from windows, that kind of thing."

"And you think she lives in Algonquin Bay?"

"Either lives there or visits there. We're not a hundred percent sure. The stuff's already on its way to you by courier. Let us know what you think. If it *is* Algonquin Bay in the pictures, we'll do everything we can to help you, but obviously the case would be yours. Now aren't you glad I remembered you?"

BUT NOT EVEN a phone call like that could distract her for long; John Cardinal kept invading her thoughts. His desk was right next to hers, and it was extremely unusual for him to miss a day of work. Even when his father had died, he hadn't taken more than one day off. It might be good for the department, she figured, but it was probably on the whole a weakness rather than a strength to be incapable of leaving your job.

Delorme recognized that she herself was much the same. She got bored on her days off, and when the end of the year rolled around she usually had a couple of weeks' vacation pay coming to her.

She looked at the photograph of Catherine on Cardinal's desk. She must have been at least forty-five in the photograph, but she retained more than her fair share of sexiness. It was there in the slightly skeptical gaze, the glint of wetness on the lower lip. It was easy to see how Cardinal had fallen in love. But what have you done to my friend? Delorme wanted to ask her. Why have you done this unforgivable thing? Then again, why does anybody do it? She could remember several cases off the top of her head: a mother of three, a social services administrator, and a teenage boy, all dead by their own hands.

Delorme opened the notebook she had found in Catherine's car, a small standard-issue spiral with NORTHERN UNIVERSITY printed on the cover. Judging by the contents, it had served as a sort of catch-all. Phone numbers and names were scrawled at odd angles alongside recipes for mushroom bisque and some kind of sauce, reminders to pick up dry cleaning or pay bills, and ideas for photographic projects: *Telephone series—all shots of people on phones: pay phones, cell phones, two-way radios, kids on tin cans, everything.* And another: *New homeless series: portraits of homeless people, but all fixed up and dressed in good suits, point being to remove as much of their "otherness" as possible. Some other way? Less contrived?* On the next page she had simply written: *John's birthday.*

Delorme had the pen as well. It had been in Catherine's shoulder bag along with the notebook, A simple Paper Mate, with very pale blue ink. Delorme wrote the words *personal effects* on a sheet of paper and compared it with the notes. It was the same ink—as far as one could tell without a lab test. And then there was the note itself. The handwriting appeared to be the same as that in the notebook. The minimalist *J* in *John*, the *t* in *other* crossed and looped over the *h* in both the notebook and the suicide note. That terrible note, and yet the handwriting did not appear to be any more emphatic or wobbly than the rest of the jottings. In fact, the note was a good deal neater, as if the decision to die had brought with it an untouchable calm. But you had a good man, a loving loyal husband. Why did you do this terrible thing? Delorme wanted to ask her. No matter how much pain you were in. How could you?

She placed all three items in a padded envelope and sealed it.

A FEW HOURS later that envelope was open on the kitchen table of John Cardinal's house on Madonna Road. Kelly Cardinal was watching her father carefully flip through the spiral notebook. The sight of her mother's handwriting made Kelly's heart liquefy in her chest. Every now and again, her father made a note in his own notebook.

"How can you stand to look at that stuff, Dad?"

"Why don't you go in the other room, sweetheart? This is something I have to do."

"I don't know how you can bear it."

"I can't. It's just something I have to do."

"But why? It's only going to make you crazy."

"Actually, it's making me feel better in a weird way. I have something to focus on other than the simple fact that Catherine's—"

Kelly reached out and touched his sleeve. "Maybe that's exactly what you should be focusing on, rather than going over her notebook. It's not healthy, Dad. Maybe you should just lie down and cry. Scream if you have to."

Her father was holding the notebook under the light that hung low over the kitchen table. He tilted it this way and that, first examining a blank page and then a page with writing on it. His concentration was irritating.

"Look at this," he said. "I mean, not if you don't want to. But this is interesting."

"What, for God's sake? I can't believe you're messing with that stuff." Thinking, I sound like a teenager. I must be reverting, under stress.

"As far as I can tell, this is Catherine's handwriting."

"Of course it is. I can tell that, even upside down. She makes those funny loops on her *t*'s."

"And it's written with this pen—or one just like it—on a page torn from this notebook."

"Surely your colleagues already determined that, Dad. Why? Do you think somebody else wrote Mom's note for her?"

"No, I don't—not yet anyway. But look. Come 'round this side."

Kelly debated whether to just go into the other room and turn on the TV. She didn't want to encourage her father, but on the other hand, she didn't want to do anything that would make things worse. She got up and stood behind him.

"See, what strikes me funny about this," Cardinal said, "is that this suicide note is not the last thing Catherine wrote in this notebook."

"What do you mean?"

"You can see the impressions back here, earlier on. They're very faint, but you can just make them out when you hold the notebook at the right angle. Can you see?"

"Frankly, no."

"You're not at the right angle. You have to sit down."

Cardinal pulled out the chair beside him and Kelly sat down. He tilted the notebook slowly back and forth.

"Wait!" Kelly said. "I can see it now."

Cardinal held the notebook steady in the light. There at the top of a page of random notes was a faint impression of the words *Dear John.* Cardinal tilted it slightly. Lower on the page, Kelly could just make out *any other way . . . Catherine.* The middle was obscured by other notes, including a reminder for Cardinal's birthday.

"My birthday's in July," he said. "Three months ago."

"You think she wrote her note three months ago? I suppose it's possible. Pretty weird to carry around a suicide note for three months, though."

Cardinal dropped the notebook onto the table and sat back. "On the other hand, there could be some perfectly simple explanation: she wrote it out one day, intending to . . . but then she changed her mind. For a while, at least. Or maybe she accidentally skipped a page in her notebook three months ago, and then, the other day, she just happened to use the first blank page in the book."

"Out of a concern for neatness? Seems a pretty odd time to be worried about using every page in your ninety-five-cent notebook."

"It does, doesn't it?"

"But it's her writing. Her pen. In the long run, what difference does it make what page she wrote it on?"

"I don't know," Cardinal said. "I truly don't know."

CARDINAL HAD LEARNED long ago that a detective thrives on contacts. In the overworked and underfunded endeavors of forensic science, the slightest personal connection can help nudge a case along quicker than the average, and an actual friendship can work magic.

Tommy Hunn had never been a friend. Tommy Hunn had been a colleague of Cardinal's back in the early days of his career in Toronto, when he was still working vice. In many ways, Hunn had been a police force nightmare: excessively muscled, casually violent, cheerfully racist. He had also been a pretty good detective right up until he got caught in a bawdy house by his own squad. He could have faced charges much more serious than conduct unbecoming had not Cardinal gone to bat for him at his disciplinary hearing. He wrote letters of support for him and, later, when Hunn was looking for a new line of work, a letter of reference. Hunn had gone back to school, and eventually managed to get himself into the documents section of the Ontario Centre of Forensic Science, where he had been leading an apparently honorable life ever since.

"Hoo, boy, it's Cardinal the friendly ghost," Hunn said, when he answered the phone. "Got to be something really special. Otherwise, I say to myself, why wouldn't he go through our central receiving office?"

"I got a couple of documents for you, Tommy. Maybe three. I'm hoping you can help me out."

"You wanna cut in, is that it? I gotta tell ya, John, we are hellaciously backed up down here. Only thing I'm supposed to work on these days is stuff that's five seconds from being in court."

"Yeah, I know."

All cops expect to have to repay a favor somewhere down the line, possibly decades later. Cardinal did not have to give Hunn any reminders.

"Why don't you tell me what you got," he said. "I'll see what I can do."

"I have a greeting card with a piece of paper glued inside. On that piece of paper there's a message that looks like it was printed out on a computer. It's just two sentences long, but I'm hoping you can give me some idea where it came from. Frankly, I can't even tell if it's ink-jet or laser."

"Either way, it's not going to get us very far without another printout to compare it to. It ain't like the old days with typewriters. What else you got?"

"A suicide note."

"Suicide. All this trouble, you're working on a suicide? Goddamn suicides burn my ass. Anyone who kills themselves is just chickenshit, far as I'm concerned."

"Oh, yeah," Cardinal said. "Complete cowards. No question."

"And selfish," Hunn went on. "There's gotta be no more self-centered act than killing yourself. All these resources get called into play: your time, my time, doctors, nurses, ambulances, shrinks, you name it. All this for someone who doesn't even want to live. It's just plain selfish."

"Thoughtless," Cardinal said. "Completely thoughtless."

"That's when they don't succeed. When they do succeed, they leave all this grief behind. I had a friend—best friend, actually—who ate his service revolver a few years back. I'm telling you, I felt like shit for months. Why didn't I see it coming? Why wasn't I a better friend? But you know what? He's the lousy friend, not me."

"Yeah, you put your finger on it there, Tommy."

"Suicides, man, I tell ya—"

"This one may not be a suicide."

"All right! Different story, entirely. Now you're engaging my attention." Hunn put on his Godfather voice: "I'm gonna use alla my skills and alla my powers—"

"I need this fast, Tommy. Like yesterday."

"Absolutely. Minute I get it. But if you're thinking of using this material or any analysis I give you on it in court, you know you gotta go through Central Receiving, and Central Receiving don't rush for nobody. God himself could come to them with a handwritten note on Satan's letterhead and they'd tell him, 'Get in line, bro.'"

"I can't go through Central Receiving, Tommy. I don't have a case number."

"Oh, boy."

"But you come back to me with something good, and I'll *get* a case number. Then I'll jump through whatever hoops you need."

There was a heavy sigh from the other end of the line. "All right, John. You're giving me serious heartburn here, but I'll do it."

8

Nausea was not quite the word to describe what Delorme was feeling. The Toronto Sex Crimes Unit had sent her about twenty images; the package had been waiting for her when she came back from lunch. She had looked them over and was now wishing she hadn't. The photographs provoked a reaction in her gut, as if she had received a solid blow to the belly. And then more complicated emotions set in: distress, almost panic, and yet at the same time an all but overwhelming hopelessness about the human species.

The sights and sounds of the office—the click and slam of the photocopier, McLeod bellowing at Sergeant Flower, the tapping of keyboards, and the chirping of phones—all diminished around her. Delorme felt a sob gathering in her chest, which she tamped down immediately. She had experienced something similar to this inner turmoil when reading certain news accounts: beheadings in Iraq, or the civil war in Africa where armed men raided villages, raping the women and chopping the hands off all the men.

She knew the acts captured in the photographs did not compare to mass murder, but the effect on her spirit was the same: despair at the depths to which human nature could sink. Even in a place the size of Algonquin Bay you heard of such pictures, but until this moment Delorme had never seen anything like them. There had been the case of a social services administrator the previous year, a man apparently well loved by his family and friends, who had been charged with possession of child pornography. But it hadn't been Delorme's case, and she hadn't seen the evidence. The man had killed himself while out on bail—apparently out of shame, even though he had been charged only with possession of the material, not with manufacturing or distributing.

The pictures on her desk, Delorme realized, were actually crime-scene photos. The criminal had taken them himself in the course of committing his crime; the creation of child pornography was unique in that respect. The girl looked to be as young as seven or eight in some of them, still with puppy fat around her neck and cheeks; in others she looked closer to thirteen. She had a sweet open face, pale blond shoulder-length hair, and eyes almost unnaturally green, the color emphasized, in several pictures, by the tears that flowed from them. There were pictures in a bedroom, pictures on a couch, pictures on a boat, in a tent, in a hotel room. In one of the photos, a detail had been blurred out; a hat the little girl was wearing had been reduced to a blue-and-white smear.

The man was careful not to show his face, so he became a collection of disparate details. He was the hairy arm, the furry chest; he was the sticklike legs, the freckled shoulder, the butt just beginning to sag. His penis, closely featured in many shots, looked scorched and red, though whether from abuse or bad photography it was impossible to tell. Delorme, no prude and no hater of men, thought it the ugliest thing she had ever seen.

It occurred to her that the man was not human; that he was mere animated flesh, a monster sprung from a madman's lab. But the spirit-crushing truth, of course, was that he *was* human. He could be anybody; he could be someone Delorme knew. Not only was he human, he was also beloved by his victim; too many of the pictures showed her relaxed and grinning for it to be otherwise. He had to be either the girl's father or someone very close to the family. That the little girl loved him, Delorme had no doubt, and it made her heart ache.

Toronto had sent two additional envelopes. The first contained exact copies of the photographs, but the girl and her abuser had been digitally removed. Now they were just unexceptional scenes: an out-of-style sofa, what looked like a hotel bed, the interior of a tent, a backyard with a grubby plastic playhouse—settings of no interest unless you knew what had transpired in them.

The third envelope contained just one picture, that of the girl wearing the hat, now enlarged into a close-up. The hat was a woolen toque, blue and white, no longer blurred. Delorme had no idea how the Toronto cops could have managed that, but she actually stopped breathing for a moment. She recognized the toque. Not all of the knitted wording was visible, but you could now clearly see ALGON . . . WIN . . . FUR. Algonquin Bay Winter Fur Carnival.

The phone rang.

"Delorme, CID."

"Sergeant Dukovsky here. You finished throwing up yet?"

"Sergeant, you may be used to this kind of stuff, but me, I feel like moving into the forest and living off roots and berries for the rest of my life."

"I know what you mean. And this guy is by no means the worst of what we get. These days we get pictures of *infants*, and they're doing this stuff *live*."

"Live? I don't understand."

"Streaming video. Guy gets himself a Webcam and abuses kids online while his brethren around the world pay to watch."

"Oh, man."

"Unfortunately, some of those pictures we sent you have shown up in the same chat room as the live stuff, so I wouldn't be surprised if it gives this guy ideas."

"Let's hope we nail him before that. Tell me about the winter carnival hat. How did you manage to unblur it?"

"We got a couple of sixty-four-bit propeller-heads here, going gaga over this image-processing tool. Real bleeding-edge stuff. I asked 'em how it worked and boy did I regret it. They started blithering about filter deconvolution and Lucy-Richardson algorithms. I'm telling you, these guys eat Athlon chips right out of the bag."

"And I thought Photoshop was cool. Interesting thing here, the name of the carnival was changed a few years back to avoid protesters. It's no longer the *fur* carnival, it's just the winter carnival."

"That could be important. Only we don't know when she got it or who from."

"In any case, it doesn't mean the kid lives here. The carnival draws people from all over the world."

"Come on. Hordes of people are crossing the globe to attend the Algonquin Bay Fur Carnival?"

"Not hordes. And they don't come for the carnival, they come for the fur auction. We get buyers from the big furriers in Paris, New York, London, places like that. We even get Russians coming to check out the competition."

"You're educating me here, Sergeant Delorme. I didn't realize Algonquin Bay was such a hive of international commerce. Did you take a look at the picture on the boat—the one where there's other boats in the background?"

Delorme shuffled the photographs, stopping when she came to the picture. It showed a cabin cruiser with lots of wooden trim, wooden floors, and comfortable-looking red seats with tuck-and-roll upholstery. The girl was lounging on one of these, wearing blue jeans and a yellow T-shirt. She was ten or eleven in this shot, grinning into the camera.

"There's a good reason why I missed this one," Delorme said. "It's one of the pictures where he's not doing anything to her. The kid looks happy."

"Check out the background."

"There's a small plane with pontoons on it. And you can just make out part of its tail number. C-G-K."

"Exactly. It's a Cessna Skylane and the whole number is CGKMC. Took us about five minutes cross-checking those letters with Cessnas and Algonquin Bay. We get a guy named Frank Rowley. I can give you his address and phone number too. I hope I'm impressing you here."

"But the plane is just in the background. There's no reason to think there's any connection between the owner of the plane and the creep in the pictures, is there?"

"No, but it's a start. Believe me, we'll hand you anything we get, minute we get it. In the meantime, maybe you can focus your logical French-*Canadian* mind on those pictures: spend some quality time with them, narrow things down."

"What if we posted a picture of the girl—just do it like a missing-person picture? We could put her face up in the post office and hope somebody who's seen her calls in. We've got to do something fast. He's destroying this kid's life."

"Problem with posting a picture is, the perp is most likely gonna see it before the kid does. Pedophiles aren't usually violent, but if he thinks she's gonna put him away for years, he just might kill her."

9

Next morning, Kelly came into the kitchen in her running gear—black leggings, mauve sweatshirt with a tiny elephant stitched on it—and grabbed an orange off the counter. Catherine bought those oranges, Cardinal thought. Did you buy half a dozen oranges when you were about to kill yourself?

He poured his daughter a coffee. "You want some oatmeal?"

"Maybe when I come back. Don't want to lug any extra weight around. God, you look exhausted, Dad."

"You should talk." Kelly's eyes looked puffy and red. "Are you managing to sleep at all?"

"Not much. I seem to wake up every half hour," she said, dropping bits of orange peel into the green bin. "I never realized how physical the emotions are. I wake up and my calves are locked up, and I feel like a wreck, even though I haven't done anything. I just can't believe she's gone. I mean, if she came in that front door right now I don't even think I'd be surprised."

"I found this," Cardinal said. He held out a photograph he'd discovered buried in an album crammed with loose pictures, a black-and-white portrait of Catherine, age about eighteen, looking very moody and artistic in a black turtleneck and silver hoop earrings.

Kelly burst into tears, and Cardinal was taken by surprise. Perhaps in an effort to ease his own grief, his daughter had been comparatively restrained, but now she wailed like a little girl. He rested a hand on her shoulder as she cried herself out.

"Wow," she said, coming back from washing her face. "I guess I needed that."

"That's how she looked when we met," Cardinal said. "I just thought she was the most beautiful person I'd ever seen. The kind of person you're only supposed to meet in movies."

"Was she always that intense?"

"No, not at all. She made fun of herself all the time."

"Why don't you come running with me?" Kelly said suddenly. "It'll make us feel better."

"Oh, I don't know. . . ."

"Come on. You still run, don't you?"

"Not as often as I used to."

"Come on, Dad. You'll feel better. We both will."

MADONNA ROAD WAS just off Highway 69, so they had to run along the shoulder for half a kilometer or so and then make a left onto Water Road, which skirted the edge of Trout Lake. The day was brilliant and clear, with a sharp autumn tang in the air.

"Wow, smell the leaves," Kelly said. "Those hills have every color except blue."

Kelly was not by nature a perky young woman; she was making an effort to cheer Cardinal up, and he was touched by it. He was indeed aware of the beauty of the day, but as they ran through the suburb, their steps seemed to beat in time with the words *Catherine's dead, Catherine's dead.* Cardinal felt the contradictory sensations of being both hollowed out and yet extremely heavy—as if his heart had been replaced by a ball of lead. *Catherine breathed this frosty air too.*

"When do you have to be back in New York?" he asked Kelly.

"Not till next week."

"Oh, you don't have to stay that long, you know. I'm sure you need to get back."

"It's fine, Dad. I want to stay."

"How about today? You have any plans?"

"I was thinking about calling Kim Delaney, but I don't know. You remember Kim?"

Cardinal recalled a big strapping blond girl—angry at the world and very political. She and Kelly had been inseparable in their last years of high school.

"I would have thought Kim would have ventured out into the big bad world by now."

"Yeah, so would I."

"You sound mournful." Cardinal accidentally brushed against a recycling bin. A Jack Russell bounced up and down on the other side of the fence, yapping elaborate canine threats.

"Well, we were best friends for a while, but now I'm not even sure if I should call her," Kelly said. "Kim was the smartest girl at Algonquin High, way smarter than me—head of the debating club, delegate at the Junior UN, editor of the yearbook. And now it's like she wants to be Queen of Suburbia."

"Not everyone wants to move to New York."

"I know that. But Kim's twenty-seven and she's already got three kids, and she owns two—two!—SUVs."

Cardinal pointed at a driveway they were just passing: one Grand Cherokee, one Wagoneer.

"All she can talk about is sports. Honestly, I think Kim's life revolves around curling and hockey and soccer. I'm surprised she isn't into bowling yet."

"Priorities change when you have kids."

"Well, I never want kids if it means you have to check your mind at the door. Kim hasn't read a newspaper in years. All she watches on TV is *Survivor* and *Canadian Idol* and hockey. Hockey! She hated sports when we were in school. Honestly, I thought Kim and I would be friends forever, but now I'm thinking maybe I won't call."

"Well, here's an idea. You feel like making a quick trip down to Toronto?"

Kelly looked over at him. There was a fine film of sweat on her upper lip, and her cheeks were flushed. "You're going to Toronto? What brought this on?"

"Something cooking at the Forensic Centre. I want to deal with it in person."

"This is to do with Mom?"

"Yeah."

For a few moments there was just the sound of their breathing—Cardinal's breathing, anyway. Kelly didn't seem to be having any trouble. Water Road ended in a turning circle. The two of them slowed and ran in place for a few moments. Beyond the redbrick bungalows, with their neat lawns and rows of stout yard-waste bags, the lake was deep indigo.

"Dad," Kelly said, "Mom killed herself. She killed herself and it hurts like hell, but the truth is she was manic depressive, she was in and out of hospitals for a long time, and it's really, ultimately, not so surprising that she wanted out." She touched his arm. "You know it wasn't about you."

"Are you gonna come?"

"Boy, you don't mess around when you set your mind on something, do you?" She gave it a second. "All right, I'll come. But just to keep you company on the drive."

Cardinal pointed to a path that looped away through the trees. "Let's go back the scenic way."

ALL THE WAY south down Highway 11, Cardinal could not think of anything but Catherine. Although *think* was not the word. He felt her absence in the beauty of the hills. He felt her hovering above the highway; it had always been the road that took Cardinal away from or back to Catherine. But she had not been there this time to wave goodbye, would not be there when he came back.

Kelly fiddled with the radio dial.

"Hey, put it back," Cardinal said. "That was the Beatles!"

"Ugh. I can't stand the Beatles."

"How can anyone hate the Beatles? That's like hating sunshine. It's like hating ice cream."

"It's just their early stuff I can't stand. They sound like little wind-up toys."

Cardinal glanced over at her. Twenty-seven. His daughter was older now than Catherine had been when Kelly was born. Cardinal asked her about New York.

For the next little while, Kelly told him about her latest frustrations in trying to make it as an artist. New York was a hard town to be broke in. She had to share an apartment with three other women, and they didn't always get along. And she was obliged to work at two jobs to make ends meet: she was assisting a painter named Klaus Meier—stretching canvases for him, doing his books—and also working as a waitress three days a week. It didn't leave a lot of time for her own painting.

"And doing all this, you never feel the pull of suburban life? The yearning for a small town?"

"Never. I miss Canada sometimes, though. It's kind of hard to be friends with Americans."

"How's that?"

"Americans are the friendliest people in the world, on the surface. At first I found it almost intoxicating—they're so much more outgoing than Canadians. And they're not afraid to have a good time."

"That's true. Canadians are more reserved."

I'm acting, Cardinal thought. I'm not having a conversation, I'm *acting* like a man having a conversation. This is how it's done: you listen, you nod, you ask a question. But I'm not here. I'm as gone as the World Trade Center. My heart is Ground Zero. He wanted to talk to Catherine about this, but Catherine was not there.

He struggled to focus.

"Somewhere along the line Americans invented a kind of fake intimacy," Kelly said. "They'll tell you about their divorce the first time they meet you, or their history of child abuse. I'm not kidding. I had one guy tell me how his father used to *incest* him, as he put it. That was on the first date. In the beginning I thought everyone was really trusting, but they're not at all. They just don't have any sense of decorum. Why are you smiling?"

"It's just funny, hearing you talk about decorum. Unconventional girl like you."

"I'm actually pretty conventional, when you get down to it. I have a feeling it's going to be my downfall as an artist. God, look at the trees."

The drive to Toronto took four hours. Cardinal dropped

Kelly at A Second Cup on College Street, where she had arranged to meet an old friend; then he headed over to the Forensic Centre on Grenville.

AS A PIECE of architecture, the Forensic Centre is of no interest whatsoever. It's just a slab tossed up, like so many other government buildings, in the era when poured concrete replaced brick and stone as the material of choice. Inside, it's a collection of putty-colored dividers, tweedy carpet, and mordant cartoons cut from newspapers and taped above people's desks.

Cardinal had been here many times, though not to the documents section, and the very familiarity of the place unnerved him. He was drowning in the deepest agony of his life; everything should have been changed. And yet the security guards, the rattling elevator, the plain offices, desks, charts, and displays were exactly as before.

"Okay, so we got three little items here," Tommy Hunn said, laying them out on the laboratory counter. Unlike the building, Tommy had changed. His hair was thinner, and his belt was hidden beneath a roll of flab, as if there were a dachshund asleep under his shirt.

"We got one suicide note. We got one notebook in which said suicide note may or may not have been written. And we have one nasty sympathy card with a typed message inside."

"Why don't we start with the sympathy card?" Cardinal said. "It's not going to be related to the other two items."

"Sympathy card first," Hunn said. He put on a pair of latex gloves, removed the card from its plastic folder, and opened it. "*How does it feel, asshole?*" he read in a flat monotone. "*Just no telling how things will turn out, is there.* Cute."

He held the note next to the window, tilting it to catch the light.

"Well, it's an ink-jet printer, I can see that right off. No idiosyncrasies visible to the naked eye. Not my eye, anyway. But let's do a little detecting." He held a loupe to his eye and brought the note up to his face. "Here we go. Printer flaw on the second line. Look at the *h*'s and the *t*'s."

He handed Cardinal the loupe. At first Cardinal couldn't see anything, but when his eye adjusted he could make out a pale threadlike line running through the crossbars of the *h*'s and the *t*'s.

"The good news is, if a printer does something like that, it does it consistently. You notice there's no flaw through the first line of type. But if we had another page the guy printed out, it would show the same flaw on the second line."

"How helpful is that going to be?" Cardinal asked.

"Without another sample to compare it to? Not helpful at all. And the bad news is, they change the cartridge, they change the flaws. Far as we're concerned, it's like they've bought themselves a whole new printer."

Cardinal pointed to the notebook. "What can you do with these?"

"Depends what you want to know."

"I'd like to be sure the note was written with the same pen as the rest of the notebook. And when it was written in relation to the last entries. If you open it to the page that mentions *John's birthday.*"

"John's birthday. Ha! Maybe she was addressing it to you!" Hunn flicked through the pages, then held the notebook up to the light the way he had the card. "Oh, yeah. You've got impressions here. I can make out *Dear John.* First thing we do is stick 'em both in the comparator."

He lifted a wide door on something labeled VSC 2000.

"Look through the window there, when I flick the switch. I can shine several different kinds of light on the samples, see what kicks up. Ink may look identical to the human eye, but even the same make and model of pen will show differences under infrared. The chemistry of different ink batches reacts differently. I can't tell you how many fraudulent wills I've busted using this gizmo. *Dear John.* Gotta love it."

Cardinal bent over to peer through the window. The writing on the pages glowed.

"These are identical," Hunn said from behind him. "Same pen wrote the suicide note and the birthday note."

"Can you tell me which one was written first?"

"Sure. First thing we do is stick it in the humidifier."
Hunn put the notebook into a small machine with a glass
front that looked like a toaster oven. "Just needs a minute or
so. Indentations will show up way better if the paper is
humid."

The machine beeped, and he took out the notebook. "Now
we'll run a little ESDA magic on it, see what we can see."

"A little what?"

"E-S-D-A. Electrostatic detection apparatus."

This was a hulk of a machine with a venting hood on top.
Hunn laid the notebook down so that the single page was flat
against a layer of foam. Then he spread a sheet of plastic
wrap over it.

"Underneath the foam we got a vacuum that pulls the air
through. It'll hold the document and the plastic down tight.
Now I take my Corona unit—don't worry, I'm not gonna
open my pants."

Hunn picked up a wandlike instrument and flicked a
switch. "Little mother puts out several thousand volts," he
said, over the hum. He waved it over the plastic sheet a few
times. There was no change that Cardinal could see.

"Now I take my fairy dust." Hunn shook what looked like
iron filings out of a small canister. "Actually, these are tiny
glass beads covered in toner. I'm just gonna cascade 'em
over my setup here. . . ."

He poured the black powder over the plastic that covered
the notebook page. The beads slid off, leaving toner behind
in the impressions. There was a flash of light.

"Now I got us a picture," Hunn said, "and we shall see
what we shall see. Have these been dusted for fingerprints?"

"Not yet. Why?"

"The toner'll often pick up prints—not as good as dust-
ing powder. They have to be pretty good prints for it to work.
Take a look."

A photograph scrolled out of a slot. Cardinal reached for it.
There was a small dark thumbprint to the left of *John's
birthday*, which now appeared in white. There was a short
straight line across the whorls where Catherine had cut her-

self in the kitchen years ago. *Catherine's thumbprint, where she braced the notebook on her lap. She was alive. She was thinking of me, planning for my birthday, imagining a future.* Cardinal coughed to cover the cry that threatened to escape his throat. The impression of the suicide note was now complete, clearly inscribed in black toner. *By the time you read this. . . .*

It's her handwriting. You know it's her handwriting. Why are you putting yourself through this?

"Okay," Cardinal said. "So we know the suicide note was written on top of the later page, which makes sense. The later pages should have been blank when she wrote the suicide note. But can you tell if the ink on the later page, I mean the ink of the birthday note, is on top of the impressions left from the suicide note? Or underneath them?"

"Oh, I like a man who thinks dirty," Hunn said. "Let's pop it under the microscope. If the white lines of the birthday note are interrupted by black, that means the indentations were made at a later time than the ink." Hunn peered into the microscope and adjusted the focus. "Nope. We got black interrupted by white—ink over indentations."

"So the suicide note was definitely written *before* the birthday note."

"Definitely. I'm assuming you know when the mysterious John's birthday occurred?"

"Yeah. Over three months ago."

"Hmm. Not your usual run of suicide, then."

"No. Can I keep the picture you took?"

"Oh, sure. That way the original doesn't have to be handled so much." Hunn pulled the original out of the ESDA machine and put it back in its folder.

"Do one more thing for me, Tommy?"

"What's that?"

"Pour some of that fairy dust on the suicide note too."

"You wanna check it for earlier impressions as well? You already have the birthday thing."

"I'd really appreciate it. My brothers-in-arms up north aren't exactly on the team on this one."

Hunn looked at him, pale blue eyes calculating. "Okay, sure."

He repeated the routine of humidifying the note, securing it under plastic, charging it. Then he poured the powder over the plastic.

"Looks like lots of impressions from notes earlier in the notebook. We can stick it under the microscope and be certain which ones came first, if you want."

"Look at this," Cardinal said. He pulled out the photo curling from the slot. The suicide note was now in white. But there was something else at the top of the photo, in the center, outlined in black toner.

"Quite a bit bigger than the other one," Hunn said, "and no scar. I'm no Ident man, but I'd say you're dealing here with a very different pair of thumbs."

A little later Hunn walked him down to the elevators, where they waited in silence a few moments. Then the bell pinged, announcing the arrival of the elevator. Cardinal got in and hit the button for the ground floor.

"Say, listen," Hunn said, in the tone of one who has been turning something over in his mind. "That stuff isn't connected to you, is it—I mean, personally? You wouldn't be the John in the notebook, would you?"

"Thanks for all your help, Tommy," Cardinal said, as the elevator doors closed between them. "Much appreciated."

TRAVELING BACK TO Algonquin Bay the same day meant Cardinal and Kelly spent a total of eight hours together in the car. The ride back was quiet.

Cardinal asked Kelly how things had gone with her friend.

"Fine. At least she hasn't turned into a vegetable like Kim. She's still involved in art, and she seems to have some idea of what's going on in the world."

Kelly twisted a strand of her blue-black hair as she stared out the window. Cardinal remembered how his own friends had changed at that age. Many had lost interest in him when he became a cop, and a lot of his Toronto associates wrote him off when he moved back to Algonquin Bay.

"You never know about people," Catherine had said. "Everybody has their own story line, and sometimes it doesn't include us—usually when we wish it did. And sometimes it does include us—usually when we wish it didn't."

And what about now, Catherine? How do I deal with your being gone?

"Like a cop," he imagined her saying, with the little half smile she gave whenever she was teasing him. "The way you handle everything."

But it doesn't help, he wanted to cry. Nothing helps.

They passed WonderWorld, a vast amusement park just north of Toronto with a fake pointy mountain and gigantic rides. Kelly asked him how things had gone at Forensics, but Cardinal mumbled something noncommittal. He didn't want to see the look of pity and frustration in her eyes.

When Orillia was behind them, she said, "I suppose this means dinner at the Sundial?"

"Unfortunately not," Cardinal said. "Sundial's closed."

"My-oh-my. The end of an era."

They had to settle for bland little sandwiches at a Tim Hortons.

It was dark by the time they got home. The hills and the trees were silent, a salve to the ears after the endless clatter of Toronto. Colder, too. A half-hidden moon lit tendrils of cloud that hung motionless over the water, the lake itself shiny and black as patent leather.

When Cardinal opened the front door, he stepped on the corner of a square white envelope. He picked it up without showing Kelly.

"I'm going to take a shower," Kelly said, taking off her coat. "Nothing like a day in the car to make you feel grubby."

Cardinal took the envelope into the kitchen, holding it by the corner. He switched on the overhead light and peered at the address. He was pretty sure he could make out a pale threadlike line running through the *M* and the *R* of *Madonna Road*.

10

Cardinal had not noticed on his previous visit how thoroughly Dr. Bell's office was set up for the comfort of his patients. The large sunny windows, with their gauzy blinds bright as sails, the floor-to-ceiling walls of psychology and philosophy texts with their reassuring smells of ink and glue and paper, the worn Persian rugs: everything about the room conveyed stability, permanence, wisdom—qualities that psychiatric patients might feel lacking in their own lives. The place was a refuge from the mess of life, a cocoon that invited safe reflection.

Cardinal sank into the couch. He noted the boxes of Kleenex discreetly placed at either end and on the coffee table—as much Kleenex as at Desmond's Funeral Home— and he wondered how many times Catherine had sat here and wept. Had she also talked about her disappointment in her husband—who didn't pay her enough attention, was not kind enough or patient enough?

"*How she must have hated you,*" Dr. Bell read from the latest sympathy card. "*You failed her so completely.*" He looked at Cardinal over tiny reading glasses. "What was your reaction when you read that? Your immediate reaction, I mean."

"That he's right. Or she. Whoever wrote it. That it's true I failed her and she probably hated me for it."

"Do you believe that?"

The doctor's mild eyes on him—not probing, not trying to x-ray—just waiting, bright squares of window glinting in his glasses.

"I believe that I failed her, yes."

What Cardinal could *not* believe was that he was talking to anyone like this. He never talked to anyone like this, except Catherine. Something about Dr. Bell—an air of gentle expectation, not to mention the wiry eyebrows and all that corduroy—compelled honesty. No wonder Catherine liked him, although . . .

"What?" Dr. Bell said. "You're hesitating now."

"Just remembering something," Cardinal said. "Something Catherine said to me one time just after she had seen you. I could tell she had been crying, and I asked her what was wrong. How it went. And she said, 'I love Dr. Bell. I think he's great. But sometimes even the best doctor has to hurt you.'"

"You thought of that now because my question hurt."

Cardinal nodded.

"There's a common saying in psychotherapy: It has to get worse before it gets better."

"Yeah. Catherine told me that too."

"Not that one ever intends to make a patient feel worse," Dr. Bell said. His hands toyed with a brass object on his desk. It looked like a miniature steam engine. "But we all build up defenses against certain truths about ourselves or our situations—against reality, essentially—and therapy provides a place where it's safe to dismantle those defenses. The patient does the dismantling, not the therapist, but the process is bound to be painful nevertheless."

"Luckily, I'm not here as a patient. I just wanted to ask you about those cards. I realize you're not a profiler. . . ."

"No forensic experience at all, I'm afraid."

"That's all right, this isn't an official investigation. But I was hoping you would help by giving me your opinion on what kind of person would write these cards. They were mailed from two different locations, but they were printed by the same machine."

"What exactly is it that is under investigation—officially or otherwise?"

"Catherine's d—" Cardinal's breath caught on the word.

He still could not say that word about Catherine, even though it was more than a week now. "Catherine."

"You mean you don't believe she killed herself?"

"The coroner has made a finding of suicide, and my colleagues down at the station agree. Personally, I find it a little harder to accept, though probably you'll tell me that's just my defense."

"Oh, no, I would never say it was *just* a defense. I have great respect for defenses, Detective. They're what get us through the day, not to mention the night. Nor would I second-guess your expertise on matters of homicide. My own experience of Catherine makes me think it indeed highly likely she killed herself, but if evidence were to show otherwise, I would not try to argue black is white. Certainly a finding of accidental death would be much easier for me to accept. But you're not thinking it an accident, are you?"

"No."

"You're thinking she was killed. And that whoever wrote these nasty cards was behind the killing."

"Let's just say I'm pursuing several lines of inquiry at the moment. I'd be willing to pay you; I should have said that right away."

"Oh, no, no. I couldn't possibly accept payment. This is not my field. I'm happy to give you my opinion, off the record, but to accept payment would imply a commercial service offered with confidence. It most assuredly is not." Dr. Bell smiled, eyes disappearing for a moment in fur. "That's a considerable caveat. Do you still wish me to proceed?"

"If you would."

Dr. Bell rolled his shoulders and shook his head. If you were going to have tics, Cardinal supposed, they weren't the worst ones to have. The doctor picked up the first card and adjusted his glasses. He swiveled slightly in his chair, bringing the card into the light. Then he went still, a figure in a painting.

"All right," he said, after some time. "First of all, what is the nature of someone who writes a note like this? Essentially, you've got someone who is sneering at you."

"A friend of mine used the same word."

"And the writer is not even sneering at you in person, he's doing it behind your back. Or she. Rather in the way of a child who calls someone names from a safe distance. He knows you can't retaliate. It's a cowardly, fearful sort of attack.

"Whereas killing someone—killing someone is very personal and face-to-face. Usually. To link these cards with Catherine's possible murder, you must assume the motive in both cases is the same: the goal is to hurt *you,* and Catherine was just a means to that end. Somehow, in order to hurt *you,* the killer somehow first got hold of her suicide note—unless you're thinking it's not in fact her handwriting. Are you in doubt about the handwriting?"

"For now, we'll assume it's genuine."

"Which would mean someone got hold of her suicide note. How could that be?"

"I don't know—at least, not yet. Please go on."

"He intends to hurt you by hurting her, perhaps follows her for a time. Possibly a good long time. Possibly snoops through her things and finds a suicide note she wrote on a particularly bad day. Possibly even finds it after she discarded it, who knows? In any case, he follows her on this night when she's quite alone and pushes her off the roof, leaving the note behind to throw everyone off the scent. If that is in fact what happened, it seems to me the person capable of going through with all that—the stalking, the waiting, and then the final violence itself—is not the sort of shrinking violet who's going to bother writing anonymous squibs. Am I making sense so far?"

"I wish the Behavioural Science guys were this fast," Cardinal said. "Keep going."

"I would say in the case of the card writer, you're looking for someone who knows you. And I emphasize *you* as opposed to Catherine. He's gone to the trouble of hiding his handwriting. And you say he's mailed the cards from two different locations." Dr. Bell sank back in his chair, rocking it with one foot propped on the coffee table. "I'd say this is going to be someone nervous and withdrawn. Someone who feels himself—or herself—a failure. Almost certainly unemployed. Self-esteem *deep* in the negative zone. Also—to judge by the first card—someone who has suffered a great loss for which you are to blame. I imagine you've already considered the possibility, Detective, that this is someone you nicked?"

"Mm," Cardinal said. "And there are a lot of those."

"Yes, but that *How does it feel* rings with a very specific intent, don't you find? Someone steps on your foot, so you stomp on his. How does it feel? How do *you* like it? My point being, it's not just someone you've imprisoned, but perhaps someone who lost his wife as a result of that imprisonment."

"We don't keep statistics, but there's probably a lot of those too. Marriages don't tend to thrive on imprisonment."

"Nor on hospitalization, though I note your own admirable exception to this."

Cardinal wanted to say, I did my best; obviously it wasn't enough, but grief closed its bony hand around his throat. He opened his briefcase and pulled out Catherine's suicide note, the original encased in plastic.

Once again Dr. Bell turned toward the window light. A few pensive scratchings among his sandy and gray curls, and then he went still again.

After a few moments he said, "That must have been painful to read."

"How does it seem to you, Doctor? Does it sound genuine?"

"Ah. So you do have doubts about the handwriting?"

"Just tell me how it sounds to you, if you would."

"It reads exactly like Catherine. A deeply sad woman, often hopeless, but also capable of great love. I think that love kept her going through depressions that by all rights should have proved lethal years earlier. Her main concern, and I heard this from her over and over again, was how it would affect you—apparently even at the end."

"If it was the end," Cardinal said.

11

Larry Burke was new in CID. He'd only been out of uniform a few months, in fact, and he very much wanted to make a good impression on his colleagues. He even worried that stopping into the Country Style at the top of Algonquin for a quiet lunch might be viewed as a complete cliché, the cop in the donut shop. But the truth was he didn't give a damn about donuts, he just liked Country Style coffee. And they were making a decent sandwich these days, when you got down to it, so why shouldn't he eat where he liked?

It was his favorite thing to do on his day off, stop into the Country Style with the *Toronto Sun*—you couldn't beat the *Sun* for sports coverage—order himself a gigantic coffee and a chicken salad sandwich, and linger for a good hour and a half. Today the sunlight streamed through the windows, and Burke was actually hot, even though it was a chilly October day. Outside, the hills were scarlet and gold.

He licked the last of the chicken salad off his fingers and took a swig of coffee. There was a bran muffin sitting there waiting for him, but he didn't want lunch to be over too fast. The truth was, days off had become a little bleak since he and Brenda had split—or, rather, since Brenda had split. Burke would have happily kept their fitful romance going for another tepid year or two.

He thought about calling her on the cell, just to see how she was doing, but he didn't want to seem pathetic. Anyway, Brenda was right: they hadn't had much of a future.

"Man, I don't believe what I just saw."

Burke looked up from an article on the Grey Cup. The guy at the next table was staring out the window at something beyond Burke's shoulder. Burke turned around to look, but all he could see was the parking lot, nothing much happening there.

"He's gone now," the guy said. "But I swear, fella just got out of that Honda Civic was carrying a shotgun. He went into the Laundromat. Looked pissed off."

"Are you sure he was carrying a gun?"

"Hey, man, I just bagged six ducks last weekend. I know a double-ought when I see one."

Burke's mouth dried. He didn't have his service firearm with him, no radio either. He flipped open his phone and hit the speed dial for the duty sergeant.

"Hey, Mo, it's Burke. . . . Yeah, yeah, I know, listen. I got a report of a man carrying a firearm into the Laundromat next to the Country Style, top of Algonquin. I didn't see him, but a hunter two seats over swears the guy's carrying a shotgun."

He heard the sergeant hitting the radio and hung up; then he went out into the parking lot and over to the Laundromat. Smells of leaves mingled with the scent of laundry detergent blowing from the building's vents. The air was cold enough to give him goose bumps. At least he thought it was the air.

He didn't hesitate. In Burke's experience, anticipation was the worst aspect of this sort of thing. These situations never improved. He was hoping the guy was either carrying a toy or just on his way to get his hunting rifle repaired.

He opened the door of the Laundromat and went in. A young man—thin, scrawny even, with a stalk of a neck and prematurely balding in his, what, mid-twenties at most—was staring at a spin dryer on the far side of a row of washers, as if it displayed college football and not a spiral of laundry. At the front of the place, in a row of plastic chairs, three women were reading magazines or listening to iPods. None of them looked up.

Under the pretense of grabbing a magazine, Burke moved toward the other side of the washers and saw that the man was indeed holding a shotgun. It dangled in a loose grip, pointing toward the floor. The guy didn't seem aware of anyone else.

Burke backed up a couple of steps. He tapped the first woman on the shoulder and when she looked up from her *Chatelaine,* startled, he put a finger to his lips. He showed her his police ID and pointed to the door. The woman opened her mouth, but Burke again gestured with his finger to his lips. She retrieved a small knapsack from the floor and went out.

By now the other two women were watching. Burke gestured to them as well to leave the Laundromat. They both stood up, but instead of going out, one of them headed toward the dryers.

"Oh, my God," she said. "He's got a gun."

Burke took hold of her elbow and spoke quietly. "Out. Now. Get out now and stay away from the windows. Don't let anyone else in until my backup units arrive. Go. Go."

The woman didn't look back; the door slammed shut behind her.

Two other people at the far end of the Laundromat hadn't heard anything over the gurgle and clatter of the machines, and the armed man sat between Burke and them. He was looking at Burke now.

"What do you want?" he said. He had an unpleasant voice, a ducklike quack that rightly belonged to a much older man.

Burke smiled. "Some guy next door panicked when he saw you had a weapon there. Thought I'd come in and check it out."

"I'm not going to hurt anybody."

"That's good. But do you realize it's an offense to carry an unsheathed firearm within city limits?"

"What are you, a cop?"

Burke nodded, gave another little smile. He looked up at the ceiling a moment, then back at the guy. He was trying to remember what the Police College at Aylmer had taught him about eye contact with disturbed individuals. Some found it threatening, but some found it reassuring. He couldn't remember which, so he tried a bit of both.

"My day off," Burke said. "Now, hand that firearm over to me, butt first."

"No. I'm not going to do that."

The people in the back were still oblivious. If Burke could get them out, he could leave too and keep the place empty till backup arrived. Where the hell were they?

"Listen," Burke said. "I'm just going to ask the other people to leave. I'm a little concerned that weapon of yours is going to go off, and we don't want any bystanders to get hurt, do we?"

"Fine. Get 'em out of here. You go too."

"Excuse me!" Burke had to yell over the washers. "Excuse me, sir, ma'am?" He held up his ID, not that they would be able to make it out from where they were. "Sir? Ma'am? Police officer. I'm going to have to ask you to leave. I need you to step outside and stay clear of the building for a little bit."

"What the hell for?" the man said. "My stuff's just about ready to come out of the dryer."

"Please step outside, sir. I need to secure this building."

The man grumbled, gathering up a knapsack and a bottle of iced tea. He grumbled all the way out the door, through which the woman had already made a less recalcitrant exit.

Burke turned back to the man with the gun, almost a boy, really.

"I'm going to ask you again. Would you hand that weapon over, please? Butt first."

By way of reply the man shucked a shell into the chamber. Burke's heart fell into his shoes.

"All right, look." Burke raised his hands. "I'm not armed. I told you, it's my day off. Just put the gun down, and we can have a dialogue about this." Have a dialogue? A *dialogue*? Be nice if I could sound like a human being, he told himself.

"Just go back outside," the man said, in that ducklike voice. "I'm not going to hurt anyone. Just myself."

"Well, at least tell me your name. I mean, we're gonna have to identify you and all that."

"Perry," the man said. "Perry Dorn."

"My name's Larry," Burke said. "Perry and Larry, how about that?" Twinning, they called it. Find some way to identify with the guy. If he lights a smoke, you light one too. If he feels like pizza, you ask if you can share it. Twinning can make a real difference; they see you as human, they see you as sympathetic. "So, where do you live, Perry?"

"Woodruff Avenue. Three forty-one Woodruff."

"Oh, yeah. That building by the old CNR station? That looks like a nice place."

"It's a dump."

"Really? You wouldn't know from the outside."

"Yeah, well. It's amazing what you don't know from the outside."

"Very true," Burke said. "That's very true. Why don't you tell me a little about what's going on with you? You look like a guy with a certain amount of stamina. Guy who can take a few hits and stay on his feet. What's going on, Perry? What's got you down? Job? Girlfriend?"

The man shook his head. One side of his mouth crept up a little, as if he was tasting bile. "If I tell you, will you go away and leave me alone?"

"I can't leave while you have a gun, Perry. I'd get in serious trouble if I did that. Why don't you tell me anyway?"

The man blinked several times. A heavy sweat had broken out on his forehead, dripping down into his eyes. It was hot in the Laundromat, but not that hot.

"I don't have a girlfriend and I don't have a job. Those are the givens. Let X be a student. A former student. I was going to go to McGill to do graduate work. But I didn't want to go unless my girlfriend went with me. Let Y be my girlfriend. Ex-girlfriend. She said she was going, but then she changed her mind after I'd already been accepted and paid my tuition and had my ticket and everything. I knew something wasn't right with this equation. Before she backed out, I knew. I knew it couldn't possibly go that well. And I was right. I got the right answer, I just didn't know how I got it."

"That's tough, Perry," Burke said. "That's a lot to handle.

You know, it might not hurt to give yourself a little time to get over this."

The man ignored him.

"I was supposed to go to McGill. They were going to pay all my tuition. All I had to cover was books and living expenses, and now I can't go. See, it wasn't just she didn't want to go to Montreal. That was not the problem. The reason she dumped me was she was sleeping with a guy I thought was my friend. Let him be Z. Stanley, my so-called friend."

Burke might have thought he was making progress here, getting the guy talking about himself and his troubles. But he wasn't speaking with any feeling. He was quacking his way through his algebra of misery and was not about to be distracted. All that mathematical jargon, like his life was just some math problem. The coldness in that voice, the lack of feeling, had Burke's heart beating double time.

"Well, hell, Perry. This just gets worse and worse. No wonder you're down in the dumps. Anybody would be. You need some time off, fella. Some time to recuperate from all the punishment you've taken."

"Time off. I was supposed to show up for my graduate course weeks ago. I've lost my slot there now. And as for my girlfriend—"

"What's her name?"

"Margaret. Everyone calls her Peg, though."

"Margaret. That's an Irish name."

The guy wasn't listening.

"She's been screwing around," he said, as if he hadn't already mentioned it. "Kinda brings a new vector into the equation. She's been unfaithful to me. For a long time now, behind my back. She says no, it's just recent. I can't prove it, but I know she's lying. It's just a feeling I get. Everything's false."

The guy should be crying now, but he's got that dead voice, that it's-all-over voice. The machines have all gone quiet, except for one dryer slamming against the back wall. Burke hears cars pulling up: the cavalry at last. He has a sudden inspiration, the kind of hunch worthy of a CID man. He points around at the Laundromat.

"Is this where you met her, Perry? Would this happen to be where you and Margaret first met?"

"A-plus *plus,*" the guy says, and gives him a big grin.

Connection! Burke figures. Now we're getting somewhere. And just as he's thinking that, Perry Dorn flips the shotgun so the muzzle is under his own chin and pulls the trigger.

12

One of the aspects of small-city police work that makes it both more interesting than big-city stuff and more frustrating is that a detective has to deal with all sorts of crimes. He or she is not a vice cop, or a homicide cop, or a bunko specialist; they take whatever gets assigned to them by their detective sergeant. With Cardinal on bereavement leave and McLeod and Burke on their days off, Lise Delorme was now, in addition to her new hunt for a child molester, covering another suicide—this time in a Laundromat that smelled of lint and hot metal and soapy water.

But Delorme could also smell the blood. The spray had hit the ceiling along with a good deal of brain matter, and there were streaks and blotches and scarlet smears where he had fallen against the washers. The pool on the floor was already dark and congealing.

"Gee," Szelagy said. "What do you suppose could be the cause of death?"

Standing next to Ken Szelagy was like standing next to the Empire State Building; he was six-four and always made Delorme feel puny, which she was not. She tended to compensate by being gruff with him, which was unnecessary, since Szelagy was the easiest-going member of CID.

They were hanging back a little so the coroner could go about his work. It was Dr. Claybourne again, reflections of fluorescent lights gleaming on his head.

Delorme flipped through the dead man's wallet. It was hard to pull out the individual cards and papers wearing latex gloves, but she finally managed to extract a driver's license, not that the stern, somewhat lopsided face in the license bore any resemblance to the carmine wreckage on the floor.

"Perry Wallace Dorn," she read. "Lives on Woodruff, if this address is still current."

"Kinda far from here," Szelagy said. "You'd think he'd at least pick his own Laundromat. Maybe a machine ate his quarter."

Delorme bypassed several credit cards, Algonquin Bay library card, medical insurance card, Chapters bookstore discount card, Northern University student card, expired.

"Here we go," she said. "Birth certificate."

She turned it over. Unfortunately, it was the short-form certificate that did not give parents' names. She handed the card to Szelagy. "Call the Registrar General, get the parents' names, and see if Perry was ever married."

Szelagy flipped open his cell phone, and Delorme reached down to take a piece of paper that Dr. Claybourne was handing to her.

"It was in his jacket pocket," he said. Dr. Claybourne's face was bright red. A matter of his complexion, Delorme reminded herself, whatever McLeod might say. McLeod was always wrong about everything; it was amazing he ever managed to make detective.

The note had been crumpled up in a tight ball at some point, then smoothed out and folded up again more neatly. In any case, it would not be going down in the history of great romantic letters.

Dear Margaret, it said. Then that had been crossed out and rewritten several times in different spots on the page. *Dear Margaret, Dear Margaret, Dear. . . .* No points for eloquence there, Perry. But then Delorme reconsidered. Perhaps that was all that needed to be said when you were going to quit the scene. No, thanks. I've had enough. You guys go on without me. Maybe Perry Dorn had distilled the suicide note to its essence: *Dear. . . .*

You'd think it would be just losers, Delorme thought, complete failures or people with no prospects at all. But she had seen enough by now to know that suicide was an equal-opportunity exit. Smart or stupid, ugly or beautiful, anyone could walk out at any time. But why this particular time? Why October? Delorme knew enough about suicide to know that the myth was wrong: there was no Christmas rush, not in Ontario. The numbers were worst in the month of February. Which made sense, because by February you were so sick of snow and cold that suicide could look like a reasonable option. Which was why, come February, virtually the entire population of Algonquin Bay transferred itself to Florida or the Caribbean.

Why kill yourself in the fall? It was so beautiful, the hills heartbreaking swells of color. The fall was the time Delorme felt happiest. It was always autumn, not New Year's, when she made her resolutions. Maybe it was just a legacy of the educational system. Fall was when you bought bright new notebooks, their fresh clean pages inviting you to write neat, comprehensive notes. Later in the year, your notes deteriorated into ambiguous little blurts that jogged the memory inconclusively, if at all. But those early autumn days when the air carried the first crisp notes of winter and the sky burned blowtorch blue, it was impossible, at least for Delorme, not to be happy. Even though every summer seemed to bring a new romantic reversal, each fall made her heart expand with hope.

Outside, the sun was so bright, the parking lot looked overexposed. Inside, everything that wasn't bloody was gray and drained of color, like clothing that has been through the wash too many times.

The door slammed on its springs and Burke came in, notebook in fist. "Checked his car. Backseat's full of new books and binders and crap."

Burke was trying to sound gruff, but his face was white and his hand was shaking.

"We have his student card," Delorme said. "Listen, Larry, why don't you go home and lie down for a while? Guy blows his head off in front of you, it's not something you're going to get over in five minutes."

"Look at this, though."

He handed her a sheet of paper, expensive letterhead with a red crest. Dated early April.

"'Dear Mr. Dorn,'" she read. "'I am delighted to inform you that McGill University has accepted you into its graduate program in Mathematics. In view of your extremely impressive record at Northern, I think I am safe in saying that this acceptance will come with a substantial grant. Subject to confirmation from the student awards department, your expenses will probably be limited to rent and other living expenses. We look forward to meeting you in the fall.' School year started ages ago. If he's accepted at McGill, why isn't he in Montreal?"

"Clearly the guy didn't have all his marbles," Burke said. "Jerk," he added, but he was not a convincing hard-ass.

"Really, Larry," Delorme said, "go home and lie down. You're not in shape to be working. Go ahead. No one's going to think badly of you."

"I'm all right. Kinda thing's all in a day's work. Kinda shit we deal with, right?"

"No, it isn't. I've never seen anyone shoot themselves, and I don't ever want to. What's that you're holding?"

"Huh?" Burke held up a PalmPilot and stared at it as if it had just been beamed into his hand. "Oh, yeah. Was in his car. Figured you might want it."

"Good thinking. Now go home."

"Maybe I'll go sit outside for a few minutes," Burke said.

Szelagy snapped his cell phone shut. "Registrar's gonna call me back."

"Might not need them," Delorme said. She was poking the stylus at the Palm, scrolling up and down through addresses. Not under *D* for Dorn, not under *P* for parents. "Here we go. Under *M* for Mom."

13

Cardinal feels a strange happiness suffusing his body. Here the three of them are—Catherine, Cardinal, and Kelly—at the Trianon Restaurant, having the best meal Algonquin Bay has to offer. The Trianon is their tradition for special occasions: birthdays, wedding anniversaries, or sometimes just because Kelly is up for a visit. And here she is, visiting from New York, and Catherine is in a great mood, the hospital a distant green-tiled memory. Cardinal's heart is aloft in his chest like a helium balloon.

He may have had a little too much to drink, because he is bubbling over with sentimentality, saying, "This is great. This is the way it's supposed to be. We could be a heart-warming TV show. *The Goode Family.*"

Kelly rolls her eyes. "Dad, really."

"No, look at us," Cardinal insists. Okay, so he's feeling all that Bordeaux, but he has to say it. "Beautiful intelligent daughter, competent husband—"

"Mad wife," Catherine interjects, and the other two smile.

Cardinal covers her warm hand with his. "I'm just so grateful," he says. "Gratitude isn't a big enough word for what I feel. I'm just so—"

"Dad, what are you going *on* about!" Kelly looks as if she's going to signal for the check and catch the first plane back to New York. "Can't we just have a normal conversation?"

"This is a normal conversation," Cardinal says. "That's what's so wonderful. I dreamed Catherine was dead, and now here we all are together, just being normal." He lays a hand on his heart, feels the warmth from that furnace of joy.

Catherine's serious brown eyes, sizing him up, tiny parentheses forming at the corners of her mouth. "You dreamed I was dead?"

"And it was so real! It was horrible!"

"Poor you," Catherine says, the honey of concern in her voice. She puts a hand on his cheek, and he feels the heat of the blood flowing through her fingers. "Are you okay now?"

"Okay? Am I okay?" Cardinal laughs. "Oh, I'm so okay, they could bottle it and sell it on street corners. It would put heroin and ecstasy out of business. I'm so okay, I could—" His voice cracks, and now he can't speak because he's crying. He's actually crying tears of happiness, tears of joy, wife and daughter rippling through his tears like computer effects.

The sensation of tears cooling on his face woke Cardinal up. He'd been sleeping on his back, and the tears were puddled in his eyes. His nose was running, his upper lip hot with a rivulet of mucus, tears cooling around his ears and neck. Such joy! He wiped his eyes and turned over on his elbow to tell Catherine.

THE DREAM SET his nerves on edge. Every move he made was amplified tenfold. The mere placing of a cup on the kitchen counter made a *clack* that hurt his ears. Water running in the kitchen sink was rough and ugly, mingling cutlery a torture. Even the newspaper, as he turned a page, made noises that were glassy and sibilant. And he could read nothing, take nothing in. Even the headlines were opaque.

And Catherine was everywhere. Every object in his house had its degree of Catherine-ness. Anything she had chosen was high on the scale; she had put effort into it, made a trip to buy it, thought about it. Anything she used daily was highly Catherined; in the bathroom: her raft of medications, the little tubes of shadow eraser and moisturizer, her hairbrush, with strands of her hair. Do you keep such things? How do you come to throw them away?

There were tulips she had brought home—was it two weeks ago?—long wilted in their vase. Cardinal couldn't bring himself to toss them out; neither could Kelly, apparently. Then there were the photographs Catherine had chosen to frame: a portrait of Kelly, a quiet shot of the two of them she had taken with a timer. The music cabinet was stacked with CDs she had chosen: the *Goldberg Variations,* the *Well-Tempered Clavier* by Gould and by Landowska. Bonnie Raitt, Sheryl Crow. *Will I ever be able to bear that music? Should I throw it out?*

In the empty kitchen, Cardinal poured himself a bowl of cornflakes. He never ate cold cereal, but he thought they were bland enough to go down without his noticing. He was staring at the flakes floating in milk when the phone on the kitchen counter rang.

He got up to answer it. There was a woman on the other end, not a voice he recognized.

"Hello, is Catherine there?"

Cardinal stood by the sink, gripping the phone, unable to move.

"Hello? Is this the right number for Catherine Cardinal?"

"Yes," Cardinal managed. "Yes, it is."

"May I speak to her, please?"

"Uh, no. She, uh—she isn't here."

"When will she be back, do you know?"

"No. I mean, I'm not sure."

"Oh. Well, if I leave my name and number, could you have her call me when she gets in? Do you have a pen?"

Cardinal picked up a pen and listened as she told him her name and Toronto number. Catherine should call her about a weekend workshop in advanced digital photography. Cardinal held the pen above the little notepad that he and Catherine used to relay phone messages, but he wrote nothing down.

HE ESCAPED TO work. Catherine had set foot in the squad room probably no more than half a dozen times. Except for her picture on Cardinal's desk, there were no reminders of her there. It was a guy place, despite the presence of Lise Delorme and Sergeant Flower and Frances and the other support personnel. The squad room was a guy place; Catherine could not claim him there.

"You're back," McLeod said. "Just when the place was beginning to seem civilized."

"I'm not here," Cardinal said. "Just came in to clear up a few things."

"Really," McLeod said. "I just came in to catch up on my sleep."

Cardinal grabbed his desk calendar and flipped it back to January. The Renaud case: two brothers who had pulled a series of break-ins. The back of their van had looked like a pawnshop when they were pulled over for a moving violation. It would have ended there, if one of their break-ins had not gone horribly wrong. One of the houses they broke into had surprised them by being occupied and, in a panic, the brothers had beaten the owner half to death. Cardinal had interrogated them over a period of weeks, finally managing to get one to turn on the other. They were both in the Kingston pen now, doing six years.

"What are you doing here?" Delorme said. She came right up and gave him a hug, and Cardinal, hypersensitized by grief, felt himself choke up. Delorme cast an investigative eye at his desk, the open calendar, and said, "Aha! Bad guys you have known and loved. Me, I'd say you're tracking down whoever's behind that horrible card."

"Cards," he said. "I got another one."

Delorme scanned his face. "Same postmark?"

"This one's from Sturgeon."

Sturgeon Falls was about half an hour west of Algonquin Bay. It only took Delorme a second before she voiced Cardinal's own thoughts on the matter. "Mattawa. Sturgeon. Assuming it's from the same person, makes me think he's probably from here. It's like disguising his handwriting."

"I'm pretty sure he used the same printer again."

Delorme's desk was right next to Cardinal's. She sat down in her chair and swiveled to face him. "You gonna show me?"

"You didn't want to know, before."

"Oh, John. Don't twist what I said."

Calling him by his first name in the office. Cardinal was surprised by how it touched him. He pulled the card in its plastic sleeve out of his briefcase.

How she must have hated you. You failed her so completely.

"Bastard," Delorme said. "Assuming it's a guy. Women can be pretty nasty too; I'm sure you've noticed. You think it's the Renaud brothers?" She pronounced it *brudders;* her French-Canadian accent tended to flower when she was emotional. "If they did this, I will personally drive down to Kingston to kick their asses."

"I don't think they did it. For one thing, how would they even know Catherine was—"

"News travels fast in prison, you know that. And they've still got family in town. Someone could have mentioned it."

"And then what? They get someone to send one card from Mattawa, and another one from Sturgeon Falls, but both out of the same printer? Seems like a stretch to me."

"Well, you know your caseload better than me."

Delorme's phone rang. She picked it up and began talking in hushed tones to Larry Burke about the boy who killed himself in the Laundromat. Cardinal had heard the news report on the radio driving in. It would be the most pressing piece of business on Delorme's calendar this week, but she hadn't mentioned it to him; she wouldn't want to upset him with talk of a suicide. Cardinal was not sure he liked being treated with kid gloves.

He continued flipping through his calendar. Every few minutes someone would come by with some variant of, "Cardinal! Good to see you back!" and Cardinal would say again, "I'm not here."

He went through his file drawer, thumbing back the tabs one after another. So many names, so many felons and miscreants, and yet very few seemed likely candidates for the position of card writer, let alone murderer.

If she was murdered. Everyone else saw suicide, despite the fact that she gave no warning. And even though her note had apparently been written months before, it wouldn't be enough, Cardinal knew. It wasn't even enough to sway Delorme, let alone the coroner, a judge, and a jury; doubts were eating away at his own heart too.

He pushed them out of his mind and reached into what he called his Halfway-In Box, which was where he put material that had to be dealt with that he never had time for. Among the notices of policy changes, upcoming conferences, court paperwork, there were Department of Corrections notices of recent releases. These were not just Cardinal's cases but all criminals from the jurisdiction.

He could hear Delorme talking quietly into the phone. "Larry, it wasn't your fault. You should talk to someone about this. You're allowed to be human."

Delorme sounded impossibly far away, as if Cardinal were underwater. He felt like a drowning man, his lungs filling with grief. These released felons and miscreants were just so much wreckage to cling to as he waited for rescue, and what would rescue consist of?

Catherine alive.

Still, he carried on, and by the time he was done he had a short list of three candidates. All were living in Algonquin Bay, all had been released in the past twelve months, and all had served at least five years in prison thanks to John Cardinal.

14

Algonquin Bay has a lot of churches, and some of them are quite attractive, but Saint Hilda's Catholic Church is not one of them. A ghastly redbrick structure on Sumner Street, Saint Hilda's has not been improved by the addition of a corrugated tin roof that is painted, unconvincingly, to look like weathered copper. Still, it is one of the benefits of the city's ever-shrinking congregations that the church parking lots provide acres of free parking.

Cardinal parked in Saint Hilda's shadow and walked along Sedgewick Street. This area was known as a "mixed" neighborhood, meaning that among its shabby bungalows and bony-looking duplexes you could find elementary school teachers, young cops, or the likes of Connor Plaskett.

Connor Plaskett had conceived an interest in glue sniffing while still in short pants. Later on he developed an affection for marijuana and alcohol in all its forms, although bottles of cheap port became a favorite, perhaps because of the sugar content. At one point, following a nasty altercation with a city bus, he had seen the light and joined AA.

He got sober, he started a business in Web design; he got married. His business grew to the point where he could support his new young wife and child quite comfortably. Then the Web bubble burst, he rapidly went broke, and alcohol provided a ready anesthetic.

Plaskett was coming out of a two-week bender when he took it into his head to rob a local convenience store. He did it with the help of a gun. He had the presence of mind to take the videotape out of the security system, not realizing that the tape he went off with was a dummy set up for precisely this purpose, so that the prospective thief would not take the tape that mattered.

So it was that Connor Plaskett appeared on the six o'clock news demanding that the teenager behind the counter hand over all the day's receipts.

It was one of the easiest cases that Cardinal had ever had to clear.

Plaskett was then unlucky in his prosecutor and his judge, not to mention his wife. He was sent up for five years. While he was away, his wife discovered that she had in fact been lesbian all her life and left him (taking the child with her) for a woman who fixed power lines for a living.

Plaskett took it badly, contriving while in prison to become readdicted to old substances and even to add some new ones. He emerged after serving his five-year sentence in worse shape than he had begun it.

Shortly after, Plaskett had accosted Cardinal one night outside the Chinook Tavern. Cardinal had just finished arresting someone else entirely—someone he could not now even recall—when Plaskett came reeling out of the tavern and recognized him.

"Fucker," he had said, spraying spit and beer fumes into the cool night air. "Motherfucker. You totally destroyed my life."

"No, Connor," Cardinal had said. "I think you deserve the credit for that."

"I had a family before you came along. I'm gonna fix you good."

Plaskett had staggered over and taken a pathetic swing at Cardinal before collapsing right there in the middle of the parking lot. Cardinal had taken his car keys away, pushed him into the backseat of his worn-out pickup, and shut the door, dropping the keys off with the Chinook bartender.

Number 164 was a tiny brown and white bungalow that leaned noticeably into the wind, as if it too were sniffing intoxicants. Number 164B turned out to be the door to the concrete block addition that had been cemented onto the house in a misguided attempt at improvement.

Cardinal pressed the bell but heard nothing from inside. He rapped on the door, onto which a picture of a Christmas wreath had been stenciled some years before.

A harsh voice, possibly female, answered, "Just a minute!" This was followed by a crash, as of a tea tray falling from a great height, and a series of unimaginative curses.

Slattern, although well within his vocabulary, was not a word that occurred frequently to Cardinal. But it certainly did when the door opened.

The woman looked as if she had been rolled to this address across a field of mud and broken glass some months before and had not yet had a chance to clean herself up. Her eyes were red, her knuckles scabbed, her hair an unnerving tangle and possible wildlife habitat.

"Whaddaya want?" A lot of that broken glass had got into her voice.

"I'm looking for Connor Plaskett."

"Good," she said. "So am I."

She opened the door, and Cardinal stepped into what had apparently been intended to be a kitchen but looked like a rag-and-bone shop.

"Excuse the mess," she said. "Got no cupboards."

In the murky light that slipped through the tiny window Cardinal could make out a sink against one wall, a hot plate sitting atop a half-size fridge, and some apple crates that formed makeshift cupboards which moisture and overuse had reduced to wreckage.

Cardinal followed the woman into the next room, which was even murkier. She sat on an unmade sofa bed so low that her chin was barely above her knees. Cardinal leaned against the doorframe. The place stank of old cigarette smoke and wet carpet.

"Where's Connor?" he asked.

"Damned if I know. Cigarette?"

"No, thanks. What's your relationship to him?"

"Fuck-buddy." Seeing his look, she gave a snort and said, "What didja think? Financial adviser?"

"And you don't know where he is right now?"

"Haven't a clue."

"Well, if you don't know, I suspect his parole officer doesn't know either, and that would put Connor in breach."

"Really," the woman said. After many tries, she had finally got her lighter to work and was sucking avidly on a du Maurier. She released a stream of smoke in Cardinal's direction. "Bummer. Whaddaya want him for?"

"It's in connection to a recent death."

"Connor couldn't kill anybody. He can barely tie his boots."

The hellish surroundings were eloquent testimony to that. While it might have made a reasonable lair for someone capable of stalking a woman and murdering her, it didn't look like the home of someone who could get it together enough to buy a card, type it out, and mail it from Mattawa or Sturgeon Falls.

But Plaskett's words rang anew in Cardinal's ears: *I'm gonna fix you.*

"Where does Connor hang out these days?" Cardinal said. "I'm going to need addresses."

"Christ, Connor doesn't go nowhere—that's what's so weird. He sits in front of that TV watching football all day and all night. I can't get him to do a damn thing. I'm gonna have a beer. You prob'ly don't want one."

"No, thank you."

She went to the fridge and pulled out a can of Molson Canadian, popped the top, and drank most of it in one go. When she went to sit back down on the bed, she misjudged and knocked over an end table, sending the phone clattering to the floor. She squinted at it for a few moments as if trying to recall its name.

"That reminds me," she said finally. "Had a funny phone conversation last night."

"Who with?"

"Christ, I don't know. I didn't know the guy. Said he was

a friend of Russell McQuaig, who's like a drinking buddy of Connor's, and Russell tol' him to call. Him and Connor take off to Toronto every now and again. Hit the big lights, you know. Personally, I couldn't give a shit about Toronto. Too dirty. Anyways, this guy tried to tell me that Connor wasn't coming back."

"What do you mean, not coming back? He took off to Toronto and some stranger called you to say he wasn't coming back?"

"Yeah, I think so. Something like that." She rubbed at her filthy hair. "Actually, now that I think of it, he even tried to tell me Connor was dead. Yeah."

"You seem to be taking it pretty well."

"Well, yeah, 'cause like I didn't know this guy from Adam. Why should I believe him? And second of all, if Connor was dead, the police and that would have had to call me, right? The hospital or whatever. They would've had to call me to, like, notify the next of kin."

"Fuck-buddy isn't generally recognized as next of kin," Cardinal said. "They would have called a blood relative first, or even his former wife, before they would call you. A hospital might not even know of your existence."

"Well, I don't know." She brushed a web of hair away from her face as if it were fog. "You think Connor's dead?"

"I don't know," Cardinal said. "It should be easy enough to find out."

"Shit, I hope he's not dead," the woman said. She tipped her head back and poured the last of her beer down her throat. She crushed the can and tried to stifle a belch. "I really couldn't face moving again."

15

Sergeant Mary Flower came into the squad room and sat on Delorme's desk. That was what she did when she wanted you to drop everything and pay attention to her. Annoying but effective.

Delorme was on the phone with the coroner's office, trying without success to determine the whereabouts of his evidence concerning a case of domestic murder that was coming to trial in two weeks. She put her hand over the phone and cocked an eyebrow at Flower.

"We got Mrs. Dorn outside, mad as hell," Flower said. "She wants to speak to you, I don't know why."

"It turns out I know her daughter."

"Good. She's here too. I love that top, by the way, is that Gap?"

"Benetton. Tell them I'll be right out."

Delorme found them in the waiting area. A woman in her fifties was standing under the clock, arms folded across her chest, one foot tapping furiously as if she were counting every split second of justice delayed. Her daughter, Shelly, was seated in a chair behind her. Shelly was an amusing red-haired friend of Delorme's from the health club. They often took treadmills next to each other and chatted to pass the time. Delorme liked her, but Shelly was married with two kids, and this was the first time Delorme had seen her outside the club. She stood up when she saw Delorme.

"Lise, I know we shouldn't show up unannounced."

"That's all right," Delorme said. "I'm sorry about your brother. He was so young."

"Yes, he was young," the older woman said, and even in those first few words Delorme could hear the agony that was coming out as fury. "He was hardly more than a boy. He was still a student, a brilliant student. He was accepted at McGill, he had every reason to live, and he didn't have to die."

"Lise, this is my mother, Beverly Dorn."

"Mrs. Dorn, I'm sorry for your loss."

"But are you going to help us with it? That's what I want to know. What are you going to do to help us right this terrible wrong? Perry was a smart person, a sensitive person, and now he's dead and it didn't have to happen. There should be an inquest, an investigation. We deserve answers."

"Mom, Lise will do whatever she can. Just take it easy."

"Why don't you come with me?" Delorme said. She showed them into a room that was often used for families under stress. Unlike the other interview rooms, it had carpeting and an almost comfortable couch. There was a scratchy-looking artwork of a mother and child on one wall, a blackboard without chalk on the other. Delorme closed the door behind them.

"Won't you sit down?" Delorme said.

"I don't feel like sitting," Mrs. Dorn said. "I'm too angry."

"Mom, you don't have any reason to be angry at Lise."

"There was another officer in that Laundromat with Perry. What about him? He was right there when it happened. He was there *before* it happened. Why didn't he disarm him, can you tell me that? Why didn't he *do* something?"

Delorme gestured once again toward the couch and waited until Mrs. Dorn sat beside her daughter. Her eyes were red and raw from the kind of crying that brings no relief, her hyperagitation that of one whom sleep has abandoned.

Delorme sat across from them and spoke softly. "Yes, there was a police officer at the Laundromat. He was in the coffee shop next door, off duty, when the man beside him saw your son going in with a shotgun. After calling for backup, the officer followed your son inside."

"Why didn't he take the gun away from him? That's what

I want to know. Why didn't he tear that gun right out of his hand? He just stood by and let it happen!"

"The officer's first concern was for the safety of everyone in the Laundromat. There were other people there. He focused on getting them to safety as quickly as possible."

"Perry has never been a danger to anyone but himself. It's obvious when you look at him. He wouldn't hurt a fly. That is literally true, by the way. He'll go to enormous lengths to get an insect out of the house without injuring it."

"The officer did not know your son. All he saw was a distraught man, armed, in a room full of people. He got the others out first, which was the appropriate action."

"And he lets my obviously distraught son kill himself. Bravo. Give the man a medal."

"Mom. Let her talk." Shelly put a hand on her mother's forearm, but Mrs. Dorn jerked it away.

"Don't patronize me."

"Nobody's patronizing you. You asked a question, and Lise is answering it. Let her finish."

"The officer then tried to—"

"The officer, the officer. Does this person have a name? A badge number?"

"He does. And you're welcome to that information, but it won't change the facts. He tried to calm your son down. He spoke quietly with him and encouraged him to put the gun down. Your son refused."

"He was just a boy! You have a trained police officer, and he can't stop a boy from killing himself? Why didn't he grab that gun!"

Delorme let the question—accusation, rather—hang there in the air for a minute.

"I think you know the answer to that question, Mrs. Dorn."

Mrs. Dorn shook her head tightly.

"The officer did not want to upset Perry any more than he already was. And he didn't want to get shot himself. I repeat, he was unarmed."

"It's a policeman's job to take risks. He should have talked calmly to Perry and got close enough to get that gun away from him."

"And I'm sure he would have done so, had it been possible. He was trying to talk him down, to calm him, just as you say. They were talking, when Perry suddenly turned the gun on himself and fired."

"And nobody stopped him."

"Mrs. Dorn, from the time your son was seen entering the Laundromat to the time he pulled the trigger took less than eight minutes. It took three or four minutes to get the other people out. That gave the officer and your son at most about five minutes to work things out."

"Time enough to save his life. Why didn't he stop him? Dear God, why didn't he stop him? He was just a boy!"

"He did his best, Mrs. Dorn. There simply wasn't time."

"Could I speak to this officer, please?"

"Mom—"

"He isn't here today," Delorme said. "The reason is, he's devastated by what happened. No police officer enters into a situation like that without wanting the best possible outcome. At that moment, believe me, Mrs. Dorn, no one wanted your son to live more than that police officer. Had he succeeded in talking Perry out of it, he would be here today and he would be on top of the world. But he isn't. He's miserable."

"Maybe because he feels guilty. Maybe that's why he's miserable. Maybe because he didn't do his job."

"I hope when you're calmer you'll see it differently."

Mrs. Dorn sniffed. She looked at the picture on the wall, then back to her daughter.

"Well, we certainly plan to demand an investigation."

"There's no longer a Special Investigations officer up here, but I'll give you their number in Toronto. If they feel it's warranted, they'll investigate."

16

It was a relief to finally escape the office and hit the road on the child porn case. Poor Burke had not been able to save Perry Dorn, but Delorme was optimistic she could find this mystery girl and save her from further abuse.

She drove out to Trout Lake and parked in the small lot above Lakeside Marina. As she went down the wooden steps, a chill breeze was blowing off the water. The air alone at this time of year was worth the drive. Pure oxygen, with the first hint of frost. It made you want to do things, embark on new projects, solve crimes.

Delorme had taken swimming lessons here as a kid—not right at the marina but just a few hundred yards away, at the Ministry of Natural Resources dock. The instructors would order their victims to plunge into the lake when the water was barely 50 degrees and practice hauling one another around with various rescue holds. She had had to practice mouth-to-mouth on Maureen Stegg; it still gave her a peculiar feeling in the pit of her stomach to think about it.

The fresh air was invaded by the dock smells of rope and creosote and gasoline. Most of the boats had already been hauled away for winter storage, but a couple of cabin cruisers lay anchored a little way from the wharf, rocking gently on the rippling water. Delorme's heart gave a little kick when she saw the Cessna shining in the sun, the tail number the same as it was in the photograph of the girl.

"Can I help you?"

The man was wearing expensive sunglasses and a Lakeside

Marina baseball cap. A hardy type, apparently, dressed in shorts, although it was not by any means shorts weather.

"I'm wondering what it costs to rent space here." Delorme had never owned a boat and had no idea of the correct terminology. Probably should have said "to lease a berth" or some such thing.

"Depends what you need," he said. Delorme saw his eyes angle down to her hand, looking for the wedding band that wasn't there, and back up again.

"Need?"

"Well, if you're going to be using power and lights and so on, that's one thing. Also, size is a factor, obviously. You from around here?"

Delorme turned and pointed to the Cessna. "Out there by the plane. Right at the end of the dock. How much would it cost to tie up there?"

"Not much turnover in those slots, I'm afraid. Those are the most desirable, the most expensive, and they're rented by the same people year after year. Even when they move away—Sudbury, Sundridge, doesn't matter—they hang on to those spots."

"So that plane, for example. It's always anchored in the same spot?"

"Oh, yeah. Planes change even less than the boats. That guy's been floating there for at least since I've owned the place, which is ten years now."

"Really? Can you show me what's so special about those slots at the end of the dock? The ones that look like they're fenced off?"

The guy grinned, big white teeth in a face still tanned from the summer. He thinks he's getting somewhere, Delorme thought. He was kind of cute with that curly blond hair and the big grin—ropy muscles, too—and he was probably used to girls on vacation paying some attention. He was certainly not the child molester: too young, too thin, and with hair the wrong color and texture.

He opened a gate and led her along the dock.

"These boats go for what," Delorme said, "forty grand?"

"Oh, you're way low. More like seventy, eighty, even more. Here we go. You see here?" He rested his hand on a blue box attached to a light post. "This connects you to all the comforts of home: electricity, cable TV, satellite, you name it."

"Don't all the docks have that?"

"No, no. Just these two. Couple of others will get you electricity, but that's it. Plus these, as you can see, have extra security. We've got the lights overhead, the extra cameras. Anyone breaks in here is going to get caught."

"And at the other docks it's open season?"

The guy looked hurt. "All our docks are secure. I'm just saying you pay extra, you get extra."

"And what's the insurance situation?"

"Insurance, you're on your own," he told her. "Obviously we have our own fire and theft and so on. And massive liability. But if your boat gets stolen or vandalized, it's your insurance going to pay, not ours."

"I see. I'm Detective Delorme with Algonquin Bay Police Services." She had her ID out, showing him. She could see the guy's interest in her cooling drastically; it was always the way. Some men may be turned on by the idea of female cops, but in Delorme's experience it wasn't many, and it was never the right kind.

"Jeff Quigly," he said, shaking her hand none too enthusiastically.

"I'm conducting an investigation into a couple of violations that may have taken place in the neighborhood, and I need your help."

"Oh, sure. Anything I can do."

Anything I can do to get you off my dock and out of sight, he meant.

"I need to know who rents these slots from you."

"What, both these docks?"

"That's right. And not just now but for the past ten years."

"Even if I wanted to tell you, I don't know if I have that information."

"You just said the tenants don't change much."

The guy had folded his arms across his chest. He was looking out across the lake now, no longer at Delorme.

"Look, I don't think I can be giving out information on our renters. That's not the way I do things. People have a right to their privacy."

"You run a marina, not a hospital. It's not privileged information."

"No, but look. Suppose I tell someone that this slot is rented by so-and-so. And so-and-so's boat just happens to be out. A thief might take that to mean so-and-so is on vacation, touring the Great Lakes, cruising down to New York, or something. And his house gets burgled. What does that make me?"

"Innocent. Mr. Quigly, I'm not a thief, I'm a police officer investigating a crime."

"Yeah. Well, see, that's another thing. What are you investigating? Sure, people drink on their boats, they smoke dope, but it's a weird time of year to be investigating that stuff, and I don't think you should be asking me to compromise people's privacy over some minor infraction."

Delorme didn't want to reveal the nature of the crime. Mention child molesting and the place would go wild with rumors. And she didn't want her quarry to get even a whiff of the investigation before she was ready to put the cuffs on him.

"I have to count on your discretion," Delorme said. "You can't be mentioning this to anybody."

"No, of course not."

"I'm investigating an assault."

"Really." He shook his head. "Must've been minor or I'd have heard about it."

"I can't give you any more detail than that. Are you going to help me? I could get a warrant, but that takes at least a day and it's just going to delay getting a criminal off the streets."

Quigly took her into the marina office. It was a cluttered place with a detailed map of Trout Lake on one wall and a gigantic model of the champion schooner *Bluenose* leaning up against the other. There were fishing photographs and enlarged cartoons of sailing jokes everywhere. He rooted through a file cabinet and came up with some manila folders.

"Rental slips going back ten years," he said. "You're not going to find them in any kind of order, though."

17

Delorme organized her list of names geographically, and that put Frank Rowley at the top. She wasn't sure what she had been expecting from a man with his own plane: an over-sized brick mansion high on Beaufort Hill, maybe. Or one of those old Victorian places down on Main West. But Frank Rowley, it turned out, lived in a plain little house of white brick just a couple of blocks from the bypass. Delorme pulled into the drive and parked behind a tan Ford Escort, a modest unassuming vehicle that did not fit with her idea of a man who flew.

A small maple in the front yard had dropped all its leaves in a colorful circle, but a trim row of holly bushes against the front of the house was deep green. Even before she got out of her unmarked, she could hear the screech and wail of an electric guitar. It sounded as if some tormented ghost had broken loose in the neighborhood.

The guitar screamed, halted, then started up again. A Beatles riff this time, but Delorme couldn't have named the song.

In answer to her knock, a completely bald man of about forty opened the front door, still wearing his guitar. Men and their toys, Delorme thought.

"Mr. Rowley?"

"That's me. Can I help you?"

She held up her ID. "Can I take up a few minutes of your time?"

The interior of the house smelled richly of something baking, and Delorme noted with approval a white scuff of flour on Rowley's bald head.

She followed him into the living room, where dolls and stuffed animals were strewn across a colorful rug like victims of some benign catastrophe. There was a child's scooter, and large gaudy books splayed open on the couch and chairs. Delorme tripped slightly on the edge of the rug.

"Sorry," Rowley said. "It's got a bad repair—only reason I could afford it."

"You have kids, I see," Delorme said. "How old are they?"

"We have one daughter, Tara. She's seven. She'll be home from school soon. Please, have a seat."

Delorme sat in a deep armchair with split-log legs and arms. All the furniture had a comfortable, country-style, lived-in look, lots of wood everywhere, and cushions and throw rugs, not to mention the larger rug with its deep blue and black chevrons. And the owner of all this, a middle-aged man with a guitar over his shoulder and a head that would not have been out of place on a billiard table. The man in the pictures had almost shoulder-length hair, and in any case Delorme had no reason to suspect Rowley, since his plane merely appeared in the background of one photograph. Also, his daughter was too young. But she sized him up anyway.

"Mr. Rowley, you have a pilot's license, is that correct?"

"That's right. I work for North Wind," he said, naming an airline that flew small planes out of Algonquin Bay to northern cities such as Timmins and Hearst.

"Business is slow these days?"

"No, I work four days on, four days off, which is why you find me here doing the house-husband thing."

"And you keep a small plane at Lakeside Marina, right?" Delorme read him the tail number from her notebook.

"Why? Did something happen to it?"

"I just want to make sure I'm talking to the right person."

"You are. Can I get you a coffee or something? I was just about to make a pot."

"No, that's all right. Thank you."

"And I've got some pretty spectacular muffins that should be ready soon. Tara's crazy about them."

Rowley switched off a Vox amplifier and leaned his guitar against the wall. It was a big black instrument with lots of knobs and chrome, and Delorme thought it would be more suited to country music than the Beatles, but guitars were not her strong point.

"Are you down at the marina a lot, Mr. Rowley?"

"Depends what you consider a lot. If I go there, it's just because I want to take Bessie up."

"Bessie?"

"Bessie the Cessna." He grinned. "That's just her name, don't ask me why. I take her up once or twice a week for maybe an hour or two at a time. Wendy—that's my wife—wanted me to get rid of it. Too dangerous, she says. But I can't give it up. I just love to fly, and it's a lot more fun on your own than it is for work."

"I can imagine," Delorme said. Rowley looked like a man who enjoyed his life, baking muffins and playing guitar surrounded by scattered books and toys. "Do you know many of the people at the marina?"

"Well, I know Jeff Quigly, the manager."

"Anybody else?"

Rowley shrugged. "Not really. I don't hang out there. I don't go to the bar afterward or anything, like a lot of guys do. Place is kind of a clubhouse, when you get down to it. But it's not a club I'd want to join—you know, guys whose idea of a good time is to get a case of two-four and go out on the lake to get absolutely rip-roaring drunk. Not something I enjoyed in my twenties, and I'm sure as hell not interested in my forties. Besides, I got a wife and kid. I don't know where these guys find the time."

"Tell me a little about them. I need to know more about the people who hang out at the marina."

"Why? What are you investigating?"

"Assault," Delorme said.

"Oh, wow. Well, when I was talking about beer parties I

certainly didn't mean to imply that any of these people would be capable of violence."

"No, of course not. It's witnesses I'm looking for. Can you tell me anything at all?"

"The only one I know very well is Owen Glenn."

Delorme wrote the name in her notebook. She had already come across it at the marina, where the records showed he did not rent any of the slots that interested her.

"Owen's a fellow flier. Owns a little Piper he likes to take up about once a month. I bump into him a lot, especially in summer, but we're not buddies or anything. He's much more conservative than I am. The couple of times politics came up, I had to politely excuse myself, you know what I mean? He's the kind of guy who wishes we were killing people in Iraq."

"So he doesn't own one of those cabin cruisers you see parked out there all the time?"

"No, he just has a little skiff, same as me."

"Do you know any of those people?"

"Just to say hi to."

"Really? But you go right past them to get to your plane, no?"

"The skiffs are around the north side of the marina. Under the deck of the bar? I just row out from there to the plane, so it's not really conducive to chatting with my neighbors, if you want to call them that."

"Do you know any of them by name?"

"Sure. There's Matt Morton. He owns a cruiser. I've known Matt since high school, although I wouldn't exactly call us friends. He was kind of a sports guy, and I was more of a—nerd, I guess you could say."

"An artistic type," Delorme suggested.

"An artistic type!" Rowley grinned. "Exactly. That's me. Now all I have to find is an art I can master."

"You were doing a pretty good Beatles impression, from what I heard. You play professionally?"

"Just a hobby. I play in a Beatles tribute band. Sergeant Tripper? We play weddings and bar mitzvahs mostly."

"Which slot is Mr. Morton in at the marina?" Delorme knew the answer, but detectives learn early always to confirm a fact when the opportunity presents itself.

"Matt's moored at the end of number three, on the north side."

"Which is where, in relation to you?"

"About as close as you can be. I mean, sometimes I can see right down into his cabin. Not that I want to, particularly."

"Why? Have you ever seen anything disturbing?"

"In Matt's boat? No, nothing at all."

"How would you describe Mr. Morton?"

"Matt? I don't know. Medium-sized kind of guy. Used to play football in high school. Brown hair going gray, like all of us. Not that I've got much to worry about." He grinned and rubbed a hand over his pate, missing the flour.

"Any kids?"

"A boy and a girl, I think. I don't remember their names."

"What about the slot opposite to Mr. Morton?"

"The south side? I don't know them. Huge boat, though."

According to Jeff Quigly and the marina's records, the slot was rented by one André Ferrier. The rent was always paid on time, but the marina hardly ever saw him.

Delorme took down the information, then snapped her notebook shut. "Like I said, Mr. Rowley, at this point I'm just looking for witnesses. You've been very helpful."

She gave him her card. On her way to the front door she tried to catch glimpses of other rooms, but there were no walls, no objects, no furnishings—nothing obvious, anyway—that matched the settings in the photographs.

"If I think of anything else, I'll give you a call," Rowley said. "But I've sure as hell never met anybody out there who seemed capable of assault."

"You might be surprised," Delorme said. "I'm constantly amazed by who turns out to be capable of what."

18

Frederick Bell finished his strawberry shortcake and scraped up the last dabs of whipped cream with his fork.

"Are you sure this is low-fat?" he asked his wife, Dorothy, who was organizing things in the fridge.

"I got it out of *Heart Healthy*," she said, her voice muffled a little by the fridge door. "It's not high-calorie."

"But that's if you only eat one serving. What if you find yourself lusting for another?"

"You don't get another." Dorothy laid claim to a large store of common sense. It had served her well in her years as a nurse, and it served her equally well as a psychiatrist's wife. "If you have another piece, you're just defeating the purpose of the reduced calories."

"I've devoted my life to missing the point and defeating the purpose. I don't see why I should stop now." Bell swallowed the last of his tea. It was cold, but he didn't mind cold tea; tea of any kind was good. Some British habits died hard.

"I found a really charming little cottage near Nottingham," Dorothy said. "I left the picture for you on your desk. I don't suppose you looked at it yet."

"Alas, I have failed you once again."

"Frederick, what's so hard about taking a look at a picture?"

"I don't know. I suppose I just haven't accepted this idea of retiring back in England."

"We've talked about it. I thought we agreed we'd both be happiest there. It's a pretty little place, a short walk from the sea. And it's near the Trent. You've always said you wanted to live near water when you retire."

"Heroic figures never retire. It's not in our nature."

"You'll have to, one day, and I'm not having you mooching around the house through these endless Canadian winters."

"England's too bloody expensive. The pound is sky-high."

"It's come down a lot. We can afford this place, and it's so cute."

On this one issue, Dorothy's common sense had deserted her as far as Bell was concerned. Here in Canada they had a huge place, almost a mansion. But back in England even the pokiest little houses cost close to half a million quid. Dorothy seemed to have an exaggerated sense of what a psychiatrist made over here. It wasn't as if they were living in the States. Oh, well, she enjoyed looking at her cottages and gardens, and it didn't hurt her to dream.

Bell put his dish and cup on the counter and pinched his wife's behind.

Dorothy turned and gave his wrist a light smack. "Don't you start with that now. It's the middle of the day."

"Nothing could be further from my mind. I've got a patient in five minutes. I must prepare my *gravitas*."

"Oh, yes. Mustn't forget the *gravitas*. Where would we be without that?"

In their early days, back in London, Bell and his wife had been tearing each other's clothes off constantly. But over the years they had settled into a more routine kind of sex life, and that was fine with Bell. They loved each other and looked after each other, and that was all he needed. Of course, Dorothy wasn't in his class—not brilliant, not even a doctor—but she was good company. And still good-looking, even in her mid-fifties. She had the kind of thin face that ages well and the slim figure of a much younger woman.

Bell washed his hands in the downstairs bathroom. He rolled his shoulders, then opened the door that separated the kitchen from the front hall and his office. A young woman with blond hair badly in need of a wash was sitting on the bench in the hall. Other patients might have leafed through a *New Yorker* or fiddled with an iPod, but this woman was just slouched in her coat, arms folded across her chest. This was Melanie, eighteen years old and the picture of misery.

"Hello, Melanie," Bell said.

"Hello."

Even in that single word he could detect a slowness, a thickness, that spoke of the enormous effort expended to express two syllables. Immediately, depression was a third entity in the room. Bell pictured it—him, really—as a silent figure, the Entity, caped and masked, invisible to the patient. Bell sometimes felt like the old priest in *The Exorcist,* fated to wrestle repeatedly with an immortal nemesis. The Entity.

Melanie followed him into the office and sat on the couch, unbuttoning her coat and letting her shoulder bag slide to the floor. She leaned back and stared at her feet. Dr. Bell sat in one of the small chairs opposite, notebook on knee, not smiling, face composed into an expression of calm expectation. It was important for the patient, after the usual pleasantries, to be the first one to speak; those first words revealed so much. But sometimes it was hard, as now, to wait for a client to overcome whatever it was they had to overcome before they could begin. The minutes ticked by.

Melanie looked a lot older than eighteen. She was small-boned and small-breasted, with something of a drowned-rat look, longish flat nose dividing stringy curtains of hair. The Northern University sweatshirt didn't do a lot for her, either. When she finally did speak, she kept her eyes focused on her outstretched feet.

"I could barely come here," she said.

"You found it difficult? Can you tell me why?"

"I don't know. . . ." A long pause while she remained still, except for one foot ticking from side to side like a metronome. "I'm just so sick of myself. Sick of thinking about myself. Sick of talking about myself. There's nothing worth saying. So why come here? Why run through it all again and again?"

"You mean you feel that you're not worth talking about? Or that nothing you say will help you get better?"

She looked at him for the first time, green eyes two pits of despair, then quickly back at her feet.

"Both, I guess."

Dr. Bell let the silence hold for a few moments, let her feel her own exaggerations, or rather the exaggerations of the hooded figure lurking in the shadows just beyond her vision. The Entity always compelled his victims to speak like this: accuse themselves of worthlessness in order to prevent them from making the slightest effort to save themselves.

"Let me ask you something," Bell said. "Suppose someone came to you—a friend, even a stranger, doesn't matter—and said, 'You shouldn't even talk to me. I'm so worthless. I'm not worth even thinking about.' What would you say to her?"

"I'd say she was wrong. That nobody's worthless."

"But you won't accord yourself the same kindness you would someone else."

"I don't know. . . . All I know is, I'm in this pain all the time. I'm sick of talking about it. Talking doesn't help. Nothing helps. I just want it to be over. I even—"

"Even what?"

Melanie started to cry. After a moment Bell picked up the Kleenex box from the end table and handed it to her. She yanked out a couple but didn't use them right away. She cried hard, hiding her face behind her hand.

"Why are you hiding?" he asked, and that only made her cry more. You could see the release in her shoulders, hear it in the jagged, breathy wails.

"God," she said, when the tears had left her.

"You needed that."

"I guess so. Phew." She sounded spent.

"You said, 'I just want it to be over. I even—'"

"Yeah." Melanie blew her nose wetly, still gasping and sighing. "Yeah. I was in Coles bookstore the other day and they had a book on suicide. Assisted suicide, I guess. It tells you how to do it—how to kill yourself—painlessly. Basically, you just tie a plastic bag over your head."

"And?"

"Well, I didn't buy it or anything. But I stood there in the store reading it for a long time."

"Because you'd been thinking about killing yourself."

"Yeah."

"Okay. Straight factual question, Melanie—I need to know this: Have you ever actually tried to kill yourself?" He was sure the answer was negative.

"No. Not really."

"How do you mean, 'not really'?"

"Well, I scratched at my wrist with a razor blade once, but it really stung. I'm completely chicken when it comes to pain. I couldn't even cut deep enough to make it bleed."

"When was this?"

"Oh, a long time ago. When I was maybe twelve or so."

"Twelve. Did you write out a note?"

"No. I guess I wasn't serious. I was just miserable."

"Worse than now?"

"No, no. Now's much worse. *Much* worse."

"How often are you thinking of suicide these days?"

"I don't know. . . ."

"You probably do, Melanie."

It was impossible to make his voice any softer. He tried to suffuse every syllable with warmth and encouragement—above all, unconditional positive regard. You're safe here, he wanted her to know; you can face any demon you can name.

"I think about killing myself a lot," she said. "Every day, I guess. Mostly in the afternoons. The late afternoons. That's when everything looks blackest to me. Another day is nearly dead and my life still amounts to nothing. *I'm* nothing. I hear my roommates laughing and talking on the phone and going out and having a good time, and they seem like—I don't know, another *species* or something. I don't think I was ever that happy. Four o'clock, five o'clock, another day down the drain. Another day trying to write an essay that is completely meaningless. Another day worrying about what my teachers think of me, what my friends think of me. That's when I really dwell on it."

"All these thoughts of suicide. Have you ever actually written out a note?"

"I've thought about it a lot, but I've never actually done it."

"If you did, what would it say?" She doesn't want to hurt her mother; it's not her fault. Here she is in absolute agony, and it'll be her mother she's most worried about.

"I guess my note would say . . . I don't know, exactly. I'd want my mother to know I don't blame her. She did her best and all that. Bringing me up, I mean. Mostly on her own."

"Melanie, I know you're finding university a little demanding these days, the written work and so on, but I'm going to give you a little bit of homework. Is that all right?"

Melanie shrugged. Tiny breasts shifted under her sweatshirt.

"What I'd like you to do is actually write that note," Dr. Bell continued. "Put your thoughts in writing. I think it would be very good for you. It might clarify exactly what you're feeling these days. Do you think you could do that?"

"I guess."

"Don't labor over it too much. It doesn't have to be long. Just write out exactly what you would say if you were actually going to kill yourself."

19

It's no secret that a certain type of man, or another type of man in a certain type of mood, will seek out exactly the person, place, or thing that is most likely to bring him the maximum pain. A drunk will head to the bar, a compulsive gambler to a loved one's savings account, a forlorn lover to the scene of parting. John Cardinal was in the basement the next afternoon, standing motionless in the dim light and chemical smells of Catherine's darkroom.

The darkroom had been hers and hers alone, and he had never set foot in it uninvited.

Although Catherine would sometimes chat about a project beforehand, she never talked about her work in the darkroom. She was like a chef who doesn't want anyone else in the kitchen, preferring to bring out the perfect meal as if it were conjured out of thin air. She liked to come upstairs with a fistful of new prints and spread them out on the kitchen table. Then she would stand back while Cardinal examined them one by one.

If Cardinal was too slow to form an opinion, she would speak her own over his shoulder. "I like the fire escape in that one, the diagonal is so dramatic." Or "Look at the cyclist in the background, heading in the opposite direction. I love accidental things like that." Half the time Cardinal sensed that he was admiring the wrong thing: how cute the little kid was, how pretty the snow. But Catherine didn't seem to mind.

There were several prints of the same photograph clipped to a line over her sinks, which Cardinal had installed for her years ago. The prints were black-and-white and showed a brick wall in the foreground, a man approaching in the background, maybe half a block away. Man and wall were equally in focus, and Cardinal knew from his own limited experience that that was hard to do. It gave a slightly dislocated feel to the image, as if man and wall were equally inhuman. The man's head was down, his face hidden by the kind of hat people rarely wear these days. An ominous picture . . . or maybe it just seemed that way in retrospect.

"What are you doing down here?" Kelly was leaning in the doorway, looking effortlessly lovely in white shirt and blue jeans. Catherine twenty years ago.

Cardinal pointed to the shelves that lined one wall, the tall closet for cameras and lenses, the wide shelves for storing prints. The bins for frames.

"I built those for her," he said.

"I know," Kelly said.

"Catherine designed them, of course. I mean, it was her work space."

"She was happy here," Kelly said, and Cardinal felt a crimp in his heart.

"I'm going to ask you to do me a favor, Kelly. Not now, but a few months from now, maybe."

"Sure. What do you need?"

"I don't know anything about photography. And to tell you the truth, I liked every single picture Catherine ever took. She saw it; she thought it was worth photographing; to me it was valuable. But you're an artist."

"Struggling painter, Dad. Not a photographer."

"You have an artist's eye. I was hoping sometime, not now, you could go through Catherine's photos and select the best ones. I was thinking—next year, maybe—we could put on a show of her work at the university or the library."

"Sure, Dad. I'd be happy to do that. But I don't think you should be hanging around down here. Everything's still too raw, don't you think?"

"Yeah. It is."

"Come on," she said, and actually took his hand and led him out of the darkroom. It all but undid him.

Kelly was right, though. He found it easier to breathe upstairs, in the domain that had been half his. He went into the living room and looked over the titles on the bookshelves. Catherine had bought most of them. The majority were photography books, but she had also bought books about yoga, Buddhism, the novels of John Irving, and a lot of psychology—books about depression and bipolar disorder. He took down *Against Self-Slaughter* by Frederick Bell.

There were several other books listed on the flyleaf, all of them with academic-sounding titles, but this one appeared to be aimed at a general audience, its tone calm, reassuring, and surprisingly self-revelatory. The first few pages related how Bell's father had committed suicide when he was eight, and his mother ten years later when he was beginning university. Not surprising that such a background might lead one to labor, as Bell put it in the introduction, "in the fields of grief and despair."

Cardinal flipped through. The book was organized around several case studies, each chapter beginning with a description of a suicide attempt that brought the patient into Bell's practice. There was also a section dealing with partners of suicides, with particular emphasis on people who had married more than one person who had committed suicide. "Some people with deep, repressed suicidal fantasies of their own," Bell wrote, "need to be near people who are able to kill themselves. Unable to hurl themselves over that mortal precipice, they need someone to commit suicide *for* them."

Cardinal decided this probably wasn't the best thing for him to be reading just then.

He went into the kitchen, where Kelly had settled herself over a sketchbook. He picked up the mail from the counter where she had stacked it. Most of it was for Catherine: a photography magazine, notices from the Art Gallery of Ontario and the Royal Ontario Museum of upcoming shows, a bill for her MasterCard, as well as various mass mailings from Northern University. There were a couple of square envelopes addressed to him, more cards.

He was looking for his letter opener when the phone rang.

It was Brian Overholt, a Toronto homicide cop Cardinal had known forever. They had worked vice together, more than twenty years ago, and narcotics after that. Together they had made an effective team, and Overholt was one of the few Toronto colleagues he missed. Cardinal had called him about Connor Plaskett.

"John, I got an answer for you. Plaskett is indeed an ex-person. Got run over by an Escalade in the club district here a couple of weeks ago. Hung in on the critical list for a while, but he died a week ago last Saturday."

"Was he into anything down there I should know about?"

"Not that we know of. His associates scattered into the woodwork when he got run over, so draw your own conclusions. They clearly didn't want to pass the time of day with law enforcement."

"You catch the driver?"

"No, but it's just a matter of time. Anything else I can do for you? Hello? You still there?"

Cardinal had opened one of the envelopes addressed to him and now he was staring at the card it had contained.

"Uh, yeah, Brian. Listen, thanks a lot. Any time I can return the favor . . ."

"Sure. Next time I'm looking for an Eskimo, I'll hold you to it. Hey, how's Catherine?"

"Gotta run, Brian. Something just came up."

This card was postmarked Mattawa, just as the first one had been, again a semi-glossy Hallmark of the sort available at any large drugstore, not to mention every stationery store in the nation. So the sender had bought at least three. Maybe he had bought them all at the same time in the same store. A clerk might notice someone who bought three sympathy cards at once.

Cardinal tried to keep his mind fixed in investigative mode and not react to the words inside the card. It was the same setup as before, original message of the card covered up with a typed message:

> *What a terrific husband you must have been. She preferred death to living with you. Think about it. She literally preferred to die. That should give you some idea of what you're worth.*

Cardinal went to the window and tilted the card this way and that in the light. Yes, he could just make out a thin line across the capital letters. Almost certainly the same printer and, even if not, almost certainly the same sender. Whoever it was, it could not be Connor Plaskett, who had died before Catherine. Connor Plaskett, as Brian Overholt had so eloquently put it, was an ex-person.

She preferred death to living with you.

"Oh, fuck you!" Cardinal slammed his fist on the fridge, sending magnets, notes, and snapshots to the floor.

"Dad, are you all right?"

Kelly had leaped up from her chair and was regarding him with dark alarmed eyes.

"I'm fine."

She put a hand to her heart. "I don't think I've ever heard you swear like that."

"You may have to get used to it," he said, shrugging on his jacket.

"You're going out?"

Cardinal grabbed his car keys.

"Don't hold supper," he said.

20

"Can you give me an address on Neil Codwallader?" Cardinal was heading into town on 63. The heat of his anger surprised him. He could feel it pulsing in his wrists, throbbing in his temples.

"Neil Codwallader is single now, John. He doesn't have anyone to beat up at the moment."

It was Wes Beattie on the other end of the line, a parole officer. Beattie had an imperturbable and comforting purr of a voice; it was hard to believe he had ever been a cop, but he had put in fifteen years with the Ontario Provincial Police before being reborn into the gentler avatar of parole officer. Whenever he spoke to Beattie on the phone, Cardinal pictured a fat tabby.

"I need to see him about something else," Cardinal said, and honked at a Focus that suddenly changed lanes without signaling. "And I need to see him now."

"You sound rather ruffled there, John. If Neil has committed some kind of breach, you'd better tell me about it. Can't go keeping secrets from our brother and sister agencies, now, can we?"

"I'll tell you after I talk to him. Are you going to give me an address?"

"Six-ninety Main Street East. But he won't be there right now. He's working two jobs."

"Let me guess: he's a volunteer counselor at the Crisis Centre."

"No, I can't imagine Neil will be consoling battered

women anytime soon, but he *is* working at Wal-Mart three days a week. And he puts in another four at Zappers."

"The photocopy place?"

"The very one. Listen, John, you're not going to go crashing around and jeopardize his employment, are you? I don't nurse any more affection for wife beaters than you do, but Neil has paid his debt to society and now he's making an honest effort to—"

"Well, what do you know? Here I am at Wal-Mart," Cardinal said, and disconnected. He swung into a parking lot the size of several football fields.

Cardinal rarely set foot in Wal-Mart. It was always so difficult to find anything, and the prices didn't seem to justify the aggravation. Half the time the aisles were jammed with obese couples pushing prams, although today they were relatively empty. In any case, he preferred to support the independent downtown stores—a goal that seemed more quixotic with each passing year.

The only thing Cardinal liked about Wal-Mart was that it employed older people. Although it had its fair share of teenagers expert in feigned helplessness, it also had a good many retirees supplementing their pensions by helping bewildered shoppers find their elusive consumer items. He asked a tiny lady who looked near seventy where he could find greeting cards.

"You're already there," she said. "They're in the next aisle over."

Cardinal zeroed in on the sympathy area. Yes, there were plenty of Hallmark cards.

"Here we go," he said under his breath. "With deepest sympathy."

He picked out a card identical to the third one he had received, and then another, identical to the second card. Apparently the first card had sold out.

"Did you find what you were looking for?" the tiny lady asked him as he walked by.

"I did. Thank you. Can you tell me if Neil Codwallader is working today?"

"Neil? Is he the tall gentleman who works in the photo place?"

"Lots of muscles, lots of tattoos," Cardinal said.

"Oh, yes. He was here earlier, but I believe he's gone home."

She directed him to the photo booth, several aisles west and one south. You really needed a moped to get around this place.

"Neil left an hour ago," the kid in the photo department told him. "He's got another job somewheres."

Ten minutes later Cardinal was on the other side of town, parked illegally on Lakeshore in front of Zappers.

Zappers was the kind of place you go to if you're from out of town and need to check your e-mail right this instant or send or receive a fax, or if you run a fraudulent business that requires an anonymous mailbox. Mostly it offered the use of obsolete computer equipment at minimal rates. There was only one customer in the place, an Asian woman typing at lightning speed.

Codwallader was behind the counter, his back to the store, photocopying an enormous stack of paper. When he turned around, he did not appear to recognize Cardinal.

His long hair and walrus mustache would have been in fashion thirty years ago, assuming he had been a rock star. Prison had not reduced the muscles that threatened to burst the seams of his T-shirt. His forearms were paisley with tattoos.

"Help you?" he said.

"You tell me," Cardinal said.

Codwallader went still, not looking Cardinal up and down the way a normal person might, but giving him the dead cold prison stare.

"I know you," he said. "You're the cop."

"And you're the wife beater."

"So you said. That doesn't make it true."

"Well, the hospital records, the doctors, and the social workers all seemed to agree. Not to mention Cora herself."

"I got nothing to say to you, pal. I don't even remember your name."

"Cardinal. John Cardinal. I'm the one who told the judge how I found your wife with her nose broken and her arm fractured and patches of her hair torn out. How both her eyes were blackened, and how her clothes had been all cut up."

"Like I told the court, I didn't do any of that shit."

"Spoken like a true abuser. Never guilty, never wrong."

"The reason I got no wife now is thanks to people like you. People who like to interfere. Right now I'm just doing what I have to do to get by, one day at a time. So if you're not gonna use a computer or something, why don't you get the hell out?"

"Actually, it was your printers I was interested in."

"Printers are over there." A paisley finger indicated a row of three machines. "Two bucks first page, after that ten cents a page. Knock yourself out."

Cardinal opened his briefcase. He took out a computer disk, slid it into one of the computers, and selected a letter he had written to his insurance broker. That policy would have to be changed now, since Catherine had been his beneficiary.

Cardinal selected printer number one, then two, then three, and printed out three copies of the letter. There were various flaws in the characters, but no hairline scar across the capitals. Of course, in a shop like this, the cartridges would be changed often. If all the messages had been printed out at the same time—say, a day or two after Catherine died—that cartridge would no longer be in these machines. For that matter, if Codwallader had done it, he could have used his own cartridge.

Cardinal put the copies into his briefcase and took his disk out of the computer.

"How much do I owe you?"

"Two seventy-five plus tax. Three sixteen."

Cardinal paid him.

"Tell me something, Cardinal. You married?"

Cardinal held up his left hand, showing the plain gold band. Catherine's name was engraved on the inside. He had always planned to be buried with it on his finger.

"You're so righteous and all," Codwallader said. "Tell me the truth. You never feel like giving your wife a tap on the head? A little smack? I'm not saying you acted on it, I'm just asking. Be honest. You don't never sometimes feel like giving her a smack?"

"No. And now I need you to answer me one question. Where were you on the night of October fourth? Tuesday before last."

"Tuesday? I woulda been right here. We're open till ten P.M. week nights. Listen, if something happened to Cora, I got no idea where she even lives or if she changed her name or nothing. So if she got beat up Tuesday night or whatever, it's got nothing to do with me."

"So you say."

"You can check the security cameras." He pointed at the tiny camera above the entrance. "They go back at least a month. Ask the manager."

"I will. Where is he?"

"Away. He'll be back next week. Fucking Cora. I thought I was through with that bitch."

21

Delorme had waited until six o'clock, when she was pretty sure Matt Morton would be home, before driving around to Warren Street, a dead end on the east side of town. She doubted if she had set foot there more than twice in her entire life.

The Morton residence was a low wooden bungalow that looked to be a tight squeeze for a couple, let alone a couple with two children, and it was dwarfed by the vehicles in the driveway. There was a Toyota Land Cruiser and a Chrysler Pacifica, and—the only car of normal size—a Ford Taurus. Beside the garage, two bright red snowmobiles were parked under an overhang.

The crowning piece was the boat, a gigantic Chris-Craft—not that Delorme would have known a Chris-Craft from a submarine, but the manufacturer's name was in big chrome script on the side. To her untutored eye the thing was quite ungainly, too much snout and not enough top, but probably it was built for speed, not a handsome profile—and who knew how it might look in the water? Delorme had no idea what kind of horsepower it might have, but the propeller looked serious.

Why would you have all these oversize vehicles and then live in a dinky little house? Delorme had often wondered about people—you came across a lot of them in police work—who seemed to spend all their money on pursuits other than their home. She had been in near-hovels that contained televisions the size of blackboards.

Not that the Morton home fell into this category; it looked to be in excellent repair.

The same could not be said of Matt Morton. If he had indeed ever been a football player, as Frank Rowley had said, there was little evidence of it now. Any muscle had long since subsided into several cubic feet of pudge and blubber. His shape was top-heavy, as if he had been squeezed tightly at the ankles and all the fat had moved up into his neck and shoulders. His hair was the same brown as the perpetrator's in the pictures, though trimmed into a neat executive cut.

Delorme introduced herself, showing her ID.

"Come on in," Morton said. "I only have a minute. We're about to sit down for dinner."

"That's okay. I won't take up much of your time." The living room, off to the left, contained nothing that she'd seen in the photographs. At the far end of the hall was the kitchen, too far to see much detail beyond a few wooden cupboards. Delorme heard kids yelling and a woman shushing them. It sounded like a boy and a girl.

"I was admiring your machines out front," Delorme said. "Particularly the boat."

"My pride and joy, that one. Better be, for what I paid. Still paying."

"Mr. Morton, I'm investigating a number of crimes that have been committed out at Lakeside Marina, and I need to take a look at your boat. Would that be all right?"

"What kind of crimes?"

"Assault, among others."

"Assault. Got nothing to do with me, I can tell you that right now."

"We're just looking for witnesses at this point."

"Well, I never saw anything that resembled an assault. Never heard anything either, for that matter. So how would it involve my boat?"

"It may not. If I could just take a quick look, Mr. Morton, that would be very helpful."

"Go ahead. I don't care."

"Thank you."

Morton put on a Maple Leafs windbreaker and led her out to the boat, walking with the careful, gliding gait of the very heavy. A man could put on a lot of pounds in a few years, however, and Delorme had not yet ruled Matt Morton out as a suspect.

"You actually need to see inside?"

"Yes, I do."

"There was no assault on this boat. I don't see what good it'll do to look inside."

"It'll help us rule a few things out, Mr. Morton. Can I just climb up onto the trailer?"

"I'd rather you used a ladder."

Delorme helped him retrieve an eight-foot aluminum ladder from the garage. The two minutes of exertion had the ex-footballer sweating and wheezing. Nevertheless, he went up first and climbed over the side of the boat. Delorme followed and stepped down onto the deck.

"Doesn't look its best right now," Morton said. "It's like looking at a racehorse in the barn. You don't really get an idea."

"Oh, I think I get the idea," Delorme said, looking around. "It must be a lot of fun to be out on the water in this."

"There's nothing like it, I guarantee you. The air, the sunshine. Not to mention the beer. And everyone's in a good mood. The kids're having fun, the wife's in seventh heaven, and I'm as far away from work as I can be."

"What line of work are you in, Mr. Morton?"

"IT. Computer networks. Used to be a good way to make a living. Not anymore. Not in this town. We were all set to buy a bigger house, but that's not gonna happen now."

"You mind if we lift the plastic sheeting off the seats there?" Delorme was already pretty sure this wasn't the boat in the photograph. The steering wheel was white, and the one in the picture was wooden. Steering wheels can be replaced, of course, but there was no wood trim visible on this boat, and she doubted that anyone would have had that changed.

Morton lifted the plastic off the two seats closest to the stern. They were the swivel kind, smooth white upholstery, with small fixed tables nearby. The photograph had shown back-to-back seats with red upholstery of the tuck-and-roll variety. The entire back of the boat was different.

"You need to see the galley too? The cabin?"

"No thanks, Mr. Morton. You've been very helpful."

"It's no trouble. Now that we're here, I mean."

"All right, then. A quick look won't hurt."

She let him show her around, Morton proudly pointing out various features for her to appreciate. A couple of times he said, "The wife would kill me if she knew how much I paid for that."

"I guess it's kind of like having a second home," Delorme said. "At least in summer."

"That's exactly what it's like." Morton emphasized the point with a finger the size of a sausage. "You said a true thing there."

Delorme had never been particularly attracted to boats, but the interior had a neatness about it that appealed to her. Lots of tiny cupboards and containers, everything miniaturized and the edges rounded off.

"Your kids must love it," she said.

"Oh, my son would stay on the boat full-time if he could. Brittney couldn't care less, though. She's thirteen."

Delorme very much wanted to see the girl but couldn't think of a way right at that moment to manage it.

"Mr. Morton, how do you get along with the other people out at the marina? Do you see much of them?"

"Not really. It's mostly families, you know. Everybody's so busy with their own kids, they don't have much time to get to know each other. We talk about the weather, that kind of thing."

"It's pretty close quarters out there. And this is an expensive piece of equipment. You ever have any complaints?"

"What, about the marina?"

"Or about the people who park next to you."

Morton thought a moment. He ran a hand over his head.

"Well, there's some Italian asshole always plays his music too loud. He's at the other end of the dock, but noise travels when you're on the water. I'd be happy if you'd arrest him or deport him or something."

"Not likely. What about the people near you?"

"The Ferriers? They're good people. We're not close, but we get along fine. André and I have the occasional beer, talk about the game. That's about it."

"They have kids?"

"Two girls: Alex and Sadie. Sadie's eight or so. Alex is Brit's age, thirteen going on thirty, way they are these days."

Thirteen years old. Delorme wanted to ask more about the girls but didn't want to draw too much attention to that angle just yet. What if Morton was the one diddling the neighbors' kids? To draw him away from that area, she mentioned Frank Rowley.

"Frank I know from high school. I got no complaints about Frank." Morton suddenly snapped his fingers. "I just remembered something. You're investigating assaults?"

"That's right."

"Guy named Fred Bell. I saved his ass one time some crazy bastard threw a punch at him."

"Frederick Bell?" Delorme had never met Dr. Bell in person, but she knew he was a psychiatrist.

"That's it. English fella. But it wasn't at the marina, exactly. It was outside the seafood joint next door."

"What was the fight about?"

"I don't know. Guy was yelling about the treatment Bell gave his son. Kid killed himself, I guess. Anyway, he was clearly out of it and swinging like a madman, so I just kinda stepped between 'em and suggested he move on. Wasn't much of an assault, when you get down to it. This was about a year, year and a half ago."

"Do you know his name?"

"I forget. Whiteside or something like that."

"Last question, Mr. Morton. You ever see or hear anything else around the marina that upset you, maybe made you think it wasn't a good place for your kids to be?"

"How do you mean? Like safety-wise?"

"Like any-wise."

Morton shook his head. "The marina's like a neighborhood. People generally look out for each other. Help out with a cup of sugar, that kind of thing, you know? Even though we don't know each other well, there's a camaraderie, a kind of trust, that you don't find in a lot of places. Perfect little sanctuary—for anybody, especially kids."

22

Cardinal was dealing with bills at the dining room table. Kelly was watching an *ER* rerun in the living room. She watched television just like Catherine, with a bowl of popcorn in her lap, making comments at the TV every now and again. "Oh, come on," she would say. "No doctor in their right mind would do that."

Cardinal had written checks for Catherine's credit cards and had scrawled on each payment stub *Deceased, please cancel.*

His thoughts drifted to the two people he had tracked down so far: one of them dead before Catherine was killed, the other still a possibility. He had yet to confirm Codwallader's alibi, but his gut was telling him that it would probably hold. Cardinal sensed he was missing something obvious. He was on an entirely wrong track. So far he had been focused on motivation and opportunity: Who had reason to hurt him through his wife? Who had recently been released from prison?

But there were more basic things to consider. Who knew his address? Who knew Catherine was his wife? Who was in a position to pounce on this information with such alacrity? Not a drunk like Connor Plaskett (even if he had been alive), and maybe not a self-absorbed loser like Codwallader either.

Cardinal's address and phone number were not listed in the phone book, and the police station certainly didn't give them out. Ever since his days on the drug squad back in Toronto, he had made it a rule to keep an eye out for people behind him, people watching. If you weren't vigilant, someone could follow you home and threaten your family. He would have known if anyone was trailing him.

He sifted through the rest of the bills. There were requests from the Audubon Society, the Sierra Club, and Amnesty International (Catherine's) and others from the Hospital for Sick Children, UNICEF, and March of Dimes (Cardinal's). There were bills from the electric company, the water department, the phone company, and Desmond's Funeral Home.

Most of these were already opened if not already paid. Cardinal examined them one by one, holding them under the gooseneck lamp beside the phone. He put on a pair of reading glasses to make sure. None of them showed the same printer flaw as the vicious sympathy cards.

All right, maybe that was too simple. Almost all of these, with the exception of the smaller charities, would be addressed by computer. No human being would even see the bills until they came back with checks attached. He opened the bill from the funeral home.

Dear Mr. Cardinal,

We at Desmond's Funeral Home wish you to know that we sympathize with you in your time of loss.

We also want to thank you for choosing us. We hope that our services have brought you some measure of comfort and security during one of life's most difficult transitions.

Our invoice is enclosed. Please remit your payment as soon as it may be convenient. And please know that if there is anything else we can do to serve your needs at this difficult time, we are always ready to help.

With thanks, and deepest sympathy.

It was signed by David Desmond. None of the capital letters showed any trace of the printer flaw.

"She is such a crackhead," Kelly said to the TV. "How could she ever get to be a nurse?"

At the commercial break she stopped by Cardinal on her way to the kitchen. "Why don't you come and watch, Dad?"

"I will in a second."

"It's such a pleasure to see people screw up their lives worse than you screw up your own. Although I guess you see that pretty much every day at work."

"I do indeed."

"I'm getting myself a Diet Coke. You want one?"

"Sure."

Cardinal was looking at the invoice that had come enclosed with the letter from Desmond's. One item in particular had caught his attention, and it wasn't the price, which came as no surprise.

Casket—Superior Walnut, Natural—$2,500.

There was a distinct line through the capital letters.

And lower down: *Payment Received—$3,400.*

The same line through the *P* and the *R.*

"The show's back on," Kelly called from the living room. "Your Coke's in here."

Cardinal pulled the three cards from his briefcase. *She preferred death.* . . . A line through the capital *S. How she must have hated you.* Same line through the capital *H.* He dug out a magnifying glass and squinted at the relevant letters. A match.

Could a funeral director get tired of sympathizing with all the pain he or she saw every day of the year? Could you get sick of all the tears, the prayers, the dithering over details of services, the relentless implication that *this* loved one was really something special, unlike, say, the other people you buried day in and day out? He supposed that, yes, you could get sick of it, and, yes, you might one day snap and start sending un-sympathy cards through the mail.

But the cover letter itself was free of flaws.

He called David Desmond at home.

A professional to the bone, Desmond didn't miss a beat. "Yes, John," he said. "What can I do for you?"

"I was just looking at my invoice from you."

"Oh, there's no rush to pay that. You've already paid half of it on deposit, and I'm sure you have lots of other things on your mind."

"I was wondering if you prepare them yourself."

"Well, we write up the initial figures, of course. But later on, after the services, we hand everything over to our book-keeping service."

"They seem to do a good job for you. I've got some rather complicated tax stuff coming up this year and I was wondering if I could get their name and address from you."

"Oh, certainly. It's Beckwith and Beaulne. Hold on a second, I've got the card here somewhere."

"Which guy do you use, Beckwith or Beaulne?"

"Neither. It's a fellow named Roger Felt."

"You're kidding."

"Why? You know Roger?"

23

Roger Felt. Cardinal had not thought about Roger Felt for at least five or six years. Roger Felt had been a stockbroker/financial adviser/investment analyst for the Algonquin Bay office of Fraser, Grant. He had enjoyed a reputation for being a local Midas with growth stocks.

Like just about every other financial adviser in town, Felt's bread and butter lay in mutual funds. He took people's nest eggs and savings accounts and rainy day funds and put them into more or less conservative allocations of five-star funds. But he had not been satisfied with that sort of program for his own retirement planning. Too many years of reading the financial press had filled his head with profiles of financial wizards who made killings and retired with sailboats and ski mansions and houses in the south of France. You weren't supposed to end up with a ranch-style split level in Algonquin Bay and a cottage on Mud Lake.

And so Roger Felt had embarked on an ambitious scheme to make the big leagues. He moved his own portfolio into the riskier stocks, the testosterone market, and he started betting on margin. And when the first margin calls had come in, he rapidly paid them off with his own cash.

Of course, this cash was also supposed to pay for his wife's retirement, not just his own. It was meant to cover assisted living for his mother-in-law and the educations of their three kids, who were all heading off, seriatim, to university. No problem. When the market turned around, as his economic savvy told him it must, he would be so rich he could pay for all of those things with pocket money.

Many losses and many margin calls later, Roger Felt found himself in the uncomfortable position of having drained not just his own accounts but those of his wealthiest clients. In Algonquin Bay, these "wealthiest" were not millionaires but retirees with plump pensions and paid-off houses who had a little extra cash. Roger Felt "borrowed" liberally from their accounts to pay off his margin calls and to place bigger investments with the intention, he later told the court, of paying everybody back—with interest, of course.

Dreams of luxury on the Côte d'Azur began to fade, dwindling into dreams of paying back the funds he had pilfered, dreams of restoring his own family to financial health, dreams of staying out of jail.

It was not to be.

One of his clients, a Mrs. Gertrude M. Lowry, wished to consolidate all her funds with another firm. When she tired of Felt's evasions, she called the police. Cardinal got the case and, since he was no financial wizard, Delorme was put on it too. She had been just a few months short of an MBA when she joined the police and had spent half a dozen years chasing white-collar criminals.

They arrested Felt on charges of fraud, misappropriation of funds, and breach of fiduciary duty. He was found guilty on all three. His lawyer, Leonard Scofield, made an eloquent request for a minimum sentence that the judge received coolly. He could do little else after hearing from the parade of witnesses: men long past their prime who had been forced to go back to work, young people whose dreams of owning a house had come to nothing, angry couples who had lost their homes, and tremulous old women now working at menial jobs to keep their heads above water. Roger Felt was banished to a medium-security prison for eight years, from which he had been paroled after serving five.

Cardinal rolled up in front of the address Desmond had given him. It turned out to be an apartment above a fabric store on Sumner. To get to the downstairs door, Cardinal had to squeeze his way through a passageway so narrow that he was forced to turn sideways.

The door had been decorated by consecutive generations of graffiti artists, the least imaginative of whom had written *I Love You* in raspberry-colored letters a foot tall. Cardinal buzzed the intercom and waited, looking around the alley with its crushed soda cans and flyaway sandwich wrappers, even a laceless, soggy tennis shoe. All in all, a long way down from the lakeside property Roger Felt had owned when Cardinal and Delorme had arrested him. He had been swinging in a hammock with a rum and Coke in his hand at the time.

A voice caused the intercom's torn speaker to flap and buzz. "Who is it?"

"Courier."

"Hold on, I'll be right down."

Heavy footsteps on the stairs within and then the door opened.

Prison had done nothing good for Roger Felt's appearance. He had always been a squarish man, not graceful, but expensive suits and a regular squash game had combined to make him look like a person you might call sir. Now he was squat and trollish. His shirt looked as if it had not been ironed for decades, and there were rings of sweat under his arms. He reeked of cigarettes and was wheezing from the stairs.

"Are you from Alma's?" he said, naming a Main Street restaurant. "I'm not really expecting anything."

Cardinal held up his shield. "Surprise."

Felt peered up at him through thick lenses. "Oh, no."

Cardinal pushed the door open. "Mr. Felt, we have reason to believe you are in breach of your parole. I need to come in and take a look around."

"Let's see a warrant first."

"You're a convicted felon on parole, Mr. Felt, and I have reasonable grounds to suspect you are in breach. No warrant required."

Cardinal pushed his way past him and went up the dark stairwell. The door at the top opened onto a cramped, lopsided kitchen lit with one of those fluorescent rings beloved of penny-pinching landlords. A cigarette sent up coils of smoke from an ashtray. Beside it there was an adding machine, a stack of files, a battered-looking laptop, and a small printer.

Cardinal pulled a sheet of paper from its OUT tray.

It was an invoice from Beckwith and Beaulne addressed to Nautilus Marine Storage and Repair. The capital N's and R's had lines running through them. Cardinal usually stayed pretty cool when it came to arresting criminals. But now, as Roger Felt came huffing into the kitchen, he felt a surge of rage. Immediately, some other part of his character locked this rage away. He pointed to the adding machine, the files, the columns of figures on the laptop screen.

"The terms of your parole are that you not be employed in the financial sector. Clearly, you are performing accountancy services. May I speak to Mr. Beckwith?"

"He isn't here."

"And Mr. Beaulne?"

"He's not available either."

"Beaulne and Beckwith are fictitious entities, aren't they?"

"It's just a name. It sounded good."

"You're running a fictitious company, Mr. Felt. For purposes once again of duping the public."

"I need clients. The name sounded good. You can't expect me to live on the income from a job in a sandwich shop."

"With your record of fraud and breach of fiduciary duty, I think a judge is going to be very interested in the fictitious Mr. Beaulne and Mr. Beckwith."

"Please don't do that. I can't go back to jail."

"Get your shoes on, Mr. Felt. That's exactly where we're going."

24

Roger Felt was booked and placed in a holding cell, after being allowed to call his lawyer. Cardinal alerted the Crown Attorney and the parole office. He wrote up his notes, finished the rest of the paperwork, and carried the boxes of material he had removed from Felt's apartment into the boardroom.

The boardroom was the quietest and most respectable-looking place in the station. The long oak table and handsome chairs gave it the feel of the headquarters of a small but prosperous corporation. Cardinal opened the first box and lifted out the adding machine, the laptop, the printer. He opened the second box and removed stacks of files and stationery.

Staff Sergeant Mary Flower came in. Mary was the kind of woman for whom the harsh word *broad* must have been originally coined. No more than five foot three but big of chest and voice, she was protective of her uniformed brood, but if she suspected a street cop of slacking, she could deliver a reprimand so fierce that the place reeked of brimstone for weeks. Over the years she had nursed a crush on John Cardinal, a fact he had occasionally used to shameless advantage in prying favors out of the uniformed division.

"Listen, John." They had been colleagues long enough to be on a first-name basis when out of earshot of her troops. "You're gonna tell me it's none of my business, but—"

"It's none of your business, Mary."

"But it is, sorta. Because it goes to proper conduct of business in the shop, and that goes very much to my bailiwick of training the juniors. But that's not why I'm bringing it up. I'm bringing it up because you're a friend and I respect you enough to tell you when I think you're making a mistake."

"I make lots of mistakes. Which one did you have in mind?"

"First of all, honey, you shouldn't be back here yet. You're still hurting, and you're gonna be hurting for a long time. The cop shop is no place for a broken heart."

"She didn't dump me. She, uh . . ." *Died*. He would never be able to say that word. Not in connection to Catherine.

"I know that, John. So allow yourself to admit that you're human. Allow yourself to admit that your judgment might be off and you might be prone to mistakes just now. I'm not a detective, I'm not gonna second-guess your investigative work."

"He's been breaching parole. Conditions either mean something or they don't. You can't have it both ways."

"See, right there, that doesn't sound like you. You're not usually an all-or-nothing black-or-white kind of guy. I'm just asking you to take some time off. You're not running on all cylinders here."

"You done?"

"Momma Mary is done, honey."

"Good. Because I have some actual work to do."

IT TURNED OUT that Wes Beattie was Roger Felt's parole officer. Although they talked on the phone quite often, Cardinal had not actually seen Beattie face-to-face for more than a year. He had grown a big bushy beard since then and was uncharacteristically formal in dark suit and tie.

"Gee, Wes," Cardinal said, "did you arrive here in a limo?"

"You've interrupted my night at the opera," Beattie purred, "thus ruining my yearly attempt at culture."

"Algonquin Bay doesn't have an opera."

"This evening it does. The Manhattan Light Opera Company is at the Capital Centre for exactly one night, and you yanked me out of it."

"Felt's lawyer's on the way, and we're also waiting for the Crown."

"No point holding your breath," Beattie said. "I've spoken to the Crown, and he doesn't want to pursue this unless I do, and I have to tell you, John, I really, really don't."

"Roger Felt is in breach of parole, Wes. He's running a financial operation under false pretenses. He's been sending me threatening and harassing letters—which you might want to see before you make up your mind, let alone the Crown Attorney's mind."

Beattie was one of those large men who seem to give off a kind of calm that is hard to resist. He stood before Cardinal, rocking gently back and forth on his heels as he listened. The whole time, he was nodding sympathetically. A parole officer—besieged by judges, criminals, victims, and lawyers, not to mention highly aggrieved cops—learns to be a good listener or he goes insane.

"Can we sit down somewhere and talk?" he said quietly. His understanding tone suddenly made Cardinal feel like a ranter.

"Yeah, sure."

Cardinal took him back to the boardroom, where Felt's accounting equipment was spread out.

Cardinal held up a sheet of letterhead. "You realize Beckwith and Beaulne is a fictitious organization?"

"Strictly speaking, John, it isn't. It's a bookkeeping operation run by Roger Felt, essentially a home business. Beckwith and Beaulne is just a name; it doesn't matter that they're not real entities. Merrill and Lynch have been dead a long time too."

"Merrill and Lynch were real people who founded a company."

"John, you're not going to make the fraudulent part stick. Roger does in fact provide the bookkeeping service that he promises. Nothing more, nothing less."

"He's doing people's taxes for them. That involves tax advice, which is financial advice, which his conditions of release strictly prohibit."

"I disagree and so will the court. He's not doing accounting, he's doing bookkeeping. That's simple record keeping and arithmetic. He has no access to accounts, no fiduciary duties. It's a worthwhile service and an effective use of his skills."

"The court may see it differently."

"John, I ran it by a judge before I gave Roger the go-ahead. He didn't have a problem with it. And the Crown doesn't either, which is why he isn't here."

"You were out of bounds heading him off, Wes."

"I'm trying to do you a favor. Believe me, you don't want this to get to court. Roger is a changed man. His crime cost him everything he had, and I mean everything. Not just his money. You saw where he's living. His wife left him shortly after he went to jail. Two of his kids want nothing to do with him. He lost his friends, you name it."

"And you think he's a changed man."

"I know it, the parole board knew it. He rediscovered his faith in prison—he's a Catholic—and while I usually don't pay the slightest attention to claims of that sort, in Roger's case it seems to be true. He's very involved in the Church now."

Cardinal pulled out several blank sympathy cards from the box.

"I found these next to his laptop." He opened his briefcase and pulled out the cards he had received in the mail. "And he sent me these. Go on. Take a look at them, Wes. Take a look at them, and then tell me what a changed man he is."

Beattie went over the cards carefully. They were open, sheathed in plastic. He held each one for a few seconds, turned it over, and let it drop to the table.

"You think he sent you these cards?"

"He used a computer so I wouldn't see his handwriting, but there's a printer flaw in the capital letters. You can see it with this."

He handed Beattie a magnifying glass. Beattie looked at one of the cards, then looked at the invoice Cardinal had received from the funeral home. He compared it with the other two cards. Beattie tapped a finger on the cards.

"John, I'm sorry you received these. It must have been very upsetting."

"Upsetting is not the word. My wife is—you know what happened to my wife. The coroner may think she killed herself, but I don't. Suppose you killed someone and made it look like suicide. That might give you the idea to write a note like this, don't you think?"

I'm losing it, Cardinal thought. I know I'm losing it. It was a mistake to mention his suspicions about murder, but he couldn't stop himself.

"Six years ago I arrest Felt for stealing people's savings. Like you say, it destroys his reputation, costs him his friends, his kids, his wife. Life as he knew it is over, and he has five years in jail to work up a hatred for me for nailing him. He figures if I hadn't stopped him, he would've been able to make that killer investment that would have made him rich and covered all he stole—*borrowed*, as he liked to put it."

"How does he get even? By killing me? No, it's too simple, too direct, and it doesn't really make it as revenge, either, because I wouldn't suffer the way he's suffered, knowing his wife left him. So he kills *my* wife to get even, then writes those cards to rub my face in it. He's scum, Wes. He always has been."

Even to Cardinal's own ears, it sounded like the shriek of a wounded animal. And now he had to suffer the awful look of compassion on Wes Beattie's bearded face. Beattie actually put a hand out and gripped Cardinal's shoulder.

"John, what are you even doing here? You should not be back at work yet."

"Why are you trying to make a case for the guy, Wes? He's already got Scofield working for him. You think it's impossible he wrote these notes?"

"No, I can see the flaws match on the cards and the invoice. I know Felt handles the billing for Desmond's Funeral Home. I can put two and two together. I can even see him writing the notes, sick as they are. The man has devious tendencies, no question. But he's the least violent guy you're ever likely to meet, so any suspicion that he hurt anyone is way out in left field. John, you don't even have a finding of murder. Take some time off. See a grief counselor."

"Even putting it in its best light, we have a parolee who's sending threatening, harassing letters through the mail. That's enough to put him back inside."

"The notes are nasty. The notes are unpleasant. The notes are mean. But do they constitute harassment? I don't know. It's debatable. But *threatening* is a stretch. You'll never get a judge to buy *threatening*. Answer me this, John. If you accepted that the finding of suicide was correct, if you had no suspicion of murder, would you even bother to chase down these cards?"

The door banged open and Leonard Scofield was standing before them, a calfskin briefcase in one hand and a letter-size document in the other. Scofield's suits always looked as if he had just come back from an appointment in Savile Row, and his shoes as if they had never been worn before. Here it was ten-thirty at night and he had shown up in a dark pinstripe suit, a snow-white shirt, and a deep burgundy tie.

Scofield also had a sonorous voice—a newscaster's tonal authority that made even his weakest arguments sound reasonable. Cardinal had managed to put two or three of Scofield's clients in jail, but never for as long as they deserved.

As if all this were not irritating enough, Scofield was also a decent human being. Cardinal, like most cops, had an innate suspicion of lawyers, even though he was smart enough to know it was unfounded. But Scofield was a guy you had to respect, even when he was tearing your case to shreds in court. He was always amenable to pre-trial discussion, always receptive to rational argument, and, even while defending his client ferociously, managed to convey a sense of absolute decency. Cardinal had often wished he would run for office.

In short, Cardinal was always dismayed to see Scofield on the other side of a case.

"Gentlemen," Scofield said, "I can't tell you how irritating it is to be summoned at this unconscionable hour."

"If you're representing Felt," Cardinal said, "you're going to wish you weren't summoned at any hour."

Scofield had dark eyebrows, very expressive and very useful in court for conveying silent but eloquent skepticism and a wide array of other, more subtle emotions, such as, in this instance, friendly concern.

"Detective Cardinal," he said, "let me say how sorry I was to hear about your wife."

"Thank you." Either Scofield was a man who was bullshit-free or he was able to fake sincerity with Hollywood's finest.

"And let me give you this." Scofield handed over several documents and then proffered copies to Wes Beattie. "This is why I was late. I stopped off at the cathedral and talked to Father Mkembe. I know he's a priest and you probably wouldn't require a sworn affidavit, but here it is anyway. Father Mkembe swears that Roger Felt was at the cathedral's fund-raiser the night of Tuesday the fourth, from eight P.M. until eleven P.M. The other affidavits are from a deacon and from Sister Catherine Wellesley, also swearing that Roger Felt was in their presence at that time. "It seems he was keeping track of the takings from their annual flea market and auction—a service, I note for the record, for which he did not charge."

Cardinal was not a self-righteous man. Having been born and raised a Catholic, he had entered adult life fully equipped with an oversize sense of guilt. He knew he was capable of doing things of which he was ashamed, even of breaking the law, so he was not a policeman who arrived at a crime scene on a high horse, ready to smite the evildoers who walk among us. Furthermore, the older he got—and the more distance he put between himself and his religion of birth—the less he trusted people who were given to righteousness: the righteous gang members who beat rivals to a pulp for trespassing on their turf, the righteous husbands who kicked and stabbed and sometimes murdered the wives who had "disrespected" them, the righteous cops who got in an extra knee or elbow when arresting those they saw as slipping through the cogs of the justice system. Cardinal spent his life in the cause of justice and had come to realize that much injustice was accompanied by just such righteousness.

And so he was appalled to find himself unmasked before his own eyes as a self-righteous cop, intent on railroading the innocent. Shame was burning its way up his neck, and a hot sweat prickled on his brow.

Wes Beattie was slow to catch on. "I don't understand. What the hell has Tuesday the fourth got to do with Roger sending cards through the mail?"

"That's the night Detective Cardinal's wife died," Scofield said. "Again, Detective, my condolences. I only raise the matter because circumstances force me to."

Beattie had been slouched in his chair, but now he shifted his weight forward and perched his enormous chest over the table. "You mean to tell me you stopped off on the way here and got three affidavits in defense of a client who has yet to be charged? Nobody even mentioned the possibility of murder—at least, not to you. And not yet."

"Exactly, Mr. Beattie. It occurred to me the moment I got your call that there could be only one reason for this unfortunate state of affairs. I've known Detective Cardinal too long—and, indeed, tilted ineffectively at his testimony far too many times—not to have enormous respect for him.

"For Detective Cardinal to go to such lengths to haul my imperfectly rehabilitated client off to jail, there must be something more at work than an unfortunate use of the mails. I have been in criminal court on a multitude of cases in the past week, and the rumors I have heard have been suggestive."

"Rumors?" Cardinal said. "Rumors that I'm off my rocker? That I'm crazy with grief and can't accept reality?"

"Nothing nearly so harsh, Detective. Rumors that the coroner was young and inexperienced, that an older man—or woman, for that matter—might well have ordered an inquest."

Cardinal was a little—not much—heartened to hear of the possibility of support, the possibility that he was not alone.

"And rumors," Scofield went on, "that Detective Cardinal

here was on a one-man crusade to find the person or persons unknown who might be behind said possible foul play. Under the circumstances, I can absolutely understand it. And that is why it seemed likely that my client was the victim of a misjudgment on the detective's part—understandable, given the circumstances, but misjudgment nevertheless. I'm hoping these affidavits will change your mind on the matter."

"You haven't seen what he sent me," Cardinal said, and pushed the cards across the table.

Scofield perused them without touching them, as if they might be infected.

"That is easily the ugliest writing I have ever seen committed to paper," the lawyer said.

Beattie spoke up. "Printer flaws on the cards match an invoice John received from the funeral home. Roger does their bookkeeping."

"Marvelous," Scofield said. "You have the ugly and the stupid combined, as they so often are. So stupid, in this case, that it seems the author of the notes wanted to get caught. Still, in light of these affidavits—"

Cardinal stood up. "Let me have a talk with him."

"I can't have you asking him questions at this point. Not without me present."

"I don't have any questions. You can sit outside and watch."

Cardinal took them both to a small kitchen. There were Coke and candy machines, and a TV monitor that showed an image of the interview room.

Then he had Felt brought in from the cells and sat him down at the interview table.

"My lawyer's here," Felt said nervously. "You can't ask me questions without my lawyer present."

Cardinal laid out the cards in their plastic wrappers one by one, in order, open to their hostile messages. And then he laid out the funeral home invoice.

"I got your cards," he said quietly.

"Oh, God," Felt said.

He looked at the cards, he looked at the invoice.

"Oh, God," he said again. And then he surprised Cardinal by bursting into tears. At first he tried to hide his face, leaning forward and covering his eyes with both hands. But as he wept longer, he sat back and let the tears flow in sheets down his face, making no attempt to wipe them away. He was trying to speak, but his voice emerged in incomprehensible fragments.

Cardinal waited.

Felt eventually found the box of Kleenex on the table, wiped his face, and blew his nose. He leaned forward, resting his forehead against his hand, and shook his head silently. His breath still came in shudders. He started to speak and then the tears took him over again, and once more Cardinal waited.

Eventually he subsided. Cardinal handed him a drink of water in a paper cup.

"I'm so sorry," Felt said. "I don't have words to say how sorry I am."

"Funny how the prospect of prison brings out the apologies."

"It's true, the thought of going back to prison terrifies me. But that's not why I'm sorry. It's just . . . seeing the words, there. Seeing them as you must have seen them. Seeing them next to the invoice for your wife's funeral service—"

Tears invaded his voice and he was forced to break off. Once more the Kleenex. Again the drink of water.

"I'm just so horrified by what I've done." He looked at Cardinal, his eyes pleading. "Have you ever done something—something that totally shames you? Something you would not want anyone to know about?" He pointed at the cards. "This is . . . this is . . . it's disgusting. How could anyone do such a thing to another human being? I did it, and yet I can't answer that question: how can anyone do such a thing to another human being?"

He sobbed a little and shook his head again. His shirt-front was soaked, as if he had just stepped in from a thunderstorm.

"My wife left me after I'd been in jail for a year," Felt

said. "She took my daughters with her. They were all disgusted with me. I thought I had finally come to accept my own guilt. I thought I had stopped blaming everybody else for everything I lost. But then, last week, I was doing the books for Desmond's and I came across your file. For your wife. And I don't know what came over me."

"It's called revenge," Cardinal said.

"I guess it is."

Felt's red eyes looked at him, no longer pleading. No longer begging for understanding. Just exhausted.

Cardinal was exhausted himself. He wanted nothing more than to be at home, asleep, as far from the police station as possible. He got to his feet and held the door open.

"Back to the cell, I suppose," Felt said.

Cardinal shook his head. "You're free to go."

"Really?" Felt looked around the room as if there might be others watching to see if he would fall for the prank. "You mean, I can go home?"

Cardinal remembered the horrible little room with the hot plate and the lopsided walls and the complete absence of anything like love. Some home.

"On one condition," Cardinal said.

"Anything. Really. Name it."

"Don't keep in touch."

25

Dr. Frederick Bell considered himself a calm, rational man, so it was disturbing to find himself more and more agitated of late. Raising his hands before his face, he noted the trembling in his fingers. It wouldn't do. He could not afford to lose control.

Dr. Bell hit the PLAY button, and immediately the trembling in his fingers eased a little. The DVD recorder was a British-made state-of-the-art Arcam, with a hundred-gigabyte hard drive, bookmarking capability, and automatic archive-to-tape functions. And it was whisper quiet—a serious consideration in a therapy session.

But the best feature was the digital videocam, a Canon slightly larger than a golf ball, completely hidden in the sconce beside the bookshelves. The wide-angle lens (courtesy of Carl Zeiss) could take in both doctor and patient with no distortion. The microphone, an omnidirectional marvel hidden in the Arts and Crafts chandelier above the coffee table, was the size of an eraser. The recording software included a feature that counteracted the distance between speaker and microphone, and the quality of the sound still gave Dr. Bell deep pleasure on playback.

He watched the beginning. When he had first started recording, he had not activated the system until doctor and patient were past the preliminary greetings and hesitations. But now he recorded his sessions entire.

He watched Perry Dorn enter the frame and sit down, daylight gleaming a little through his thinning hair. He listened to the polite exchanges, his excitement growing. Then there was a pause, his on-screen patient so still and silent that Dr. Bell imagined for a moment that he had accidentally hit the freeze-frame.

Every therapist has to learn what to do with pauses in the conversation. Some believe that if patients are hesitant, it is not the therapist's place to prod them into speech. Five minutes, ten; let them blow the whole fifty minutes if they want. You go at the patient's speed and no faster.

Others won't let a pause last much beyond a minute. Patients can misinterpret the therapist's return silence as hostility, as letting them twist in the wind. The appropriate response may be a gentle question, nothing too probing, or perhaps a quiet summary of where they left off at the previous session. Still others, more hands-on, will ask about any "homework" they may have assigned.

It's young Perry who breaks the silence. Poor Perry.

"I'm so sorry I called the other day," he says. "I'm sorry I interrupted you."

"That's all right," Dr. Bell says. "I'm sorry I couldn't be more attentive just then. It simply wasn't possible."

"Oh, I know that. I can't expect people to drop everything every time I get depressed. I felt bad about calling. I just—I really thought I was going to do it, you know. I really thought I was going to. . . ."

How long to let that silence hang? Speak his thought for him? Or let him hear it ringing over and over in his own head? Dr. Bell had seen a movie when he was a boy, an old sword-and-sandals epic in which one poor unfortunate had a giant bell lowered over him. His tormentors then proceeded to beat on the bell with hammers. When it was lifted up again, blood was trickling from the victim's ears. Sometimes maintaining a silence could have the same effect as that bell: *kill myself, kill myself, kill myself,* ringing inside the skull over and over again.

Then it was end-game. Bell watched it with the pleasure of a chess champion reliving a recent victory. At each step, since he was winning, he had more and more options, more

plays available to him. But for the patient, who was losing—
who was not even aware there was a game in progress—each
move left fewer and fewer choices, until eventually he had
none.

On-screen, Dr. Bell lets the silence bloom.

Perry lowers his head.

Dr. Bell lets the silence expand to fill the room like gas.

Perry starts to sob.

Dr. Bell slides a box of Kleenex across the coffee table.
Knight to Queen-4.

Perry takes a Kleenex and blows his nose. "Sorry," he
says.

"You were feeling desperate," Dr. Bell says. "You wanted
to kill yourself."

Perry nods.

"But you didn't."

"No."

"Why not?"

"Too chicken, I guess. Chicken to the tenth power, that's
me."

Perry gives a little snort of self-derision. This results in
the need for another Kleenex.

It was amazing how filled with self-hatred a person could
be and yet still be walking around, Dr. Bell thought. By all
rights Perry Dorn should have killed himself years ago, but
no, he hung on day after day, month after month, year after
year, wallowing in misery.

"Surely it's more than a matter of being chicken," Dr.
Bell says on-screen. "After all, what was there to be afraid
of?"

A shrug. "The pain. Partly the pain. Also, I'm scared I
might make a mistake and just blow my face off without
actually killing myself."

"That could happen, I suppose, if one were not careful.
But perhaps there was something else about the plan that
didn't seem adequate?"

"I don't know what you mean."

"Well, what would Margaret think if she were to find out you'd killed yourself?"

"Honestly?"

"Honestly."

Perry thinks a few moments.

"Well, in the short term she'd be upset, I suppose."

"And then? In the long term?"

"Long term, I don't think she'd give a shit. She'd just think it was another sign of my. . . ."

"Defectiveness?"

"Exactly. My defectiveness."

"She'd feel well rid of you."

"Exactly. Like she'd made a smart move by dumping me."

Suicide as revenge, Dr. Bell had thought but not said. To voice that observation would have hauled an unspoken motive to the surface. Perry could have examined it, perhaps even rejected it. Certainly, if your objective were to keep the patient alive at all costs, that would indeed be the thing to do.

"You want her to know what she's done to you. How she's destroyed your happiness."

"Right, right. I didn't used to be like this!"

Bell had had his doubts on that score and still did. There was suicide in Perry's background, a history of antidepressants. There was the angry mother, the more competent sister.

"Have you had any other thoughts since, on how you might change that? Enhance the effect, so to speak?"

"Hey," Perry says, and there's almost a smile on his face. Almost. Perry has never actually smiled in Dr. Bell's office. "Aren't you supposed to be talking me out of this?"

"Oh, I certainly don't want to talk you into anything. My job is to help you recognize patterns in your life. To analyze your feelings about them. And to help you discover alternatives to these patterns that bring you so much pain."

"You mean like my pattern of getting dumped by women I worship."

"That's one. Harshly put, but yes, that is one."

"And my habit of destroying anything good that comes into my life. Academic future, et cetera."

"Again, harshly put."

"You know, I've been thinking about something you said long ago. When I first came here. You said, 'We can find happiness in our work. Or we can find happiness in love.' And some lucky few, you said, I guess like movie stars and so on, may find happiness in both."

"But I also said, 'It's possible, indeed common, to find happiness in one but not the other.' Many people are happy in their work but wretched in their marriage. Or the reverse. And they manage to have fulfilling lives."

"Exactly! That's what you said way back. And you said it's very difficult to go on if you don't find happiness in love *or* in work. And I just realized the other day that that describes me to a T. I mean, it's obvious. I like being a student, but I can't even consider going to McGill with Margaret here in Algonquin Bay. My graduate career is over."

"Costing you one source of happiness."

"Right. And then Margaret dumps me."

"Costing you the other."

"So what's the point of going on? I mean logically. I'm not trying to whine or gain sympathy or anything. I'm just saying it's like there's no point in my living anymore. I have zero source of happiness. I'm a black hole for happiness. What's the point of staying alive? I'm just in agony all the time."

"I can't answer that for you, Perry. No one can. We all have to find our own grounds for living. I mean, if you really wanted me to, I could offer all sorts of reasons: you're young, you're good-looking, you're intelligent, things can change, clouds part, flood waters recede."

"Happy talk, you mean. I don't want happy talk."

"No."

"I want the truth."

"I know you do. That's why I say you don't really strike me as 'too chicken' to do anything. I think you can complete whatever you set your mind to. The question is, how to know when your mind is really set on something. Clearly, the other day, when you didn't pull the trigger, it wasn't set. It wasn't satisfactory. Margaret wouldn't know it was about her."

"That's true." Perry sags even deeper into the couch. "Nothing I say or do reaches her. Never did, I guess. She had me fooled for a while, though. For a while there, I actually thought I mattered to her. I actually thought I existed."

In the long silence that follows, Perry shoves his hands between his knees and all but curls up on the couch. His face goes blank, and every angle of his bony frame expresses despair.

Dr. Bell froze the image. Most psychiatrists would have judged Perry a sure candidate for hospitalization and a course of antidepressants. History, posture, ideation, and personal circumstances would all go under the REASONS FOR ADMISSION heading. And yet it was so unnecessary to prolong his suffering. He was banging his head on an open door.

Dr. Bell unfroze the image.

"Did you do the homework we talked about?" he says on-screen. And, when there's no answer, "Perry?"

Perry stirs. "I tried to."

"And what happened?"

Perry reaches into his pocket and pulls out a balled-up piece of paper. In a move that appears to exhaust him, he sits up and rolls it across the table to the doctor.

Dr. Bell opens it up and smooths it out.

"Dear Margaret," Dr. Bell reads. "Why did you give up after *Dear Margaret*?"

"Because what's the point? She doesn't want to hear from me. She doesn't want to know my thoughts. She doesn't want to know I still love her. She wants me out of her life. That's why I think I should save her the trouble and take myself out of her life for good."

"And yet you haven't."

"Not yet. Part of me is afraid that blowing my head off will just make her and Stanley happy."

"Do you mean that?" Bell said. "Do you really think it

will make them happy? Suppose I put it another way: What do you think will be Margaret's reaction when she first hears the news? And when she gets your note? Such as it is."

"Shock, I guess. She'll be upset. Mostly because she'll worry that people will blame her. But they won't. They'll be all concerned for her—everyone looks after Margaret—and tell her it wasn't her fault. 'Oh, you were so kind to him.' 'Poor Margaret, you tried so hard not to hurt him.' The problem was with me. There was something wrong with me. I had *issues*."

"Will she believe them?"

"Oh, sure. She believes everything negative about me."

A silence descends.

Dr. Bell felt now, watching the disk, just as he had felt then: he knew Perry's suicide plan was not adequate. It was not going to have the punch the young man wanted it to have. Really, it was like shaping a theatrical performance. Tweaking the dialogue, blocking the scenes.

"Something's missing," Dr. Bell says, and tilts his chair back, contemplating the ceiling as if he were a philosopher chewing away on the meaning of life, testing his own theory for weaknesses. "No, that's not right. . . ."

"What?" Perry sits up, a cat hearing the rattle of its bowl.

"No, really. It's nothing. Stray thought."

"No, what? Really. What were you going to say?"

"Well, I was just thinking of the Laundromat. I was thinking how, when you started going out with Margaret, it seemed symbolic. You said yourself it was like you were starting out clean. I remember thinking that a witty remark. Neither of you carrying germs, you said—I'm sure that was your word—of previous relationships. And I was wondering. . . ."

"The Laundromat," Perry says. He tosses a ragged Kleenex onto the coffee table. "Yeah, she'd have to notice the Laundromat."

26

In all the time she had worked with Cardinal, Delorme had never had the slightest reason to doubt his sanity. But when she heard about his hauling in of Roger Felt on suspicion of having murdered Catherine—the story got around the squad room instantly—she began to wonder if grief were pushing him over the edge.

But she couldn't think about him right now. Somewhere there was a twelve- or thirteen-year-old kid who had been horribly abused and was likely to keep on being abused unless Delorme, with the help of the Toronto Sex Crimes Unit, could find her. Which was why she was at the home of André Ferrier on Sunday, her day off.

Delorme was no one's idea of a great housekeeper. There were days—all right, weeks—where the laundry piled up, the dishes didn't get done, and tumbleweeds of dust gathered under the furniture. Living alone—well, no one cared if you didn't clean up all the time. So she was not overly judgmental when it came to other people's housekeeping habits.

But the Ferrier household? The Ferriers took messiness to a whole new level. Their venetian blinds were down and set so that the overall gloom was sliced by slats of light that hit the ceiling rather than the floor. There were mirrors and photographs and artwork everywhere. But the clutter itself was not artful, it was random and uncomfortable.

As if for contrast, Mrs. Ferrier herself was a neat, trim woman, whose dark hair was secured by an uncompromising snood that allowed no strand to escape. She ushered Delorme into the living room and urged her to sit on a chair that was suffocating under an avalanche of cushions.

"Oh, sorry," Mrs. Ferrier said, and heaved armloads of them onto the floor, one, two, three. Then she excavated a place for herself in the middle of the couch and sat, her feet disappearing into a floor-level nebula of cushions, toys, and sleeping dogs—nothing Delorme recognized from the photographs. There was a Saint Bernard snoring near a radiator, apparently stone deaf, a gray poodle that raised one eyebrow at Delorme before falling back to sleep, and a brown and white sheltie that may actually have been defunct. The air carried a distinct aroma of hound.

Delorme, with no known allergies, began to itch.

"Now, what was it you wanted to ask?" Mrs. Ferrier said. In contrast to the chaos of her living room, she looked positively antiseptic in a plain pale sweater and blue jeans. Mid-thirties, but with the air of someone older. To the childless Delorme, anyone with children seemed impossibly mature.

She told Mrs. Ferrier about the marina, the assault.

"Well, I'm shocked. We've certainly never had any trouble out there. When did this happen?"

"We're not certain of the exact date," Delorme said. She wasn't about to say possibly two or three years ago.

She asked the questions she had asked the others: about the neighbors, any complaints, ever see anything suspicious. The answers were much the same: neighbors at the marina were friendly but not close, there were occasional disagreements, there was nothing that ever made her think the place was in any way unsafe.

Delorme's eye fell on the photographs covering one entire wall.

"What does your husband do, Mrs. Ferrier?"

"He's a car salesman. Down at the Nissan dealership? But that's his real passion," she added, waving a trim hand at the wall. "André's a born shutterbug."

A blast of TV noise from upstairs, ray guns firing and barked commands involving futuristic weaponry. Fast foot-steps on the stairs, and then a little girl was in the room with them. She looked seven or eight, blond hair pulled back in a ponytail that made her eyes appear slanted.

"Mum, can I go over to Roberta's? Tammy and Gayle are going."

"I thought Roberta was coming over here."

"Oh, please, Mummy, please!"

Mrs. Ferrier looked at her watch. "All right. But I want you back here for lunch."

"Yayyyy!"

The girl did a little dance and dashed out the door.

"Cute girl," Delorme said. "Bet she keeps you busy."

"Sadie's still a little kid, thank God. It's her sister that's starting to give us headaches. Do you have kids? I'm guessing not, judging by the shape you're in."

"Not married," Delorme said, and moved to the wall for a closer look at the photographs. As she did so, she tried to get a view of the next room, but the door was half closed and it was dim.

"Nice pictures," she said. There were images of boats, pictures of people, pictures of trees, houses, trains, buildings. The photographs were much better quality than the pornographic ones Toronto had sent her. Not that that meant much. Even a pro might let his standards slip in the grip of lust.

Mrs. Ferrier got up and joined her, a sudden whiff of lemony soap.

"That's Sadie," she said, pointing to a photo of a four-year-old sitting on the back of the Saint Bernard. "That was taken a few years ago, when we first got Ludwig. Oh, she tormented that dog. The poor thing had to ride her around as if he was a pony. No wonder he sleeps all the time these days, don't you, Ludwig?"

"And you have another girl, you said?"

"Alex. Alex hates having her picture taken. She even took down the old ones we had of her. Thirteen-year-olds are so . . . passionate about everything."

"Is Alex home right now?"

"No, she's spending the weekend at her cousin's in Toronto."

There was the sound of the front door opening.

"Here's André now," Mrs. Ferrier said. "He'll be able to tell you more about the marina."

There was a loud sigh from the front hall and the noise of shoes being removed.

"God, am I beat." This from the front hall.

"We're in here," Mrs. Ferrier called.

"We?" Mr. Ferrier came in and held out his hand to Delorme. "André Ferrier," he said, before his wife could introduce them.

"Lise Delorme."

"Ms. Delorme is a detective," Mrs. Ferrier said. "She's investigating something that happened at the marina. An assault of some kind."

"At the marina? God, who got assaulted? I suppose you can't tell me that."

"No, I can't. Do you mind if I ask you a few questions, Mr. Ferrier?"

"Not at all. As long as I can put my feet up. I just played nine holes out at Pine Grove, and my dogs are barking."

"Isn't it a little cold for golf these days?"

"Tell my boss that. He's a fanatic. Honey, do we have an extra Diet Coke or something for the detective?"

"That's okay," Delorme said. "I'm fine."

André Ferrier settled himself into the chaos of the couch. He was average-sized, broad in the shoulder, but in better shape than one might expect of a salesman. Medium-brown hair just covered his ears and collar.

It's possible, Delorme thought. He could be the guy in the pictures, though with shorter hair. She wanted to see his boat, wanted to see it right away, but didn't want to put him on his guard. She trotted out her questions once more. By now she was practiced at making them sound as if she were circling around an assault that might have happened at a wild party, maybe teenagers out of control.

Mr. Ferrier sipped lazily at his drink as he answered the questions. He didn't seem worried in the least.

"You have to be on your feet a lot?" he said at one point. "With what you do, are you standing a lot of the time?"

"Not anymore," Delorme said. "That's the best thing about getting out of uniform."

"I'm standing in the showroom most of the day, talking to customers. You'd be amazed how exhausting it is. That's probably why my boss has us playing golf all the time. Born sadist."

"But I see you have your own hobby," Delorme said.

"What? Oh, my photographs. Yeah, I love photography. That's my idea of the perfect afternoon—go out somewhere I've never been before, couple of cameras on my shoulder, and just shoot pictures all day."

"You hardly ever do it anymore," Mrs. Ferrier said. "You should get out more often."

"It's hard, with kids," Ferrier said. "They don't want to hang around while you frame your shot, decide on a lens, all that. Let alone watch you take multiple shots of the same thing. But that's what you have to do. When you see something you want to shoot, just fire away as many times as necessary. No point saving film."

"A couple of cameras, you said? Digital or film?"

"I'm just getting into digital. Tell you the truth, the technology isn't quite there yet. For the kind of results I want, I'd have to spend thousands of dollars on a camera—and then it would be obsolete in a couple of years anyway. I have a little point-and-shoot digital, but that's not why I take two cameras with me. You take two so that you don't have to change lenses all the time. I keep a wide angle on one, a telephoto on the other. Little trick I learned from a great teacher I had."

"Can't you just use a zoom?"

Ferrier winced. "Heavy. Clumsy. Too much glass."

"And you develop your own pictures?"

"Oh, yeah. That's the only way you get any control."

"Mr. Ferrier, it would greatly assist in our investigation if you were to allow me to look at your boat."

"Hey, wait a minute. You think somebody got beat up on

our boat? Sorry, but that's nuts, Detective. Nobody ever goes
on it except us."

"Even when you're away?"

"Nope. We keep an eye on things for each other out there.
If I tell Matt Morton or Frank Rowley I'm gonna be away,
they'll make sure nobody messes with the boat."

"But it's not like a house—they're not there all the time."

"True. But there's all sorts of security out there. Has to
be. They had a run of break-ins a few years back and now
they have cameras."

"You're certainly within your rights to expect a search
warrant," Delorme said, and stood up. "Mrs. Ferrier, thanks
for your help."

"I don't think André meant to say you couldn't look at the
boat, did you, dear?"

"Well, no. Not really. I just think it's a waste of time,
that's all."

"Even if we just rule it out as a crime scene, that's useful," Delorme said. "Our problem right now is that most of
the boats are already out of the water. Where do you keep
yours in winter?"

"Four Mile Marina. Other side of the lake. They have a
lot more room and they're a lot less pricey."

"Is that off Island Road?"

"Take Island. Make a right at Royal. Go about half a kilometer, you'll see a sign. Can't miss it. I'll tell 'em you're
coming."

ISLAND ROAD WAS four miles out of town, north on
Highway 63. Delorme had to drive past Madonna Road on
the way. Following Trout Lake's western edge, Madonna
Road curved back along the highway after a few hundred
yards. Cardinal's house was a dark rectangle below brilliant
clouds of colored leaves. She wondered if his daughter was
still there or if she had gone back to New York.

Work wasn't the same without Cardinal around. Delorme
liked to do all the footwork, cover all the bases, and keep her
supplementary reports up to the minute. Cardinal was all for

narrowing the focus as soon as possible, and he was right almost every time. Then he would go back and cover all the bases, just like Delorme. "Working together," Chouinard had said to them one time, "you two might add up to a decent investigator."

The two Ident guys lived in their own world. Szelagy was such a chatterbox, it was practically like having a radio going all the time. McLeod was always making the world a present of his opinions—and his opinions were insufferable. At least once a day Delorme prayed he was only kidding with some sexist or racist or anti-civilian remark. She hadn't realized how much Cardinal kept a lid on such things at the office until he was gone.

She made the turn onto Island Road, wondering how Cardinal was coping. Never having had a husband, Delorme had never lost one, but she remembered how she had grieved when her mother died, a dozen years ago now. Delorme had been a student at Carleton University in Ottawa. But she still remembered how it hurt, day in and day out, for weeks and months. She hoped Cardinal would soon begin to feel some respite.

A daydream visited her. She saw herself having dinner with Cardinal at an expensive restaurant. In Montreal, for some reason. And then they were walking on Mount Royal, the city spread out below them. She was giving him a hug, just to comfort him, and then he was hugging her back, and her heart stirred with something more than friendship.

"Jesus, Delorme," she said aloud, and slammed on the brakes. She had missed the turn onto Royal Road. She backed up, provoking honks of protest from an oncoming Jeep, and wheeled onto the dirt road.

FOUR MILE MARINA: SALES, SERVICE, STORAGE. The sign came up sooner than she expected, at the foot of a driveway wide enough to accommodate boats and trailers.

A young man in cargo pants and elaborate running shoes showed her to the boathouse. The structure resembled an enormous shoe rack with rolling metal shutters for doors. It was two levels high, and Delorme was glad to learn that the Ferriers' boat was stored on the lower level.

"I better get back to the office," the kid said. "Gimme a holler if you need anything."

"I will. Thank you."

The place was deserted. A light rain began to fall, rattling on corrugated tin and intensifying the surrounding smells of pine and wet leaves. Delorme opened the padlock and pushed up the shutter. She found a light switch and flipped it on.

The boat was up on its trailer, which made it seem enormous. The hull alone looked to be about six feet deep, all blinding-white fiberglass. The upper cabin was crowned with aerials, lights, and a satellite dish.

Delorme stepped onto the trailer and then onto the little chrome ladder attached to the stern. When she could see over the edge, she paused. Except for the wooden trim of the gunwales (if that was the right term), the entire deck of the boat was swathed in opaque plastic sheeting fastened with yellow cord looped through a border of grommets.

Ten minutes, fifteen, went by while Delorme fiddled with knots. Eventually she managed to loosen the covering and pull it back far enough so she could climb into the boat.

She stood and looked around at the wooden floors, the polished wooden trim. She climbed into the upper cabin and examined the wooden wheel, surrounded by brass fittings. Toward the stern, there were back-to-back seats in red tuck-and-roll upholstery. It was the boat in the photograph.

She stepped back down to the deck and sat on the bottom step. This was where he had sat to take the picture. The girl, not more than ten or eleven at the time, had sat on the front-facing rear seat. Frank Rowley's Cessna had been off to the right, the south. Delorme made a picture frame, film-director style, with her fingers and held it in front of her face. Yes, it was easy to picture the plane angled in the corner of the shot. Despite his care to remain anonymous, the photographer was so wrapped up in his pornographic project that he missed the identifying feature of the plane's tail number.

She had her crime scene—one of them, at least—and she was getting closer to her criminal. But it was his victim she most wanted to find.

27

Dr. Bell came out of the downstairs bathroom, drying his hands. There had been no need to scrub up, he wasn't a surgeon, but it was a habit he had got into long ago, during his medical training. Whenever he was about to see a patient, he washed his hands. He kept the mildest soap possible for this purpose: Caswell-Massey glycerine soap, faintly scented with almonds.

It was a ritual that helped him feel in control, and he needed it now, because lately his mind seemed somehow not entirely his own. Maintaining his equanimity was becoming harder and harder, and unwanted thoughts were intruding into his mind. These days he found himself clenching his hands, ready to batter some of his patients into submission.

He called Dorothy's name, but then he remembered she was out for the afternoon, though he couldn't for the life of him say where. Old age creeping up.

He opened the door into the public part of his house. Melanie was seated in her usual spot, although not in her usual depressed posture. She was reading a *Toronto Life* she must have brought with her. Dr. Bell took *The New Yorker*.

Melanie was so absorbed in the article, she didn't even look up right away. Bell suspected she was in a comparatively good mood. An interest in the outside world was always a sign of abatement in depression.

"Hello, Melanie," he said.

"Oh, hi." She stuffed the magazine into her knapsack and followed him into the office.

"Is it okay if I sit there for a change?" She pointed to a chair beside the couch.

"Of course."

Melanie plunked herself down in the chair. "Just seeing that couch, I suddenly felt depressed, and I thought, Why not sit somewhere else, somewhere you might sit if you weren't depressed?"

"I see."

"I mean, I get so tired of myself. So tired of my moaning and groaning. And I think part of it is I see myself as this pathetic person—a hopeless patient wailing on her shrink's couch—and I thought, Why don't I just not do that for a change?"

"A fresh perspective, so to speak."

"Exactly. Yeah. I feel good today. Better, anyway."

"So I see. Is that why you asked for this extra session?"

"Uh-huh. I have something important to tell you, but first I just want to say the normal stuff."

"By all means. Bring me up to date, Melanie."

Brighter affect was evident in every aspect of her behavior. Great actors understand the physiognomy of the emotions instinctively. Bell was an expert partly by instinct and partly by long study. Young Melanie was at this moment almost a cartoon of—not happiness but a mixture of relief and excitement. It was visible in the unaccustomed animation of her features: the twin commas of her eyebrows riding high above her glasses instead of in their usual furrowed V. It was there in the bigger gestures: the small hands flying away from her body, this way and that, as she described her week to him. It was there in the loose-limbed way she crossed one leg over the other, ankle on thigh, not her usual defensive clench. She bounced one knee up and down as she talked. He felt a surge of frustration and rigorously suppressed it.

"I actually managed to read a whole novel in the past couple of days," Melanie said. "You know, I was way behind in my English Lit survey, but I suddenly got so into it. It was this E. M. Forster thing, and I just didn't want it to end. I loved the characters, I loved his descriptions, and I loved not thinking about myself for a change."

"You turned your mind to things other than yourself."

"Exactly. And the amazing thing was that it was so easy."

She sat forward and swung her long hair to one side—hair that had been freshly washed, Bell noted. The drowned-rat look was now a pentimento beneath the eager face before him.

"The amazing thing about reading that book—which I had been putting off and putting off because I was afraid I wouldn't be able to follow it and it would end up depressing me—the amazing thing is that it was easier reading it than not reading it. You know what I mean? I was in such a state about getting behind and putting it off and waiting for just the right time to start and feeling so guilty and depressed. But once I started, it just went great."

"That's good to hear," Dr. Bell said. "Do you have any idea what accounts for the change?"

"That's the funny thing. Because what happened to me was something that should have upset the hell out of me, but it didn't. I mean, it did, but not in a way that depressed me. I haven't told anybody about this, and . . ."

Bell waited.

Melanie let out a deep breath, small shoulders dropping. "I haven't told my mom. I haven't told Rachel."

Rachel was her sometime best friend and current room-mate. Melanie had already told Bell lots of things she had never divulged to Rachel—or to her mother, for that matter—and she would tell him this too.

"I saw the Bastard," she said.

"You did? You saw your stepfather?"

"*Former* stepfather. I can't call him that. I'll just keep calling him the Bastard, which is what he is."

"Call him what you like. But I thought he had moved away."

"He did—not very far. To Sudbury."

"Where did you see him?"

"At Algonquin Mall. He was coming out of RadioShack.

I was just coming out of the Shoppers Drug Mart, and he was coming out of RadioShack. I can't believe he's back in town."

"And yet you said it made you happier?"

"Did I?" She looked at him blankly for a moment. "I guess I did."

"This was the man who molested you repeatedly. Used you as his sex toy for years and years. Can you think why it made you happy to see him?"

"I expressed myself badly. It didn't make me happy to see him. In fact, it felt like a kick in the belly at first. I literally almost doubled over. But then I followed him. He didn't look at me. And maybe he wouldn't have even recognized me if he had. But I followed him out into the parking lot. And I watched him get into his car. There was no one else in it. I wrote down his license plate number."

"Why did you do that?"

One of the hands stopped its fluttering. "I don't know. I didn't think about it. I just did it. I took out my pen and wrote it down on my hand. Isn't that weird?"

"You think it's weird?"

"Well, not weird maybe. But it was completely instinctive. And my heart was hammering away the whole time." She thumped her small fist up and down on her sternum. "*Boom, boom, boom.* I could actually hear it. And when he drove out of the parking lot, I followed him. Isn't that wild?"

"Go on."

"I followed him home. He's living in this completely suburban-looking brick house. Big garage and all. I watched him park in the driveway. I just stopped a little way back on the road and pretended to, like, look around, as if I was trying to find an address or a street or something, but I saw him go into the house. So I know where he lives now. At first I was gonna call Mom and tell her all about it, but then I decided against it. It would just upset her too much. She can't bear to hear his name as it is.

"So I didn't call Mom, I just went straight back to the

rooming house and put on the new Radiohead CD. I just sat on the end of my bed and listened to it right through from beginning to end."

"What were you thinking while you did that?"

"Nothing. I don't think I was thinking anything whatsoever."

"How were you feeling?"

"Good. Better, anyway. Like—I don't know—as if this huge rubber band that had been squeezing the life out of me had suddenly been undone somehow. Like I could breathe again." She looked at Bell, eyes searching his face. "Why would that be?"

"Well, on one level you liked him, remember?"

"I suppose."

"He was very seductive. He got you to like him, to trust him. He took you to these great places."

"That's true. He took me to WonderWorld."

"And to see the Musical Ride, you told me. Things a little girl was bound to love."

"That's not why I felt good after I saw him, though."

"Why, then? Can you tell me?"

He knew why, of course. Sighting her stepfather would have done two things for Melanie. First, he would be cut down to size; he would no longer be the giant monster of her imagination. He had become a human being, a man who buys his batteries at RadioShack, who gets into his car in a parking lot like anybody else. This was good; Bell could work with this. It wasn't the setback he'd feared. But there was something else she was struggling now to articulate.

"Did your stepfather see you?" he asked. "You said you followed him out into the parking lot. Did he see you?"

"No." Spoken emphatically. Not a trace of doubt.

"You saw him, but he didn't see you. How did that make you feel?"

"Like I had an advantage."

Bell nodded.

"It was like I was watching a bird or something. I mean, I

was frightened. My heart was pounding, like I said. But part of me was not scared at all. In fact, part of me felt pretty good."

"Like he was a bird," Bell said, "and you were a . . ."

"Cat," she said.

"A hunter," Bell said.

"Exactly. Not the hunted, for once."

She flopped back in her chair, pleased with herself, hands open, relaxed. Let her have her triumph. Next thing you know, she might even have a plan of attack. Totally out of character. It wouldn't change the ultimate outcome, though. The whole art of therapy was to help patients see their choices, allowing them to pick the right one.

Bell would gently bring her to a point on the precipice where she could see that, yes, one step and all the pain would cease. To do that he would have to keep calm, yet once again the biochemicals of anger were making his heartbeat tachy, his respiration rapid and shallow. He had a sudden vivid image of slapping Melanie across the face, the scarlet imprint of his hand on her cheek, but he took a deep breath and held it at bay.

"Are you thinking of hunting your stepfather in some way?"

"As we're sitting here now, I'm starting to feel awfully angry at him. I wouldn't mind an apology from him. Some acknowledgment that he hurt me."

Pretty feeble, considering that Melanie had already told him things that would put her stepfather in prison for years. If she chose to become a huntress, she could get her apology and a good measure of revenge as well. But then that would reduce her own guilt and depression, which wouldn't do. She would just become a perpetual whiner and a burden to everyone. For now he let her natter on about letters she might write, calls she might make, but they would have to go over those early events in more detail.

"Our time is almost up for today," Bell said, when she finally slowed down.

"I know. I always start to feel lousy when the hour's almost up."

"A couple of points I want you to think about before next time. First, you didn't write me the note you promised."

"The suicide note? I forgot all about it. I mean, after I saw my stepfather I really didn't think about it again."

"You were thinking of what you might say to him."

"I still am."

"We can talk about that. But first I want you to write that note. If you want to vanquish your depression, it's crucial to articulate it. One must name the beast, so to speak."

"I'll do it. I promise."

"Second thing. You're feeling an advantage over your stepfather at the moment, that you might be able to wring an apology out of him. It might even be a good thing to do. I can find you a dozen textbooks that would say exactly that. But let's not rush into it."

"Why not? Don't you think he should apologize for what he did? Look at me. I'm eighteen years old, and most days I can barely get up in the morning. Half the time I'm thinking I'd be better off dead."

"If I were a surgeon, would you want me to rush an operation?"

"No."

"If you had a tumor, would you want me to cut short your chemotherapy? Even if it nauseated you?"

"No, but I'm not sure this is like that."

"Well, let's leave it all up to you, Melanie. You're the surgeon here, not me. I'm just advising you that it might be better if we examine exactly what your stepfather did to you. In detail."

"Tell you the exact details? Oh, God. Now I do feel nauseous."

"As long as you don't articulate them, they will continue to have power over you. Also, you may be somewhat confused over just what he has to apologize for, just what he's guilty of. I'd like to see you absolutely clear on these matters."

"I know you're right. It makes perfect sense, but . . ."

"But?"

"I was feeling so good when I came in. And now I feel so lousy."

"Self-knowledge is rarely good news. But you're a strong young woman."

"I don't think so. Right now I feel horrible."

"So." Bell stood up. "Next time we'll have a lot to talk about. We'll have your note, and we'll have a precise history of what you did with your stepfather. You can write that out too, if you like. It might be easier than saying it face-to-face, though of course we'll have to talk about it."

"I don't think I can say some of the things he did to me."

"There's absolutely no rush," Bell said. "We'll go at your own speed and no quicker."

Melanie gathered up her backpack and got to her feet. The energy had drained out of her; the drowned-rat look was back.

"Okay," she said. "I'll see you next time, I guess."

"Bye-bye, Melanie."

28

Dr. Bell was only trying to help, Melanie understood that. He was a wonderful doctor, even with those funny little tics of his, the way he was always rolling his shoulders and shaking his head. Half the time she expected him to woof like a big mutt. And he kept that funny little antique engine on his desk. He had even showed her how it worked one day. As he named the parts and flipped the levers, he was like the best kind of father, the kind she had never had.

So, he was sincerely trying to help, but Melanie wished he hadn't set her such a difficult piece of homework. How do you write a suicide note when you're not actually planning to kill yourself? Three or four weeks ago she could've written one, no problem. Three or four weeks ago the only thing that had stopped her from killing herself was that she didn't have the energy.

Down the hall she could hear her roommates Rachel and Laryssa laughing about something. Melanie and Rachel had been best friends when they were younger, but over the past few years Rachel seemed to have cooled a little—no doubt because Melanie was always so depressed. She and Laryssa were very different from her, always with their doors open, always heading out to some social event or other.

Melanie had just started studying English Literature this year at the university, and she decided to think of her suicide note as a literary rather than a therapeutic exercise. When she had been close to offing herself, she had composed—in her head, at least—several suicide notes. Sometimes they were addressed to her mother, sometimes to her stepfather, sometimes to the natural father she had never known, and sometimes to the world at large. But she had never actually written one down.

It wasn't exactly a literary form you could study up and learn from the pros. She had read Sylvia Plath's *Ariel* poems— one long suicide note, as far as she was concerned, a letter from a Lady Lazarus who decided she would just as soon step back to the other side. A suicide of white-hot anger.

And then there was Diane Arbus. Melanie had been struck by her pictures of freaks: the man with the flea circus, the transvestite, the Jewish giant. Clearly the photographer had felt like a freak herself. On the whole, Melanie felt more like an Arbus than a Plath; she had the feeling she and Arbus would have been good friends.

In any case, Melanie thought, I'm not a poet. I wouldn't have a clue how to write like Plath even if I wanted to. And all Arbus had written, before taking an overdose and cutting her wrists, was *The last supper.* It was as if she didn't want to bother anyone with a note. The last supper.

Well, Melanie had just had a peanut butter and jam sandwich, and she wasn't about to write *The last lunch* and take it in to Dr. Bell. She had the feeling he already thought she might be a little dim; she wanted to impress him.

It's just too painful to go on, she wrote. That would be to the world at large, she supposed, as if the world cared. It was about as uninteresting a thing as you could possibly say, also the truest. It stated the case, so why waste words? Perhaps that was why a lot of artists committed suicide. It is, if nothing else, the most eloquent and yet economical statement. Words might be redundant.

Dear Mom, This is going to hurt you terribly, so I want you to know beyond a shadow of a doubt IT ISN'T YOUR FAULT. Whoever my father was, he did a bad thing by leaving you alone to have a baby, and I think you did a great job, considering. Much better than I would have done. You made one mistake, marrying the Bastard, as we call him, but I realize now you were a single mom, alone with a little kid, bored and afraid with no joy in your life, and when he came along offering love and protection and a few laughs it must have been the most tremendous rush. He hurt you terribly, and I'll never forgive him for that.

No point telling her mother what the Bastard had done to her. Not in a suicide note.

I'm so sorry to repay all the care and comfort and joy you gave me in this awful way. But I seem to suffer from terminal sadness the way other people suffer from terminal cancer. My quality of life is gone. I can't enjoy food or sunshine or even sleep anymore. I wake up each morning with nothing but dread and weariness. And even though I see a wonderful psychiatrist, I understand now that there is no hope of recovery.

It was almost dark now. The house was quiet: Rachel and Laryssa had either gone out or settled down to study. Melanie remained in the gathering gloom, pen poised in the air, and fell into a blank space. She did that sometimes, sat absolutely still, staring into space, her mind an empty white mist. Sometimes an hour would pass, sometimes two. This time it was only half an hour.

So she got up and went down the hall to the bathroom. Tiny dabs of brown and black and blue dotted the sink, as if it had developed multicolored measles. Laryssa had obviously been experimenting with makeup again. She was always revising her face, Laryssa, which was something Melanie might do if she could ever stand looking in a mirror long enough.

When she got back to her room, she pulled out her cell phone.

"Mom?"

"Hi, Mel. You want to come over for supper? I've got lamb pie in the oven."

"Um, no, that's okay. But I was wondering if I could borrow the car for a little while."

"Of course. I don't need it this evening. I do want it back tonight, though. I need it for work in the morning."

"Yeah, I only need it for a while. Just wanna go out to the Chinook with some friends, and it's such a drag waiting for the bus."

"You know, if you lived at home, honey, you'd actually have a lot more freedom."

"I'm too old to live at home, Mom."

She put on a jacket and walked the few blocks to her home, as she still thought of it. She would never think of the boardinghouse as home, no matter how kind Mrs. Kemper was. Her mother asked her all sorts of questions about her classes and her roommates, and it took forever to get away.

But now here she was, parked a little way down from the Bastard's place, waiting for—well, she wasn't quite sure what for. His car was in the driveway, and the lights were on inside the house. It didn't look like the kind of place where a single person would live, far too big and suburban-looking.

If he came out, she would speak to him. Just come on out, you bastard, and I'll tell you exactly what I think of you. Let me tell you what it cost me, the things you did to me. How I've felt sick and ashamed and guilty my whole life. If he came out, she would tell him how she could not so much as kiss a boy without thinking of the Bastard, seeing his face in front of her, his penis, his huge hands. The hands that had gripped and probed and bound. The hands that had held the camera.

She would tell him how she could not use the Internet these days without wondering if her pictures were on it somewhere. Why else would he take all those photographs? She would tell him how she burned with shame to think of them. Even now, the shame crept up her back and over her shoulders and up her neck like a rash, burning her ears.

She thought she would be sick, but the wave of nausea became a wave of sorrow rolling upward through her chest and into her eyes until the tears prickled. She would not cry; she refused to cry. She stared at the brick house with its big yard and its big garage and thought, You bastard, if you have a new wife in there, I'm going to tell her everything. I'm going to tell her exactly what you did to me, and she'll leave you and maybe even report you to the police, which is what I should have done years ago.

Yes, I hope you have a wife. I hope she's young and beautiful and I hope you adore her because, when I'm finished, she's going to drop you so fast you're going to feel your ribs break.

"ARCH YOUR BACK, honey. Come on, Mel. Arch your back. That's right. Oh, you look so beautiful like that!"

The camera *clicks, clicks, clicks* as he moves closer, closer, sometimes only inches away. And then more instructions.

"Okay, lie down on your belly and pretend you're asleep."

The smell of bleach on the hotel sheets, sheets creased and crisp, not the comfy kind at home. Sunlight spills through the windows along with rollicking music from the fairground: calliopes, organs, glockenspiels, and rock music. The shouts of children whooshing down the waterslide, the screams of young mothers on the Tilt-A-Whirl, the Slingshot, the Wild Mouse.

"Daddy, can we go on the Wild Mouse?"

"Soon, baby. Just close your eyes now."

Click, click, click.

With eyes closed: "Daddy, now can we please go on the Wild Mouse?"

"Soon, Mel. Okay, let's pull that sheet a little lower."

Click, click, click.

"Daddy, you promised."

"I know, sweetheart. Oh, you look so beautiful, I could just eat you up!"

Click, click, click.

A frolic then, sloppy kisses on her neck and tickling her ribs till she can hardly breathe. Such fun! And then he leaves her breathless and excited.

She jumps off the bed and looks for her shorts and the rest of her clothes.

"What are you doing, Mel?"

"Getting dressed. I wanna go on the Wild Mouse."

"Honey, we're going to go on the Wild Mouse, just like I promised. But right now you have to get back on the bed."

He hoists her from under her armpits and lowers her back where he wants her. He isn't wearing any clothes now, and she knows what's going to happen. She knew it all along but didn't want to think about it. She wanted this trip so bad. WonderWorld!

"I don't want to be in bed now. I want to go on the rides. You promised."

"I'll make a deal with you, Mel. We're going to go on the rides. But which rides we go on depends entirely on you. Now, you can earn each ride by doing certain things for Daddy. You do one thing, you get the Tilt-A-Whirl. You do another thing, you get the Slingshot. And if you do something really super special for Daddy, you get the Wild Mouse. But first let's snuggle up close."

He holds her tight, and it's like a boa constrictor wrapping itself around her chest. "You remember what I said about this, right, honey? About it being our secret?"

"I know."

"You can't tell Mom or anyone. No one. You remember?"

"I remember."

"Never, ever, right?"

"Never, ever."

"And what will happen if you do?"

"The police will come and take me away and put me in a home for bad girls."

"That's right. And we don't want that, do we? Okay, now we're going to be special, special friends."

MORE THAN A decade later and Melanie's in her mother's car watching the Bastard's house, hoping he'll come out. She roots around in her backpack for a Kleenex, finding an old crumpled pack. She wipes her eyes, blows her nose. She never cried, back then when he was doing those things to her. Well, only once or twice when he actually hurt her, his full-grown body too large for her not-yet-developed one.

But mostly he didn't hurt her, physically. WonderWorld. How she'd wanted to go there. All her friends had gone and raved about it. And then, as a surprise for her eighth birthday, he took her. Somehow he had arranged it so her mother hadn't come with them. Melanie had been so excited, she hadn't worried about anything. It was like waiting for Christmas.

But the minute they set their bags down in the hotel room, a sourness grew in her stomach and she felt shaky all over. She hadn't had a word for it back then, that swampy feeling in her belly. That dread. That fear, chemically enhanced with excitement. Her heart was in complete confusion because, when he did those things to her, he was also so *nice*. Attentive. Kind. Funny. He'd do anything she asked—play with her dolls, have tea parties with imaginary guests—as long as she did what he wanted.

Then there were the fishing trips. He would take her out to the smaller lakes in a flat-bottomed boat. He was good at showing her how to attach the hooks and lures. He was patient, teaching her to cast the line from the small rod he bought for her. He showed her how to clean the fish they caught and how to fry them up so that they tasted wonderful.

Of course, it wasn't free. In the tent at night, she had to earn all that attention and instruction and fun. In the tent, she was expected to pose and perform. In the tent, her job was to please him. And he was always finding new ways for her to please him.

One day, years later, her friend Rachel had shocked her by opening some images she had discovered on the computer she shared with her older brother. Rachel had clicked from one to the next, wide-eyed and giggling and appalled and fascinated. They had both been twelve years old at the time.

"Oh, gross!" Rachel would cry.

"Oh, gross!" Melanie would say too, trying for the same tone. But she could tell she wasn't seeing the pictures the way Rachel was seeing them. It was obvious from her shock and amazement that Rachel, unlike Melanie, was innocent.

"Do people really do that?" Rachel cried. "It's so disgusting!"

"Weird," Melanie said.

"This is just like the most perverted stuff I've ever seen! I think I'm going to barf!"

No, Rachel had never seen such things before. But Melanie had not only seen them, she'd been doing them since she was seven years old.

OCCASIONALLY A shadow rippled across the curtains in the picture window. A man's shadow.

"Come out," Melanie said in the car. "Come out, you bastard, and I'll tell you what I think of you now."

That day with the computer images had put a distance between her and her best friend. Rachel had been so disgusted that Melanie was forced to wonder, What would she think of me if she knew? She would be horrified, repulsed. She wouldn't want anything to do with Melanie ever again.

A new fear had slithered into her heart. Here were all these pictures on a computer: images of ordinary people, some of them teenagers. For the first time Melanie worried that there might be hundreds of pictures of her on the Internet, just waiting for a friend to discover. She had lived with that fear of discovery ever since.

All those pictures, countless pictures. Because it didn't happen only on special trips. Even at home, whenever her mother was out for a couple of hours, the Bastard would come after her. When hugs and attention were no longer enough, he'd use money. How about some cash for that new CD? Could there be a pair of Guess jeans in your future? We'll just have to see how things go. A few days later her mother had asked about the jeans: Those are expensive. Where did you get the money for them?

"Oh, Mel helped me tidy up the basement," the Bastard said, "and I gave her some money toward them."

Then there was that time on the boat, that beautiful cabin cruiser the Bastard had borrowed from someone. The three of them in the same cabin, cruising around Trout Lake for days.

Mom and the Bastard sleeping on one side, Melanie on the other. She would have been about eleven. In the middle of the night she had awoken with a start. He was sitting on the edge of her bed with his hands in her pajamas, her mother not three feet away. He must have put some drug in her mom's wine. That night Melanie earned a new pair of Nikes.

AND NOW THE sick Bastard was coming out of the house. Five years hadn't made much difference to his appearance. His jacket was different, a light blue nylon windbreaker, and he had a baseball cap on his head. He never used to wear baseball caps. He came a few steps down the driveway, tilting his head back, breathing in the cool evening air. He stopped, hands in pockets, waiting, stepped over onto the lawn to examine some flaw or other.

Just like a normal person might do, Melanie thought. As if you're just like everybody else.

She put her hand on the car door and took a deep breath. She would tell him; oh, boy, would she tell him. Then she stopped.

A woman came out the side door of the house and joined her former stepfather. She was pretty, maybe forty, with dark hair curling to her shoulders. Her denim jacket and khaki trousers looked good on her. She still had a real figure. Better looking than Mom, Melanie thought, and it made her sad.

I'm going to tell this new wife everything, absolutely everything. Even if he denies it, even if he calls me insane, she's going to know it's true. That pretty face of hers will crumple in shock. The happy gleam in her eye will turn to suspicion, anger, loathing.

Melanie opened the car door. There was no other traffic, no other pedestrians. The happy couple were turned back toward the house now, their postures expectant. Well, here's something they won't expect.

Melanie was twenty yards down the road from them, crossing at a diagonal. She ordered her heart to calm down. She did not want to look crazy; it was important that this woman believe her, that she sound rational. Her pace was brisk, businesslike, a young executive headed to a meeting.

The side door of the house opened, and a little girl came out carrying a Nerf ball and paddle.

"Where are we going?" she said, in a piping little voice.

"We're just going for a walk," the woman said. "It's such a nice night. You won't be able to see that ball in the dark, though."

"Yes, I will."

"Okay, hon, but you forgot to close the door."

The little girl stopped and turned back to look at the house.

"Go on and close it, sweetie."

The girl went back toward the house uncertainly.

"I'll do it," the Bastard said, and headed toward the girl.

The blast of a car horn made Melanie jump. Her feet literally left the ground for a split second. She turned just as a car stopped less than a yard from her knees.

"Sorry," she managed to say. She headed back to her car. "Sorry, sorry . . ."

The man in the car shook his head and drove on.

Melanie got back into her mother's car, quivering. The key refused to fit in the ignition. All three members of that pathetic family were staring in her direction. She finally managed to start the car and drove past them, face averted, pretending to fiddle with the radio.

Her pulse pounded in her ears, and she missed the turn back onto Algonquin. She pulled into the parking lot of a Mac's Milk and sat with the motor running, trying to catch her breath. The Bastard had a new daughter, seven years old or thereabouts. The Bastard had another little girl.

29

Kelly put the prints back and closed the drawer.

"I think that's the last batch," she said, "at least here. She's probably got tons of prints up at the college. Negatives too, I bet."

"Oh, yeah," Cardinal said. "She has a couple of filing cabinets up there."

He had been sitting on a trunk in a corner of the darkroom, watching, even though Kelly had asked him to go away and do something else. He couldn't help it; he wanted to be around his daughter, especially while she was doing something for her mother.

"You might want to check with the school," she said. "There may be someone there who's up on what she was doing. They might have better insights into her work than me."

"No way, Kell. You're an artist, you're her daughter. Who could know better?"

"A fellow photographer. Someone who worked with her all the time. I just think you might want to check first. If it still seems like I'm the best person to organize a show, I'll be happy to do it. In fact, I'd love to do it."

"She always worked alone. She didn't like company when she was taking pictures. Or in the darkroom."

"Please just check, Dad. We want to do what's best for her work."

"I will. I'll let you know."

"It's a bit of a surprise to me," Kelly said, touching the

white chest of drawers she had just closed, "but Mom was actually a very organized person."

"Oh, yes. She liked to know where everything was. Liked to get things done on time. She had her problems, but she wasn't scatterbrained."

"She has all her contact sheets here, filed and dated, and the negatives attached. Prints have negative numbers on the back."

"Yeah, she'd get very upset if she couldn't find the exact image she wanted. And she was always ordering her students to keep things shipshape. She wouldn't tolerate sloppiness."

Kelly touched a file cabinet with her index finger, her smallest gesture reminiscent of her mother's.

"Even the more recent stuff. The digital stuff. She's got disks filed with them, and lists of file numbers inside the jacket. I wish I was that organized."

"That's funny. She often wished she was a painter, like you. 'I'd love to just get down in the mess sometime,' she'd say. 'Photography seems so clinical sometimes. All this damn equipment.'"

Kelly opened the tall cupboard in the corner. Inside, neat rows of lenses and filters were interrupted by gaps for the equipment Catherine had taken on her last—her final—project.

THAT EVENING, KELLY trundled her small suitcase out to the car and Cardinal drove her to the airport. She had seen him through the funeral and his first two weeks alone; what more could he ask? He tried to make conversation, but her mind was already traveling ahead to New York. New York. Not so far geographically, but psychologically she might as well have been in Shanghai.

He stayed in the waiting area with her until it was time for her to go through security. She hugged him fiercely and said, "I'll call you soon, Dad."

"Look after yourself down there."

"I will."

Cardinal drove slowly back down Airport Hill, but not slowly enough. He didn't want to go home, didn't want to face that silence. Instead of making the left onto Highway 11, he continued straight into town.

He drove to Main and from there along the waterfront. Beneath a moon misshapen by clouds, scattered joggers trotted along the shore and dog walkers stood in small groups surrounded by sniffing, leaping canines. Cardinal turned back into the west end of town and drove back and forth along the side streets. Pretty pathetic, he thought, to be afraid of going home.

He found himself driving past Lise Delorme's place, a small bungalow on the corner of a quiet crescent off Rayne Street. Her lights were on, and he wondered what she was doing. He had a strong urge to pull into her driveway, knock on her door, but what would he say? He didn't want to look pathetic in front of Delorme.

What would she be doing, reading? Watching television? In some ways he knew Delorme very well, they had worked so many cases together. They got on well, laughed a lot. But when you got down to it, he didn't know how she spent her spare time, didn't even know if she had a boyfriend right now, although he had seen her chatting with Shane Cosgrove a little more amiably than necessary.

Her company would have been good, though, in this evening hour that didn't even feel like a particular hour in a particular place, but more like a space between hours, an interregnum between two lives: his life with Catherine and whatever was left.

He stopped at the traffic light on the corner.

"Pathetic," he said aloud. "Haven't even been alone five minutes."

He sat there for quite a while, until he realized the light was green.

HIS HOUSE WAS silent in a way he had never known. The absence of sound was so deep it seemed to be not just around him but inside him, through him. It was as if, except for whatever space he occupied at any given moment, the world had disappeared.

There was no sound of Catherine in the other rooms. No footsteps of any kind, no slippers, no bare feet, no tap of dress shoes, no stamp of snowy boots. From the darkroom below, no sound of Fleetwood Mac or Aimee Mann. No rattle of developing trays, no whine of hair dryer. No sudden call: "John, come and take a look at this!"

Cardinal tried to read and found he could not. He flicked on the television. A CSI team was busy destroying evidence. He stared at the screen for a while, taking nothing in.

"Trying to act normal," he muttered.

He took Catherine's photograph from the bookshelf where Kelly had placed it. It was the one of her in the anorak, with two cameras slung over her shoulders.

Did you kill yourself?

All the times she had railed at him for taking her to the hospital, cursed him for interfering in her mania, bridled at his checking on her medication. All those cries and tears over the decades—had she meant them, after all? Had that been the real Catherine? He could not bring himself to believe that the woman he had loved so long could have thrown that love back in his face, could have said, No, your love is not enough; *you* are not enough; I'd rather die than spend another minute in your company. That was what Roger Felt had said on his cards. He couldn't believe it.

And yet he had no proof that it was otherwise. Roger Felt, his number one suspect, had turned out to be nothing more than a vengeful loser. And Codwallader's manager had confirmed that he had been at work when he said. The security tapes would confirm it.

You wrote the note. But could you really have killed yourself?

Had Catherine had enemies? Cardinal had investigated enough deaths to know that people can surprise you on this count. A small-time drug dealer may turn out to have been the kindest person in the neighborhood, his death caused not by rivals but by his own pharmaceutical miscalculation.

And then you could have the saint, the woman who does all the charity work, who is always the first to get friends and associates to "sign the card for Shirley," to organize visits to the hospital, to raise money for the summer camp. Such paragons could turn out to have slept with the wrong woman's husband, pilfered money, suffered delusions, nursed compulsions—and they end as victim or perpetrator of a homicide.

But Catherine? All right, yes, she had had her turf wars up at the college. Lost them all, too. God knows she could have a sharp tongue when she was angry; it was just conceivable that some rival in the art department had been outraged by some ill-considered remark. And she had won prizes for her photography—several provincial, one national—and her work had been exhibited locally many times and every couple of years in Toronto. When a person wins a prize, someone else may feel robbed.

Cardinal went into the kitchen and made himself a drink. The clink of the ice, the glug of the whiskey, sounded absurdly loud in the silence. He switched on the radio and heard a split second of country music before he switched it off again. He never listened to the radio at night, it was just desperation.

He sat at the kitchen table. Nights when he could not sleep, he would come in here and scrounge up some cookies and milk. The room hadn't seemed bleak then, with his wife sleeping in the other room. He opened her case file. It was thinner than any other case file he had ever worked. By definition, if you had a case, you had notes, you had leads, you had some direction. But this file contained almost nothing.

There were the bogus sympathy cards, useless now. There were his notes concerning Codwallader and Felt, footsteps into the same cul-de-sac. And there was the page torn from Catherine's notebook. The pale blue ink from her favorite Paper Mate. And her handwriting, with its unadorned *j*'s and looped *t*'s.

By the time you read this. . . .

The file contained two versions of the note: the original in blue ink and the copy that Tommy Hunn had made at the

Forensic Centre, white writing on a graphite background, where the toner had brought out the fingerprints invisible on the original. There was Catherine's thumbprint along the edge, with the small white line where she had cut herself years ago. And the smaller prints along the edges would be Catherine's too; it would be simple to check.

But then there was that thumbprint at the bottom of the note, too large to be Catherine's. And Catherine was right-handed. When she went to tear the page from the notebook, she would have grabbed it by the right-hand side and pulled. But whose thumbprint was on the bottom of the page, in the middle? If it was not the coroner's and not Delorme's or anyone else's who had been on the scene, who had held Catherine's suicide note in his or her hand?

30

Dead Mother and Child. The Edvard Munch painting was Frederick Bell's favorite, and he knew exactly why. The still form of the dead mother, pale, almost transparent, on the bed and the family members attending to her, ignoring the little girl in the foreground, her hands wavering about her head as though to cover her eyes—or perhaps her ears—to shut out the reality of her mother's death. The mother had died of consumption, Bell knew, when Munch was still a boy, and it had colored his whole life. It had made him miserable, and it had made him an artist.

Consumption. Medicine had come a long way in the past hundred years. Consumption, or tuberculosis, with the help of antibiotics, had been virtually erased from the planet. Depression, of course, was flourishing.

Munch had had his deathbed. Bell had known two.

The first had been his father's, when Bell was eight years old. Every day he would have to sit with his father for an hour, between the time school got out and the time his mother got home from her job as a nurse.

His father had been a dark man: thick mustache, a single lintel of brow above his eyes, and curly black hair. Black Irish, his mother had called him, and the young Bell had wondered if that meant his father had had a background in the Troubles of Northern Ireland. Later, he realized his father had never set foot in that country. Later, he learned all sorts of things.

But back then at Deathbed One, his father's dark good

looks were made even more heroic by the swaths of white bandages wrapped around his head, covering one eye. He looked like a soldier just back from a war, wounded in the defense of his brothers, struck dumb by the horrors he had witnessed.

An accident, his mother had told him. A terrible accident while cleaning his pistol, a Luger liberated from the dead hand of a German soldier in 1945.

The door to his father's study hung open, as it never had before. His father's study had always been a place you did not venture into uninvited. The young Frederick had been inside only a few times, once to receive congratulations for having come first in his class, other times to receive punishment.

His father had terrified him—such black moods, such tantrums—yet he could also be kind. One summer he had taken Frederick out into the fields to catch and classify butterflies, an afternoon that was to become one of his happiest memories. His father taught science at a nearby grammar school; indeed, he always seemed happiest when he was teaching something.

Those evenings when he took it into his head to instruct his son, he was transformed into a different man: patient, good-natured, and knowledgeable about a wide range of subjects (the history of flight, the principles of internal combustion, the intricacies of cellular reproduction, the diatonic scale). He would sit beside the lad for a couple of hours, explaining, giving context, analyzing, even suggesting what Frederick might want to write down or draw to help him remember. Every once in a while he would lay a hand on the boy's shoulder and say, "Don't roll your shoulders like that, son, it'll develop into a habit."

Bell still had the model steam engine his father had passed on to him; it had been a gift from his own father. A simple elegant toy, it consisted of a miniature brass boiler suspended on brass brackets above an oak base. You filled it by unscrewing a tight-fitting brass cap and pouring water from a measuring cup into a tiny hole. A single piston, a drive-shaft, a flywheel, and that was it. You placed a tiny lamp filled with methanol under the boiler. When the water boiled, it moved the piston and the piston drove the shaft that cranked the wheel. The best part was a miniature valve at one end of the boiler that you could open with a lever, causing it to emit a surprisingly throaty whistle.

Those pedagogical afternoons and evenings were infrequent. Mr. Bell was prone to depressions that sent him into his study for days on end. When he was like that, you didn't want to disturb him. Even if you were lonely and bored and all your friends had gone away somewhere for the holidays, you didn't dare knock on that door. Sometimes Frederick would sit on the hall chair just outside the study, swinging his feet, not doing anything, waiting for his father to emerge.

Sometimes he would hear weeping, papers tearing, a book being thrown, even though no one was in there with his father. The sobs tore into Frederick, frightening him. His mother would sometimes tap with a light hand on the door. The sobbing would cease and she would enter, and then Frederick would hear her voice, questioning, soothing, pleading, and his father's laconic, unintelligible replies.

Nobody called it anything back then, at least no one in his family's circle. People had moods, some people had severe moods. That was all. This was England and they had come through the war; nothing else could be as bad as that. You were supposed to keep your chin up, stiff upper lip, mustn't grumble, and under no circumstances suggest that you had any complicated emotions. No one uttered the word *depression*.

So when his mother told him that his father had suffered a terrible accident with his pistol, Frederick did not question her, although he was surprised. On one of his more instructive afternoons, Mr. Bell had invited Frederick into his study to show him how to clean and care for a gun. It was a manly sort of endeavor, involving manly smells of oil and metal. His father had explained how you never kept a pistol loaded, and you never stored the ammunition in the same location as the pistol. He admonished him never to point the barrel at anyone, yourself included, not even in jest, not even in the most transient gesture. Instead, you held it pointed toward the floor—toward the corner, in fact—while you removed the various cunning parts and set them out on a cloth.

Much later, after he had become a doctor, Bell realized that the bullet must have entered toward the posterior nasopharynx, crashing through the palate, probably fracturing the eye socket, before exiting through the anterior of the skull. Emergency rooms were not then as skilled as they would later become at dealing with gunshot wounds. Today such a wound would probably send a man home with impaired speech and eyesight. In the fifties, the damage was enough to kill, but not immediately.

His father lingered. A hospital bed was set up in the living room. A visiting nurse came every other day to check his condition and change his bandage. Frederick was always ordered out of the room when she did this. Sometimes his father muttered things, irrelevant words and sentence fragments. "Dragon's foot," was one phrase. "On the wire," was another.

Frederick's mother was so riven with grief she was little help to her young son. Indeed, it was he who tried to comfort her, bringing her tea and sandwiches that his various aunts had made. She would smile wanly at him, and her eyes would overflow. Frederick felt himself to be invisible during this time. His aunts talked as if he were not there, and more than once he heard one of them—Aunt May, it was—whispering into the phone the phrase "shot himself," in a way that made it sound, well, not accidental.

The invisible boy would sit in the gloom at the top of the stairs, listening. Whenever anyone came up to use the bathroom, he would scuttle back to his bedroom and pretend to be reading. He heard more phrases, and several times his mother wailed, "Why did he do it? Why!"

"He must have been in terrible pain," Aunt May answered.

"He was not in his right mind," said Aunt Josephine.

And so the young Frederick came to understand, with a sick feeling in his stomach, that his father had shot himself on purpose. There was nothing he could do with the information. There were no priests or nuns to consult, not that they would have done any good; he had been brought up without religion. And he couldn't go to his mother, because she still insisted that it had been an accident. He was like the girl in the Munch painting, bewildered, alone, and with nowhere to turn.

The sick feeling stayed in his stomach and hardened into something else. At school, the teacher began to sound very far away, as if talking to him from the edge of a deep well into which he had tumbled. He had no urge to climb out. His fellow pupils no longer interested him with their silliness and their games. During recess he took to sitting under a tree, counting stones or bits of grass or reading one of his science biographies.

His father sank ever deeper into unconsciousness. According to the nurse, things were taking a grave turn. A doctor came—they still made house calls then—and then another doctor. Both said there was nothing they could do; Frederick's father would either wake up or he wouldn't.

Nothing to Be Done.

Dr. Bell often reflected that if Munch had painted a picture of himself as a boy sitting by that deathbed, that's what he would have titled it. *Nothing to Be Done.* Nothing to do but mourn and be consumed by all the emotions that were not to be mentioned in a 1950s British household. As a psychiatrist, Bell knew he must have experienced tremendous rage at his father for abandoning him in this hideous way, for the torment he had inflicted on his mother. But he never felt it, not then, not now.

It was on a Friday afternoon in March of 1952 that Frederick Bell's father died. The boy was not actually in the room with him, nor was his mother. His Aunt May had been on duty at the time. According to her (the eavesdropping boy heard her telling someone sotto voce on the phone), it had been the most terrifying event. Mr. Bell, who had barely moved for the past three weeks, suddenly sat up in his bed, staring straight ahead with his one uncovered eye. Aunt May had been too frightened to move. Her brother sat there, bolt upright, staring for a few moments, perhaps not even a minute.

"Then he spoke," she said. "It was as if someone had just

handed him some bad news. *Oh my God,* he said, but not in a way at all religious. I don't believe he had a revelation of that sort. It was the tone you would use if someone told you a school had burned down, a kind of horrified wonder. *Oh my God,* he said, and lay back down. I went to his side and tried to speak to him, but he didn't say anything else; he just gave a kind of gasp and that was it. It's been massively hard on Jane, of course."

Jane was his mother, and it had been just the two of them after that. Eventually she turned his father's study back to its original function as a parlor, but neither of them ever set foot in the room again. Shortly after that, financial pressures forced them to move to much meaner accommodation, a dark cold flat where they lived for the next ten years. One day Frederick came home from his part-time job assisting the local pharmacist and found a note in his mother's handwriting on the door:

Frederick, don't come in. Please go round to your Aunt May's and have her call the doctor.

And so, Deathbed Two, this one comparatively brief. His mother had taken an overdose of sleeping pills, but she had thrown up. Consequently, it took her three days to die instead of the hour or two she had no doubt intended. In the end, so much brain function was suppressed that the other organs failed.

Frederick had to move out of the flat and into a basement room at Aunt Josephine's. While cleaning out his mother's papers, he found an old envelope with just one word scrawled on it in his father's handwriting: *Jane.* This was inside:

Dear Jane,

I'm going to kill myself and end this farce. I'm sorry to leave a mess. I just can't seem to get control of myself.

No signature, no expression of love, no mention of their son. Frederick Bell, eighteen years old, sat down in his mother's bedroom, surrounded by the overstuffed bags and boxes, and stared at his father's handwriting—stared for a long, long time.

LUCKILY, HE WAS an intelligent young man and determined to succeed. He put himself through university entirely with scholarships and part-time jobs. Thanks to Aunt Josephine, his living expenses were minimal while he attended Sussex University.

Calm and jocular on the outside, on the inside he was launched on a private crusade. As he put it to himself, he wanted to cure blindness—the blindness of the medical profession to the problem of suicide. He had lost two parents, both of whom had been seeing family doctors, and neither of whom had been diagnosed as depressed, let alone suicidal.

He wanted to perfect that treatment himself. He was fascinated both by the prospects of pharmaceutical treatment and also by the various kinds of talk therapy. Except for his occasional foray onto a nearby river in a small rowboat, he had no other interests. Essentially, he entered the university library one September day and emerged years later an M.D. Another four years at London University, and he was a board-certified psychiatrist, armed for battle with the Entity.

Through his various residencies, his supervisors noted the young doctor's particular affinity for depressed patients; his evaluations were uniformly excellent. His final residency was at the Kensington Clinic, where at the end of six months he was offered a staff position. He was dedicated, sensitive, and up-to-the-minute on the latest medications. His results spoke for themselves.

His first year was all work and success. Somehow along the way he found time to court Dorothy Miller, a nurse at the hospital. She found him a gentle and amusing bundle of nervous tics, what with his shoulder rolling and head shaking, and she admired him. For his part, he found Dorothy attractive and liked it that she forced him to go to the occasional movie or dinner out, insisting that he live like a human being now and again.

It was during his second year as a full-fledged psychiatrist that he began to experience difficulties. Even thirty years later he remembered the first time the change had really taken hold. For some weeks he had been having more and more trouble listening to his patients. He would suddenly be startled to find they were asking him a question and he hadn't heard it. Or they had just finished telling him something important and he had not responded. The patient would be sitting there looking at him expectantly and he hadn't a clue what for.

Then one day a middle-aged man, married twelve years and a father of three, was telling him how deathly depressed he was, how he woke each morning with a groan and a curse because he could not face another day. And Bell felt a surge of anger in his belly. He couldn't account for it; it seemed quite anomalous. His life was going well, he enjoyed his work, and his patient had said nothing in particular to irk him, and yet he had felt anger radiating up from his belly and into his chest—so much so that he had a split-second fantasy of crossing the room and grabbing the man by his collar and shaking him. Hard.

That day, the feeling passed quickly, but these surges became more and more frequent. And it wasn't just this one patient who provoked them; it was all his patients—at least, all the depressed ones. It was an alarming development that threatened to become debilitating, and he was afraid to discuss it with any of his colleagues.

It became increasingly uncomfortable for him even to face his patients. He could not bear to hear how they hated themselves. Could not bear to hear them summarize their lives with deep derision. Could not bear to hear how the future held nothing for them, how they were sick of everything, sick of themselves. Especially themselves. It was torture.

And then one day it happened. The anger broke through.

Edgar Vail was a thirty-six-year-old commercial artist, admitted to the clinic after he had tried to kill himself by drowning, only to discover that he was a better swimmer than he remembered. There was suicide in his family's past, and the isolation of life in the present. Contributing factors were the sorrows of a recent divorce and a series of career disappointments. Plenty to be sad about, in other words.

He wanted to paint serious art. In fact, he did paint serious pictures; he just couldn't get a gallery to handle his work or a single soul outside his immediate circle of friends to buy anything. He was going on about it, staring at the floor and shaking his head and mumbling that he didn't know why he bothered painting at all, he should just throw away his brushes and give up entirely. It was a perfect mirror of his romantic life, he went on, all this effort, all this struggle, and nothing to show for it.

"Why don't you just kill yourself?" Bell burst out. "Why not just do yourself in and make a thorough job of it this time?"

Vail looked up sharply. The shock in his usually haunted eyes frightened Bell.

He had tried to recover, saying, "Well, I mean, I certainly didn't intend it to sound so harsh. I just meant, there you were, you had a bottle full of Seconal at home, and yet you jump into water knowing perfectly well you can swim. My point being that you could have ended all this pain, this terrible pain you suffer from, right there with a few pills and yet you chose not to. Why don't we concentrate on what was behind that choice?"

The shock had dwindled in Vail's eyes.

"I thought for a second there you were actually attacking me."

"Good heavens, no. Last thing on earth I want to do. Please continue."

The reassurance seemed to work. Vail sank back into the couch and into the comfortable assumption that his psychiatrist was trying to help him.

Over the next few months, Bell set himself the task of learning to hide the anger. He tried reminding himself of happy events just before he had a scheduled session. That didn't work; he simply forgot them in the face of his patients' misery. He tried exercise, taking up rowing again. It made his muscles ache so much that his temper actually became worse—with everybody, not just patients.

But eventually he mastered his anger by training himself not to feel it. The way he did this was to behave just like any other psychiatrist. It came to him one afternoon when he was about to go rowing. He stopped, the oars in his hands, and sat down heavily on a bench beside the water.

The Thames shimmered, silver fringed with fire in the last of the afternoon light. He heard the lapping water, the breeze through the leaves, and all the million individual traffic noises. For some moments he had the sense that he was hearing a conversation taking place blocks away. A moment of hideous confusion, one might think, but Bell recognized it as absolute razor-sharp clarity.

What he had realized in that instant was that you could use the tools of therapy in a brand-new way, just as a surgeon might choose to employ his blade. You could ask the same questions, raise your eyebrows in just the same way, show great empathy, positive regard, all the rest of it. And yet you could skew it all just slightly, change the angle by a few degrees, and you could steer your patient in quite a different direction.

The next time Edgar Vail left his office, with a prescription for yet more sedatives, Bell spoke aloud to his booklined walls.

"Kill yourself and get it over with, you pathetic waste of space."

The words seemed to echo in the empty room, and Bell felt giddy. He began to laugh. It was all so simple; why hadn't he seen it before? He laughed with surprise, with shock, with recognition, but also with the sheer hilarity of relief.

IT WAS AMAZING how easy it was. Pick a patient who is desperately unhappy, take a few sessions to establish trust and empathy, then prescribe a month's supply of sleeping pills. Barbiturates, they were, back then. Handled correctly, absolutely lethal.

In certain cases, like Edgar Vail's, where the patient was

consumed with self-loathing and yet still fully functional, you had to be sure they were aware of the right dosage. Too much—as Bell knew from his mother's experience—and they throw up, possibly surviving. Too little, and they just get a bad hangover.

In other cases, where a patient was prostrate with the inarticulate grief that had eaten his father alive, Bell had to be a little more artful. In these cases what he did was schedule them for a Monday or Tuesday and send them home with a scrip for one of the tricyclics, something fast-acting. Come the weekend, the patient has the energy to pick up the gun, to climb to the roof, to tie the noose. It was like lighting a fuse. Of the first twenty suicides under his care, probably half came to their end this way. Another twenty-five percent (including Edgar Vail) chose sedatives. The rest had been so far gone they probably would have killed themselves anyway. Bell didn't take credit for those.

But there were problems with the pharmaceutical approach. The simple fact was that it was *too* easy. Really, the drugs did all the work; any psychiatrist could have managed it. Also, it was risky. A large prescription for sedatives does not look good in the medical history of a suicidal patient, as the "wake-up-and-die" effect of tricyclics is well known. He got into a spot of trouble in Swindon over this. Later on, in Manchester, there had been rumors of an inquiry, but that was about his mortality rate, not about overprescribing per se. In any case, Bell had thought it prudent to move to Canada. He had long ago eased up on the chemicals and now relied solely on his skills as a therapist.

31

Melanie Greene had only a few weeks to live; that was Dr. Bell's professional estimate. She had done her homework this time, bringing in three—count 'em, three!—suicide notes. Not that he would need them. If he couldn't manipulate a miserable teenager into topping herself, he might as well take down his shingle. There would be no mistakes this time.

She told him about driving to her stepfather's place, about her plan to tell his new wife about his sexual proclivities, and how seeing the little girl had prevented her. Such failure of nerve was typical with Melanie and might prove a minor obstacle in getting her to make a decent exit. But only minor.

"What made you stop?" Bell said. "You were going to tell his new wife, why not tell his new daughter what he had done?"

"Well, she's only around six years old, for one thing. Maybe seven."

"You didn't think a six-year-old should hear about such things?"

"No, of course not."

"These things that were done to you at a similar age? When you were seven?"

"I don't think little kids should even know about them, let alone do them. I mean, do *you* think people should be talking to six-year-olds about oral sex?"

"It's *your* feelings that matter, Melanie."

"Well, I'm not gonna talk to a little kid about that stuff. But the reason I stopped was just pure shock. I mean, bad enough the Bastard's married again, and he's probably going to put this woman through hell. But to have another little kid. I was just, like, stunned. I nearly got run over by a car. She's going to go through everything I went through—on those fishing trips, on the boat, at WonderWorld."

Dr. Bell felt his control slipping. There was a sudden heat in his hands and he realized he was imagining choking her, shaking her, screaming in her face. *Can't you see? You don't belong here. Do us all a favor and kill yourself once and for all.* It was a struggle to quiet the pounding in his chest. He decided to take Melanie out of the present and back to her traumas.

"What was the worst part of it? Back then, back when you were a little girl. What was truly the worst? Was it the physical pain?"

Melanie shook her head.

She'll start chewing her knuckles in a minute, Bell thought.

As if he had willed it, her left hand rose to her mouth and paused there as she gnawed on a knuckle.

"There wasn't usually any physical pain. Just once or twice when he, when he . . . you know. Oh, God. From behind."

"Anal sex?"

"Um, yeah."

"Did you bleed?"

She shook her head, stared at her feet. Bell saw her shiver as the Entity slipped into the room. The shadowed, hooded figure composed of ice and death folded the young woman under his caped arm.

"He was usually very careful that way," Melanie said. "And mostly it was oral. My lips would be numb. Sometimes I was sore between my legs. A few times, when I couldn't sleep, my mother asked me what was wrong, and I wanted to tell her. Oh, I wanted to tell her so bad."

"But you didn't."

"No."

"Because . . ."

"Because I was too afraid. He told me if anyone found

out, the Children's Aid would come and take me away. And he would go to prison."

"So it wasn't the physical pain that was the worst. Would you say it was the fear, then?"

Melanie nodded, hugging herself as if it were freezing in the room, though in fact the sunlight through the windows had overheated the office.

"I was afraid all the time. I was terrified of being found out."

"Because of the consequences you just mentioned?"

"Yes. But also—this was later, when I was thirteen or so— I was afraid of Mom finding out. Because I knew it would hurt her. And because I knew I was taking something that was hers. I was doing something wrong to my own mother."

"You were sleeping with her husband."

That should open the spigot, Bell thought, noting the gulping movement in her throat.

"It's like I was the other woman. It's—"

The tears would not be stopped. They burst from her with pitiful cries.

Dr. Bell handed her the Kleenex box and waited. He marveled at the power of guilt. Properly administered, it was far more potent than any drug.

When there came a lull in Melanie's sobs, he said, "So you had to deal with the fear. You had to deal with the guilt of stealing your mother's man. It's a lot for a little girl to cope with. But let's go back to WonderWorld. Something you said earlier made me think that WonderWorld might be the worst, but we haven't gone into any detail yet."

Melanie nodded. Tears had reddened her eyes, streaked her makeup. The Entity had transformed her into a rag doll.

Generally, in therapy, patients are allowed to move at their own speed. It's usually counterproductive to push, the risks being twofold: either the material is too much for patients to digest, causing them to develop an even thicker armor of denial, or it can unleash a torrent of emotion for which they are not adequately prepared. Depending on the presenting neurosis, this can result in any number of ways of acting out: running away, rages, and, of course, suicide.

And so Dr. Bell prompted his patient for detail. Melanie was young and passionate and had a strong drive to be rid of her pain. He knew he could count on that.

"First, let me be sure I understand you correctly. You were dying to go on all the rides at WonderWorld, and that's exactly what he promised you. So you get down there, he has you in a hotel room, and he won't let you go on the rides until you satisfy him. For you to get the rides, you had to give him sex."

"Right."

"You hinted at this, I think, when you said he had asked you ahead of time for a list of your favorite rides. Sort of a Christmas list. You mentioned the Tilt-A-Whirl."

"That's right. If I wanted to go on the Tilt-A-Whirl he, uh . . ."

"Take your time, Melanie."

She pulled out the whole array of delaying tactics: looked at her feet, examined her fingernails, heaved deep sighs, stared out the window, looked at the clock. Finally, when there was no option left short of complete catatonia, she said—and this in a voice so tiny Bell had to lean forward to catch it—"If I wanted to go on the Tilt-A-Whirl, I had to give him oral sex."

Her right hand rose, fanlike, to cover her face.

"So, it was like a contract. A negotiation, perhaps."

A shake of the head. "There wasn't any negotiating. He just told me the way things were. I was seven years old, for God's sake. I didn't question him. He was my father. I thought of him as my father, anyway. He'd been living with us a couple of years by then."

"And did he get what he wanted?"

"Yes."

"And you got the Tilt-A-Whirl."

"Yes."

Bell let her weep again, watched the face crumple and the

mucus run, listened to the ugly cries. He didn't let it go on too long; he needed the momentum.

"And there was the waterslide," he said. "I believe you indicated that that was on your list."

Melanie nodded. "I'm feeling a little sick. Do you think maybe . . ."

"Would you like to lie down? Sometimes going over old pain can be overwhelming."

"Um, maybe I will." Melanie got up unsteadily. "It seems like such a cartoon—you know, lying on a psychiatrist's couch—you see jokes about it all the time. But I'm feeling really dizzy."

"Lie down, then. No jokes, I promise."

She lay down gingerly, feet politely hanging off to one side. She took one of the cushions and was about to place it on the floor, thought better of it, and placed it over her genital region. Sometimes patients could be so eloquent without knowing it. A shaft of sunlight made her hair shine.

"You were talking about the waterslide."

"Yeah. I really wanted the waterslide. I think the single most fun I ever had as a kid was flying down that slide. It's such a thrill, but it feels completely safe at the same time."

"What did he suggest you do in exchange?"

"He didn't *suggest* anything. There wasn't any maybe about it. He just laid down the law."

"But didn't you say he told you that if you wanted to go on one ride, you'd have to do this? If you wanted to go on another ride, you'd have to do that? Wasn't he in effect giving you a menu of choices?"

"I suppose so."

"And you chose the waterslide?"

"Right."

"Chose it. You weren't forced to go on it, were you?"

"I guess not. Oh, God."

"And what did it cost you? What was the going price of a ride on the waterslide that particular summer day?"

"I had to let him . . . well, intercourse, I guess."

"Full intercourse. Vaginal intercourse."

"Yeah."

"And you did that?"

He had to wait a long time while she wept.

"And then there was the Wild Mouse," Bell said. "Your absolute favorite, you said. You couldn't wait to go on it."

"Anal sex," she said, just like that, her voice dead. "If I wanted to go on the Wild Mouse, he had to get anal sex."

"And did he?"

"Yes. He turned me into a little whore. Just turning eight and already a prostitute."

"Keep in mind, Melanie, the age of consent in this country is fourteen years old. Almost twice the age you were."

It cost Bell a lot to say that, and Melanie received it like balm. He could see the effect right away: her lower lip began to quiver. It cost him, but anything less might have struck her as callous, which could provoke anger and resistance he would only have to break down again. So if a little kindness and understanding added a week or two until end-game, that was just the price of being a professional.

"That's in Canada," he went on, "and a lot of people in this country think the age of consent should be much higher. In most other places, it is. In the U.K., anyone under sixteen is considered to be incapable of giving an informed consent. You were seven, Melanie. Not even eight years old."

"It's not like I didn't know what he was doing. By the time he took me to WonderWorld, he'd already introduced me to all of it."

"Nevertheless, Melanie, we're talking about rape here."

"All right."

It was hard, sometimes, to be so comforting. It went against the grain, felt as if he were working against himself. But it was also necessary. They had to believe you were on their side, that you were saving them from themselves.

"So, would you say, then, we've gotten to the worst of things, Melanie? He made you feel like the other woman. And he made you feel like a whore. It's as if he turned WonderWorld into a house of horrors."

She sat up suddenly, gripping the edges of the couch.

"WonderWorld wasn't the worst," she said. "Despite everything that happened there? WonderWorld wasn't the worst, not by a long shot."

"I must have misunderstood, then. You're telling me there were other times, other places, when your stepfather did even worse things to you?"

"No. Not things he did. WonderWorld was as bad as it got, physically. But he did those same things to me in other places. Even at home, if you want to know the truth. Even in my mother's bed, sometimes. Can you imagine? That bastard. In my mother's bed. But even that wasn't the worst." She lay back again, her rib cage rising and falling with labored breathing. "The worst was the boat."

"The fishing trips you mentioned before? The camping and so on?"

Melanie shook her head. "No. This was a different boat. A beautiful cabin cruiser. I think he must have borrowed it, or maybe he was looking after it for someone. It was just a couple of times, when I was about eleven. There was the time my mother was on the boat. But there was another time when it was just me and him. It was toward the end of the whole business. He took a lot of pictures."

"Sexual poses like before?"

"Some of them were normal. I guess so he could show them to Mom—you know, 'Here we are still in the marina. Here we are at the island.' But a lot of them were completely pornographic. I just hope to God he didn't put them on the Internet. That's all I need, for someone I know to come across them."

"Do you think that's likely?"

"I don't know. He used to spend a lot of time on his computer. I mean, you hear about stuff like that."

"Tell me more about the boat. What do you remember most, when you think about those times?"

"Lying in the bed at night. It was Trout Lake, you know, dead calm most of the time. And once it got quiet, dead dark. The rocking was just so gentle, it was like you were suspended in some warm sweet place where nothing bad could ever happen to you. And yet . . ."

Dr. Bell let her have the hesitation. Her momentum toward revelation was palpable.

"And yet," she said again. "Oh, I feel sick, remembering. . . ."

"You're safe here. Truly safe. Not like the boat."

She looked up at him. "You know what I think about all this stuff, don't you? I mean, you know that I know it was wrong. That it was sick and perverted and illegal and all the rest of it."

"Yes, I know you think that. But just because a thought occurs to you doesn't make it true."

That one went right by her, as he knew it would. She was turned so inward at this moment, he could have nominated her for sainthood and she wouldn't have heard it.

"Like I say. It felt wonderful to lie there in the dark. To listen to the little waves against the hull, I guess you call it. To hear the breeze flapping the little pennants on the back of the boat. It should have been the most peaceful, restful feeling in the world. But there's no way I could sleep. He was in his bed on one side of the cabin, I was in mine on the other. It was hot, so I was wearing just pajama bottoms, and he never wore anything to bed; he always let it all hang out. So quiet, but I couldn't sleep a wink. I was completely tense and wide awake."

And it wasn't because you were afraid, that you couldn't sleep, Dr. Bell was almost tempted to say aloud. It wasn't because you were afraid of what he would do, and it wasn't because you wanted your mother. That wasn't why you couldn't sleep. Eleven, twelve years old, doesn't matter. It wasn't because you were angry. I know exactly why you couldn't sleep. The only question is whether you can bear to reveal it to me. To reveal the worst part of yourself and have it accepted, not judged, was the very crux of therapy. Without those moments there is no therapy, no progress, no healing; there's just talk. Hours and hours of talk.

Bell's voice was as soft as it could be while remaining audible, the gentlest beckoning:

"Can you tell me why, Melanie? Can you tell me why you

couldn't sleep? What were the feelings that kept you awake?"

"Well, um . . . I knew it was going to happen. I mean, it always did, whenever he had me alone. Especially at night."

"You were a child, Melanie."

"I was eleven years old! Maybe twelve! I should have known better by then!"

"Why? How could you have known? Did someone hand out an instruction manual, 'How to Tell Mom That Your Stepfather Rapes You'? Have you ever observed twelve-year-old girls on the street? At the movies? Wherever?"

"Well, yes. . . ."

"And what are they like?"

"Airheads, most of them. Complete ditzes."

"Kids, in other words."

"Kids. Right."

"So there you are, eleven years old, maybe twelve, a child lying in the dark in this completely safe and secret environment with a man who professes to love you. Maybe in his way did love you. No one else is around. What was that little girl feeling?"

"I'm going to be sick."

"Feel like you're going to throw up?"

A tight nod. She's pale and quivering, gripping the edge of the couch.

"It's the words you need to throw up, Melanie. The secrets. Tell me this one thing and the feeling will pass, I promise."

"No, I'm really going to be sick."

"You're lying in the dark. You're eleven or twelve. There's a full-grown man beside you. You know he's going to come over to your bed. You know what he's going to do to you. What are you feeling? Tell me this one thing, Melanie, and the nausea will pass. You know he's going to come to you. What are your feelings before he crosses that dark space and comes over to your bed?"

"He didn't! That's just it, don't you see? He didn't come over to me!"

"What happened, then, Melanie? Tell me."

"I can't! I can't! I don't want to!"

"Yes, you do. You wouldn't be here otherwise."

"Please. I just can't."

"He didn't come over to you, you said. He didn't come over to you . . . and then?"

"I can't."

"He didn't come over to you. . . ."

"Oh, God."

"He didn't come over to you, and . . ."

"I went over to him!"

The tears that came from her then drowned all the tears that had gone before. In all his years as a psychiatrist, Dr. Bell had never seen anyone cry harder.

"I wanted it! I'm so sick! I'm so sick! I wanted him to do it! I wanted him to do it! I did it to him! I did it to him that time, do you see? Oh, God, I deserve to die, I'm such a fucking whore!"

Bell watched her cry and cry until there were no tears left.

"I'm so sick," she said weakly. "Really, I don't know why I'm still walking around." She looked smaller, as if guilt had taken up physical space in her small frame.

"I'm afraid that's all we have time for today."

"Oh, God."

"Stay another minute or two, if you like."

"No, no. That's okay. I'm all right."

Melanie smoothed her hair and stood up, tottering a little. She gathered her things, still sniffling, and moved toward the door. She opened it, then stopped.

"God. I don't know how I'm going to make it till next week."

"Oh, that reminds me. Sorry, Melanie, I should have told you at the top of the hour."

"Told me what?"

"I'm not going to be available next week."

32

After lunch, Cardinal took the note with its thumbprint to the station to speak to Paul Arsenault. He was not yet ready to declare himself officially back at work. If he did, there would be a stack of assignments he would be expected to deal with, and pursuit of non-police business would become difficult if not impossible.

Arsenault took a swig from a coffee mug bearing his last name under the Acadian flag. "You want me to run this for you on the q.t.?"

"You know it's not orthodox," Cardinal said. "It's not officially a case."

"You're right, John. It's not."

The use of his first name was a bad sign. The use of his first name meant pity or maybe even something worse. Arsenault would have heard about his arrest of Roger Felt. He put his patriotic mug down, got up from his desk, and closed the door that separated Ident from the evidence room and the rest of the station.

"Look, John. You come to me with this, your wife's suicide note, and ask me to run prints. I want to help. Of course I want to help. And I'll do it if you really want me to. But the coroner looked into this. Delorme looked into it. The pathologist. We all looked into it. There's just no reason to think anyone else was involved."

"So humor me. Do it out of pity, I don't care. As long as it gets done. I want to know who touched that note other than Catherine."

"But it's not a fake, John, you said so yourself."

"All the more reason why there shouldn't be any fingerprints on it other than Catherine's."

"Suppose it comes back and it's the coroner's thumbprint? Where's that gonna get anyone?"

"If the coroner or some uniform made a mistake, fine. People make mistakes, I don't care about mistakes."

Arsenault gave it a beat, contemplating the last of his coffee. "You really think she was killed, John?"

"I think someone else read that note. I want to know who."

"ALL RIGHT, KIDS. Take ten!"

Eleanor Cathcart came down from the stage wiping imaginary sweat from her brow and sat down in the front row of the Capital Centre auditorium. Cardinal had been here many times as a kid, back when it had been the biggest movie theater in town.

"My God, we open tomorrow night and our Torvald still has a closer relationship to the prompter than he does to me. What brings you here? I'm so sorry about Catherine, by the way. That woman will be *missed*."

"I just wanted to talk to you," Cardinal said. "You were the last person to see Catherine alive." *As far as we know*.

"Yes, I feel in some way responsible. If only I hadn't raved about my wonderful views! If only I hadn't let her in! If only I'd stayed!"

"It must be very hard on you."

"Well, I carry on, you know, but it does have a dampening effect on one's joie de vivre. I have of late and wherefore I know not lost all my mirth, so to speak, though of course I know very well wherefore. Catherine's gone; she'll come no more. I have already told your distaff colleague everything I know, of course."

"This is personal. I'm just trying to clarify a few things in my mind."

"Yes, of course, poor man." She laid a benevolent hand on his wrist. "I know exactly how you feel."

Cardinal asked the questions he knew Delorme would have already asked. Catherine had expressed interest in photographing the view from her apartment building; a date was arranged; Ms. Cathcart let her in and went off to rehearse with the Algonquin Bay Players.

"Did you see Catherine a lot? Up at school, I mean?"

"Not really. Just bumped into her now and again. Said hello. That kind of thing. We weren't palsy-walsy or anything. Just cordial. I admired her from a distance, I suppose you could say. There was something beautifully self-contained about Catherine."

That was true, Cardinal knew, when she was well.

"So you wouldn't know about her other relationships at the college."

"No. I have my own little province in Theatrical Arts. Doesn't overlap terribly much with photography."

"Did you ever see her with a stranger? Or anyone else that seemed out of place around the college?"

"No. She was usually alone or with students when I saw her."

"Did you ever see her upset with anyone? Or anyone upset with her?"

"Never. I mean, people worried about her, you must know that. And, well, sometimes other instructors had to fill in for her. But I'm sure they accepted that this was not a matter of caprice." Ms. Cathcart touched her forehead with elegant fingertips. "Of course, she did have rather a contretemps with Meredith Moore."

"Tell me about that," Cardinal said. He had heard Catherine's side of the story many times.

"Oh, it was just college politics as usual. Control of a department becomes available; out come the knives. Really, the Borgias have nothing on academics. When Sophie Klein got hired away by York University, both Catherine and Meredith wanted to run the art department. They were probably equally qualified: Catherine had more honors for her creative work, but Meredith had an edge in administrative experience. The stupid thing was, Meredith seemed to take it as a personal affront that Catherine would even apply. I mean, she seemed to think the crown should have just automatically descended upon her anointed head, God knows why.

"And Meredith was not above pointing out Catherine's—um, psychological vagaries as a disqualifying factor. There was even a rumor that the dean had received a copy of Catherine's medical records anonymously, but that something smacks of urban legend, at least to me. The outcome you know."

"Meredith got the job."

"And I always admired the way Catherine handled it. She never said a bad word about Meredith or expressed any resentment. But Meredith—"

"But Meredith what?"

Ms. Cathcart flashed a thin blade of smile. "You know what they say: people can never forgive you the wrongs they've done you. I'm sure Meredith would have loved to have Catherine replaced. She could barely stand to be in the same room after that and was always sniping at her behind her back. Dry old stick."

AND YET, WHEN he went to see her, Meredith Moore was graciousness personified. She clasped Cardinal's hand in both her woody little palms, looked him in the eye, and said, "It's such a shame about Catherine. Such a tragedy."

"Have you found somebody to teach her courses?"

"In the middle of the semester? Not likely. We have somebody filling in, but it's not the same as having the person who prepared the course."

"I've heard you weren't particularly happy with Catherine. That you were probably looking to replace her."

Meredith Moore had a brittle appearance at the best of times: hair that looked as if it might break off, and a face of fine crepe. Cardinal could almost hear the crackle as she set her mouth in a thin line.

"Whoever you heard that from," she said, "did not know what they were talking about. Catherine had nothing but excellent evaluations, and her photographs were highly respected."

"So you weren't looking to replace her."

"I was not."

"How would you characterize your relationship with Catherine? How did you get along?"

"Fine. We weren't close friends, but I'd say we had a collegial relationship. I have to say, I know you're a policeman and maybe the manner sticks with you whether you want it to or not, but this feels very much like an interrogation."

"You said Catherine's student reviews were excellent. Do you know if there was any student in particular who was giving her trouble? Someone who might have taken offense at a low grade?"

"Not that I know of. And I rather doubt it. She was a good teacher but an easy marker. Some people are too severe, some are lenient. I try to be somewhere in the middle myself. Catherine was on the lenient side, I think she'd agree with me on that."

That was true, Cardinal knew. Catherine hated to give anyone who made the least effort a bad grade and would get upset when she had no choice.

"Did you ever have a student come in here, upset, and ask you to change a grade Catherine had given?"

"No. Mind you, it's too early in the semester for people to be worried about failing."

"Catherine wanted to be chair of the department too."

"She certainly did. She made a strong case for herself."

"I imagine that could put quite a strain on your collegial relationship. Did it?"

"Is that what Catherine said?"

"I'm asking you."

"It's safe to say it made us both a little tense. That's understandable, don't you think? I don't imagine the police department is free of competition."

"Well, no one's gone off a roof so far."

Ms. Moore's mouth opened with an audible snap. "You think she killed herself because she didn't get chair?"

"No, I don't."

"Good. Because she showed no ill effects from it that I'm

aware of. And Catherine was a—well, a sensitive soul, wouldn't you say?"

"Yes. Did you see her the day she died?"

"I saw her in the hall here, around lunchtime. She was heading into her noon class."

"What about in the evening?"

"She doesn't teach on Tuesday evenings."

"That isn't what I asked."

Ms. Moore was turning red, but from the set of her mouth it was the heat of anger, not embarrassment.

"The answer is no."

"Were you here at the school?"

"I was at home watching *Antiques Roadshow*. Look, I don't know how to say this to you. I'm sorry about what happened to Catherine, I truly am. But my sympathy does not extend to being cross-questioned like a criminal."

"I realize that," Cardinal said, and headed for the exit. "Criminals don't like it either."

33

Dorothy Bell was bundling up the newspapers for the recycling when an article caught her eye. She spread the paper out on the kitchen table and peered at it nearsightedly. According to the article, over two hundred mourners had attended Perry Dorn's funeral. Perry Dorn, it said, a recent graduate of Northern University, had had many friends and the respect of his professors. The newspaper quoted several people who had known him.

"He was a very generous guy," one said. "Whatever Perry had, he'd share it with you. Even when he was broke."

"Always looking out for others," said another.

"A very sharp intellect," according to a professor of mathematics. "You had to work hard to keep up with Perry."

The reason the *Algonquin Lode* was giving the funeral so much space, of course, was that Perry Dorn had shocked the community by blowing his brains out in a Laundromat.

Long subject to depression, the paper said.

"But lately he seemed to be getting better," said a fellow student. "He was looking forward to doing graduate work in Montreal. He was very excited about McGill."

One of the subheads read ROMANTIC REVERSALS, and under this a former roommate stated that Perry Dorn had had a tendency to become emotionally entangled with unattainable women. "The shame of it was, he could have had lots of girlfriends. There were lots of girls who would have gladly gone out with him, he was so smart and gentle. But he always went for the ones who weren't interested. Then he'd get depressed and wouldn't eat or sleep or even talk for days. It could get kinda spooky."

Shelly Lanois, the young man's sister, said only, "We're all too devastated to comment."

The name Perry Dorn didn't mean anything to Dorothy Bell, but she might have recognized his face in the picture sooner had he not been wearing the graduation cap. It hid his prematurely thinning hair, but it did not hide the scrawny chicken neck, the outsized Adam's apple, the deep-set mournful eyes of the young man she had seen several times in the waiting area outside her husband's office.

The moment she did recognize him, her heart began to pound. A young man on the verge of graduate school chooses instead to end his life—and in a spectacular manner. A young man who had many reasons to be happy and optimistic. A young man who had been a patient of her husband's.

When Dorothy had first met Frederick—well over thirty years ago now—she had been deeply impressed by his intelligence. She was no slouch herself, winning excellent marks in nursing school, but he had the kind of brilliance she had known she would never possess. He was dark and handsome—no beard, no specs—with a charming array of nervous tics. Even in his twenties he was a bit of a star at the London hospital where they worked.

When one day he asked her to go out to dinner with him, she had trouble forming the words to answer him. She turned around to look behind herself, to see if there were some other young doctors in the hallway who were in on the joke. But there was no one.

Neither of them had any money in those days. He took her to an American-style joint on the King's Road with jukeboxes and bottles of Heinz ketchup in each booth. Hamburgers were an exotic treat in London in those days. Long after they were married, Bell told her that the place had turned out to be much more expensive than he had anticipated. He had had just enough to cover the meal, no tip.

"Never dared set foot in there again," he liked to tell friends when he recounted the story. "Too embarrassed."

From the first, Dorothy enjoyed his intelligence and his sense of humor. He liked her sensitivity and the way she could transform a dreary duplex apartment into a real home. They were so contented, they saw no reason to disrupt the pleasantness of their life with children. That, at least, was the way Frederick had put it. Dorothy would have liked to try, but she sensed from things he said that he was not a man who would enjoy fatherhood.

She could still think back on those first few years with nostalgia. They amused themselves with weekend forays to obscure English villages and the odd walking tour.

Gradually—she couldn't have said when it started exactly—the early happiness began to be marred by a certain instability in Frederick's professional life. He had been overjoyed to be on the staff of the Kensington Clinic; it had a great reputation, and he was lucky to be there. But after only eighteen months he'd suddenly announced that they were moving to Swindon, where he was going to join the Swindon General Hospital. It was a pleasant enough place to work, and Dorothy enjoyed the other nurses there, but it had seemed a considerable step down. This was not a view she aired aloud.

It was while at Swindon that Frederick was investigated for overprescribing. As he had explained it to her, all he had done was prescribe a tricyclic for a depressed patient, hardly an exotic line of treatment, but the patient had almost immediately swallowed a bottle of sleeping pills, also prescribed by Dr. Bell. The bereaved family claimed Bell had ignored obvious cries for help, that the boy should have been hospitalized. The hospital's inquiry merely found him somewhat lax in follow-up and gave him a reprimand. Even so, he had been outraged.

"Idiots," he had cried. "Morons! What do they know? Depressed people kill themselves all the time. For all they know, that kid would have been dead months ago if it wasn't for me. Suicide is what depressed people do. Hiding their intentions is also what depressed people do. They get good at it. If the charge is that I failed to read his mind, fine. I plead guilty."

Of course, reading minds is exactly a psychiatrist's job, Dorothy thought, even at the time. But Frederick was her husband and she stood by him, sharing his outrage. The young doctor had been so grateful that this early adversity strengthened their marriage.

Despite this episode, Frederick managed to find himself a better position soon after, this time in Lancashire, at the Manchester Centre for Mental Health. It suited him much better. They became active in the community, made many friends, gave enviable parties. Just when Dorothy had begun to think they were really set, really secure, the Centre informed them there would be another inquiry into Frederick's practice. The hospital had become concerned by the number of suicides among the patients under his care.

But it was brief and largely exculpatory. No abnormalities were found in his prescribing. If anything, he made less use of drugs than his contemporaries.

"We overprescribe, in my opinion," he told the committee. "I believe the optimum treatment for depression to be a combination of psychotherapy and medication. Neither alone is enough, not for severe cases, but the risks of relying on medication are high, because the treatment proceeds at the speed of the drug rather than at the speed of the patient's capacity to heal."

In this, he was ahead of his time. By then he was known as one of the foremost authorities in England on the causes and treatment of depression. He took on a herculean caseload and specialized almost exclusively in depression. This, the review committee noted, was bound to result in a high number of suicides among his patients.

Still, Frederick had been offended by the whole debacle. "The insult, the ingratitude," he said, over and over again. "The incredible stupidity. They have to mount a committee of inquiry to discover the obvious: sad people kill themselves."

Soon after, the couple had emigrated. Despite the hospital's clearing of her husband, Dorothy had found her faith in his abilities shaken. She knew enough of hospital politics to know that the administration would be quite capable of keeping a lid on scandal. When, in the course of packing, she discovered a letter from the National Health Service announcing that it was beginning proceedings for yet another investigation—this one into the entire term of his practice from Swindon to Manchester—she had been thoroughly shocked.

The letter was dated just after the Manchester investigation, and yet Frederick had said nothing.

She could not bring herself to discuss it with him. She did not want him calling her *idiot, moron, fool.* But from the moment of their arrival in Toronto, Dorothy Bell had told herself that, without snooping, she would keep a closer eye on what happened with her husband's caseload. Obviously, patient confidentiality precluded her knowing the names of most of his patients. Occasionally, though, she would overhear him on the phone. And a couple of times, when someone had died, he had said to her, "Patient of mine. Poor fella."

She noticed that he clipped the obituaries.

Frederick never took to Toronto, and after a short stint at the Queen Street Mental Health Centre he had accepted a post with the Ontario Hospital at Algonquin Bay. He told his wife he was sick of city living, that he wanted to live in a smaller town, and she had no reason to disbelieve him.

That had been two years ago. Since then Dorothy had become aware of three suicides under her husband's care: Leonard Keswick, a social services administrator; Catherine Cardinal, a teacher and photographer; and now this Perry Dorn. All three had been in the paper, one because he had been charged with a crime, one because she had been found dead next to a brand-new building, and the last one because he had killed himself in such a public manner. It was hard to admit, but Dorothy knew it was likely there were more.

And this young man, this Perry Dorn. Why had Frederick not mentioned that he had been a patient? It had been all over the news and the local paper. An expression of shock or dismay might have been in order, but he had said nothing, not a word.

Dorothy put the article aside and finished tying up the last of the newspapers. It was time to do the grocery shopping, before the late afternoon rush. On her way out, she paused in front of Frederick's closed office door. You couldn't hear much through solid oak, but she could hear his voice and quieter responses from a patient. He didn't have a patient now; the next one wasn't due for another half hour. No, he was watching a recording of a session. He did that a lot.

She had asked him about it once. Why did he go over his sessions so much?

"Self-improvement," he said, in his jaunty way. "You're never too old to get better. When I replay sessions, I see subtle cues I missed, body language I didn't notice at the time. And, of course, it helps me remember things better."

It's gone way past self-training, she thought as she locked the front door behind her. Frederick now spent every spare minute watching his recordings, retiring to his office late at night when other people might be reading or watching television or getting ready for bed.

There was something unhealthy about it.

34

Police Chief R. J. Kendall did not tend to be a harsh man. Cardinal had seen him give members of the force second, third, even fourth chances when he himself would have yanked badges and guns. But Kendall was also inconsistent to the point where you wondered if inconsistency was a policy with him, a way to keep staff on their toes. When provoked, he would shout abuse loud enough that the whole station could hear. Then a week later he'd be saying what a good job the former malefactor was doing.

Kendall was seated in his big leather chair now, the light from the window behind him turning his thinning silver hair into a dull halo. He had not asked Cardinal to sit down.

"It's not that I'm unsympathetic," he said. "If my wife were to die in similar circumstances—God forbid—I would probably be tempted to do the same thing."

"Chief, I saw her just three hours before. She was fine. She was looking forward to working on her project. Not the kind of thing you expect from someone about to do herself in."

"We have a coroner's finding of suicide."

"A young doctor. Inexperienced as a coroner."

"You read the note yourself. You identified the writing. I don't think we have to go into her history, do we?"

"She was doing fine, Chief. She was not in any emotional distress."

"Delorme, McLeod, Szelagy—all of them were there with the coroner. None of them found anything inconsistent with suicide. Nor did the pathologist. There is nothing to investigate. We have no case."

"Her note was written months ago. I had a guy in Documents confirm it."

"Which you should not have done," the chief said, a warning flush of crimson forming at his jawline. "That's called a misuse of police resources. We have no case."

"In order to believe it was suicide, you have to believe that she wrote a note three months ago. That she went on with her life as usual, giving no sign of her intentions. Then one night, in the middle of a photographic project, she takes along the note to leave at the scene before jumping off the roof."

"We have *no case*!" Kendall was on his feet now, his face a brilliant cardiac red. He was not a tall man, but he made up in decibels what he lacked in centimeters. "You will not come in here and tell me how the entire law enforcement community is wrong and you are right. And you will refrain from cross-questioning the chair of a college department as if she were a member of the mob! Do I make myself clear?"

"Chief, there are reasonable grounds to—"

"You were not even on the job, Cardinal, you were on leave. And you interrogated this woman as if she were a subject in a murder case. But there is *no such case*! Your behavior would be out of line if she were a streetwalker, if she were a drug dealer. But Meredith Moore is chair of a college department and you do not interrogate such people when you have no warrant, no justification, and *no case*!"

Cardinal started to speak, but the chief raised a traffic-stopping hand.

"I don't want you to go out of here thinking this is going to be a matter where I'm going to give you another chance. It isn't. You want to be back at work, fine, you're back at work. But you are here to pursue cases that I and your detective sergeant approve. Everything else is unlawful use of police resources, and I will not tolerate it. Do you understand me?"

"Yes."

"Good. I hope this matter is now closed."

"I just have one question."

"What is it?"

"What would it take to make you open a case on Catherine?"

"More than you have."

WHEN HE RETURNED to his desk, Cardinal found new e-mail waiting for him.

To: parsenault, lburke, rcollingwood, ldelorme, imcleod, kszelagy
From: rjk

I know that you are all deeply saddened by John Cardinal's tragic loss, and I share that sadness. However, I must remind you that there has been a finding of suicide in the matter and as a result no police file has been opened. Therefore there is no investigation. I repeat, there is no investigation. Anyone using police resources to pursue a different finding is in breach of the Police Services Act and will be dealt with accordingly.

RJ Kendall
Chief of Police

Cardinal's own name was conspicuously absent from the address list; the message had been forwarded to him by Arsenault. Arsenault was now waving him over to the hallway connecting CID to Ident.

"I wanted to talk to you about the Zellers break-in," Arsenault said, loud enough for everyone to hear.

Cardinal followed him into Ident. Collingwood was out, and except for the two of them, the place was empty.

"I ran the print," Arsenault said.

"Obviously we can't talk about it right now."

"Why? The air belongs to Police Services?"

"The time does."

"It's okay. R.J. has left the building." He jerked a thumb toward the parking lot. "Just saw him take off in a limo."

"Thanks for forwarding the e-mail. I don't want to get anyone else in trouble."

"Forget it. R.J.'s a pussycat. Anyway, just wanted to let you know we came back negative on the thumbprint."

"Nothing at all?"

"Nothing local, nothing national. Total bust."

"All right. It was worth a try."

"I got a few more avenues I can explore. You want me to keep trying?"

"Just make sure R.J. doesn't find out."

Cardinal picked up his mail and phone messages and sat down at his desk. From a brass-framed photograph, Catherine smiled at him—the same smile that had sent his heart spinning way back when they had first met. Cardinal opened his middle drawer, put the picture inside, and closed the drawer.

He began sorting his in-box: notices to appear in court, office memos, notices of parole committee hearings, missives from his pension plan and the payroll department, and various unclassifiable material that went straight to the recycle bin.

He opened the middle drawer, took out the photograph, and set it once more in the corner.

"Are you really here this time?"

Delorme was dropping her briefcase onto her desk. She looked tired and frustrated, a slight pout forming on her mouth, but that was not unusual for her.

"I'm back," Cardinal said. "At least physically."

Delorme sat down and rolled her chair up close. "Let me tell you about a case that might take your mind off things."

"Oh, yeah?"

She began pulling file folders from her briefcase. "I've got a crime scene but no witnesses, no victim, and no perpetrator. How familiar are you with child porn?"

"Haven't had that many cases. Keswick: remember him?"

"Keswick was nothing. Get ready for a real stomach-turner."

35

Leonard Keswick leans forward on the couch, gripping and twisting a shredded tissue. He is a roughly spheroid man and looks weak and dispirited, like a partially deflated soccer ball. His eyes are large and watery, slightly protuberant—a bloodhound's eyes. He looks up mournfully at the unseen camera.

"I don't know what to do," he says. "I don't know where to turn with this problem."

"Well, you've turned here," Dr. Bell says, on-screen. "That's a start, isn't it?"

"Yes, but I don't seem to be getting over this. It's been months now, and I'm not getting any better."

Dr. Bell, watching this a year later, nodded his agreement. "Because you don't want to get better," he said quietly, although not on-screen. "You just won't admit it."

The office phone rang and Dr. Bell froze the image. He had set the voice mail to pick up on the first ring so he could monitor the message. He knew who it would be. She had already called twice, the second message considerably more distraught than the first.

"Dr. Bell? It's Melanie. Oh, God, you're probably at the hospital or with another patient. Please call me as soon as you get this. I'm feeling really, really bad."

"Of course you feel bad," Dr. Bell said to the room. "You always feel bad."

"I'm afraid I might really do it this time. I can't stop thinking about it."

Bell clasped his hands behind his head and spoke to the ceiling. "Sounds like real progress to me."

"Please call me when you get this. Please. I'm sorry. I just need—I just—please."

"Please-I just-please-I just-please-I just," Bell mimicked her. "Gimme, gimme, gimme. I, I, *I*."

"Something about seeing my stepfather again really put me over the edge. Everything is just black, absolutely black, and I can hardly breathe. Please give me a call when you get this."

There was a timid click as she hung up.

Bell sat back and pressed PLAY.

"What I can't get over," Keswick says, "is how helpless I am over this. And it came on so suddenly. I mean, I looked at porno magazines as a kid, same as everybody else. Looked at them right through college and even a little after. But magazines are different. Magazines, it's just normal: adult women, adult guys. It's not as if I went searching for the stuff I'm staring at these days!"

"I believe you," Dr. Bell says. "There are people addicted to eBay, to shopping online, gambling online—people who had no problems with these areas before the Internet came into their lives."

"Yes, because you used to have to go way out of your way to do them. Let's face it, it used to be difficult to be a shopaholic in Algonquin Bay. What are you going to do, buy up the entire collection of ski pants? Same with gambling. There's no casinos here. The most damage you could do to yourself was with the lottery. But this stuff is right in my home. It's as if they filled my drawers and closets with an endless supply of pictures."

"Is it just pictures?" Dr. Bell says on-screen.

"What?" Keswick looks bewildered, as if the doctor has suddenly addressed him in Farsi. "Well, yeah. I would never touch a kid. I never thought about kids sexually before. I still don't—not actual kids I see on the street. And I know the damage sexual abuse can cause. I would never do that to a kid. Never."

"Well, let's talk about exactly what it is you *are* doing."

"I'm looking at pictures. That's all. I get them from file-sharing sites."

"Do you ever post any pictures yourself?"

"God, no."

"Do you pay for the pictures you look at?"

"No. And I never would. That would be encouraging the whole enterprise."

"All right. So tell me, what is it you do that's so terrible? You haven't molested any children. You haven't taken pictures of any children. You haven't paid anyone else to take them. You haven't sent them to anyone."

"No, I just look at them. But it's sick! It's sick! I shouldn't be looking at them! Oh, God, I'm so ashamed. So ashamed."

Keswick is weeping now, tears filming his cheeks. He takes his glasses off and tries to put them on the table but drops them. He doesn't stoop to retrieve them, just sits there in a soggy rumpled heap, crying.

Finally, when he is able to speak again: "I have kids of my own, that's the real kicker. Jenny and Rob. They're three and five—younger than the pictures I'm looking at—but still, it makes me want to throw up. I can't imagine what I'd do if I found out someone was taking pictures of my kids. I think I would even be able to kill someone in that situation."

"This has been going on how long, a year? Eighteen months?"

"About eighteen months. It was, like, instantaneous with me. The minute I stumbled onto that site, it was like a lock turned inside me. Like these tumblers clanked into place and suddenly I go from being a more or less normal human to being a sex fiend. A pervert."

He cries again, and Dr. Bell watches him in silence.

"I've tried twelve-step, like you suggested. I found a site online. It's better than nothing, I guess, but it's only once a week and sometimes hardly anyone logs on. There's no sex addiction groups here that I know of. And even if there were, I could never tell them what I've been looking at."

"You've told me. Why couldn't you tell them?"

"That's different. You're a doctor. Our conversations are privileged. There might be people I knew at the meetings. I would die if this ever got out. Literally. I would have to kill myself."

"Well, perhaps we should work on reducing some of this shame you're suffering from."

"But it *is* shameful. What I do *is* shameful."

"Let me finish. With all addictions there's a cycle of shame that seems to operate. Take heroin, for example. An addict has resolved to quit using, but he's feeling a little nervous, a little jumpy. Eventually he goes out and buys some dope and shoots up. Magic. All that anxiety is gone. It's a powerful thing. But it wears off, of course, and then the addict is left with his shame at having used the drug again. Then he needs something to counteract the shame—and what's the first thing that comes to mind?"

"More dope."

"More dope. Exactly. And that's one of the reasons twelve-step programs enjoy some success. Being in a room full of people who accept you and your weakness, who even share it, is a powerful way to reduce shame. It's certainly a pity, as you say, that there's no such group here in town. Suppose we were to have a couple of sessions with your wife—"

"Never. Don't even think that. She doesn't even know I'm seeing you."

"But you've said many times you have a loving relationship with your wife. Wouldn't that love survive the possible disappointment of finding out you have an unfortunate weakness?"

"She would hate me. She would dump me. She would leave me and take the kids, and I'd never get to see any of them again."

"Are you sure?"

"Oh, yeah. I've heard her talk about it. You know, when there's a story in the paper or on TV, about a teacher or a priest or whatever. She's always completely disgusted. She says stuff like, 'Oh, they should boil that guy in oil.' 'They ought to castrate that man.'"

Dr. Bell is the calm voice of reason. "But priests, teachers—those are people who are responsible for lots of children. They're in positions of trust."

"Look, I work for ComSoc. Social assistance. I'm surrounded by social workers. You think they're going to tolerate having a child porno addict in their midst? I'd be out of there in five seconds."

"We were talking about your wife, not your colleagues. This would only be sharing the information with your wife. Is there not any possibility she was exaggerating her response to the stories you mentioned? One often says things like 'They ought to hang that man.' But one doesn't necessarily mean them."

"She may have been exaggerating. Meg isn't one to hold back her feelings. She may have been exaggerating about the punishments, castration and so on, but she wasn't exaggerating her disgust. I could hear contempt in every word. If she ever felt that kind of contempt toward me, I couldn't live with it. I'd sooner die, I swear. I'd sooner die."

Bell froze the image, savoring his patient's horrified gaze, his absolute helplessness, then hit the OFF button. Keswick had been a lamb to the slaughter. A little too easy, really, to be completely satisfying. Still, there was a neatness about it, an almost Greek inevitability, that one could appreciate.

The phone rang again.

"Hello, Melanie," Bell said, without picking up. "Little distressed, are we? Lurching toward an actual decision?"

"Dr. Bell, it's Melanie again. I know you said you'd be unavailable this week, but I thought you'd be checking messages. This is pretty critical—"

He could hear a sniffle, loud and wet. He got up and took the DVD out of the player, slipping it into a numbered sleeve.

"Please call me back, Dr. Bell. My thinking gets so distorted. I think maybe I should go to the hospital. If you could just get me into the hospital. I actually have the pills. I have them in my room and it just seems like the best thing to do, but I don't know."

Dr. Bell took out a CD of Haydn's *Seven Last Words of Christ*. "Eli, Eli, why hast thou forsaken me?" An agony of ropes and nails and abandonment.

"Oh, God. I can't stand this anymore. I don't know why I'm alive, I truly don't." There was a messy disconnection as she had trouble hanging up.

Bell pushed PLAY and lay back on the sofa.

36

Cardinal woke up the next day and Catherine's absence sucked his breath away, as if his bedroom were adrift in deep space and someone had thrown open the airlock.

As he stumbled through his morning routine—toast and coffee and the *Globe and Mail*—he forced his thoughts toward work: Delorme's case of the child pornographer, Arsenault's series of break-ins.

At one point he looked up from his newspaper and stared into the emptiness across the table.

"I don't want to think about you," he said. "I don't want to think about you."

He went back to the *Globe* but could not concentrate; his eyes were scratchy from a night of fitful sleep. The sooner he went in to work, the better. He put his plate in the dishwasher and tossed the rest of his coffee down the sink. He rushed through his shower, threw on his clothes, and headed out.

The mornings were getting crisper now. There was a scent of winter, a hint of ice, even though there was no ice on the lake, nor would there be for another month or so. He shivered in his sports jacket. It would soon be time for a heavy coat. The sky was dazzling blue, and he thought of how Catherine would have loved it. Her PT Cruiser sat empty in the driveway.

"I don't want to think about you," he said again, and got into his Camry.

He was backing out of the drive when a car pulled up and blocked his exit. Paul Arsenault rolled down the window and waved a gloved hand.

"Morning!"

Cardinal knew he must have something good. No way Arsenault would stop by before work unless he had something pretty tasty to share. Cardinal got out of his car and went over to Arsenault's window.

"Thought I'd stop by so we don't use up any of that precious Police Services time."

"You get something interesting?"

"Well, yes and no. I don't know how you're going to take it."

"Just give it to me, Paul."

"In the end, I got it from the Immigration database—and no, I'm not going to tell you how. We got a British national, moved here a couple of years ago." He handed a printout through the window.

It showed two thumbprints. The photograph above them was kinder than the general run of such documents. In the curly hair, the salt-and-pepper beard, it captured the canine amiability of the man. Frederick David Bell, M.D.

WHEN CARDINAL GOT to work, he called Bell and arranged to meet him on his lunch hour up at the psychiatric hospital.

He drove out along Highway 11 and turned in at the all too familiar driveway of the Ontario Hospital. Cardinal had been here countless times—professionally, because it often housed criminals, and personally, because of Catherine. Usually when she was booked in here, it was the dead gray month of February.

The redbrick building was nearly lost amid the glory of the leaves. A crisp wind blew over the hilltop, and the poplars and birches dipped their heads like dancers. All of Cardinal's history with the place blurred into one long ache, all the times Catherine had been taken here because she was manic and spouting some loony idea as if it made perfect sense, or because she was so depressed she was an inch away from sliding a razor across her wrist.

He took the elevator to the third floor. Dr. Bell's door was open. He was in his chair, looking out over the parking lot and the hills beyond. He sat very still, and Cardinal was put in mind of a dog at the window, waiting for its owner to return.

He knocked—loudly, with the intent to startle—and was gratified to see the effect. Bell's shoulders shot up and he turned around. He stood up when he saw Cardinal.

"Detective. Please come in. Have a seat."

Cardinal set his briefcase on the floor and sat down.

"You were right about the cards," he said. "They weren't from a murderer."

"No, I thought not."

"They were from a guy I put in jail for fraud a few years back."

"Well, that makes perfect sense. Fraud is such a sneaking, knavish thing. Fits in with the style of the poisoned pen. And did he lose his wife as a result of your efforts?"

"Yes. You were right about that too."

"Probably not by suicide, though."

"No. But how would you know that?"

"Because—at least on the face of things—the shame in such a case would be all with the criminal and not the criminal's family. Different story if, say, the crimes were a long-standing series of sexual assaults, or racist violence, something a spouse might be expected to know about or at least suspect. Do you have something else for me? Is that why this sudden trip up here? I was thinking, just before you arrived, that it would be painful for you to come up here. All the memories of Catherine."

"It doesn't make any difference where I am."

Cardinal opened his briefcase and pulled out Catherine's suicide note. This time he handed the doctor the version that had been through the ESDA machine. It was encased in plastic, the writing a ghostly white script on a background of graphite, Catherine's small prints dotting one edge, and a fat splotch of thumbprint at the bottom.

Dr. Bell put on small reading glasses and peered at the note. "Mm, you showed me this before. I see it's now been processed in some way."

"Right again, Doctor. And that's your thumbprint at the bottom."

Cardinal was watching Bell's face for any reaction, but there was none. Of course, he was a psychiatrist, trained to keep his own emotions hidden while others wept and wailed.

Bell handed the note back. "Yes. Catherine did show me such a note a few months ago."

"Funny, you didn't mention that when I brought it to you last week."

Dr. Bell winced and removed his glasses, massaging the bridge of his nose. Without the thick lenses he looked oddly vulnerable, a lemur in daylight.

"I've gone and put my foot in it, haven't I? Detective, I'm so sorry. I admit I wasn't keen for you to know I'd seen this. I was afraid you'd think I'd been negligent in some way, that Catherine had written a suicide note in a pitch of agony and I had blithely ignored it."

"Now, why would I think a thing like that?" Cardinal said. "After all, it's only a suicide note. She only has a history of serious depression."

"Well, of course, now you're angry—"

"She even shows you the note, hoping against hope that somehow you will help her with these terrible urges. You have a little chat, and at the end of the hour you hand it back."

"It's easy to make it sound bad in retrospect."

"And during the next three months, as these suicidal thoughts are apparently building up and building up, and Catherine is coming to see you two or three times a month, you never see fit to hospitalize her. You don't even see fit to call me in for a consultation. After all, I'm only her husband, I've only lived with her for decades, why should you bother to let me know? So, as far as the rest of the world is concerned,

Catherine is doing fine. You, on the other hand, happen to know she's planning to kill herself and you choose to do nothing about it."

"Detective, you're making exactly the sorts of assumptions I was afraid you'd make. I labor in the fields of grief and despair—with people who are unbearably depressed. Sadly, they often want to end their lives, and sometimes they succeed. It's no one's fault. Families get upset and they can rush to judgment. I'm sure it happens in your line of work too. I read in the paper that the Dorn family is extremely upset with the way the police handled that young man's suicide."

"The difference is, the officer did everything he could to stop that guy."

"And I did everything I could to help your wife."

"Allowing her to carry around a suicide note for three months. So that one night, when she's in the middle of an interesting photographic project, on impulse, she pulls it out and jumps."

"Detective, I've been dealing with depression for over thirty years now, and believe me, at this point there's nothing that would surprise me. The only certainty with this disease is that it *will* surprise you."

"Really? Personally, I've always found it hideously predictable."

"Forgive me, Detective, but clearly not. You didn't see it coming any more than I did. As to her using a note she'd written earlier, it's most likely an example of Catherine's thoughtfulness. She wanted to use words she'd written when she was not too overwrought, a note that would express her feelings less harshly than something scribbled in the heat of the moment. Most suicide notes, as you probably know, are not full of concern for those left behind."

"Did you even think about calling me after she wrote that note?"

"No. Catherine was not upset when she brought it in. We discussed it as we would a dream or a fantasy. She was emphatic that she had no imminent plans to harm herself."

"I believe her. I would have seen it coming."

"You're still suggesting there's some other explanation for her death? The original reason you suspected she might have been murdered was that you were receiving those nasty cards in the mail. You thought that only someone who had killed your wife would do such a thing. And so you tracked down the person who wrote them, and it turned out he hadn't killed anyone. Isn't that right? Or am I missing something?"

I'm off my game, Cardinal thought. The shrink has me nailed: I have no hard evidence. Nothing.

"She wasn't upset the day she died," was all he could manage. "She gave no sign that she was thinking of suicide."

"Over the years, she gave every sign. I've read her medical records, Detective. Catherine has stayed in this hospital more than half a dozen times—once for an episode of mania, but all the other admissions were for unmanageable depression. All those times she was feeling that she wanted to die, that suicide was the only way out for her. It seems clear to me that she decided to actually do the deed when she was in a relatively lucid state, when she could carry it out with some degree of control, some forethought."

"I would have seen it coming," Cardinal said again, knowing how lame it sounded. *Catherine, what have you done? What have you done to me?*

"Surely in your line of work, Detective, you've had occasions where people miss the obvious about people they live with?"

Cardinal thought of the mayor and his trollop of a wife. *Am I that blind? Does everyone know the truth but me?*

"Is it not possible, Detective, that you, in your grief, are missing what is obvious to everyone else? Why not allow yourself the possibility of being wrong? You've lost your wife, your thinking is bound to be clouded at best, and who wouldn't be subject to the palliative effects of denial? The nasty cards were sent by a resentful ex-con; there's no reason to believe anyone killed your wife. I knew Catherine for going on two years, and I can't imagine her having any serious enemies. You've known her for decades—have you come up with anyone who might have a motive?"

"No," Cardinal said. "But motives aren't always personal."

"Psychopaths, you mean. But there's no reason to suppose this was the work of a serial killer. Especially not one who had handy access to her suicide note and could leave it behind at the scene of the crime.

"If you believe Catherine was murdered, then knowing that she wrote a suicide note three months earlier would not have prevented it. If you believe she committed suicide, then you have nothing to investigate, unless you intend to sue me for malpractice. As I say—and as you say—she gave no indication she was intending such an act. None. And so I treated the note at face value. It was the answer to a question I posed to her."

"What question was that?"

"We were talking about the reasons why she *hadn't* killed herself, despite years of emotional suffering. Her biggest reason was what it would do to you—to you and your daughter. My question was, What would you say to your husband if you *did* commit suicide? What would you say in a note? I wanted her to articulate the feelings right then and there, but Catherine didn't answer me. She said she would have to think about it. And then, to my surprise, she brought a note in, next session. As you see, it clearly expresses her love for you."

Cardinal's throat felt swollen shut. And then, to his horror, he found that he was weeping.

"You might think about taking some more time off," Dr. Bell said gently. "Clearly you haven't yet had time to grieve properly. Maybe you should consider allowing yourself that kindness."

37

Normally, Delorme loved the morning meetings. All six CID detectives would assemble in the boardroom with their coffee and muffins and discuss the status of their various cases with the whole team. What with Ident and the two street-crime guys, the intelligence officer, the joint forces officer, and the Crime Stoppers coordinator, some days there could be as many as sixteen people in the room, although today there would just be seven.

The point of these meetings was to focus the day's tactics and assign various tasks to individuals. It was always interesting, and sometimes appalling, to hear how other detectives handled their cases, and there was usually a lot of humor. If there were going to be any laughs in the course of a day, this was where they would come. McLeod might go into one of his patented full-tilt rants, or Szelagy would come up with some earnest observation that just cracked everybody up. And Cardinal could be funny too, though his humor tended to be quiet and self-deprecating.

But today Cardinal's presence was casting a pall. While they were waiting for Chouinard, everyone just kept to themselves, pretending to read over their notes or look at documents. McLeod was reading the *Toronto Sun* sports pages. Cardinal himself just sat quietly, his notebook open to a clean page on the table before him. He must have been aware of his effect on the room, and Delorme's heart went out to him.

Chouinard breezed in, carrying a giant Tim Hortons mug

in one hand and a thin file folder in the other. If oatmeal could be a person, Ian McLeod liked to say, it would be Daniel Chouinard. The detective sergeant was dull but dependable, bland but reasonable, solemn but solid.

"Don't get up," he said. He always said that, because of course no one ever did.

"See, that's why I want to be detective sergeant someday." McLeod snatched Chouinard's thin file and held it up. "We're all lugging fifty-pound briefcases and he's carrying a lunch menu."

"It's the natural order of things," Chouinard said. "Didn't you study the divine right of kings?"

"I musta been out that day."

"All right." Chouinard took a huge sip from his coffee and found it good. He opened his file to the single typed sheet he always carried into the meetings. "Sergeant Delorme, ladies first, why don't you enlighten us on what's happening with your little boat girl?"

"I've found the cabin cruiser where at least one sexual assault took place. It's currently in storage at Four Mile Marina. I searched it with the permission of the owners, the Ferriers, but I haven't informed them of the finding yet. The little we can see of the perpetrator isn't enough to absolutely rule out Mr. Ferrier. Also, he's got a daughter who is blond and thirteen, but I haven't been able to interview her yet. It's possible she is the victim, maybe by a friend of the family or an acquaintance."

"So we have a crime scene. You didn't make any effort to preserve it?"

"It's years old—the girl's about eleven in those pictures—and it's been in wind and water and storage since the crime took place. I don't think we're going to get anything off that boat. Even so, I'd like a watch to be put on the storage facility to make sure no one tampers with it."

"That's easy enough. We'll get that right away."

Delorme opened a manila envelope containing two more pictures Toronto had sent. There was another one of the boat. In this one the girl was dressed, smiling, and in the background there was the hill they now knew to be the hill beside Trout Lake. Part of Highway 63 was visible, snaking off into the trees. The other picture showed her as a much younger girl, naked this time, giggling at the camera, lying on a rug. There was a section of blue sofa in the background.

"That's her home, we figure," Delorme said. "That blue sofa appears in a lot of the shots."

"That's Highway Sixty-three in the background?" Chouinard said.

"Right. Toronto thinks this one is about two years old. Some of the others show her that age. So we're looking for a thirteen-year-old girl, blond, green eyes."

"Toronto thinks this picture is two years old?"

Everyone looked at Cardinal. Delorme could feel the relief in the room that he had spoken. Spoken about business, something day-to-day.

"I'm not sure what they're basing that on," Delorme said. "Other than the fact that we have no pictures showing her older than about thirteen."

"You're not looking for a thirteen-year-old," Cardinal said. "She's going to be eighteen or thereabouts."

"Why do you say that?"

"Look at the highway lights. Those are the old sodium lights. Don't you remember when they replaced those with the new white ones?"

"You're the only one who lives out that way," Chouinard said. "Why don't you remind us?"

"I can tell you exactly, because I'd just bought my car, and it's a 1999 model. Day I got it, I'm driving home and this rookie OPP pulls me over for driving too fast for conditions. The lights were all out. He was giving me a lecture about how I should be more careful, nice brand-new car and all. I could've killed him."

"He actually gave you the ticket?" McLeod said.

"He did."

"See, that's the problem with the OPP," McLeod said.

"They train 'em all wrong from the beginning. They see the *rules,* they don't see *reality,* they don't see the *situation.* Gimme two weeks in Orillia, man, I'd turn that place around."

"Upside down is more like it," Chouinard said.

"So, if she was eleven or twelve in 1999," Cardinal said, "she's got to be seventeen or eighteen now."

Delorme was still trying to process what Cardinal had given her. It was like having a bone reset; it would take her a while to get used to it. She was no longer looking for a thirteen-year-old. She was looking for an eighteen-year-old.

"I asked Toronto to send me more pictures," Delorme said. "They say I should have them today. Apparently they've just hauled in about a hundred disks from some perv, and our girl appears in a lot of the images. I'm hoping the backgrounds in the new shots might be useful."

"All right," Chouinard said. "Cardinal, you work with Delorme on this. I really want to nail this bastard, but I'm not sure we need the whole department on it. It's not like we're dealing with a major porn ring here. As far as we know, it's one guy victimizing one girl. That's bad enough, but I don't want to squander resources. And Delorme, please, let's treat these pictures with serious security. Strictly a need-to-see basis, all right?"

"Of course."

"What about the people at the marina? Nobody remembers anything suspicious?"

"Nothing. It's a pretty peaceful spot. I've just been telling them I'm investigating an assault, so they're not thinking child rape. Only violence anyone's mentioned wasn't actually at the marina. Some guy tried to punch out Frederick Bell outside the restaurant next door."

Cardinal looked up.

"The psychiatrist?" Chouinard said.

"Right. This was a little over a year ago. A distraught father. Bell had been treating his son, who committed suicide." Delorme couldn't bear to look at Cardinal as she said the word, but she could feel his eyes on her.

"I know how that goes," Burke said ruefully, and made

things worse by adding, "Some people really don't want to live."

"You did all you could. I told Mrs. Dorn that," Delorme said. Then, praying could they please, God, get off the subject of suicide, she turned to Chouinard. "D.S., I know Perry Dorn's older sister. I think I should have another word with her."

He shook his head. "It's not an open case, and the family is threatening legal action."

"I could talk to her informally. We're good enough friends for that. As it happens, her brother's shrink was also Dr. Bell."

"Fine. But do not discuss it on police property or using a police telephone. What's next?"

Delorme had to sit through Arsenault's list of suspects on the Zellers break-in. And McLeod had a series of assaults he was working where none of the witnesses would talk. Naturally, this was McLeod's cue for a detailed rant on the multicolored wall of silence.

Cardinal spoke to her the moment they were back at their desks.

"This guy that attacked Dr. Bell," he said quietly, "What was his name?"

"Burnside," Delorme said. "William Burnside. His son's name was Jonathan."

"I remember that case. Did you know Bell was Catherine's psychiatrist too?"

"It was in the coroner's report."

Cardinal was looking at her with an intensity she found unnerving. Usually he was such an even-tempered guy, a little morose sometimes, but mostly calm and good-natured.

"Jonathan Burnside, Perry Dorn, and Catherine. Don't you think that's a lot of suicides for one guy's caseload? What are the odds of three suicides in that amount of time?"

"Four," Delorme said. "I was going over our previous child porn cases yesterday."

"Of course," Cardinal said. "Keswick."

"Leonard Keswick. Shot himself when he was out on

bail. Which was pretty surprising, since it was a relatively minor charge: a few pictures on his computer, mostly teenagers, and it wasn't like he was taking them himself, he was just looking at them."

"I remember. Apparently the shame was too much for him."

"Losing your job doesn't help."

"Remind me," Cardinal said. "How did we get on to Keswick initially? If he wasn't selling child porn or trading it or even buying it, why did we even know about him?"

"It was an anonymous tip. Somebody just phoned it in. Maybe one of those computer vigilantes you hear about."

"Yeah," Cardinal said. "Maybe."

38

Cardinal helped Delorme with her child porn case that morning and afternoon, but thoughts of Dr. Bell kept running through his mind like a persistent radio signal. Several times he had to ask Delorme to repeat something she had just said. Even so, the investigative work brought him some relief—relief enough that he found himself dreading going home.

For Cardinal, home had turned into a house made of knives; there was nowhere he could move that did not hurt. That night he lay in bed, but sleep was out of the question. After a while he got up and hauled the television into the bedroom and set it on top of the chest of drawers. It was a bad viewing angle, and he didn't much like the idea of a TV in the bedroom, but he had a faint hope of perhaps watching an old movie until he fell asleep.

He flipped through all forty channels before he gave up. He went into the kitchen, poured himself a glass of milk, and stood in bathrobe and slippers contemplating Catherine's computer, a slim silver laptop that sat on a little desk beside the telephone. She was much more computer savvy than Cardinal, and used her Mac for everything, from paying bills to making travel arrangements to buying camera equipment.

But a computer was private, and Cardinal had never touched Catherine's. He didn't like to use computers at home anyway. Whenever he needed to check e-mail on a weekend, he logged on to a dial-up network on a clunky old PC in the basement.

But now he sat down and opened the laptop, and it came

right up with Catherine's desktop screen, a dreamy turquoise. He clicked on the Web browser icon, which opened to Catherine's home page, a photographer's site that offered a button for today's HOT SHOTS. Cardinal ignored this and clicked on the pull-down menu of bookmarked sites. She had everything neatly sorted into folders. He clicked on one labeled HEALTH. He knew there was an online support group she liked, for people who suffered from bipolar disorder.

He found something labeled bipolar.org and clicked on that. A window opened up asking for a log-in name and password. The log-in slot filled itself in with the name Ice-Fire, but the password field was blank. He knew Catherine used the word *Nikon* as a password on some of her accounts, but when he typed it in, the site informed him in red type that it was incorrect. He tried to remember the make of her digital camera. He typed in *Cannon* and was once again scolded. He retyped it, this time omitting one *n*, all lower case.

The screen flashed and took him to a LIST OF THREADS. There were themes of medication ("Why I hate/love Lithium"; "Suicidal reactions to SSRIs"), themes of resolution ("High Goodbye: Saying yes to sanity"), and finally one that looked more promising: "Shrink Raps."

He opened the thread and scrolled down for postings bearing Catherine's log-in. The first one he found was a reply to someone else's thread.

"Sorry, sweetheart," Cardinal whispered, and clicked on the message she had written:

If you're not comfortable with your therapist after six sessions or so, I'd look for someone else. You don't want to give up too soon, because it takes awhile to establish rapport. On the other hand, if the relationship isn't productive by then, there's a good chance it may never be.

That was Catherine: cool and deliberate and decisive about the things that mattered. She had written this just three days before she died.

Cardinal read a few more of her messages. None was

about Dr. Bell. Mostly they were replies to queries, telling people where to turn for referrals or recommending books she had found helpful.

He clicked on a NEW MESSAGE button and wrote the following:

Urgent: I need to hear from anyone who has had experience with Dr. Frederick Bell, currently in practice in Algonquin Bay, Ontario, formerly in Toronto, and before that in England. Any comments, positive or negative, gratefully received.

He read the message over, hit ENTER, and closed the computer.

WHEN HE WOKE the next morning, he went straight to the kitchen and logged on. The Web site informed him there were three replies.

IceFire, I saw Dr. Bell for about six months in Toronto, just before I moved back to Nova Scotia. I found him to be sensitive and intelligent and I was sorry to lose him. I was coming off a manic binge at the time, so mostly our meetings were around medication that would keep me grounded. Can't say how he'd be with someone whose difficulties were more to do with depression. Hope this helps.

The next one began:

Hey, thought you loved your shrink. What gives?

The third was from England.

IceFire, if you are considering seeing Frederick Bell for bipolar disorder or depression I would *strongly* advise against it. There's no denying the guy is intelligent—he's very well respected in his field—and he may keep you from flying off into the outer limits of mania, but I saw him for close to three years after I tried to kill myself with a bottle of sleeping pills (*bad idea*!). In those three years, I would say that not only did I not improve, I was getting steadily, but quite subtly, *worse*. It's hard to put my finger on it, but I began to feel that he did not want me to get better. Think about that. He did not want me to get better. In case you're wondering, paranoia is not one of my problems. I tend to be too trusting and it has got me into trouble many times in life. But I was treading suicidal waters the whole time I was seeing Bell, and his interest seemed to me, frankly, morbid. Once or twice I even got the feeling he was encouraging me to view suicide as a viable option. One example: I'm a struggling writer, poetry mostly, and one day he brought up Sylvia Plath. He was subtle about it, but he was kind of leaning on the idea that her suicide had made her famous. A small thing, you might say, but if you were a psychiatrist treating a struggling writer for suicidal tendencies, would *you* bring up Sylvia Plath?

There were lots of things like this—in themselves, maybe nothing much, but cumulatively I think they had an extremely negative effect on me. I now see a psychologist for therapy and a psychiatrist for prescriptions, and the difference is night and day. My therapist really reflects back at me my negative thought patterns, but in such a way that I see them for what they are, which is *lethal*! The result is my thoughts tend far less in that direction now. I'm no Sunshine Sally, but suicidal thoughts are definitely gone and I'm far more productive than I ever was. Maybe other people have had a good experience with Bell, but frankly I doubt it.

By the way. The clincher that made me dump Bell? When I was in a really black period—I'd just been rejected for a grant, my dog had died, and my husband was having an affair (*arrrgh!*)—he suggested I write out a suicide note. Actually write one out. Nice, huh? Why not hand me a .45 while you're at it?

Cardinal closed the computer and reached for the phone. The number for Dr. Carl Jonas at the Clarke Institute was still on the list of frequently dialed numbers on the fridge. There were several numbers for Dr. Jonas, including his cell, he was that kind of doctor. It was eight-thirty in the morning.

Cardinal dialed his cell phone, not really expecting to get hold of him.

"Hallo! Jonas!" the doctor yelled. It was always the way he answered the phone. Forty years in Canada, he still sounded as Hungarian as goulash.

"Dr. Jonas, it's John Cardinal calling."

"John Cardinal. Hold on a moment, you've just caught me trying to avoid being decimated by a lady parking her sport-futility vehicle. I could drive right inside this machine and still have room to turn around. Hah! She's given up. Looking for a landing strip to park in, I suppose. Such monsters, they are, it's an incredible. What I can do for you? Catherine is all right?"

When would he get used to this question? Even knowing it was going to come was no defense.

"No," was all he could manage.

"No? What means this no? What's going on with Catherine?"

"She's dead, Doctor. Catherine is dead."

There was a long pause.

"Doctor, are you there?"

"Yes, I'm here. I'm just so—If you're calling me, I'm thinking she did not die by accidental means."

"She went off a nine-story building. Leaving a suicide note."

"Oh, I'm so sorry. What a sad, sad thing. I don't have what to say, Detective. Such a brave, creative woman. It's too sad. I was very fond of her."

"Well, you meant a lot to her, I hope you realize. She could never say enough good things about you. In fact, she referred someone to you just the other day. Really, you would blush to read the things she had to say about you."

"You make my heart glow," the doctor said quietly. "Tell me, Detective, if you don't mind, was Catherine hospitalized?"

"No. Out for a year now."

"But she was seeing the Englishman, was she not? Dr. Bell?"

"Yes, and frankly, she seemed to like him okay."

"Naturally, you believe he failed her. Perhaps you believe the same of me too."

"Not at all. You hadn't seen her for a long time."

"Was she despondent before she died?"

"No. I thought she was in good shape. You know, busy, working on a project."

"Sadly, this is often the way. They make up their minds and—*boom!*—they leave the rest of us to cry. I never expected this of Catherine, though, I must say. She loved too much to do this, I always thought. That's why, despite the severity of her problems, she always managed to get to the hospital in time. She wanted to survive, and above all she did not want to hurt you or your daughter. Ach, so sad it is. Was there something I can do for you, John?"

"I just have one question. And since you treated Catherine for many years, I hope you'll be able to give me a clear, solid answer."

"I'll do my best. Though things, as you know, are not so often black-and-white. What is your question?"

"Would you ever ask a manic-depressive to write a suicide note? Or a depressive of any kind?"

"Never. Absolutely not."

"Not even as part of therapy? Maybe to get their suicidal thoughts out on the table?"

"Never. The first question one asks of a depressed patient is, Have you ever considered suicide? And if the answer is yes, there are two follow-up questions: How often? Have you taken any concrete steps? That is how you gauge the seriousness of suicidal ideation, if they have taken steps. By getting them to write out a note, you are making real what was previously only fantasy. They are taking a concrete step."

"Put that in context for me. Is this your personal view or is it general practice?"

"No, no, it's basic, basic, basic. Anyone trained in psychotherapy will tell you the same. A suicidal patient is seeking help with such thoughts. Asking them to write a suicide note would be sending the message that writing suicide notes is a healthy thing to do. It is not. Suicide notes are intended either to accompany the patient's extinction or they are meant as a cry for help. Since in the first place we don't want the patient to become extinct and in the second place they are already crying for help, such a note would serve neither of these purposes.

"Look, a terminal cancer patient in terrible pain, no quality of life, a few weeks left to live, by all means, if you want to end your pain, that's a legitimate choice, maybe a positive choice, so practice a few notes, say exactly what you want to say. But as therapy for suicide? Please. It's like suggesting to a pedophile, Why don't you draw me a few pictures of your fantasies? Or to a serial killer, Why don't you write out a nice description of your ideal victim and we'll talk about it? I'm sorry, I make depressed people sound like criminals now, and I don't mean to, but you get my point. Perhaps it's more like saying to someone killing themselves with anorexia, Why don't you bring me in some pictures of the models and actresses you'd most like to look like? They already suffer from extreme negative self-image, extreme body dysmorphia, and you're going to help them by such an enterprise? No, no, it's an incredible."

"All right. Well, that's clear. But isn't it possible another therapist would see it as a way of clarifying a patient's negative feelings?"

"I sincerely hope not. It's completely irresponsible. Are you saying Bell asked this of Catherine?"

"Her suicide note had his thumbprint on it. He admits seeing it before she died, but he says she brought it in on her own. It was her idea."

"Well, that's totally different. Obviously—"

"The thing is, I'm not sure I believe him. Another patient told me he *asked* her to bring in a suicide note. She was extremely depressed at the time and he *asked* her to write one out—for therapy—and to bring it in. She dumped him because of it."

"Well, I'm sitting here shocked, Detective. The parking enforcement is eyeing me suspiciously and I'm sitting here not knowing what to make of this. It strikes me as extremely bad therapy, if true. I can't believe. And anyway, even if he *didn't* ask for Catherine's note, he should have hospitalized her when she wrote it. There was no discussion of this?"

"None that included me."

"I can't believe. Okay, so question is what to do. Suppose he did ask for the note, it's now a legal matter on which I can't advise you. He's negligent? It's malpractice? Those are questions for lawyers and ethics committees. You're planning to pursue such an avenue?"

"Ethics committees?" Cardinal said. "No, I have something a little different in mind."

39

Dorothy Bell went to the hairdresser in the morning, and in the afternoon spent a tranquil hour raking leaves and bagging them for recycling. She was back inside, watering the houseplants, when she heard a patient leaving, and then the connecting door opened and Frederick came in.

"What a nice surprise," he said, and kissed the top of her head. "I thought you were going downtown."

"I've been downtown. I'm back."

"Gosh, only four o'clock and I'm starving. Those sandwiches at the hospital are so skimpy. A person could starve up there and no one would know."

He was rooting around in the cupboard.

"What are you looking for?"

"Biscuits, my dear! Biscuits! My kingdom for a biscuit!"

"They're in the other cupboard. Red tin."

"Hiding them again," he said cheerfully. "Keeping them from me."

"That Dorn boy," she said. "The one who shot himself in the Laundromat. He was one of your patients, wasn't he?"

"Yes, he was. Poor fellow."

"I'm surprised you weren't more upset about it."

"I was upset about it."

"You didn't mention it."

"I didn't want to worry you, that's all."

"Why would it worry me?"

"I don't know. You're worried now, it would seem."

"I just wonder why you didn't mention it. It's a pretty

dramatic way to lose a patient, after all. It was in all the papers."

"Oddly enough, Dorothy, I see it as *my* job to worry about my patient, not yours. Some young men want to kill themselves; it's a fact of life. Lots of them come to me when either it's too late to do anything for them or they don't really want to change. That is to say, they really, *really* want to kill themselves. And so they do."

"And that's fine with you?"

"Darling, what's got into you?"

"I just find it appalling that you can have a patient go into a public place and blow his head off and you say not one word about it."

"I talk to people all day, I listen to people all day. Sometimes I don't feel like talking at home. No doubt there are doctors who drag their entire caseload home with them and worry their families with it day and night. I'm not one of them. End of story." He put the milk back into the fridge and picked up his glass and plate. "I don't have another patient until five. Until then I'm going to be writing up some notes."

He closed the door after himself, and Dorothy listened to his footsteps recede.

DR. BELL SET his milk and cookies on the coffee table and inserted a DVD into the player. He had had to leave the kitchen immediately, all but overwhelmed by the urge to strike his wife, something he had never done—or even wished to do—in his life. Her accusations rattled him. Dorn's departure, it was now obvious, had been too flamboyant to be considered a hundred-percent optimal outcome.

Bell used to have endless patience; he could allow his flock to move at their own pace. But he was losing that now, and it unnerved him. He had dealt with enough obsessives to know they rarely remained stable; they got worse and worse until their lives spun horribly out of control and they ended up hospitalized and doped to stupefaction. He yearned to be back the way he was, before everything had begun to slip from his fingers.

"Leonard Keswick," he said aloud, to clear his head. "Further adventures of."

Keswick would cheer him up. He fast-forwarded to the good bits. On-screen, Kleenexes were snatched up and used. Keswick's hands covered his face, then flew away in a jerky peekaboo. Then Bell hit PLAY.

"It's my worst nightmare," Keswick says on-screen. His voice is fogged with tears, hushed with shame. "You know what my wife did when she found out?"

"I'm sure you'll tell," Bell said, and bit off a piece of cookie. Peanut butter. Not his favorite.

"She spit on me," Keswick says. "She actually spit on me. In my face. My own wife."

The Dr. Bell on the TV is all therapeutic patience and understanding. The one in the office made masturbating motions in the air.

"How did the police find out?" Keswick wails. "How could they have known?"

"Didn't they tell you? Surely they have to give you some idea of the evidence?"

"Evidence? The evidence was on my computer! It was full of pictures of thirteen-year-old girls!"

"Boys too," Bell said, over a mouthful of cookie. "Let's not forget the boys, you old ponce."

"All they would say was they were 'acting on information received.'"

"What do you suppose they mean by that?" Dr. Bell says.

"I don't know. Maybe something to do with the Internet portal or provider or whatever they call it. Not that it matters. I'm going to lose my job, I'm probably going to lose my family. And I'm in hell, Doctor, that's the truth. It's like I've already died and gone to hell, and I just don't know what to do."

Dr. Bell gulped the last of his milk and wiped cookie crumbs from his lap. "Oh, I think you know what to do, *Lenny*. I think you know exactly what to do."

The phone rang, and he heard the voice of Gillian McRae, a receptionist at the hospital.

"Doctor, it's Gillian. Have you not gotten back to Melanie Greene? She's called twice this afternoon. She sounds really distraught, and I think you should talk to her first chance you get."

"Absolutely, Gillian," Bell said, without picking up. "I'll get right on it."

40

Delorme slid the file across the table to Cardinal. Her brown eyes, those earnest brown eyes, gave nothing away.

Cardinal opened the file and his immediate reaction was two words: "Oh, no."

"It gets worse," Delorme said.

If D.S. Chouinard was trying to take Cardinal's mind off his loss by assigning him to help Delorme, he couldn't have picked a better case. Cardinal had seen some wicked things in his decades as a policeman—disgusting, evil things—but he had never seen anything that shocked him more than the pictures he was looking at now.

He shook his head, as if to physically shake the taint from his mind. "She can't be more than seven years old in some of these."

"I know," Delorme said, examining her thumbnail absently, as if she dealt with this kind of masculine evil every day. "And it goes on for years. At least until she's thirteen."

In the later pictures, the tears were gone. In most of them the girl wore a blank expression, like a sheep being sheared. Perhaps she was turning her mind somewhere else, trying to think of arithmetic problems, the names of rivers, anything to take her mind off what this man—her father or guardian, most likely—was taking from her. The things she would never get back.

"I don't know about you," Delorme said, "but me, one of the sweetest moments in my life was my first kiss. Donny Leroux. We were so young—not even teenagers yet. I think I was twelve, maybe only eleven, he was probably the same. We were in his guesthouse. His family lived out on Trout Lake, on Water Road, and they had a tiny guesthouse down by the water. Just a cabin, really, with two sets of bunk beds.

"I went with my friend Michelle Godin, and I forget who the other boy was. And somebody pulled out a bottle and started spinning it. I'd heard of spin the bottle before but never played it. And you know, the funny thing was, I hadn't even really thought about being kissed. It wasn't something I was yearning for or wondering about. I must've been just eleven, because I sure thought about it later.

"Anyway, it ended up Donny kissed me. Just, you know, closed mouth and only for maybe a microsecond, and I'll never forget it. Well, here it is twenty-five years later or whatever and I still remember it, the sweet thrill of it. Like tiny threads of electricity snaking all over my body, down to my toes and fingertips. Like being tickled, only from the inside, somehow."

"Sounds like love," Cardinal said.

"Oh, no. I thought about it and thought about it afterward, but I didn't want to do anything more with him. I don't think I had the concept of dating yet, but I don't remember particularly wanting to know him better or spend lots of time with him. It was like having seen the northern lights for the first time. You remember them, you never forget them, but you don't build your life around them."

"Maybe the boy felt differently."

Delorme shrugged. "Who knows if it was the first time for him? Anyway, my point was that our mystery girl will never have that experience. The man in the picture has robbed her of that. When she kisses a boy her own age, it will be an entirely different thing."

And that may be the least of it, Cardinal thought, as he shuffled through the rest of the photographs.

"Toronto's come up with some great stuff." She pointed to one of the pictures, a hotel room to judge by the plain symmetry of the bed and its two night tables. "They figured out that it's the Travellers Rest Motel just north of Toronto."

"I don't know it," Cardinal said.

"I didn't either. But apparently if you have little kids, you know it. It's the closest inexpensive motel near Wonder-World."

"Nice," Cardinal said. "Takes her on a special trip and then does that to her. And they traced them to Algonquin Bay how, the plane?"

"Yeah. I talked to the owner of the plane, guy named Frank Rowley. Doesn't look like our perp. No hair, for one thing. He's got a wife and kid and a serious guitar habit in addition to his plane. He gave me a lot of stuff on his neighbors at the marina, but he never saw anything that made him suspicious."

The squad room door opened and Mary Flower came in with another padded envelope.

"You wanted me to let you know the minute it got here?" she said. "It just got here."

"More stuff from Toronto," Delorme said. "Those guys have been working hard. They'd love to see us nab this guy."

Delorme slit open the envelope and pulled out more photos. "No motel this time. No boat either."

"All the same house, looks like," Cardinal said. "You've got living room, kitchen, bedroom—"

"I know. Unfortunately, none of it matches any of the houses I saw. I tried to catch glimpses of other rooms when I could, but none of them looked like this. None of the kitchens had blue tile, for example."

"What about these curtains?" Cardinal had pulled out a photo taken in a living room: the little girl on the couch, behind her the edge of a curtain that looked blue with a gold medallion motif.

"Those weren't visible in the earlier pictures. But I'm pretty sure none of the houses had curtains like those. Of course, people change their curtains all the time."

Cardinal shuffled through the rest of the pictures. The images draped a whole other layer of sadness over his own personal grief. This poor girl. He had little doubt that the man in the pictures was her father or stepfather—her face was too full of delight in the non-sexual pictures, too full of trust. And then to have that trust ripped from you and torn in pieces. How would you ever learn to trust again?

"Let's arrange all the photographs according to her age," Delorme said. "You set these out and I'll go get the others."

Cardinal laid the pictures out on the table one by one. With each image his heart grew heavier. Leaving aside the question of how a man could lust after a child nowhere near puberty, Cardinal could not understand how he could have looked at that sweet face and betrayed the growing spirit behind it. How could you hold that little hand, receive the innocent kisses of the Cupid's-bow mouth, and then abuse her? He could not comprehend the mind of someone capable of such treachery toward a child.

From what Cardinal could see, the man appeared to be in his thirties, with long, almost shoulder-length dark hair. Although they showed everything else, none of the photographs showed his whole face. An eyebrow here, an ear there, a bit of nose. It was impossible to tell from such fragments, but he seemed to be a reasonably good-looking man, able to have a sex life in the normal way. So why plunder the childhood of a little girl in your care?

Delorme had brought the earlier pictures in and added them to the arrangement on the table.

"Well, she never looks any older than the later one on the boat," Delorme said. "And if that was taken five years ago, it could mean a number of things. Possibly the kid got sick and tired of being his sex toy and told him to drop dead. Or maybe even told someone else."

"I doubt it," Cardinal said. "I'm not sure why—maybe it's just the way she clearly loves the guy in some of the non-sexual shots—but I can't see her turning him in. Not back then, anyway."

"Me, I think it's possible. Which means this guy could already be in jail."

"It's a happy thought . . .," Cardinal said.

"What? You look distracted."

"I'm just trying to think what it means, these pictures

being five years old. I read somewhere that the average family these days moves every five years."

"Which makes it unlikely that any of the homes I visited was the actual crime scene." She gestured at the pictures and corrected herself. "Scenes. And not only that, the family could have broken up. Seems likely, given the problems this guy has."

"And causes." Cardinal shook his head. "A guy like that could destroy a lot of families before he's through."

The two of them stood with arms folded, heads bowed like wartime strategists surveying pictures of bombed-out cities, smoking ruins. There were enough photos now to cover most of the boardroom table.

"People take furniture with them when they move," Delorme said. "I keep hoping to recognize a chair, a table, books, *something*."

"He was pretty careful to keep out any identifying features."

"Yeah. He's sickeningly fond of close-ups."

"What about the sofa in this one?" Cardinal held up a picture of the girl asleep on a love seat. It had red plush seats and interesting wooden trim.

"No. I'd have remembered a piece of furniture like that."

"What about this?" Cardinal held up a picture that included the leg and corner of a coffee table in the Swedish modern style. "The table's pretty distinctive."

Delorme peered at it and shook her head. "The Ferriers had something a lot bigger, in darker wood. And Rowley's was some kind of country look, sort of a split-log effect. He's a real whole-wheater, that guy."

"There's a fireplace in this one," Cardinal said, holding up another shot.

Delorme shrugged. "I didn't see any fireplaces. Anyway, as you say, after five years, chances are they've moved, and the fireplace is no longer part of the picture."

"Yeah, but the implements might be. The brass poker and shovel."

"I didn't see anything like that."

"I wish I'd gone with you to the houses. Two heads are better than one, and we could have split up—you know, one of us uses the bathroom while the other takes a gander at the kitchen."

Delorme didn't respond. She was standing, head bowed, chin in hand, pondering the table. She reached for a photograph, put it back. Reached for it again. Cardinal and Delorme were not partners—the Algonquin Bay police service does not have partners as such; personnel are assigned to a case as needed—but he had worked with Delorme enough to know when an idea was forming behind those serious brown eyes. She would go quite still, tuned to her own private station.

She picked up another photograph and held the two together, side by side. "Look at this," she said.

Cardinal put down the boat picture he had been looking at and came to stand beside her.

"Frank Rowley has a rug like this," she said. "Navajo kind of thing."

"Well, I'm no rug expert. I couldn't tell you if that's an expensive item that someone would be likely to hang on to."

"It looks expensive to me. In fact, I noticed a rug at his house, the colors were so rich. Those blacks and blues. Everything in that house is made of wood, and it looked really good against the colors of that rug. But I don't think this is the same one."

"Why? Just because you liked the guy?"

"No, his had a repair in it. In fact, I tripped on it. It had a jagged line, like a scar running through the pattern."

Cardinal had been scanning the other photos on the table, looking for any that might include the rug. He found one. You could hardly expect to notice the corner of rug right away, overshadowed as it was by a scene of child rape. He picked up the photo.

"You mean a jagged line like this one?"

41

Wendy Merritt put the last of the dishes in the dishwasher, loaded the little compartment with detergent, and slammed the door shut. The timer was set to start after midnight. It was noisy, but it used energy when it was cheapest. She was very energy conscious, especially since she and Frank had started living together.

What a huge decision that had been, and only a year and a half after her husband's death. He had died of a heart attack after running a marathon in Toronto, and the shock had left her stunned and weeping for two months solid. After that, she was just stunned. Without Tara, she would almost certainly have settled into the long decline of the dedicated alcoholic, but she pulled herself together in order to look after her little girl, eventually even beginning to appreciate the sweeter moments of life as a single mother.

But Wendy did not want to be single forever. She took to eyeing the personal ads and went to church functions where there were likely to be single men. She even went out to the pub occasionally with her friend Pat to size up the local talent, as Pat called the men who hung around the Chinook Tavern and the Five Bells.

The cliché had proved sadly true: the best men really were married or gay. Honestly, the single men in this town are just pitiful, she and Pat used to say. They'd have their two beers at the bar, talk to whoever talked to them, and then head off to their separate homes, faintly depressed by the whole exercise.

Lots of the men who spoke to them seemed to be outright crazy. It wasn't that they had outlandish hobbies or behaved in a threatening manner, although some of them were pretty rough around the edges. No, for the most part it was just that these lonely men were vacant, like abandoned houses. You had the sense that there might have been a person in there a long time ago, but then something happened and that person had never developed. Instead you got the guy who bought you a drink and then stared at the bottles behind the bar, saying nothing. Then, just before it was time to leave, he'd put a hand on your leg as if you'd been having the most intimate, exciting conversation of your life. Most of them hadn't read a book in ten years, never read the newspaper except for the sports pages, and had no opinion on anything that mattered—because there was no one living behind their blank eyes to take an interest. Even if Wendy had been interested in sleeping with any of them, or befriending any of them, which she was not, there had not been a single man among them whom she considered worth introducing to her six-year-old daughter.

Tara had weathered her father's death as well as could be expected. At first Wendy had thought the tears would never end. But gradually Tara had got used to their new life and eventually stopped asking about her father. In a way, that had made Wendy even sadder.

So: a year and a half of single motherhood. Her love for Tara became a golden bridge across a dark chasm, the thing that kept her alive. And although she would never have thought it possible, it seemed her love for her daughter grew deeper. She worried about it sometimes, that her daughter had become almost *too* important to her, as if she were becoming a surrogate for the missing husband. That was one of the reasons she had so wanted to find a man and had been so dismayed with the local talent—until she met Frank Rowley.

Wendy liked to say that Frank had flown into her life like somebody out of a movie—a white knight wafting out of the sky to save her and Tara—but the truth was much less interesting. She and Tara had been just ahead of him in the checkout line at the No Frills. He had made some sort of inconsequential comment, and she hadn't thought anything of it beyond thinking he was cute for a bald guy. (These days she thought he was *super* cute, and she thought his bald head was one of the sexiest things about him.)

Afterward, she and Tara had been in the parking lot, about to drive away, when Tara said, "Here comes that man, Mommy."

"What man, sweetheart?"

"The man in the store. He's running."

Wendy had turned to look, and he waved at her and came up puffing. A grin. The window rolling down, the forgotten grocery bag handed over, the thanks. It all took less than a minute, and she would not have given it another thought if it hadn't been for their next encounter.

And this time he *was* a white knight.

She and Tara had gone out on Trout Lake. She had rented a small aluminum boat from the marina, just a fifteen-horse on the back. They'd had a wonderful day, putt-putting around the tiny islands near Four Mile Bay. Wendy had beached the boat on a sandy point and the two of them had become absorbed in a game of Indians. Mostly it was a game of hide-and-seek, but it stretched on and on, and Wendy had not noticed the storm clouds coming up.

They were only a few hundred yards from the island when the motor quit. Wendy tried and tried to start it until her arm was just about falling off; then she found a bad rip in the fuel line and knew they wouldn't be going anywhere unless it was by rowing.

But the oars turned out to be heavy and unwieldy, and they hurt her hands. She simply could not get the boat moving with any speed. The air grew thick and dark, and there were flashes of lightning beyond the hills. Pulling with all her strength on the oars, Wendy overbalanced and fell backward off the seat. Both oars came out of the oarlocks and went into the water. She and Tara went paddling after them by hand, but Tara's efforts were more counterproductive than useful, and Wendy was becoming genuinely frightened. In a matter of minutes the wind had blown them a long way from shore, there were few houses visible, and there wasn't another soul on the water. Everyone else had had the sense to clear off.

She heard it before she saw it: a low roar, louder and louder. She looked up, and there was nothing but the gray and purple turmoil of clouds. Then the plane dropped down and nearly deafened them as it flew by; disappearing to the north between two more islands. Wendy had a faint hope that the pilot would report their lack of power to someone at the marina, who could come and get them. By the time she had retrieved the drifting oars and put them into the locks, raindrops had begun pelting down, heavy drops the size of marbles.

"Wow," Tara said, over and over again. "I'm not scared, Mommy. Hey, Mommy, I'm not even scared."

"That's good, honey," Wendy had said, although she considered it more rational to be frightened at this point, both of them soaked through, lightning pogo-ing over the hills toward them, and their aluminum boat the highest point on a flat surface.

Blisters were stinging the palms of her hands when they heard a motor again, much quieter this time.

They had rounded the point that took them into the main bay when they saw the plane plowing its way toward them, pontoons sending up white frills on the black water. It came within twenty yards of them, propellers roaring. The plane seemed to pivot on one pontoon, then the tiny side door opened and a man leaned out.

"Storm's gonna break any minute, and it won't be pretty. You better let me tow you in, all right?"

In no time at all he had tossed them a rope that Wendy tied to the metal ring on the prow. They were no more than twenty feet apart when she did this, and she could feel Frank staring at them.

"Do I know you?" he said. "Have we met somewhere?"

"Possibly. It's not that big a town, is it?"

He snapped his fingers. "The No Frills. You were ahead of me at the checkout line. You forgot one of your bags."

"I remember you," Tara said. "You brought our bag."

"That's right," Frank said. "I remember you too. Are you ready for a tow?"

"I am!" Tara said. "Are you going to take us up in the air behind you?"

"No. I'm just going to drive across the bay here on the pontoons."

"Oh." Tara plunked down on the aluminum seat, disappointed. The rain made her hair cling to her perfectly round skull.

"We're ready," Wendy said.

Frank closed the door, the propellers roared again, and soon they were following along in the V of his wake. The wind from his propellers competed with the winds of the storm, whipping wet strands of hair across their faces. It was nearly as dark as night. Along the shore, photosensitive dock lights winked on.

"I wish he'd fly up in the air," Tara said. "That would be awesome."

"I don't think the plane's strong enough for that, honey."

"We could fly over the hills and all the way home in the boat."

It took less than fifteen minutes to cross the bay, a distance that would have taken them an hour of rowing. Frank hooked his plane onto his buoy at the marina and then hauled their tin boat in.

"Can you make it to the dock from here?" He had to shout over the thunder. "I have to take my little skiff in, or I'll have no way of getting to the plane next time."

"I think we can make it," Wendy said. "Thank you so much!"

He hauled them toward the plane as he coiled up the rope. Wendy untied it and he reached down to shake her hand.

"Frank Rowley," he said.

"Wendy Merritt. And this is Tara."

AND THAT WAS how Frank Rowley had flown into their lives.

Wendy started scouring a pot that was too big for the dishwasher. Frank came in wearing his wig. His sixties tribute band was playing the Chinook this week, and he liked to wear his John Lennon wig onstage. That was how his hair had looked before he lost most of it at the early age of thirty; he'd shown her pictures.

"Are you off to your gig?" Wendy said.

"In a minute. Stuff's already in the car. I want to show you something." He pulled two coupons out of his back pocket. "Bob Thibeault gave me two free passes for Wonder-World this weekend—well, actually Friday and Saturday."

"Oh, that's too bad," Wendy said. "I can't go next weekend. It's the conference."

Wendy had the autumn teachers' conference coming up. On Friday the schools would be closed for a professional development day.

"I know, honey. But I wanted to run something by you. I've been thinking—we've been together eight months now, and I think Tara and I are getting along pretty well."

"More than pretty well, honey. She's crazy about you."

"Do you think?" Frank said, visibly pleased.

"She always wants to know where you are. Always asks when you're coming home. I think she still doesn't quite believe you're real. And she thinks maybe you'll disappear like her other dad did."

"Well, that's kinda what I was thinking. Tara and I haven't had a chance to really do any bonding stuff, just the two of us, you know?"

"But you've taken her up in the plane, you've done a couple of hikes. And you took the cruise on the *Chippewa Princess*."

"That's true. But those are just a couple of hours. I think it would be really great to spend a couple of days together. I think it might really make us a unit, you know? A real dad and daughter."

Wendy leaned back against the counter, arms folded. The thought of Tara going away for a couple of days—to another town—made her nervous. Her daughter had been to day camps. And she'd slept over at friends' houses. But she'd never gone out of town without Wendy. And WonderWorld was two hundred miles away, almost in Toronto. She said as much to Frank.

"Well, okay," he said, disappointed. "If you feel she's not ready. I just thought it was a great opportunity. But hey, I can give these away, no problem."

"No, no, don't do that."

"Well, if we're not going to use them . . ."

What am I worrying about? Wendy chastised herself. Frank's the most responsible guy I've ever met.

"I'm just being silly," she decided. "Of course she can go. I think the two of you would have a great time. Except—are you willing to spend two days at an amusement park?"

"I have to admit, it wouldn't normally be my idea of a good time. But it seems like such a great opportunity for me and Tara to get to really know each other."

The television went off in the living room. Tara came in, clutching a stuffed lion. She laughed when she saw Frank. "You're wearing your hair!"

Frank primped a little. "How do I look? Ozzy Osbourne?"

"I love it," Tara said, tugging at it.

"Oops, careful, honey. It'll fall over my face and I won't be able to see where I'm driving."

"Mommy, can I get a cell phone? I want a Harry Potter cell phone."

"No, you don't. You've just seen a commercial."

"I do! I do! Then I could call Courtenay and Bridget."

"You can call them now."

"It's not the same. Mommy, please, can I?"

"Actually, Frank has something better. You want to tell her, Frank?"

Frank crouched down to be on Tara's level, the way he

always did when he spoke to her. "How would you like to go to WonderWorld this weekend, just you and me?"

"WonderWorld? Are you serious? That would be triple awesome!"

"Well, think about it a second," Wendy said. "Would you be okay just going with Frank? Mommy can't go, because of work."

"I wanna go! I wanna go! When? Tomorrow?"

"Friday," Frank said. "We'll have all day Friday and all day Saturday together. Won't that be fun? Maybe I'll even wear my hair for you."

42

Patients turning up dead and Frederick completely unconcerned. It's Manchester all over again, Dorothy Bell thought, as her mind tumbled back to their life in England. In England, Frederick had been unconcerned when three patients killed themselves in little more than a week. He had been unconcerned when the mother of one young suicide stood outside the hospital with a sign that read DR. BELL MURDERED MY SON. And he had been unconcerned when his colleagues pointed out the high rate of death among his patients.

He developed some stock responses. You try to help people and this is the thanks you get, he would say, with a heavy sigh and a world-weary shrug. Nobody understands what a lethal killer depression is, he would say. Most doctors won't even take it on. He painted himself as a swashbuckling surgeon venturing with his knife into hostile territory where others feared to tread.

And yet he had been unconcerned in Swindon when a teenage girl in his care had blown up her entire house in the course of gassing herself. And unconcerned when a man in his late fifties, about to become a grandfather, had blown his head off in his daughter's backyard. And unconcerned when nurses at the Manchester hospital, where Dorothy also worked, began referring to him as Dr. Death. She had told him about it, and he had merely shrugged that world-weary shrug and said, "Against stupidity, the gods themselves labor in vain."

The only time Frederick had seemed at all worried was when colleagues at Manchester had demanded an inquiry from the National Health authorities into his habit of prescribing seven times more sleeping pills than psychiatrists with similar caseloads. "There are no psychiatrists with similar caseloads," he had fumed, even as they were packing for Canada. "Depression causes sleeplessness. What am I supposed to do, let them go psychotic with insomnia?"

This was around the time Dr. Harold Shipman had been on trial for murdering some 250 patients with massive overdoses of heroin. Shipman had been known as a good kindly doctor who made house calls. Indeed, many of his patients died even as he was visiting them, or shortly afterward. His plump wife had stood stolidly by him, attending his lengthy trial every day, never saying a word to the media.

And now here was Frederick, with that boy who'd killed himself a couple of summers ago, and Mr. Keswick, and that policeman's wife, and the poor Dorn boy who'd shot himself in the Laundromat. How could her husband be so untroubled by it all? Of course, he wasn't Harold Shipman, he wasn't going around killing people, but he must be doing something wrong for so many of his patients to be killing themselves.

She remembered saying to herself, when Shipman was convicted, that unlike Mrs. Shipman, *she* would have known, *she* would have done something.

I'm doing something now, she told herself, as she slipped into Frederick's office. She wasn't entirely sure *what* she was doing, but she could not—no, *would* not—sit still again while bodies started piling up. She was not going to be Mrs. Shipman.

She unlocked the closet where Frederick kept his session recordings. So obsessive, the way he watched them. Years ago, back when he had been using videotape, she had worried that they were pornographic movies, but a few listens at his office door had quelled that particular fear. No grunts and groans, no cries of not quite credible ecstasy. The only sounds that issued under and around his heavy door were the murmurs of confession, the voice of reassurance, the tears of despair.

The disks were identified by file numbers, not by names; it would be a simple matter to match them up to the files in his cabinets.

Frederick wasn't due back from hospital rounds for hours. She took the first disk out of its sleeve and popped it into the player. Then she went over to the couch, where so many of her husband's patients had wept and confided, and sat down to watch.

43

Even though Cardinal's caseload was lighter than usual, he still had to pay attention to the petty crimes that are the usual fare in a small city. Break-ins, robberies, and assaults demanded investigation, and reams of paperwork had to be completed for court.

In the morning, he had helped track down the former Mrs. Rowley, but Delorme didn't need him at the moment, so he was making quiet inquiries on the background of Dr. Bell. Internet searches led him to abstracts of papers the doctor had given, boards he had belonged to, degrees he held, and all his affiliations, past and present. He focused on the earliest of Bell's associations, the Kensington Clinic in London, England. Unfortunately, both the doctors who had been there during Bell's tenure informed Cardinal that they were far too busy to discuss a former colleague.

He had better luck with Dr. Irv Kantor at the Swindon General Hospital. Dr. Kantor spoke in the sorrowful tones of a former friend.

"I thought Frederick was a good psychiatrist," Dr. Kantor said. "Hardworking, smart, productive, caring. Nobody had a better understanding of depression. No one."

"But you sound doubtful," Cardinal said.

"Well, then there was all the trouble."

"What kind of trouble?"

"Frederick was a resident here, but he received a reprimand for overprescribing—which meant he would never get a staff position."

"Overprescribing what?"

"Sleeping pills. I think the disciplinary committee thought he must be an addict himself from the amount he was prescribing, but he wasn't. He was just giving them to an awful lot of patients. A number of them committed suicide with the pills he prescribed."

"Was he charged with malpractice?"

"One patient's family tried to bring a charge, but they couldn't get any psychiatrist to testify that it's a gross error to prescribe sleeping pills to someone who is not sleeping— even if they are depressed. The most any of us could say is that we might not have prescribed so *many* pills. It might have been misjudgment but not malpractice."

"I'm surprised you're telling me about it, then."

"If that were all there was to it, I wouldn't. But we live in a post-Shipman world—you're aware of the physician who killed hundreds of patients?"

"Yes, I read about it. There had been suspicions about him for some time, as I recall, but one hospital did not inform another, is that right?"

"That's right. Nobody talked to each other. And there was more about Frederick. He left Swindon shortly after the committee's report. We had all liked him, but we also all breathed a sigh of relief when he left. He joined the Manchester Centre for Mental Health; it's the biggest psychiatric hospital in the north. A couple of years after he went there, they had an extraordinary number of suicides, something like four times the rate in similar hospitals. There was a story in the papers and demands for a National Health investigation, but it didn't happen for some reason. Frederick moved away, and I believe the matter was dropped."

"Where did he move to?"

"I don't know. Once he left here, our paths never crossed again."

Cardinal put in a call to the Manchester hospital. The personnel department would tell him only the years of Bell's employment, the Standards and Practice Committee chair refused to say anything at all without a British warrant, and the chief of psychiatry did not return his call.

Cardinal knew the relationship between those who diagnose patients and those who actually look after them is often bumpy, if not openly hostile. Which was why his next call was to the head of nursing.

Police in Ontario are not normally allowed to gain information by outright subterfuge, and it was an indication of Cardinal's overstressed state of mind that he, usually a stickler in matters of procedure, gave it barely a moment's thought.

The Manchester head of nursing was a woman named Claire Whitestone, who had a mannish voice and a tone that suggested she had fifteen other things she would rather be doing than talking to one George Becker, assistant chief of nursing at Algonquin Bay Psychiatric.

"Algonquin Bay," Sister Whitestone noted. "Sounds like a place where you might run into igloos and polar bears."

"Bears and Indians," Cardinal said. "No igloos."

"What can I do for you?"

"We've got a serious problem over here and I need some help from your outfit. Some information. And your administration, your physicians? Well, it's like talking to a brick wall."

"You'll get no sympathy from me, mate. I bang my head on those same walls every single day. Banes of my bloody existence. What's the problem?"

"I need background on a psychiatrist who used to work with you. He had problems with a previous employer on matters of overprescribing."

"I already know who you're talking about. If you want dirt on Frederick Bell, I can't give it to you. Despite all the Shipman fuss, there are still all sorts of rules about sharing disciplinary records. It can be done, but it can't be done quickly, and it can't be done through me. You have to go through the—"

"Through the National Health Service. I know that."

"They're not going to give you anything over the phone, and neither am I. I assume you have laws against slander and libel in your country?"

"Yes, of course."

"Then you'll understand why I can't tell you anything negative about that wonderful, wonderful man, that inspired physician, that shining beacon to us all."

Cardinal definitely got the feeling she wished it were otherwise. He had an answer prepared.

"We're going to request every record under the sun," he told her. "But, as you say, that's going to take time. Meanwhile, we've got people dying over here and you may be able to save us a lot of time and actually save some lives."

"Get on with it, Mr. Becker. We're shorthanded over here, it's already been a hell of a day, and I'm facing another shift."

"I can put it to you very simply. We have a situation here where we have a suspiciously high number of suicides. All treated by the same psychiatrist."

"Are you getting complaints from patients? Patients' families?"

"One family member took a swing at the doctor; I'd call that a complaint. And another former patient says he kept encouraging her to write out a suicide note."

A snort and its slight echo were transmitted to Cardinal via satellite.

"So let me put it to you this way: if we *were* to get a detailed report from your National Health Service on this doctor, would it be likely to show a similar pattern? Notice I have not named any doctor."

"Noted and appreciated, Mr. Becker. If the National Health ever got off its collective arse and did a detailed investigation, it would indeed show similar occurrences here."

"Was there any suggestion of foul play?"

"Other than negligence? Nothing official. But, you know, in my book, when someone jumps off a building—"

"Someone jumped?"

"I'm no bloody forensic expert, but I always found that one suspicious. Mind you, that's just me. There was in fact a note and everything. But you say he was *asking* for notes, your doctor?"

"Yes. In at least two cases."

"That doesn't sound like good therapy to me. How does it sound to you?"

"Worthy of further investigation."

"Frankly, Mr. Becker, you don't sound like a nurse. What are you, exactly?"

"I'm a husband." The word *widower* would not come to his tongue. It did not even enter his mind until *husband* was already out. "My wife went out one day to take some photographs. It appears she jumped to her death, leaving a note."

There was the briefest of pauses.

"I'm sorry to hear that, Mr. Becker. I'm going to hang up now. You put your question simply, so I can answer it simply. Would an investigation show similarities between our caseload and Algonquin Bay Psychiatric's? The answer to your purely hypothetical question is a very unhypothetical *yes*."

When he got back to the station, Mary Flower held up a plump padded envelope addressed to him.

"Looks like Christmas arrived early for you, John," she said, and then she colored. "Sorry. Stupid thing to say," she muttered, and turned away.

There was no return address on the envelope. Cardinal took it back to his cubicle, opened it, and slid the contents onto his desk. Six shiny DVDs.

44

The DVDs were in plain white sleeves with clear plastic windows—no labels save for a white strip on the back where a number was written in blue ink. The numeral seven was written in the Continental style, with a cross through the shaft. Cardinal shoved the disks back into the envelope and went into the boardroom, shutting the door behind him.

There was a large television on a trolley with a combination VCR/DVD player underneath. It was used for reviewing interviews with suspects, procedures at a crime scene, and so on. Cardinal pulled a disk from the envelope and stuck it into the machine.

On-screen: Dr. Bell's office—the books, the rugs, the oak furniture, the comfortable chairs, all beckoning you to sit down, relax, reveal your heartbreak. All is soft and welcoming here. A young man with thinning sandy hair is seated in the middle of the couch, one ankle crossed over a knee and one hand clasping that ankle. On the surface it's a posture of comfort and informality, but the jiggling foot gives away a certain nervousness, and the jerky movements of his head speak of someone who is uncomfortable in this office, in the world, perhaps in his own body: Perry Dorn, who killed himself in the Laundromat. Cardinal recognized him from pictures on the TV news. Off to one side sits Dr. Bell, notebook propped open on one knee.

The young man spills out his anguish: how he had loved mathematics, how he had turned down an offer from McGill University in order to stay near the woman he is obsessed with, and how she has dumped him. Despair cries out in every crack in his voice, in the defeated slump of his shoulders. The acid of self-loathing burns and sizzles over his words, even those of forced cheer. But the good doctor doesn't suggest a hospital admission. Instead, he asks for details on how Margaret, the young man's beloved, has devastated him.

And then they talk about how he can't be sure Margaret would even notice his suicide, she's so preoccupied with her new lover.

"I was just thinking of the Laundromat," Dr. Bell says. "I was thinking how, when you started going out with Margaret, it seemed symbolic. You said yourself it was like you were starting out clean. I remember thinking that a witty remark. Neither of you carrying germs, you said—I'm sure that was your word—of previous relationships. And I was wondering . . ."

"The Laundromat," Perry says, and tosses a Kleenex onto the coffee table. "Yeah, she'd have to notice the Laundromat."

Cardinal replaced the disk with another. Leonard Keswick, the civil servant who had killed himself after child pornography was discovered on his computer. As a senior administrator at Community and Social Services, Keswick had crossed paths with Cardinal at various civic functions, and Cardinal had often seen him on the evening news.

He fast-forwarded through the preliminaries.

"You know what my wife did when she found out?" Keswick says. "She spit on me. She actually spit on me. In my face. My own wife." He bursts into tears. Dr. Bell waits patiently in his chair until howls subside into sobs, sobs into sniffles.

"How did the police find out?" Keswick wails, muffled behind a Kleenex. "How could they have known?"

"Didn't they tell you?" Bell asks with apparent concern. "Surely they have to give you some idea of the evidence?"

"Evidence? The evidence was on my computer! It was full of pictures of thirteen-year-old girls. I don't know how they found out. All they would say was they were 'acting on information received.'"

"What do you suppose they mean by that?" Dr. Bell says. He shifts in his seat, rolls his shoulders, and cocks his head this way and that, his doglike tics becoming more pronounced.

"I don't know. Maybe something to do with the Internet portal or provider or whatever they call it. Not that it matters. I'm going to lose my job, I'm probably going to lose my family. And I'm in hell, Doctor, that's the truth. It's like I've already died and gone to hell, and I just don't know what to do."

Keswick had always seemed such a self-possessed, confident person, and now here he was unraveling on his psychiatrist's couch.

Cardinal began to understand now how Bell's patients could be completely taken in by his surface warmth. His manner spoke of open arms, a glowing hearth, unconditional positive regard. Cardinal himself had dissolved in the presence of that manner when he had first come to Bell; he had even asked him for advice. All these patients—Catherine too—coming to the doctor with nothing but a wish for help, for a strong dependable hand to extract them from the tar pit of despair. Who would suspect that the man who extended it would at the same time be pushing them back down? It brought to Cardinal's mind the classic definition of seduction: warm manner, low intent.

The date stamp in the corner of the image put the Keswick interview about a year ago, the month of his suicide.

Cardinal ran the disk back a little and hit PLAY.

"All they would say was they were 'acting on information received,'" Keswick says miserably.

And from the doctor: "What do you suppose they mean by that?"

"As if you didn't know, Doctor." Cardinal hit the STOP button. "As if you didn't know."

He pulled another disk out of the envelope. There was a yellow sticky on the front, on which was written in neat script, *I'm so sorry for your loss.*

A moment later Catherine appeared on the television

screen, and Cardinal's breathing stopped. His hand, without his willing it, reached out toward her.

Catherine sits in the center of the couch, hunched forward with her hands clenched between her knees, a posture habitual with her when discussing something of intense interest, the earnest student.

Bell is relaxed, thoughtful, one leg crossed over the other, notepad as always on knee.

"I've been feeling much better lately," Catherine says. "Remember last time I was worried that I was on the edge of a depressive episode?"

"Yes."

"Well, I don't feel that way now. It was just a little anxiety about my project. I'm going to be doing a series of shots at different times of the day—starting with night shots. But it's going to be precise times of the day: nine A.M., six P.M., and nine P.M."

"I believe you told me they would be aerial shots of some kind?"

"High shots, not aerial. I wanted to take the first set from the cathedral spire, but they won't give me permission. So I'm shooting my first night photos tonight—you know the new Gateway building just off the bypass?"

"Oh, yes. I didn't think it was finished yet."

"It's mostly finished. I have a friend who lives there, so I'm heading over tonight with my cameras. She's going to take me up onto her roof—they have a deck out there—and I'm going to take shots over the city. Supposed to be a moon tonight too, so it should be pretty spectacular."

Cardinal could hear the enthusiasm in her voice. The doctor could not have missed it either.

"Your friend will be there with you?" Bell says. "I thought you always worked alone."

"She's just going to get me out to the roof and then she's off to a rehearsal. So I'll have the roof all to myself."

"So what's changed from last week? Last week you were feeling hopeless about your work." Bell flips back through his notebook. "'I don't know why I bother,' you said. 'I've never done anything worthwhile. Nobody cares about my pictures, and they probably never will.'"

Her own words hit her hard. The change in her face is dramatic, the sudden droop at the corners of her eyes, her mouth open slightly.

She trusts you, Cardinal thought. She's completely open with you. Catherine is usually far more guarded, especially about her work. But with you she opens right up. She wants your help. She wants your help to fight off her own dark impulses. How did you repay that trust?

"That was . . .," she begins, then sags a little. "That was . . ."

"You were thinking you should quit photography altogether. That it was pointless to go on with it. I don't mean to be harsh, but it's your deepest feelings we have to bring out in the open here."

"No, no, I understand," Catherine says. "I'd forgotten how bad I was feeling last week."

"Mm-hmm."

"But I think it was just pre-project blues. I get those. We've talked about that before. Whenever I'm starting on a new project, I get anxious and I start thinking of all the reasons not to do it. Once I start thinking that way, I just see my life as a series of failures, and I get blue."

"'Nothing I've done has any value,' you said. . . ."

Bastard, Cardinal thought.

"That sounds more than a little blue," Bell continues. "Nothing you've done has any value?"

"That was . . . I mean . . . I was thinking—I was thinking. See, that's what happens when I get nervous about a project: I think of all the reasons not to do it. And the main reason is, Who cares? It's not like I have a long string of successes behind me. You know, by my age Karsh was famous for his portraits, André Kertész had done the most beautiful street scenes as well as these wild experiments, and Diane Arbus had already had an exhibit at the Museum of Modern Art. Why should I bother?

"That's how I was thinking. But then all those thoughts

drop away, and I just think about the work—the technical challenges, how interesting the various exposures will be—and I forget everything else."

"Interesting you should bring up Diane Arbus."

"She was great. Here she was, this nice little girl from the Upper West Side, and she's going off into the scariest corners of New York City taking pictures of transvestites and dwarves and God knows what else. She was brilliant."

"Probably the most famous photographer of the last century."

"I don't know about that. Most famous female photographer, yes. That's true."

"After she killed herself, anyway."

"That was so sad," Catherine says, as if she has lost a personal friend. "I've read everything about her. She and her husband were just so powerfully in love. After they broke up, she was just never the same. She never got over it. I don't think any amount of work or praise could fix that for her. Not that she blamed him, she still loved him. He still loved her."

She speaks about her as if they had known each other for years, as if they talked and worked together every day, Cardinal thought. How could I have missed that? Was I just not listening?

"The fact remains," Dr. Bell says quietly, "she killed herself, and she may not be the most famous photographer, but she's certainly one of the most famous suicides, and it affected how her work was seen. You've obviously thought about her a lot."

"I love her. Her work has meant a lot to me. And you're right: the way she died does affect the way her work is seen. It's as if every photograph is accompanied by this huge red exclamation mark. Like it's underlined in blood."

"It increased her fame."

"Yeah. Still sad, though."

"And so—and don't take this the wrong way—I wonder if that might not be somewhere in your mind when you think about killing yourself. Do you think that might be part of the attraction?"

"Oh, God," Catherine begins. Then a long pause as she looks away, staring offscreen. "Could I really be that shallow? Kill myself to get famous?"

"It's not totally unrealistic, right? There are precedents."

Bastard, Cardinal thought again.

"I don't *think* that's a factor. I mean, maybe it is, but it's not conscious, if so. No, when I think about suicide, it's because I'm in such pain I just want the pain to stop. I want it to be *over. Done.* That, and I think what a burden I must be to John, how he must hate the sight of me, and I just think, Oh why not take this weight from around his neck?"

"Oh, honey, no," Cardinal said aloud. "No."

"But then I think how it would hurt him, how sad he'd be, and I can't do it." Catherine shakes her head, flinging away the dark thoughts. "And you know what? I'm never going to kill myself. There've been lots of times when I've been close, but I don't know—I seem to have this inner core of strength, and I know deep down I'm never going to do it."

"I see." Dr. Bell sits back so that his face is in shadow. "And you don't think this is just because you're in a good mood today?"

"No. This is the real me. This is who I am. Last week was just pre-project anxiety. I'm into it now, I'm ready to work, and I feel—nervous, yeah, I'm always anxious—but I want to get down to work. I want to see how it's going to turn out."

WITH THOSE LAST words searing their way through his heart, Cardinal drove over to the Crown Attorney's Office on Slater Street.

A DVD player was trundled into a meeting room, and he and attorney Walter Pierce sat in silence watching the work of Dr. Bell unfold beneath a portrait of the Queen as she had looked thirty years previously. Cardinal played him the last sessions of three patients.

Pierce was a big man, barrel-chested, with pale skin and

very small eyes that blinked a lot with some nervous disorder. It gave him a gentle, molelike appearance that had deceived more than a few felons into thinking they could withstand cross-examination from such a harmless-looking creature. Pierce's greatest asset in court was his voice, a velvet whisper that made the most far-fetched argument seem a reasonable idea that had occurred to you—and a jury—after the soberest reflection.

"The woman is your wife, I believe," he said, as Cardinal pulled the last disk from the player.

"That's right."

"I'm sorry for your loss, Detective. I'm surprised you're back at work so soon. It must be unbearable for you to watch this."

"Someone has to stop Bell from killing any more patients." Cardinal could hear the rumblings of rage in his own voice. He added, more softly, "He needs to be put away."

Pierce leaned toward Cardinal. He hadn't made a single note on the yellow legal pad before him. "Listen," he whispered. "We've presented some difficult cases together, you and I—won most of them too. Largely because you're very good at organizing your cases and finding evidence to back up evidence."

"I have Bell's thumbprint on—"

"Let me finish. I can't even begin to imagine what you think there is in these recordings that might lead to a criminal charge. If you were new on the force, I would be on that phone right now to Chief Kendall asking him where the hell he found you. Because you don't have here even the semblance of a case."

"I have his thumbprint on my wife's suicide note. I have forensics that prove it was written months ago—back in July—and he didn't suggest hospitalization, didn't mention it to anyone." Careful, he told himself, keep it calm and rational.

"Even accepting what you say at face value, that might be construed as malpractice—a civil matter. No one would bring that case to court based on a thumbprint on a note. No one from my office."

"We're not talking about one case here. You saw him with Perry Dorn. The kid is completely suicidal, yet again and again he turns the conversation back to the most painful subjects: she left you, she rejected you, you gave up your future. He's rubbing his face in it."

"I agree with you. He appears almost sinister in some of his remarks."

"The whole time he puts on this pseudo-warm demeanor. So kind, so concerned. Then he knifes them."

"Hardly, Detective."

"These people are completely vulnerable. And even when they're not—look at Catherine." Cardinal took a deep breath, but he could not calm the pounding in his chest. "She goes in, she's in a good mood, she's excited about her project, and what does he do? He says, 'Last week you hated yourself and everything you've ever done.' Do you find that therapeutic?"

"It's surprising, I grant you. But a therapy session is not a casual chat. He's not there to discuss photography, he's there to help with depression. Perhaps in his judgment the best way to do that is to bring the patient back to the most painful subjects."

"Look at Keswick. You remember Keswick."

"I remember Leonard Keswick."

"How much time was he facing? Tops."

"Well, the law allows for as much as five years, but realistically, he was looking at eighteen months suspended."

"Eighteen months suspended, and the man is dead."

"Being charged with possession of child pornography is not going to be good for anyone's self-esteem. He lost his family. He was certainly going to lose his job."

"Exactly. And how did it come about? Look at his file. He had maybe a dozen images on his computer of teenagers having sex. How did he ever get charged in the first place? We certainly weren't looking for him. It was an anonymous call."

"And you're saying Bell made that call?"

"I think so."

"Can you prove it? Do you have the call on tape?"

"No. All it says in the file is two anonymous calls. Both from a middle-aged male. The second one claimed to actually have seen the pictures on Keswick's computer. We wouldn't have acted on it otherwise. Who else could it have been? This computer was at home, not at work."

Pierce took off his glasses and rubbed the bridge of his nose. Without the spectacles his face looked even more like a benign creature out of Beatrix Potter, snout twitching. "At this point, you have nothing," he said. "And if you were thinking clearly, you would know you have nothing. I can only put it down to your bereavement."

"It's a hands-off murder," Cardinal said. "Murder by proxy. He knows exactly each patient's most vulnerable point and he goes right for it. Look at Perry Dorn. Bell even suggested the venue, the Laundromat. What more do you need? We can't just sit here and do nothing. The bastard did everything but sell tickets."

"Now you're raving." Pierce stood up. "Detective, my wife died two years ago. Not in the same circumstances as yours— it was a car accident, a trucker asleep at the wheel. It was out of the blue and it was not her fault and I was absolutely devastated. I stayed away from work for a month. There was no way on earth I would have been able to do my job during that time. We tend to forget how big a role the emotions play in our thinking. There is no such charge as hands-off murder, as I'm sure you know."

"There's criminal negligence. At the very least, criminal negligence. He asks them to write out suicide notes. You don't think that's reckless disregard?"

"Human error or misjudgment is not criminal negligence. You'd need him to prescribe some preposterous dose of medication, something along those lines. Notice I'm not even raising the issue of how you got hold of those disks."

"They were sent anonymously—probably by Mrs. Bell."

"Makes no difference. There's nothing in them that would make a homicide charge stick."

"Please don't tell me the Crown Attorney's Office is going

to do nothing. Are you really going to sit back and watch this guy push his patients into killing themselves? People are dying here."

"Well," Pierce said softly, "if you really want to nail him, you could bring the disks before the medical board. They'll almost certainly give him a stern talking-to."

45

The little brass wheel gleamed as it rotated, and the tiny engine made the puffing sounds of a miniature locomotive. Frederick Bell had used a nail clipper to trim the wick of the tiny burner below the boiler and filled it with methanol. The cylindrical boiler was so small it held less than a half cup of water. All the brass parts shimmered in the window light, and the flywheel spun.

This stationary engine was the only memento he kept of his father—or, rather, the only one he kept in plain sight. It stayed on his desk, to be started up occasionally when the doctor found himself in a contemplative mood.

He was in such a mood now, contemplating Melanie Greene. Bell was almost certain he had nudged the young woman over the edge. There's nothing like a history of sexual abuse to bring on low self-esteem and depression. Getting her to talk about it, and to admit her own ancient ambiguous feelings about it, was just the most basic psychotherapy. His master stroke, of course, was the timing of his rejection. He had seen the trust in those green eyes, the yearning for acceptance. He was fairly sure she was now in the grip of a despair so deep she would no longer reach out for help. Today was the first day she hadn't called since their last session.

But it made him edgy not to be one hundred percent sure. He couldn't begin to savor a victory until it was beyond doubt.

Playing with the little steam engine usually calmed him. It summoned his best memories of childhood, when his father had been teaching him his beloved facts of science. The steam engine presented opportunities to talk about Boyle's law, momentum, and the history of steam power in general. At such times his father had seemed, in his boy's eyes, to be another Alexander Graham Bell. He even had the same dark hair and beard.

Sometimes, when he worked the little steam engine, he would have a complete change of heart about his negative therapy. He would resolve to help people recover, as he had in the beginning, help pull them back from the cliff's edge instead of nudging them over. But it would only be a matter of two or three sessions, sometimes the very first after his new resolution, before he would shift back to his previous attitude.

"I hate them," he muttered. He pressed a tiny brass lever, and the engine emitted a cheerful toot. "I just hate them."

He held the lever down until the whistle dwindled to a hiss and the wheel stopped turning. The engine was not calming him today, and he certainly wasn't making any resolutions. He extinguished the little blue flame and set the engine on the bookcase next to the picture of his mother, a picture of her smiling in the backyard in one of her shirtwaist dresses, her hair still swept to one side in the style of the forties. The picture had been taken by an aunt just a week before his mother swallowed the pills that killed her and left her eighteen-year-old son to make out however he could.

No, no, even reveries about early childhood would not calm him today, not while he was waiting to find out if he had rid the earth of another useless whiner. It was important work, a kind of sanitation, but he only got real satisfaction out of getting them to do it themselves. He was enough of a psychiatrist to know why this was so, but the self-knowledge changed nothing. This of course was the dirty little secret of psychiatry: you could come to know exactly the genesis of your particular neurosis, obsession, or fetish and still be no closer to being free of it.

No, the real satisfaction was getting these snivelers to remove themselves from the face of the earth. The world was better off, and he had committed no crime. Catherine Cardinal had not been at all satisfactory in that regard. He had had to resort to heroic measures with that one, and he hadn't been the same since. It was the first time he had actually killed someone, and that way, he knew, lay madness, incarceration, death.

He did not see himself as a violent man, but Catherine Cardinal had driven him to it. All that insistence on love and art as the saving graces of her life. What life? Going to hospital every other year for months at a time? Living on lithium? How could she not *see* that death was the only cure for her? It would destroy the game if he no longer had the patience to let them kill themselves. If he resorted to such personal interventions, the law would be bound to catch up to him. Just his luck that his first hands-on victim should be the wife of a detective.

He had been careful to remain unseen. Through that all-but-abandoned parking lot and the vacant storefronts, he had moved like a shadow within shadow. Up the freight elevator and onto the roof, and not a soul to see him. Then it was done and he had left the note at the scene and removed the evidence.

He went to the cabinet where he kept his session recordings. He wanted to watch Dorn again. All right, his exit had been too spectacular, but it had been inevitable. A young man who was determined to come to no good, Dorn: a born pisser and moaner, always conceiving these passions for women who couldn't care less. Left untreated, he would have gone on plaguing women with unwanted adoration and friends with tales of his misery. Cut that one off at the knees and no mistake.

The moment he opened the cabinet, he saw that disks were missing, half a dozen at least. His first thought was that a patient had somehow learned of the camera and decided to steal some. But then he realized that the patients concerned— Perry Dorn, Leonard Keswick, Catherine Cardinal—were all dead. There were two disks missing for each of them.

"Dorothy!" He went out to the hall, calling her name. "Dorothy, where are you!"

Blood pounded in his temples. The hall seemed to narrow

itself into a black tunnel. Somewhere a part of him recognized rage. I'm in a rage, he thought from a distance: the tunnel vision, the pounding pulse, the quivering in my legs, are the effects of rage. He couldn't have suppressed it now even if he had wanted to. The threshold had been crossed; the release was thrilling.

He flung open the door to the kitchen. Dorothy had her hand on the back door, about to go out. She turned, and her eyes were two dark little holes of dread. Munch's eyes. *Dead Mother and Child.*

"I think you have something of mine," Bell said. His words throbbed as if they had pounding pulses of their own.

Dorothy gripped the doorknob. "You're doing something wrong," she said evenly. "I stood by you in Manchester when people started dying. I told myself, He must be right, it must be just that he has a difficult caseload; he tries to help people who are really beyond help and it ends up looking bad."

"What have you done with my disks?" Bell said.

46

When he left the Crown Attorney's Office, Cardinal drove straight over to Bell's house. He stopped the car across the street and sat looking at the dark gables outlined against an evening sky of mauve. The silver BMW parked in the driveway would seem to indicate the doctor was home, but there was no way to be sure.

Although he could employ violence when the occasion demanded it, Cardinal was not a violent man. No matter how angry he got at the thugs and wretches he was called upon to arrest, he always managed to find within himself that rational, controlling part of his mind that could rein in his feelings. Now, as he sat staring at Bell's house, it took every ounce of control not to break right in and beat Bell into a lingering death on a ventilator. Finally he put the car in gear and drove through the crush of evening traffic to the one place he had thought he would never set foot again.

When he got there, CompuClinic was just closing. A woman came out of the dry cleaner's carrying an armful of plastic-shrouded clothes and got into her car. Cardinal parked and walked around the side of the building. He knew he shouldn't be there, that he was not ready—the quivering in his hands told him that, as did the sudden swelling sensation in his throat.

Catherine's blood had been washed away. The crime-scene tape was gone, and all the little bits and pieces of computer had been swept up. You would never know a life had ended here. He circled the building, looking for entrances.

Like most buildings under construction, security was not nearly as tight as it might be when the building was finished. There were two different fire exits, both closed at the moment, either of which might have been propped open by a lazy workman or a careless smoker; the alarms were almost never active at construction sites. The empty storefronts were boarded over, but some of these boards required no more than a sharp tug to come away. It took him all of ten seconds to open up a space big enough to walk through.

Inside, there was enough light coming through the glass door at the rear to see by. The space was essentially a concrete box with thick wires extruding from the walls and ceiling. Two-by-fours were stacked in a neat pile by one of the walls, and the place smelled of concrete and raw wood.

The door led to a plain hallway bright with fluorescent lights. At the end of this, a door marked STAIRWELL led to the basement and a freight elevator sitting empty and open. Cardinal put on leather gloves before stepping inside and pushing the button for the roof. In less than two minutes he had got himself to the rooftop without being seen, just as a killer could have done. The door to the patio was locked now, but there was a loose brick right next to it that could be used to prop it open. Probably one of the last things Catherine had touched on this earth.

He went down using the regular elevator and exited through the front lobby. He stood once more in the parking lot, staring at the place where Catherine had been. Would that image of her lying there be with him for the rest of his life? Her tan coat, her bloodied face, the smashed camera?

All the way home he tried to replace it with another image. Of course, he could recall thousands of different moments with Catherine, but he could not hold any of them in his mind long enough to erase the horror of that parking lot. The only image he could retain for more than a split second was the one of her in the photograph, looking slightly annoyed, two cameras slung across her shoulders.

Two cameras.

If it were not for that memory, that photograph, Cardinal

would probably not have ventured down to Catherine's dark-room again for months. He didn't want to hover among her sinks and trays and strips of film as if *he* were the ghost. He had not even yet considered the possibility of clearing the place out. Catherine's darkroom had to stay exactly as she had left it. She would be upset, otherwise. She would be unable to work.

Despite having held her dead body in his arms, despite the weeks-long absence, he still, somewhere in his being—everywhere in his being, it felt like—expected Catherine to come back.

The scene from Bell's session recording was replaying in his head, this time in detective, not husband, mode.

"You know the new Gateway building just off the bypass?" The enthusiasm climbing in her voice. "I'm heading over tonight with my cameras."

Cameras. Plural.

He opened the narrow white closet where she kept her gear. No cameras. A few black lenses, long ones, lay on the shelves, lenses for her old battered Nikon. She would have taken the smaller lenses with her. The Canon was missing.

Cameras plural.

He went to the other part of the basement, his worktable where he had put Catherine's things. Her last things. The plastic bag from the hospital containing her clothing: her watch, a bracelet, her sweatshirt, jeans, and underwear. No camera.

Outside again, he checked Catherine's car—floor, trunk, glove compartment. No camera.

When he was back in his own car heading into town, he called Ident. Collingwood kept a schedule as strict as police work would allow; he did his shift and then he was gone, like a mechanical figure on an antique clock. Arsenault seemed to have been selected for the job purely for contrast, because you never knew when you would find him in. He often worked late into the night, so much so that there was a lot of speculation at the office on his personal life, or lack thereof.

Arsenault picked up on the first ring.

Cardinal didn't bother with preliminaries. "I need to

check the boxes from Catherine's scene," he said, passing a pickup truck that straddled two lanes. "I need to know if there's a camera there."

"I can tell you that right now. Yes, there was a camera there. A Nikon. Lens smashed all to hell."

"Just the one."

"Yeah, John. There was just the one." Arsenault sounded surprised.

"Is there anyone still in the evidence room? Can you sign the boxes out for me? I'm on my way in."

"No need. They're right here in Ident. Closed case, remember? Figured you'd ask for 'em sooner or later, though."

"I'll be there in ten minutes."

Cardinal swerved around a Honda Civic and shot past Water Road. Luckily, most of the traffic was going the other way.

The station was quiet. He could hear someone, probably Szelagy, typing in his cubicle, but other than that, CID was deserted. He walked straight through to Ident. Arsenault was at his desk, tapping on his keyboard. Collingwood's desk was dark.

"Hey, John," Arsenault said, without looking up, "stuff's on the counter."

Two boxes, one large, one small, stood open on a counter that ran along one wall. Cardinal hit a switch and the counter was bathed in bright fluorescent light.

He peered into the smaller box. Catherine's Nikon, with its shattered lens, lay among other items that clearly had belonged to her: her camera bag and the contents that may have spilled out of it—a notebook, the flat disks of filters, and a few more lenses. One of these was silver and labeled Canon.

There was no camera in the bigger box. Cardinal stood still, thinking. The only sound was the click of Arsenault's keyboard. Assuming Catherine had been following her custom and taking pictures with both cameras, that meant someone had taken the Canon: either someone who had happened onto the scene afterward or her attacker.

A thief of opportunity seemed unlikely. How many people, happening onto a dead body, are likely to steal a camera from it—a camera that was almost certainly smashed up? And if you're going to take one camera, why not take the other? Assuming her attacker stole it, that could indicate one of two things: Catherine had been mugged for her camera, the nice shiny new Canon, and the robber had pushed her from the roof when he grabbed it; or her attacker had taken it from the scene afterward. Cardinal could think of only one good reason to do that.

The bigger box contained items that had been found near the body but were not necessarily connected to it: a cigarette pack, several butts, an Oh Henry! wrapper, a paper cup from a nearby Harvey's. There were also many bits of electronics, junk from the computer repair center on the ground floor. Beside the Dumpster, the driveway had been littered with stray cards, drives, and chips. Collingwood and Arsenault had dutifully gathered them up and tagged them.

Each item was in a plastic Baggie, numbered and labeled with the date, the initials of the Ident person who had found it, and the distance and clock position relative to the body. Cardinal looked at several of these through the plastic. He was no computer whiz, but he knew memory cards when he saw them. The ones he was seeing were pretty old-looking, probably from computers beyond even the ministry of CompuClinic, Inc.

He pulled another couple of items from the box: a CD drive, a pair of headphones, another tiny Baggie encasing a chip. He turned this last item over. It was a chip about the size of a postage stamp, green-colored and ridged with tiny teeth. The other side was obscured by the label. He opened the Baggie and slid the chip out onto the counter. Pale gray lettering on the green surface of the chip spelled out the word CANON.

"Hey, Arsenault," Cardinal said, "do you guys have a camera that will take this chip?"

Arsenault looked up and shook his head. "Ours take memory sticks. Different shape. Why?"

"I think this is the chip from Catherine's camera. I want to see what's on it."

"That Nikon's not digital."

"She had another camera with her. A Canon."

"Really?" Arsenault looked up from his keyboard. "In that case, the printer will show you what's on the chip."

"Don't you have to plug a camera into it?"

"Nope. It's got a tray you can stick the chip in."

Arsenault swiveled away from his desk and rolled his chair over to the printer. He pressed a button and a little tray with several indentations slid out. "Just drop it in there," he said, pointing to the smallest indentation, which was square. Cardinal pressed the chip into the slot and Arsenault slid the drawer in.

"If there's anything there, it should show up on the preview screen." He tapped a glowing rectangle on the printer about the size of a playing card.

The rectangle turned black and the Canon logo appeared, then the first photograph. It was a high shot of the city, the lights bright pinpricks. Cardinal could make out the twin belfries of the French church in the distance. These were the last things Catherine had seen.

"You can cycle through them," Arsenault said. "Just push the NEXT button."

Cardinal hit the button and the image changed slightly: the same view, a little closer. The next picture was a different angle. Off to the right, the red warning lights glowed on the post office communications tower. There were several shots of this and then back to the French church, and Cardinal saw why she had wanted to take pictures that particular night. The orange harvest moon was just beginning to roll into view beside the church towers.

"Nice," Arsenault said quietly.

In the next shot the moon was half hidden. And in the one after that, it was just beginning to appear between the towers. Another moment and the moon would be caught between the towers like a pumpkin. But the next shot was something else entirely.

It looked accidental, as if she had been jostled or startled: a wall, slightly blurred, a streak of light from overhead, and in the right-hand corner, someone's arm. A man's arm. You could just see a shoulder, arm, glove, and the side of his overcoat.

Cardinal hit the NEXT button and heard Arsenault suck in his breath.

They both stared at the image glowing before them.

"She got him," Cardinal said quietly. "She got him cold."

The man's arm was raised in greeting. The light above the roof door threw a sharp shadow of his arm, raised like a warning, to the ground. Despite the shadows, he was clearly recognizable, with that wide smile and his open features like a large, friendly dog. He looked like the sort of man anyone would want for a friend or a teacher—or even a doctor.

47

The pills were on her desk, little blue lovelies the soothing indigo of late evening. There were nearly thirty of them, just under a month's supply, kindly prescribed by Dr. Bell when she had first started seeing him. What a blessing they were when sleep deserted you. When the night stretched ahead and the inside of your skull seemed lit up with floodlights, they soothed your brow like a mother's warm touch.

A tall glass of water stood on the desk beside them, drops of condensation beading on the sides. Melanie lifted it up and put one of her Northern University notebooks underneath.

Saying goodbye was taking longer than she had expected. She had intended to write just a brief farewell and then be gone. But she found she could not do that to her mother. Or to Dr. Bell, who had tried so hard to help her.

She spread the pills out in a line on her desk, tiny blue pillows. Twenty-five of them. Using a ruler, she divided them into groups of five. She lingered over this process for a few minutes, arranging the pills into little star shapes.

Don't ever blame yourself, she wrote, *this is not your fault in any way. You were always a good mother to me, you always gave me everything I needed. Anyone else would have grown up into a happy, well-adjusted young woman.*

She swept five pills off the desk into the palm of her hand and tossed them to the back of her throat. Two swallows of water and they were down.

I love you very much, she added in neat script, and paused.

A few moments went by, during which she just stared, not at the note but through it. Then another five pills. She would have to be quick now, or she would just fall asleep and wake up feeling worse than ever. She didn't want to wake up.

Dr. Bell, I don't blame you for turning away from me. Some of the things I said to you were pretty disgusting, and it's understandable they would make you sick.

She tossed another five pills into her mouth and picked up the glass of water. The memory of the things she had told Dr. Bell last time made her choke. She got the pills down, but had an uncomfortable coughing fit and had to drink nearly all her water to calm it. Her eyes stung with tears. But I won't cry, she told herself. I'm done with crying. Forever.

Being a good doctor, I guess you saw that I was beyond help, even though you tried so hard to help me and couldn't bring yourself to tell me I was terminal.

Another five pills.

I'm sorry.

Another five pills.

So sorry for everything.

48

Despite what he recognized as his previous misbehavior, Cardinal was a firm believer in procedure. And the proper procedure on this frosty night—still no snow and yet the temperature heading toward freezing—would have been to call his detective sergeant and tell him the evidence he had. If Chouinard agreed the evidence warranted immediate arrest, the D.S. would assign other detectives to assist him. If not, a discussion with the Crown might be arranged to see what more was needed.

As he drove past the cathedral toward Randall Street, Cardinal knew very well he was violating procedure by not calling his D.S. But then, he was violating procedure by working on the case at all. And he was violating procedure by not calling for backup. He could see D.S. Chouinard's face forming in the frost on his windshield. He could hear his angry words somewhere within the blast of the Camry's heater.

But none of that stopped him.

The Camry zoomed through a red light, cherry flashing on the roof. No siren. He didn't want the doctor to hear him coming.

Three minutes later he was pulling to a stop a few doors from Bell's house. There were lights on at the back and upstairs. He went around to the rear, passing the kitchen windows; there was no shadow of movement inside. The BMW was still parked in the driveway.

Cardinal stepped silently onto the back porch. The upper part of the back door was glass, mostly covered by gingham curtains on the inside. He peered through a small gap and saw the far wall, with its fridge and calendar, a cuckoo clock above the far door, which was closed. And, changing his angle a bit, he could see the still form of Mrs. Bell, curled up on the floor in a dark pool of blood.

He broke the glass with his elbow and reached in to open the lock.

Cardinal paused for a second in the doorway, listening. The house was huge, and the kitchen door was closed. If Bell was home, he might not have heard the window break.

Cardinal tiptoed around the blood and touched the side of Mrs. Bell's neck. She was still warm, but there was no pulse, and the size of the dark pool beneath her indicated there never would be. There were defensive wounds on her forearms, and a terrible gash across her throat.

Not your best work, Cardinal thought. You're used to having people kill themselves for you. She took your disks, stole your precious trophies, and you went into a rage. The question is, What do you do next? What does a man obsessed with suicide, and guilty of at least two murders, do next?

Cardinal turned the handle of the kitchen door and moved silently into the front hall, the waiting area. It was lit by a small elegant chandelier, but the doctor's office, off to the left, was dark, as was the living room on the right. He tried the office door. Locked. The stairs were carpeted but old. He stepped on the edges to minimize creaking, his Beretta in his hand.

Upstairs, the only light flowed from the front room. Four steps, and Cardinal was there, gun at the ready, safety off, right hand cradled in left palm. The room was large but overfurnished, with two armoires, an antique vanity, and a vast bed covered in a red quilt on which a suitcase lay open, half packed with men's clothes. A quick check showed no one behind the door, no one under the bed, no one crouched in the armoires.

Cardinal worked his way swiftly through the other rooms. A bedroom set up as a sewing room. A guest room, spicy with the scent of potpourri. And two other rooms done up in subtle color schemes, one a small TV room, the other a comfortable-looking library with a small billiard table and a fireplace.

There were two more doors leading off the hall. The first proved to be a closet.

A creak. Was that a floorboard overhead? Someone on the third floor? It could have been nothing, just the kind of noise an old house makes, but Cardinal went dead still, listening.

49

Finding Frank Rowley's previous wife required no subtleties of police work. A few phone calls, a check of marriage records, and Delorme found herself at the home of Ms. Penelope Greene. Few houses in Algonquin Bay were smaller than Delorme's bungalow, but this one managed it. It was a tiny brick cottage hunched between two much larger brick houses like a toddler between its parents.

The pretty woman who answered the door was in her forties, with hair fighting to stay more blond than gray. Her face had a wary expression, the green eyes narrowed, but that was less likely to be pure physiognomy than the result of finding a policewoman on her doorstep.

"Mrs. Rowley?" Delorme said.

"Not anymore. I changed back to my maiden name years ago."

"I'm Sergeant Delorme."

"Melanie's not in any trouble, is she?"

"No, your daughter hasn't done anything wrong, but I need to talk to you about something that almost certainly involves her."

Ms. Greene showed her into a miniature living room. A doll-sized love seat and two compact armchairs seemed to jostle one another for breathing room, but the place had a comfortable dog-eared charm. Delorme sat on the love seat, which was so low-slung that her view of Melanie's mother was framed by her own knees. As she sat down, Delorme realized it was the love seat from one of the photographs:

intricate wooden trim around red plush cushions. And through the doorway beyond Ms. Greene, a partial view of the kitchen showed the distinctive blue tiles that had appeared in several of the pictures. Yes, Delorme had come to the right place, but it did not make her happy.

"Ms. Greene, how old is your daughter?"

"Melanie's eighteen. She'll be nineteen in December."

"And she has blond hair like you?" This was probably an unnecessary question. Ms. Greene had the same green eyes as the girl in the photographs, the same perfect eyebrows, the same upturned nose.

"Well, it's much blonder than mine. It's like mine used to be. Why could you possibly want to know that? There hasn't been an accident, has there? Tell me right now. She's all right, isn't she?"

"No accidents. As far as we know, she's all right. Her father is Frank Rowley, is that correct?"

"Stepfather. He came into our lives when Melanie was just starting school. He left nearly five years ago, though. Married life didn't suit him, it turned out—or so he said. He moved away to Sudbury and didn't keep in touch. He should have kept up some relationship with Melanie, at least, but he didn't. He's living in town again now. I've seen him a couple of times, but I crossed the street to avoid him. He has a new wife and a stepdaughter who looks about six. I haven't even told Melanie he's back. I should, though. It'll upset her if she bumps into him."

Delorme took out the file of pictures and selected an enlargement that just showed the girl's smiling face, aged seven or eight.

"Is this your daughter?"

"Yes, that's Melanie. Where did you get this? I have tons of photos, but I don't think I've ever seen this one."

Delorme selected another enlargement. Head and shoulders, the girl at thirteen, the same wary gaze as her mother.

"Yes, that's Melanie too. She would have been thirteen. Sergeant Delorme, you're scaring me. Why do you have pictures of my daughter—old pictures—that I've never seen?"

Delorme pulled out another two photographs, carefully cropped to show only the perpetrator, not what he was doing or to whom. Long hair, naked torso, turned mostly away from the camera.

"Ms. Greene, do you recognize this man?"

She took the pictures from Delorme with excessive care, as if they were germ cultures. "This is—this is Frank. My husband, Frank. Former husband."

"You're sure? The pictures don't show much."

"Well, I just know it's him. The way you do, when you've lived with someone for years: the tilt of his head, his jawline, even his stance—that slight bend to his shoulders. Besides which, he's got those three freckles on his shoulder." She tapped the photograph. "His left shoulder. They're like Orion's belt, a slight triangle. This isn't going anywhere good, is it?"

"No, I'm afraid not, Ms. Greene. Can you tell me where I can find Melanie?"

"She has her own place now. It's just a boardinghouse, but she wanted to be on her own once she went to college. I'll give you the address. But not until you tell me what's going on." Ms. Greene stood up and clenched her hands open and shut, as if preparing for a terrible fight.

"You might want to sit down," Delorme said. "What I have to say is going to upset you."

"Please just tell me, Detective."

"I'm sorry to have to say this, but we have other photographs of Frank and your daughter. Photographs in which he is having sex with her. They were found on the Internet."

Ms. Greene's right hand rose to her chest. "What?"

"There are at least a hundred of these photographs. Where he posted them originally, we've no idea. People who collect porn often like to trade it. The result is that now, when the Toronto police arrest someone for possession of child porn, they often find images of your daughter among all the others on the suspects' computers."

Ms. Greene still had not moved, the hand wavering uncertainly above her heart in the hopeless quest to protect it.

"We need to speak to your daughter to see if she'll testify against Mr. Rowley. We're dealing with serious crimes here, and it seems there's now another little girl to worry about."

But Ms. Greene was barely hearing her. Delorme watched the process of shock turning into heartbreak, pity, sorrow, and regret, and a thousand other emotions that could only be guessed at. It was like watching the slow-motion toppling of a building: both hands rose to cover her face and she gave a muffled cry, her legs gave way, and she crumpled back into her chair, tipping forward over her knees.

Delorme went into the kitchen, which was as tiny and neat as a ship's galley, and made tea. By the time it was ready, Ms. Greene's weeping had subsided into sniffles, and as she sipped delicately at her cup, misery was shifting into anger. "I'll kill him," she said at one point. "I'll absolutely kill him."

"You can't do that," Delorme said gently, "but you can help make sure he never does this again."

Anger became self-recrimination then. "I should have known. Why didn't I catch on? My poor little girl. Oh, God. All those times I left them alone together. I let him take her camping! Boating! I let him take her out of town! It never occurred to me he would do something like this."

"He would have made every effort to make sure you never suspected."

"I should have known, though. Now that you tell me and you show me these pictures, I have no trouble believing it. I know that what you're saying is true, so why didn't I figure it out for myself? Oh, all those times he wanted to take her places on his own—I'm such an idiot! Oh, poor Melanie."

More tears, more tea, and when finally the tears no longer came, Ms. Greene reached for the phone and dialed.

"Not answering," she said, and dialed again. She dialed three times before Delorme suggested they just drive over to Melanie's boardinghouse.

"I DON'T KNOW why she isn't answering her phone," Ms. Greene said for the fifth time as they drove across town. Like most people in the grip of bad news, she was veering between expressions of anguish and hope. "I'm sure she's all right," she said next.

Delorme turned off Sumner onto MacPherson. "What I'm hoping," she said, "is that Melanie will testify against Mr. Rowley."

"Surely the pictures are enough to convict him? That bastard. He needs to be castrated, that's what he needs."

"The pictures will go a long way," Delorme said. "But Melanie's testimony would remove any trace of doubt from a jury's mind. And if she doesn't testify, they'll wonder why not. It could be used in his favor."

"But it would be so horrible for her. All these years she's wondered why she's so unhappy, and here she was traumatized by a man she adored. He uses her like . . . like a—oh, I can't even say it—and then he cuts her out of his life completely. Testifying will bring back all those memories."

"Ms. Greene, I've worked with a lot of rape victims over the past ten years or so. In almost every case—I can't say all—but in almost every case, they found that testifying against the person who hurt them was a positive experience. Embarrassing, yes. Painful, yes. But not nearly as painful as staying silent. And if they work toward it with a good therapist, it can ultimately be very healing."

"She's seeing a therapist now. Dr. Bell? He's supposed to be very good."

Delorme made a left onto Redpath and they drove two or three blocks in silence. Then Ms. Greene pointed to a foursquare redbrick house with an electric garden gnome glowing in a heap of leaves.

"That's it. Melanie likes it because it's just half a block to Algonquin, and the bus stops right at the corner. She can get to Northern in ten minutes, which is good because she has a couple of eight o'clock classes. Eight A.M., can you imagine? I hope she's home. I'm sure she is.

"It's just a rooming house," she went on, as they walked up the front path, "but Mrs. Kemper, the lady who runs it, seems very nice. She keeps an eye on the kids—I think all her renters are students—but she doesn't boss them around.

"Melanie's on the second floor to the left. Oh, her lights are on; she must've got home as we were driving over."

They went into the closet-sized vestibule and Ms. Greene pressed a buzzer. "Those are her boots, with the furry seams. Mrs. Kemper makes them take their boots off at the door."

They waited a minute or two, and she pressed the buzzer again.

Footsteps of someone coming down the stairs. Ms. Greene had a rather too-big smile ready, but when the inner door opened, it drooped into polite-greeting mode.

A young woman wearing a hooded Northern U sweat-shirt and three rings in her left nostril opened the door. She let out a little cry of surprise.

"Hello," Ms. Greene said, catching hold of the door and holding it open. "Ashley, isn't it? I think we've met. I'm Melanie's mom?"

"Oh, yeah. Hi."

"I think Melanie just came in. We were heading up to see her."

"Melanie's been in all night, far as I know," the girl said. Then, with a "See ya" tossed over her shoulder, she was out the door.

Delorme followed Ms. Greene up the stairs. The house was a considerable cut above the places she had stayed in her own student days: carpeting on the stairs, nice wallpaper and, best of all, everything clean. Delorme had a sudden memory of a basement room in Ottawa, grit on the stairs, and the smell of mold everywhere.

Ms. Greene tapped on a solid white door with a brass number four on it.

From inside, an old rock song finished playing, and then Delorme recognized the announcer from EZ Rock, an ad for a local Toyota dealer.

"She must be home," Ms. Greene said. "Her boots were downstairs. And it's not like her to leave lights on and a radio playing."

Delorme rapped sharply on the door. "She could be in the shower."

"The shower's right there." Ms. Greene pointed at an open door. "Shared bathroom. Oh, where is she?"

"Melanie?" Delorme slammed at the door with the flat of her palm. A door down the hall opened and a young female face beamed hatred at them, then was withdrawn.

Ms. Greene leaned against the door and spoke through it. "Melanie, if you're in there, please answer. We don't have to come in, if you don't want. If you need privacy, that's okay, but just let us know you're all right."

"Go downstairs and get the key," Delorme said.

A look of panic.

"Hurry."

Delorme continued shouting through the door. From the floor above, a female voice yelled, "Shut the fuck up!"

A moment later Ms. Greene came up the stairs, stumbling in her rush. She tried to fit the key into the lock, but Delorme had to take it from her and do it herself. When they stepped inside, Ms. Greene let out a cry.

Melanie was on the floor by her desk.

Delorme saw at once the empty pill bottle, the glass of water, the note. She knelt beside the girl and felt for a pulse.

"She's alive. Take her feet and we'll get her onto the bed."

Ms. Greene obeyed numbly, her eyes hollowed out with dread.

Delorme turned the girl over onto her stomach and stuck a finger into her throat. A sudden retch, and scalding vomit spewed over her hand. She did it again. Another retch, but nothing came.

Awkwardly, using her left hand, she took out her cell phone and called for an ambulance. They were not more than half a dozen blocks from the hospital.

50

Frank Rowley lifted his guitar case into the trunk of the car and laid it flat. Then he loaded the miniature pink suitcase decorated with Disney creatures for Tara. She was standing in the driveway now in her pink ski jacket, the wind whipping her blond hair across her face. Finally, he wedged his own suitcase in beside the guitar. He had packed it carefully, sliding his laptop between a couple of pairs of jeans and hiding the new webcam in a pair of balled-up socks. Soon he and Tara would be on the road, alone together, and Rowley's heart was pounding at the prospect.

"Pretty big suitcase for two days," Wendy said. She hadn't bothered to put on a coat. She stood behind Tara, hugging her daughter's oversized teddy bear to keep warm.

"You know me. I always overpack."

"It's so windy," she said. "Maybe you shouldn't set out tonight."

"Nonsense," Rowley said. "Best time to go. No traffic, and we'll get there in plenty of time to have a good long sleep. Then first thing in the morning we're gonna be banging on WonderWorld's gate to let us in. Aren't we, Tara?"

"Yes! Yes!" Tara shouted. "Wild Mouse!"

"It's gonna work out great," Frank said to Wendy. "We get all day Friday at WonderWorld, and Saturday morning, and then Saturday afternoon I play my wedding. She'll be fine. They only booked us for two hours, and Terry'll look after her."

Terry was the bass player's wife, who insisted on coming

to all the gigs, her husband being a solid musician but a way-ward mate.

"The wind's blowing your wig all crooked," Wendy said.

"I know, I know." Rowley reached up and adjusted the hairpiece.

"It looks cool!" Tara said.

"I don't know why you're wearing it. You're not playing till Saturday."

"Because Tara likes it, and I promised I would. Didn't I, Tara?"

"Yes, you did."

"Okay, Hotshot. Hop in."

"I want to put Teddy in first."

Wendy opened the back door and the bear was solemnly strapped in. Then she buckled her daughter into the front passenger seat.

"You be good, now, you hear?"

"I will."

Wendy gave her a hug and a kiss on the head. "I'm gonna miss you, sweetums."

"Mommy, it's only for two days!"

Frank smiled at Wendy with a kids–what-can-you-do? sort of smile.

"Don't worry," he said. "I'll look after her."

A car swung into the driveway, followed by a black-and-white patrol car. Rowley shielded his eyes with his forearm against the headlights. The silence of their approach, the decisiveness of their stopping—he knew the police were not here by mistake. He also knew there was only one thing it could be about, and felt the first prickle of fear on his skin and sweat breaking out between his shoulder blades.

"Can we help you?" he said, before he recognized the woman coming toward him. "Oh, hey, I remember you. You're the detective from the marina."

"That's right," Detective Delorme said. But she turned immediately to Wendy and introduced herself, holding up her ID. "Ma'am, is that your daughter in the car?"

"Yes, why?"

"Would you take her inside, please?"

"Why? What's going on here?"

"Take her inside, please. I'm here to arrest Mr. Rowley, and I don't want to do it in front of your daughter."

"Arrest him! You can't arrest him. He hasn't done anything."

"Go ahead and take her inside," Rowley said. "I'll sort it all out at the station."

"But what's going on?"

"Honey, take her inside."

Rowley watched Wendy scoop Tara out of the front seat. The howls of protest started before they were halfway to the house.

"Frank Rowley, you're under arrest for the production and distribution of child pornography. We'll be seizing any computers, cameras, hard drives, disks, or other storage devices in your possession. Further charges of child abuse and sexual assault will be laid at the discretion of the Crown Attorney."

"I don't know what you're talking about," Rowley said. "I never touched that girl."

"We're not talking about this girl," Delorme said, and snapped the cuffs on him.

51

Cardinal waited, listening. Old houses creak; it might have been nothing. Bell could already have fled, taken a cab to the airport.

A definite footfall.

He crossed the hall in three silent steps and opened the remaining door. A half flight of stairs led to a landing. Once more keeping to the edges, he moved toward the third floor. He could see nothing beyond the landing. When he reached it, he took a deep breath and turned toward the next flight, Beretta up.

"I thought it would be you," Bell said.

The doctor was seated on the top step, an automatic in his hand—a Luger, if Cardinal was not mistaken—pointed right at Cardinal's chest.

Had it happened a few weeks previously, Cardinal knew, the sight of Dr. Bell's Luger pointed at his chest would have made him tremble. But standing on the steps below the doctor, he realized that at this moment, he didn't care.

"One thing you should know," he said. "I have a significant advantage over you right now."

"Why? Because you don't care whether you live or die?"

Once again the doctor had read him perfectly.

"I assure you," the doctor continued, "I am quite at the same point. I too have lost a wife."

"*Lost* isn't quite the word, is it? I know why you murdered your wife. She took your trophies. You've been collecting them for years. Mementos of your triumphs. Your victories."

"If you are referring to my disks, a more intelligent man would realize they are a teaching aid."

"You don't have any students."

"Teaching aid for myself. Some of us do try to keep learning, you know, by reviewing sessions with particularly difficult clients."

"Easy to gloat, too. To see how you encouraged your patients to kill themselves, all the while pretending to help them."

"What I do is clarify. By reflecting a patient's true feelings back at him or her, I give them the power to act on those feelings. New options can open up. Some may find new ways to ease the pain, if not to find earthly bliss. Others may choose to kill themselves, and that's entirely their choice and their right."

"Those disks clearly show you pick and choose which feelings to reflect. All the negative ones. Their blackest thoughts. You encourage them. 'Write me out a suicide note. Let's make it real, here. Let's put it into words. Let's take a real step toward actually doing it. Think of all the good things that'll come out of it. An end to pain, for one. Ease the burden on your family, for another.'"

"True, in a lot of cases. Those are legitimate concerns."

"And you make sure they have a lot of pills handy, in case they're squeamish about blood or—"

"Or what? Disfigurement? Yes, when they jump, it does terrible damage to the facial bones, doesn't it?"

Cardinal's finger tightened on the Beretta.

"Or you put them on an antidepressant. And then suddenly change it or take them off it. Excellent way to put people over the edge."

"Detective, if I made all my patients feel suicidal, I'd have no practice at all. If I really made people feel worse, no one would come back to me."

"They don't come back to you. They die."

"Wonderful. Sherlock Holmes uncovers the truth about depression. Depressed patients kill themselves."

"Yours do. They have to, don't they?"

Bell raised the Luger so that it was now aimed at Cardinal's face.

Cardinal jerked his Beretta up to firing position.

"I could kill you now," he said, "and it would be justifiable homicide. I wouldn't even have to lie about it."

"Go ahead, then," Bell said. His gun hand was wavering.

Cardinal noticed as from a great distance the fury burning through him, as if he were observing a wildfire from a helicopter.

"I know you want to kill me," Bell said.

"And you want me to. It's called suicide by cop. That's what this is all about, isn't it? I read in your book how both your parents killed themselves; that might be a good reason for studying the treatment of depression. On the other hand, it might be a good reason for hating people who get depressed. And it might be a good reason for wanting to kill yourself."

"You read that in my book too. The so-called suicide gene."

"You've wanted to kill yourself for a long time, but unlike so many of your patients, you can't do it. Just like you say in your book: some people need to be around people who are capable of killing themselves. You need them to do it *for* you. You egg them on, maneuver them, manipulate them, all the time pretending to help them. But it's you you're trying to help. You're trying to finish the one suicide you've always wanted to commit but never had the guts to follow through on. I wonder if you knew that, way back when you first became a psychiatrist."

"What have you got, Detective, a grade-ten education? Do you really imagine you can analyze me?"

"I don't have to. You can do it yourself. Why else would you devote your life to people you clearly hate? It must have been quite a strain keeping up that concerned, caring front all these years."

"You don't know anything about the people I treat. They're scum. Whiners. Utterly useless. Utterly selfish. They've never done anything for anyone else in their entire miserable lives. Human garbage."

"How does it make you feel, Doctor? Isn't that your favorite question? How does it make you feel when they finally kill themselves? These whiners, this human garbage. It must feel—"

"Wonderful," Bell said. "There's no feeling like it. I couldn't describe it to you. Better than sex. Better than heroin. I love it. So why don't you kill me?"

"And when they won't kill themselves," Cardinal went on, "if they're too strong, like Catherine—"

"It's not my fault she didn't get it. She was desperate to kill herself; she just wouldn't admit it. How many times does she need to be hospitalized before she catches on?"

"That must be very . . . upsetting for you. It must be extremely—what's the right word here—frustrating?"

Bell's face was a portrait of contempt.

"Infuriating?"

Bell shook his head tightly. "You don't know anything about me. No one does."

"They know in Manchester. Or they will know, when they finally open their investigation."

"You think so."

"I know it. I also know you killed Catherine. Because, as you say, she just didn't get it. She didn't get that her therapist *wanted* her to commit suicide, and when she wouldn't give in, it was intolerable for you and you had to kill her yourself."

"Wouldn't you like to think so? If she committed suicide, what does that make you, right? The big detective. The knight in shining armor. What becomes of him if he can't save his own wife? If she can't stand living with him anymore? If she hates him so thoroughly she can throw away the rest of her life rather than spend it with him? That's unbearable, isn't it, Detective? No wonder you have to believe I killed her."

"I didn't say I believed it," Cardinal said. "I said I know it."

He held up the tiny Baggie.

"What's that supposed to be?"

"It's a memory chip, Doctor. From Catherine's camera."

"Why should I care about that?"

"She took your picture when you came out onto the roof. She always did that—photographed whoever was around when she was taking pictures. She photographed everyone. She was essentially a shy person. Her camera was a kind of defense. You knew she took your picture and that's why you took the camera with you when you left. You went down to where she fell and you took it away. I imagine you were too excited at the time to realize it had broken open and the chip had flown out. You must've been awfully disappointed when you got home and realized the camera was empty. I would have loved to have seen that moment. Better than heroin, for sure. Well, I've seen what's on that chip, and your life is essentially over."

"She was bipolar, Detective. Had been for decades. How many hospital admissions were there, all told? A dozen? Twenty?"

"I didn't count them."

"She would have killed herself eventually."

"Is that what you tell yourself? Is that how you get to sleep at night?"

"Go ahead, then. Shoot me."

"You want me to?"

"Go ahead. I'm not afraid."

"Sorry, Doctor. No one's going to do it for you ever again. You're just going to have to shoot yourself."

Cardinal lowered his gun so it was pointed at the floor.

Bell's gun hand shook harder.

"I'll kill you," he said. "You know I can do it."

"I'm not the one you want to kill, Doctor. I'm not one of your patients. One of your whiners, as you so compassionately call them. Killing me won't stop the pain."

With a jerk of his elbow, a marionette move in its suddenness, Bell aimed the Luger in a diagonal at his own temple.

"All these years," Cardinal said, "it's what you've really wanted, isn't it?"

Beads of sweat sprang out on Bell's brow. He squeezed his eyes shut. A single tear rolled down his cheek and into his beard.

"Go ahead. You don't really want to spend the rest of your life in prison, do you?"

Hand and gun trembled. Bell's whole body was shaking. Sweat rolled down the reddening face.

"You can't do it, can you?"

Bell groaned, and a sob escaped from his woolly beard. The Luger dropped to the floor and tumbled down the steps. Cardinal picked it up.

"I think we've done some good work today, Doctor. I'd say we've got to the root of your problem. Now you'll have a couple of decades in Kingston to work on it."

52

The days go by, and the last of autumn shades into winter. Mid-November now, and not a single leaf remains to fall. Every stem has closed; every branch is black and bare against the clouds. Fallen leaves have gathered along the sides of roads and in the culverts; they have gathered on porch steps and around garage doors. They have gathered on decks and cars and windowsills. It has rained, and the lawns are no longer covered in fluffy multicolored layers. Now the leaves are plastered in flat jagged collages on the sidewalks and on the driveways and even in the wheel wells of Algonquin Bay vehicles.

The temperature has dropped, and John Cardinal is wearing his heavy leather coat, the one with something like fur for a lining. After the beauties of October, November is dour, the pretty girl replaced by the sourpuss. Another week or two and the leather coat will be replaced by the down parka, his full Nanook, as Catherine called it.

Cardinal is coming back from a morning walk along the hiking trail that curls up the hill behind his house, a walk he has taken countless times with his wife. Delorme had called him earlier, berating herself yet again for jumping to conclusions about Catherine. Then she told him that Melanie Greene was out of the hospital and living at home with her mother. Her new therapist was optimistic.

Mr. and Mrs. Walcott are coming along the other side of the road, walking their horrible dog. They stop bickering when they see Cardinal, in deference to his loss.

"Supposed to snow," Mrs. Walcott says.

Cardinal agrees with a wave and heads up the slope to his house. Smells of wood smoke and bacon mingle with the smell of snow. Snow has been about to fall for at least a week now. It's late this year.

He enters his house and hangs up his coat. He struggles to undo the wet laces of his boots, gets one off, and then the phone is ringing in the kitchen and he walks clump-footed with one boot still on, laces flapping, to answer it.

It is the only person he wants to hear from right now.

"Kelly, how are you? What are you doing up this early?"

"I got your message last night, but it was too late to call."

Cardinal pries the boot off his foot and takes the phone into the living room. The line is not great, full of mysterious crackles, but he sits in his favorite chair and tells his daughter that Frederick Bell's bail has been set so high he won't be getting out of jail pending his trial for murder in the first degree.

A moment later he can hear his daughter crying, her sobs echoing up the increasingly bad line from New York. Kelly has still not made the adjustment demanded by the knowledge that her mother is dead not by her own but by another's hand. Bitter either way, and Cardinal wishes Kelly were with him so he could give her a hug and tell her it was all right and everything would be okay, even though it wasn't and it wouldn't.

"Kelly?"

The sobbing has stopped, but so has the crackling of static.

"Kelly?"

The line has gone dead.

Cardinal presses the FLASH button and dials her number, getting only a busy signal.

Outside, the snow is falling now, small rainlike flakes that fall fast on a slant. If she were there, Catherine would be gathering up her camera, putting on her boots. The first snow always got her outside taking pictures even though they were too "calendarish," in her opinion, to be any good. Cardinal hears a scrabbling on the roof. Taking the phone with him, he goes to the back door and opens it, surprising a squirrel in the act of chewing insulation from an air-conditioning line.

"Beat it," Cardinal says, but the squirrel just regards him with a black glistening eye. Flakes of snow are melting on his ears and tail.

Cardinal raises the phone to him and the squirrel scampers away, a black squiggle among the leaves, and then there is silence. Or near silence. A soft wind threads itself through the birches, and snow ticks on fallen leaves.

The phone rings in his hand. Cardinal answers it, and the line to New York is open once more.

ACKNOWLEDGMENTS

I wish to thank Greg Dawson of the Centre of Forensic Sciences for details on the handling of suspect documents.

I am also grateful, once again, to Staff Sergeant (Ret.) Rick Sapinski of the North Bay police for information on police procedures. Any errors that remain are despite his generous efforts.

On a cool night in late June the traffic on Highway 101 was not heavy—not for a Saturday night, anyway—and moved along at a steady clip, people cruising out to restaurants or movies or to spend the evening with friends.

There was one car traveling north from the city—a midnight-blue Lexus. An old man was driving, his considerable belly pressed up against the steering wheel, and the passenger seat was only partially filled by a weed-thin boy who looked to be in his late teens.

As the Lexus rounded a curve, it broke away from the rest of the traffic and veered across an entire lane. A sharp left, and then it bounced into the parking lot of a gas station, and made a swift circle so that it came around again, nose pointed toward the highway.

Inside the car, the boy took his hand from the dash where it had been bracing him against becoming a highway statistic, and said, "Would you mind telling me what that was all about?"

"Final wardrobe check."

"We already did that, Max. Why do we have to do it over and over again?"

"It's your hide I'm looking out for, Owen, me lad. You know I never give a thought to myself—I've been accused of it many times. 'Max,' the doctor said to me—cardiologist, I hasten to point out, knows a thing or two about this sorrowful organ we call the human heart. 'Max,' he said, 'The fact is you are suffering from magnacarditis. Your heart's too big. An albatross borne down by giant wings. You care too much for other people and it's driving you to an early grave. Have a care for yourself,' he said, 'It's all right once in a while to look out for number one.'"

"You're always looking out for number one," the boy said. "The only thing getting bigger on you is your belly, and if you had a decent doctor—not that I believe you ever went to see a doctor—he'd tell you to cut back on all the Guinness, the single malts, not to mention the hamburgers, the milkshakes, and the shepherd's pie."

"It pains me to hear such cynicism from one so young." Max placed a hand over his heart as if to protect that overworked organ. "The world is a barren, comfortless place when a sixteen-year-old—"

"Seventeen."

"When a seventeen-year-old addresses his mentor this way—insulting the sage and learned man who's raised him up as his own and taught him everything he knows."

"I know lots of stuff you didn't teach me. The capitals of Africa, the rivers of South America, how to calculate the area of an irregular surface."

"Trivia," Max said. "Tell it to Roscoe. But you wound me, boy." He tapped a plump finger on his heart and sighed. "I'm a gentle creature, beset by a heartless teenager, no doubt an incipient gangbanger. You, of course, are a warlike American, whereas I remain your humble Warwickshire yeoman, and ever shall."

"I'd like to visit Warwick one day. I'd love to hear from somebody other than you what you were like as a kid. I have a feeling they'll be telling a very different story about Max Maxwell over there."

"Nonsense. They would recall a heroic figure, just as you see me today."

The boy examined himself in the rear-view mirror.

"Okay, so how do I look?"

Max squinted at him, ginger eyebrows furrowing. "Terrifying. Perfect young Republican."

They had decided on a dark wig for Owen, one with

vigorous curls and neatly trimmed sideburns. Gorgeous black Armani jacket and pants and, instead of the usual white shirt and bowtie, an expensive white t-shirt that showed off his fat-free abdominals. Owen's first draft had been red hair, freckles, and polka-dot bowtie, but Max had overruled him: too on-the-nose, he called it, a parody. And besides, it was important to make optimal use of Owen's heartthrob potential. The curls did give the boy's profile a touch of the Greek god, not that Owen believed that heartthrob business for one minute.

"You don't think the hair's too dark for me?"

"It's perfect. Gives you a touch of the Kennedy—to which even the most granite-hearted Republican is not immune. And me? Not a hair out of place, mind."

Max smoothed his ginger mustache. Even up close it looked completely natural.

"I'd say you were a real bastard. Kind of guy who owns several mines and seriously mistreats his workers."

"Thank you."

"Hey, Max, I brought you a little present."

"No time, boy, no time." Max started the car again. "We must get a wiggle on."

"Hang on. You're gonna love this." Owen pulled it from an inside pocket and held it out.

"A cell phone?" Max furrowed his new ginger brows. "Why in the name of heaven would we need another cell phone?"

"We don't. Try to make a call from your cell."

"Owen, time is of the essence." Max gunned the motor, eyeing the traffic whizzing by. "We dare no longer stay."

"We've got plenty of time. Try to make a call."

Muttering, snorting, Max extracted his cell phone and dialed Owen's number.

"Nothing happening," he said. "Completely dead." He showed the tiny screen to Owen. No signal.

"Exactly," Owen said. "Because what I have here in my hot little hand is not a cell phone. It's a cell-phone *jammer*. Good for up to five hundred yards, too."

"You actually found one?" Max said. "Sweet boy, you are my very Ariel."

Owen put on a thin reedy voice—he was good at voices—this one made him sound like a tiny alien. "*All hail, great master! I come to answer thy best pleasure, be it to fly, to swim, to dive into the fire!*"

Max laughed. "You're a good lad, Owen. Truly, it's not every boy who's cut out for a life of crime."

The old man slid the gear shift into drive, and the Lexus eased back onto a highway peopled with innocent civilians.

THE HOME OF Margot Peabody was lit up like a Chinese lantern, all four stories of it, a beacon to the rich, the Republican, and the reprobate. It was an ornate wooden structure located in the most exclusive segment of Belvedere, purchased by pulp and paper magnate Cyrus Peabody (now defunct), some ten years previously for a comparative song. Expensive automobiles gleamed in a semicircle of driveway, their uniformed drivers absorbed in the sports pages.

Owen's usual stage fright kicked up a notch.

"We're gonna be coming right back out," Max said to the teenager directing the traffic. His accent was now American, a touch of the East Coast in it, but not much. "Put us somewhere we can make a fast getaway."

"Sure thing, sir. Just park it over there under that tree. I won't let anyone block you."

"First class, kid," Max handed him a rolled-up bill. "First class."

At the door they were met by an Asian houseboy in white livery. His hair was so slick, his skin so flawless, he looked as if he had escaped from a wax works.

"Good evening, sir. What name shall I say?"

"Carter and Christopher Gould, but it's hardly worth the bother," Max said, "we can't stay."

In the vast cathedral of space before them, men in dinner jackets mingled with well-tended women too thin for their hairdos. Owen looked up at the beautiful redwood beams supporting a ceiling that had to be at least forty feet high, but Max had taught him never to comment on such things: "We take luxury and service for granted. We don't notice them."

Nevertheless, Owen was eyeing an interesting architectural detail. A redwood mezzanine that ran around the entire great hall, the massive twin skylights overhead. The butterflies in his stomach took flight up into his chest. But Owen loved this moment, this sense of balancing on the edge of the high dive, poised to plunge into triumph or disaster.

"Turn around, kid," Max said to the houseboy. "Just let me use your shoulder, I'll write a check right now, and we'll be out of your hair."

The houseboy obligingly turned, tilting his head slightly, and Max whipped out a checkbook.

"This state has had a Republican government for nearly eight years and I want to make sure it stays that way. Twenty thousand should help. If it was legal to give more, I'd do it in a shot. Carter, your turn."

Owen pulled out a checkbook and wrote out a similar figure, signing it Carter P. Gould with a flourish.

"Now, where do we drop these?"

"In the large bottle by the stairs, sir, but I must tell Ms. Peabody you're here."

"Relax, kid, put your feet up. Margot!"

Max waved to a woman just emerging from the crowd in an ivory summer dress tied at the waist that, with the sandals laced elaborately round her ankles, hinted at ancient Greece, besotted fauns, and massive hedge funds.

"How lovely to see you," she said with a smile that gave no hint that they had never met. Max was always meticulous about his research, and had assured Owen that Margot Peabody was renowned for a spectacular collection of jewelry. It was not much in evidence tonight: a single strand of pearls, perfect milky spheres, circled her throat. "Come and have a drink on the lawn. I'm sure you'll find scads of people you know."

"Sorry, Margot. Can't stay. Gotta be in the capital first thing in the morning." He waggled the check at her, and popped it into the bottle.

"Oh, stay for one drink, I insist. I'm trying to remember where it was we met."

"Hah! You've got me, there. The Leonardo drawings?"

"The Getty! Of course, of course! And is this your son?"

"Nephew. Carter Gould—doesn't like to use the numerals. Grumpy teenager, way they all are."

"A handsome teenager nevertheless." She reached out a hand that was pure gristle. "Are you really such a grump?"

"Not at all, ma'am," Owen said. "Pleasure to meet you." He inserted his check into the mouth of the bottle and tapped it home.

"You're both too, too kind. Now follow me."

She led them through the crowd toward a pair of French doors. Owen noted earrings, necklaces, brooches, watches; your honest, God-fearing Republicans were not averse to a little ostentation. What's the point of owning diamonds, after all, if you never wear them?

Under a snow-white canopy out back, a cover band was doing an earnest version of "Born in the U.S.A.," the singer sounding in imminent danger of aneurism. Sausalito glittered across the black water, and off to the south, the arc of the Golden Gate. In the dark of the waterfront, the house seemed to blaze and shimmer.

Ms. Peabody led them to the bar and made sure they got their drinks—gin and tonic for Max, Coke for Owen. She introduced Owen to a busty debutante who shook his hand and smiled shyly. He tried to engage her in conversation, but she blushed and looked at her feet.

"To be perfectly honest," Margot Peabody said to Max, "I don't think we're in much danger of losing in November, but we do want to be on the safe side, don't we?"

"Absolutely," Max said. "Have to generate a healthy investment climate, get those returns growing again."

"Well, yes. And property values."

"Excuse me," Owen said, "back in a minute." He headed into the house at a clip that suggested serious discomfort.

"Poor kid," Max said. "Ever since the accident he's had the bladder of a little girl."

"Accident?"

"High-strung filly. Took a nasty tumble."

Ms. Peabody spread that gristly hand, fanlike, over her heart.

"A riding accident! He's lucky he didn't end up paralyzed, or in a coma."

"He was wearing the regulation helmet, thank God."

"He was playing polo? There's nowhere near here, is there?"

"Cirencester, UK. Charity match. Three princes there that afternoon and I guarantee you not one of *their* horses balked. I was ready to blow a gasket, but you know you can't say anything to a royal—raise an international stink. They did send a nice card, I'll give 'em that."

"The least they could do, under the circumstances. You probably could have sued them."

"Nah," Max said. "Polo's a tough game. Have to expect to get knocked around a little."

"How delightfully macho," his hostess said, and gave a musical laugh.

INSIDE, OWEN BOUNDED up the front stairs two at a time.

"Sir! Sir!" the houseboy called after him, "there are plenty of restrooms down here."

Owen found a sumptuous five-piece bathroom halfway along the hall. He stepped in and checked himself out in multiple mirrors. Owen didn't care a lot about clothes, but the black Armani looked great, he had to admit, and the new curls seemed to be working wonders with the female element. He flushed the toilet and set the tap running in the sink so the bathroom would sound occupied, then shut the door from the outside. At the end of the hall a pair of double doors was closed, but under Max's tutelage he had developed an instinct for such things.

If you want to rob a Republican, your best time is supper time, Max had taught him. They always have company, the place is full of strangers, and every alarm is exactly where you want it: off.

Five minutes, he wouldn't need more.

The master bedroom was all rustic wood and white fabric, but Owen wasted no time in admiration. He made straight for the dressing room, a compact chamber redolent with aromas of cedar, Guerlain, and shoe leather, and got it right on the first guess: the set of library steps gave her away. He reached up into the space between the ceiling and the top shelf and pulled out a high quality wooden chest secured with a paltry lock that he snapped in less than two seconds.

Inside, there was a diamond brooch that had to be worth thirty or forty grand, an exquisite jade cameo, and a gold and ruby bracelet. But the real showstopper was the pair of emerald earrings, emeralds being more valuable even than diamonds. Both gems looked free of inclusions and at least twelve carats, the light and clear green of a cat's eye. Hundred and twenty grand on a bad day.

"God, I love this job," Owen said softly. He stuffed his pockets, closed the doors, and returned to the bathroom to shut off the water.

When he emerged, a somewhat off-kilter babe in a shimmery blue dress was having trouble making it up the last few stairs, pressing a cell phone to her ear with one hand and clutching a martini in the other. She snapped the phone shut, eying Owen.

"What are you doing up here?" she said, an edge in her voice.

"Bathroom."

"There are bathrooms downstairs," she said, slurring a little.

"They were occupied."

"Yeah?" She looked him up and down, taking her time about it. She was pretty in a hard way; her frown looked like it might be permanent. "Who are you?" she said. "Why haven't we met?"

Owen put out a hand. "Carter Gould. Who are you?"

"Melinda Peabody. Unfortunately."

"Why unfortunately?"

She waved a limp hand. "Long story. How old are you, anyway? I'm twenty-five." She looked ten years older.

"I'm eighteen," Owen said. "Well, I will be."

"Too young," she said, "which is too bad, because you're so cute you're making me dizzy." She steadied herself against the wall.

"That must be the martini," Owen said. "I better be getting back downstairs." Max would be wondering where the hell he was. A missed cue could ruin the whole show.

"No, really," Melinda said. "People must tell you that all the time, right? That you're totally fucking devastating?"

"Never," Owen said. "This is the first time."

"Liar. Get out of here before I jump you." She flung open the bathroom door, nearly toppling herself, and shut it behind her.

Owen stopped off at the mezzanine on the way down. The band was taking a break, and Margot Peabody was herding everyone into the great hall below where a bulky bear of a man in a tux was seated at a grand piano. Max looked up at Owen, and Owen pulled out the jammer and flipped it open. He pushed the ON button and held it to his ear as if answering a call. Then he scowled at it, and put it back into his pocket.

When she had got the crowd quiet, Ms. Peabody told them they were in for a terrific surprise.

"We are honored to have a very special guest with us tonight, one who needs no introduction, seeing how she's come here straight from the stage of New York's Lincoln Center. Ladies and gentlemen, I give you Evelyn del Rio."

Max was always hauling Owen off to the theatre—he'd seen more productions of *Hamlet* than he cared to think about—but Owen had never been to an opera. Even so, he knew who Evelyn del Rio was. He was disappointed that she was not fat. She was a trim, blond woman in a plain black skirt with a sparkly top that drew attention to her chest. When the applause died down, she nodded at the piano bear and he began to play, a set of dark, dour chords. Over these the famous voice came hovering, floating at first, and then sweeping upward into the ceiling, sending a thrill up Owen's spine. It was something, a voice of pure silver at such proximity; he'd never heard anything like it. One of the great things about robbing the rich was you got to see some first-class entertainment.

It was a sad aria, not too long, and when it was over, the audience couldn't stop grinning and applauding. Melinda Peabody had made her way back downstairs and was off in a corner, stabbing repeatedly at her cell phone and frowning. Owen looked around. Max's caterers, as he called them, were in place at the two exits. They wore livery much like the houseboy's and stood with folded arms, looking serious and professional.

Before the applause had quite died down, Max stepped into a spot right below Owen and raised his hands. Owen's adrenaline levels shot up several levels, heart hammering.

"Well, that was stupendous, wasn't it?" Max said to the crowd. "Beautiful music, beautifully rendered. But, before we go any further, I also have an announcement to make, and I want you to promise not to get upset. It's the kind of thing people can get hysterical about, so let me tell you up front that such a reaction is totally unnecessary. You are here to part with money, after all. This gathering is being robbed. That's right, you heard me. Robbed."

The whole mansion seemed to darken, although the lights stayed on. There were murmurs and catches of breath and questioning, worried looks.

"Rest assured that I myself, not to mention the able assistants you see at various points around the room, are fully— by which I mean lethally—armed. Still—"

A couple of men started to speak up, but Max silenced them by pulling out a .38 Special, which he did not point at anybody. He didn't have to.

"Still," he continued, "there is no reason in the world why this has to be a totally negative experience. I urge you— strongly urge you—to simply drop your valuables into the sack we'll be bringing around. Watches, brooches, necklaces, jewelry of any kind. Unprovoked, we're not brutes—wedding rings are not required unless extraordinarily valuable— worth, say, over five thousand."

"Bullshit," someone said. Owen didn't see who it was; he was more worried about a small, lean man moving slowly, almost imperceptibly toward Max from behind. Owen unhooked the elegant velvet rope that reached upward to the skylights all the way from the lower floor. He took a pair of leather gloves from his pocket, put them on, and slowly slid down the rope to the floor below, planting himself firmly between Max and the approaching man. Pure Errol Flynn.

"Don't even think about it," he said, and the man went still.

Max handed Owen a sack emblazoned with a red Republican elephant. Owen began going to each of the women in turn, holding it open.

"No tricks, mister," Max said to the man, still in his East Coast accent. "The usual restrictions will be strictly enforced. Nobody moves, nobody leaves. This'll only take a few minutes. Look, you were only going to donate the dough to a corrupt old codger, anyway. I don't see why you shouldn't donate it to me. Now, don't spoil it for everybody," he said to the lean man. "This is very much a money-or-your-life situation."

"Try and stop me."

The guy was heading for the door now. Roscoe, one of Max's caterers, reared up to his full height, which was considerable, and the man veered toward another door. Pookie, Roscoe's colleague, stepped forward. The man kept coming. Pookie was reaching for his weapon, but Max fired first, a single shot into the ceiling that made an enormous noise. They always used smokeless blanks that were even louder than the real thing. It made Owen jump every time.

"The next one won't be a warning."

"Look," Evelyn del Rio said, "if we're going to be robbed anyway, we should at least have some music. Giorgio?"

"You expect me to play?" said the bear. He seemed more shook up than his diva.

"What else are we going to do?" she said. "I'm damned if I'm going to crumple up and cry."

"Marvelous," Max said. "And I know that a woman who sings like you has just got to be a magnificent dancer. I beseech you, Giorgio—a waltz."

Giorgio shook his head, but he turned back to the keyboard and started to play. Owen recognized the tune, though he couldn't have named it. Some Viennese thing.

Max put his gun away and took Evelyn del Rio's hand. As Owen stepped from guest to guest accepting "donations," Max twirled around the floor with the soprano, who looked as cool as ivory.

"The ring, too," Owen said.

The girl, who was about twelve—a breastless vision in Calvin Klein—started to cry, and handed it over.

"It's just a ring," Owen said. "A material object. There's no reason to get worked up over it."

"My daddy gave me that ring," she said, a Southern girl, maybe Arkansas, "'fore he died. It was my momma's engagement ring."

"Well, why isn't your mother wearing it, then?"

"Because she's dead, too, you snake."

Owen took her hot little fist and opened it, placed the sparkling ring into her palm, and folded her fingers over it.

"You don't know me well enough to call me that," he said.

He looked over to Max, still spinning around the floor with Evelyn del Rio. There was an abstracted air on his face that worried Owen. Lately the old man had been having spells of vagueness—usually not more than a few minutes—during which he forgot where he was and what he was doing. Max should have been collecting loot in a second bag, thus doubling their speed, but instead he was dancing with an opera star. Not good.

A couple of the men glared as if they would take him apart, but the rest were exceedingly cooperative. One of the things that had surprised Owen when he had first become involved in the lively pursuit of robbery was that men were generally as terrified as women. They didn't cry and carry on, but they trembled a lot. He wished they wouldn't; he wished they understood how truly safe they were, provided they didn't try anything violent.

"I suppose you want credit cards, too," said one fellow—he had a lot of freckles though he was much older than

Owen. He looked like the type of guy you'd enjoy tossing a Frisbee with.

"Just cash and jewelry," Owen told him. "But thank you for asking."

"Fuck you."

"Settle down, man. It'll all be over soon, and you'll have a great story to tell your grandchildren."

Another two minutes and it was done. Owen signaled to Max, but Max was lost in his dancing, a blissful smile on his face, and missed it completely. Pookie had to bull his way through the crowd and take Max by the elbow. Max came back down to earth, bowed deeply, and kissed Evelyn del Rio's hand.